THE SHADOW OF THE SUN

A. S. Byatt was educated in York and Newnham College, Cambridge. She was a lecturer at the Central School of Art and Design and is a regular broadcaster on BBC radio. Until recently she was a lecturer in English and American literature at University College, London. She has a distinguished reputation as a critic and her books include four novels – *The Game, The Virgin in the Garden, Still Life* and *Possession*, which won the 1990 Booker Prize – *Sugar and Other Stories, Degrees of Freedom*, a study of the novels of Iris Murdoch, and *Unruly Times: Wordsworth and Coleridge in Their Time*. She was awarded the CBE in the New Year's Honours List, 1990.

She is married and has three daughters.

'Mrs Byatt feels deeply for her characters and has a thoughtful unhurried way of conveying precisely why they are worth caring about. *The Shadow of the Sun* ... suggests that before long Mrs Byatt may achieve a considerable reputation.'

Times Literary Supplement

'As the book develops, through the medium of a prose closely modulated to psychological niceties, I am reminded of George Eliot's *Middlemarch*. That may be an extravagant compliment to offer a novice, but the maturity of vision and observation in this first novel compels me to compare Mrs Byatt's quiet, patient examination of emotions, motives and reactions among the personalities of her characters, to the massive intellectual deployments of the great novel that was the crown of George Eliot's achievement.'

Richard Church, *Country Life*

'She gives one of the few convincing pictures of genius I have ever met, rightly putting agonised impatience to be working at the heart of it. Her descriptive passages, which at first seem too long and elaborate, reflect the heroine's visual intensity which she inherits from her father. The book is promising ... there are passages which seem to speak in a maturer voice, the voice perhaps of Mrs Byatt's third or fourth novel.'

Punch

A. S. Byatt

THE SHADOW OF THE SUN

A Novel

VINTAGE

VINTAGE
20 Vauxhall Bridge Road, London SW1V 2SA

London Melbourne Sydney Auckland
Johannesburg and agencies throughout
the world

First published by Chatto & Windus Ltd, 1964
Vintage edition 1991

© A. S. Byatt 1964

Set in 10½/12 Sabon by Intype, London

Printed and bound in Great Britain by
Cox & Wyman Ltd, Reading, Berks

ISBN 0 09 988960 9

FOR I. C. R. BYATT

INTRODUCTION

This novel was published in 1964, when my two elder children were four and three years old, but it was written, at least the first draft, when I was an undergraduate at Cambridge between 1954 and 1957. It is the novel of a very young woman, a novel written by someone who *had* to write but was very unsure whether she should admit to wanting to write, unsure even whether she ought, being a woman, to want to write. It was written in libraries and lectures, between essays and love affairs. I remember getting the idea for it during one of John Holloway's lectures on D. H. Lawrence, and scribbling busily, so busily that the lecturer looked fixedly at what must have seemed to him an earnest female acolyte and remarked sharply 'You don't need to take all that down. It's not *that* interesting.' I have no idea what he was talking about, but the novel does have its ideas about what was and wasn't interesting about Lawrence, in Leavis's Cambridge.

Reading it now, or skimming it and remembering it, I re-experience a kind of fear. I didn't want to write a 'me-novel' as we scornfully labelled them then, literary sophisticates, inexperienced human beings. But I had the eternal first novelist's problem. I didn't *know* anything – about life, at least. I remember thinking out the primitive first idea of it, which was that of someone who had the weight of a future life, amorphously dragging in front of her, someone whose major decisions were all to come, and who found that they had got made whilst she wasn't looking, by casual acts she thought didn't impair her freedom. That the battle fought itself out between sexuality, literary criticism, and writing, was inevitable. The way in which it shaped itself was more instinctive.

My problems were both human and literary. The human problems were to do with being an ambitious woman, in the English version of the world of Betty Friedan's feminine mystique.

We wanted marriage and children, we wanted weddings and romantic love and sex, and to be normal. ('Normal' is a word my characters puzzle over in book after book, a word dated now, full of ancient pressures to conformity, backed by a crude psychoanalytic chatter.) We had fought, much harder than the men, who outnumbered us eleven to one, to be allowed to study at Cambridge, and we were fatally torn, when thinking of our futures, by hopes of marriage, and hopes of something, some work, beyond getting to university at all. Men could have both, work and love, but it seemed that women couldn't. No woman of my generation would have expected any putative husband to consider her work prospects when making his own decisions. I myself went on to do academic research, and had my grant taken away when I married. Men in my position had their grants increased, to provide for their households. I always knew, as my heroine didn't, that I must contrive to *work* (to think, to write). It is only now, looking back, that I see how furtive, how beleaguered, how publicly *improper*, I imagined this contriving was going to have to be. I tried to write a thesis at Oxford under Helen Gardner, who believed, and frequently said, that a woman had to be dedicated like a nun, to achieve anything as a mind. I didn't want to be, and wasn't capable of being, an unsexed mind. I meet women now who work in different places from their husbands, and meet at weekends, to talk, and I envy them what I believe to be their certainty that they have a right to this. It was appallingly confusing, the battle to win scholarships, the closed future after them.

My own mother had herself studied English at Cambridge, and I might, in the 1960s, have felt I should have written about the generations of women who faced the same problems. As it was, I avoided approaching her perpetual rage, depression, and frustration, which were, in fact, the driving force that made sure none of her daughters became housebound. We wanted 'not to be like her' and I am only now, some years after her death, beginning to dare to try to imagine what went on in her inner mind. I wrote a novel about a girl with an ideal and unapproachable father, who, being male, could have what she and I felt we perhaps ought not to want, singlemindedness, art, vision. Henry Severell has little or nothing to do with my father –

what they have in common is an incapacity, usual enough in the hardworking man, to notice what is going on inside others.

Henry Severell is partly simply my secret self, someone, as a man I was in love with once said to me who didn't 'need drugs or anything because you've got mescalin in your blood, so to speak.' Someone who saw everything too bright, too fierce, too much, like Van Gogh's cornfields, or Samuel Palmer's overloaded magic apples, or the Coleridge of the flashing eyes and floating hair, or the Blake who saw infinity in a grain of sand. Or, in some less satisfactory, and more corrupt and dangerous aspects, the sunworshipping Lawrence. This vision of too much makes the visionary want to write – in my case – or paint, or compose, or dance or sing. The other thing I wrote at Cambridge, over and over, was the story of Cassandra who was loved by the sun god, also Lord of the Muses, and wouldn't give in to him, so couldn't speak, or not to be believed by anyone. Female visionaries are poor mad exploited sibyls and pythonesses. Male ones are prophets and poets. Or so I thought. There was a feminine mystique but no tradition of female mysticism that wasn't hopelessly self-abnegating. There is no female art I can think of that is like what I wanted to be able to do. Virginia Woolf is too full of nervous sensibility. All strung up, like my mother, it occurs to me as I write.

My mother's background, which she had rejected, was nonconformist and Puritanical. The best thing that had happened to her was English literature, but in her misery she was suspicious of it, tended to dismiss artists gloomily as exploiters, self-indulgent, frivolous. In some way these suspicions became connected in my mind, at that time, with Dr Leavis's moral ferocity which dismissed all literature but the greatest, which was great for *moral* reasons. He could show you the toughness of a sentence, the strength and the grace of it, the way another one failed and betrayed itself, but you paid a terrible price for this useful technical knowledge. It went without saying in his world, as later in Helen Gardner's, that anything you wrote yourself would fall so woefully short of the highest standards that it was better not to try. What writing was for was to be taught, in order to make the world better, more just, more discriminating. In his shadow his pupils, would-be critics and would-be poets and novelists alike shrivelled into writing-blocks. A good kind of teacherly moral seriousness flourished. It went in that place in those days with what I experienced as a good kind of moral classlessness — my friends were not angry young men, the best of them were just sure that the sillinesses of the British Class System were withering into irrelevance. They were the meritocracy, and the literature class was their pulpit, in schools, in evening classes, in colleges. But there were others who felt aggressive, scornful, assertive of 'working-class' values.

Oliver comes out of that — someone with a chip, who can think, who is thinking, who makes too much of literature in one way, and doesn't understand its too-bright aspect. He represents I suppose, if I'm seeing the novel as an allegory of my own life, which it isn't, of course, it has its own — he represents a kind of public vision of what I was about, a scholar, a critic, a *user* of literature, not a maker, a natural judge. In all my novels there are characters whose thoughts the reader shares and those whose thoughts are opaque, who are seen from outside. Oliver is one of the latter, the Other. He would have been the hero of any male version of this story, l'homme moyen sensuel, suspicious of Henry's wilder edges, guilty about his wife and the girl, but essentially 'decent.' This novel doesn't see him quite that way. It is afraid of him, though I only understand now how much.

What I said at the time was that the novel was about the paradox of Leavis preaching Lawrence when if the two had ever met they would have hated each other. It was about the secondary imagination feeding off, and taming, the primary to use Coleridgean terms, since the one person I was sure I admired and loved at that time was Coleridge.

I had awful problems with the form of the novel. I had no model I found at all satisfactory. I should say now that the available models, Elizabeth Bowen, Rosamund Lehmann, Forster, Woolf, were all too suffused with 'sensibility' but that I disliked the joky social comedy of Amis and Wain considerably more than I disliked 'sensibility'. I know that there is a considerable stylistic influence from *Bonjour Tristesse*, which I read in

French the summer before Cambridge, and which is against sensibility, and also concerns final decisions made casually and by accident. Between the first Cambridge draft and the final one, made in Durham in 1962–3, I had read Proust and discovered Iris Murdoch, both of whom combine a kind of toughness of thought with a sensuous awareness that is part of their thought. I had also written a partial draft of *The Game* which is about the fear of the 'woman's novel' as an immoral devouring force. But the underlying shape of *The Shadow of the Sun* is dictated by Elizabeth Bowen and Rosamond Lehmann, and a vague dissatisfaction with this state of affairs.

There is also Lawrence, whom I cannot escape and cannot love. His background is something I know, better than Leavis did, having been brought up in the north midlands as he was, of mixed working-class and intellectual lower-middle-class stock, with low church Christianity for myth and morality, with a terrible desire for something *more*. I brooded and brooded about how Lawrence cheated with Birkin, who is only explicable if he is Lawrence and a driven artist (i.e. someone who has to *make* something) but who remains a school inspector driven by a need for sexual honesty and personal freedom. Anna is a descendant of Birkin, a portrait of the artist with the artist left out. I learned from Lawrence that you can stop the action of a novel and move it into another dimension with the vision of a place, or an event, or a ceremony. But I couldn't love the man who wrote the *Plumed Serpent* and I couldn't condone the God of Leavis's creed of wholesomeness and wholeness, partly because I was a woman, and partly because the two didn't in fact coincide, the priest and his creed, the God and his creed. He is violent and savage, as Proust is not, and coercive, as Proust is not, and altogether Proust has more to teach on every page, but is not close to my blood, as Lawrence is. I choose the words advisedly.

I did not know, when I chose my title, just how powerful a metaphor, or myth, personal and universal, I was tapping. I loved the poem by Ralegh, *False Love* , and I thought the verse I chose as an epigraph was a wry comment on the female belief in, or illusion of, the need to be 'in love' which was the danger which most threatened the autonomy of my heroine. All those desiderata of the feminine mystique, the lover, the house, the nursery, the kitchen, were indeed a 'goal of grief for which the wisest run' and my mother was there to prove it, saying frequently 'What I hope for you is that you will be as happy as your father and I have been.' 'A substance like the shadow of the sun' was a good phrase, and more than that. Coleridge saw the human intellect as a light like the moon, reflecting the light of the primary consciousness, the Sun. My Anna was not even a reflected light, she was a shadow of a light only, who had partial visions in clouds (like the *Dejection Ode*) or stormy moonlight, or the glare of Cambridge's blood-coloured streetlighting. I feared that fate.

The novel was finished when I was a very desperate faculty wife in Durham. I had two children in two years – I was 25, and thought I was old, 'past it'. I was surrounded by young men who debated in an all-male Union from which the women students were excluded, though there was nowhere else for them to meet. I was lonely and frightened, and Cambridge, with its equal talk, and its flirtations, and above all its *library* and *work* seemed like a dream of the earthly Paradise. I began contriving – I sat rocking my son with one hand in a plastic chair on the table, and wrote with the other. I had a cleaning-lady, and ran across the Palace Green to the University Library for the hour she was there to write, fiercely, with a new desperation. The children were human and beautiful and I loved them. Anna and her vague fears took on a useful distance. My husband paid for the heaps of manuscript to be typed, and I sent them, at John Beer's suggestion to Chatto and Windus.

I was invited to lunch by Cecil Day Lewis in the Atheneum. Goddess Athene over the door, women confined to the dark basement, affable poet murmuring 'boarding house food, boarding house food' and swapping quotations from Yeats. Outside on the pavement, in brilliant sunlight, he said 'This has been most enjoyable' and I gathered up all my courage and said 'Yes, but will you be going to publish it?' He laughed at me, and said that of course he would, but the title would sound better if it was 'Shadow of a Sun' and not, as I had it 'The Shadow of the Sun.' I would have agreed to anything, then. Now, I should like to restore my original title. It is more what I meant, and I prefer its grittiness to the mellifluousness of Day Lewis's version. The sun has no shadow, that is the point.

You have to be the sun or nothing.

What I write is heliotropic. I don't think I knew that when I chose my title, despite being already involved with Cassandra and her inability to contain or transmit molten light. My unfinished Ph.D thesis was partly about the neoplatonic creation myths, where the Sun is the male Logos, or Nous, or Mind, that penetrated inert Hyle, or matter, or female Earth, and brought it to life and form. This is both exciting, because in a way physically true – life does depend absolutely on light – and depressing because false in its analogies – there is nothing intrinsically male about the sun, or female about the earth. There is a Lawrentian version of this in *Sun*, where a city woman bathes naked in Mediterranean sunlight and feels power pouring into her, removing her from the scope of her grey, timid, city husband. This is powerfully moving at one level, at least to a sun-worshipping winter-light-deprived depressive like me. Lawrence's sun shines out with gold and blue and white fire. But 'he' is also 'like a big shy creature' and the woman is convinced that he '*knew* her in the cosmic carnal sense of the word.' Her desiderated state is blind wholesome passivity. There is something also powerfully repellent about Lawrence's sexual imagery for what the sun is doing to the woman.

And then there is the question of the moon, the silver, cold savage moon, a purely reflected light, usually female in Western mythologies.

My subsequent novels all think about the problem of female vision, female art and thought, using these images (amongst others, and not without interest in the male too). In *The Game* I called the character who had taken Helen Gardner's monastic advice Cassandra, and she, like Anna, saw moons through glass. In *The Virgin in the Garden*, the imagery became complicated. The helpless visionary who saw too much light was male and a mathematician. The power figure was female, Queen Elizabeth I, who presides over the pale world of her successor, all ruddy and shining. Elizabeth wrote a poem which is very close to

Ralegh's *False Love* – 'My Care is like my Shadow in the Sunne – Follows one flieing, flies when I pursue it – '. But she was mythologised by her poets and courtiers as a complex virgin *moon goddess*, not only, as Frances Yates pointed out in *Astraea*, the queen and huntress chaste and fair, Diana, but the Eastern goddesses of earth and harvest, turret-crowned Cybele, Astarte. Because she was born under Virgo, and because Virgo is a high summer sign, she goes with harvest and plenty, she carries sun-ripened corn, she brings in the Golden, not the Silver Age. Ralegh apostrophised her in *The Ocean to Cynthia* as the goddess drawing all to her, like the tides. The novel includes a parody of the comical and magical chapter in *Women in Love* where Birkin apostrophises the full moon, reflected in a pond, 'Cursed Astarte, Syria Dea' and breaks up her fullness with stones, only to see it reuniting, pulling itself together again into wholeness.

There is more power in this image, but it is still on condition of being virginal and moony, reflected if pulling tides.

In *Still Life* the central figure turned out to be Vincent Van Gogh, rather to my surprise, a whole-hearted sun-driven, light-driven maker (but who also had problems about sexuality and work.) Like Cassandra he was mad with too much light, but he got something done, he made something. In *Possession*, where there are two poets, both of whom can and do write, and can and do feel sexual passion, even if tragically, the sun becomes quietly female for both of them. This is because I had noticed – to repay debts – that the sun is female in Tolkien, and this made me remember that in my earliest and first-loved book, *Asgard and the Gods*, the Sun Chariot is driven across the sky by a goddess. In Norse and in German the sun is female. My poets both quietly accepted the personification, destroying the old Nous-Hyle creation myths without even shouting about it.

In writing this introduction to a thirty-year old book, I have realised something else I have never thought out before. The visual image that always went with the idea of 'The Shadow of the Sun' was that of Samuel Palmer's Cornfield with the Evening Star – an image I now associate with Van Gogh's Reaper, working his way through a seething furnace of light and white-gold corn. The Palmer is nocturnal, warm but bright, lit by a reflected moonlight which nevertheless contains the partial sickle within the possibility of a complete circle of light. I see suddenly that images of harvest are also an intricate part of my private-universal imagery. When I was writing *The Shadow of the Sun* I read a wonderful article in the *Manchester Guardian* about the turbulences in ripe corn, and incorporated it into Henry Severell's vision of harvest fields, including several words I'd only learned from there, such as the 'awn' of the barley (which caused a farmer my mother knew to say he liked the book, the language was accurate, it was clear I knew about agriculture.) I think I was also partially remembering the magical scene in *The Rainbow* where Will and Anna meet in moonlit cornfields, which are a kind of creative paradox. For the ripeness and the growth of the corn, the harvest, are brought about by the heat and light of the sun, and yet here they are seen in this milder, darker, colder light, which I think I did take, at that time, for an image of women's creativity. I wanted my harvest, both in my life and in my work, and I was afraid that my light was a lesser one, a cold one, that could only mildly illuminate, however hauntingly. But I did go on from there, to Queen Elizabeth as Corn Goddess, to Van Gogh's Death the Reaper working happily, to a poem in *Possession* by Randolph Henry Ash about the Norse Creation myth, in which the light that gives life to the first man and woman, Ask and Embla, is a *female* sun. And in his poetry too Ash accepts that the 'golden apples' of the underworld dark goddess Persephone, are, according to Vico, the corn that springs from the furrow. It is interesting to reflect, looking back at those first suns, moons and corn how instinctively they were found, how long, although I had all the material for doing so, they took to understand and work out.

A. S. Byatt
1991

A fortress foil'd which reason did defend,
A siren song, a fever of the mind,
A maze wherein affection finds no end,
A ranging cloud that runs before the wind,
A substance like the shadow of the sun,
A goal of grief for which the wisest run.

SIR WALTER RALEGH

PART ONE

ONE

THE HOUSE WAS in waiting; low, and still, and grey, with
clean curtains in the long windows, and a fresh line of white
across the edge of the steps. They had repainted the door in the
spring, a soft colour, between blue and grey, which seemed to
retreat coolly before the sparkle of the wide lawns under the
sun. It was very hot; the air hung, rising and shivering in little
fountains over the hedges and the gateposts, snaking in busy
rivers across the lawns, and curving round past the steps into
the shadows, where it suddenly became invisible again. The
roses, massed tidily in beds upon and around the lawns, were
damp with it, the petals weighed softly against each other where
yesterday they had been crisp, standing out as though they were
sugared. But the grass, greener here than at the back of the
house where it was less shadowed, was violent; it thrust itself
into the sun in neat metallic ranks, its blades shorn away and
the fine planes of it catching the light, throwing it about on the
lawn like crossed threads of spun glass, silver, green and white.
There were no daisies; one of their minor tidinesses was this
expanse of lawn, formal in front of the formal house. At the
back, where some nineteenth-century owner had added an
untidy terrace with a verandah, and where they played croquet
or badminton all summer, there were hundreds of daisies and
a thriving patch of plantains. But it was here at the front, here
in the unbroken order of house and garden and drive, that the
waiting was apparent – a certain tension in the placidity, the
stiffening of the formation before the attack. It was that time
between lunch and tea, when everything is very still, and heavy
enough to be sleepy; but here, outside in the silence, the brilliance of the sun gave an extra sharpness, an extra clarity to
everything, made it all so definite that it had the brittle quality
of a mirage, and it was somehow only too easy to feel, given
the transitory lucidity of English sunshine, that it might shatter

3

like a mirage, might flake away and dissolve under pressure, into something grey and ordinary and dispersed.

In the hall, inside, Caroline Severell stood over a white bowl of flowers, and pushed delicately at the blue spike of the tallest delphinium. Her mind ran wordlessly over her preparations; the little tablets of soap, the clean towels, the lavender bags in the drawers, the carafe, the bowl of roses in the spare room followed each other, rapid little pictures across her inner eye. She had collected and disposed of all the books which her husband had scattered across the drawing room, along the landings, in the bathroom. It was only a matter of time until he discovered their loss, and reclaimed them to pile them up again in some more awkward place, but by then the arrival at least would be over. She had removed her daughter's riding crop and boots from the kitchen table, a pile of her dirty under-wear from the bathroom floor, two filthy Aertex shirts from the banisters where they were hanging – this with a certain distaste – and her son's electric railway from under the dining table with some compunction – she saw, after all, that it was reasonable for him to need space to play with it – he made so little mess for a boy of his age – but visitors were visitors, and the trains could come out again later. The dinner was prepared, the tea-tray was set, and the kettle was filled and ready on the stove. Caroline thought coolly that that was all; she gave a final organizing twitch to the stems of the flowers, already bitten securely by the wire mesh in the bowl, and untied the strings of her apron. It had all been managed very neatly.

She looked at her watch. Three ten. Time was slipping away. There was an unwritten rule that her husband was never to be disturbed when he was in his study, which Caroline took pride in keeping, but she was aware without bothering to wonder how, that he had entirely forgotten that he had promised to fetch the visitors from the station, which was some miles away. She went to hang her apron in the kitchen, to give him time, to make quite certain, and then came back through the house and knocked firmly on the study door.

There was no reply, but she had not expected one. She waited a moment for politeness' sake, and then walked in.

The study, for a study, was very large, and full of light, which flooded in through a large french window which opened onto the terrace at the back. It had nothing of the dark leather and silver and tobacco comfort of the gentleman's study, no steel cabinets, on the other hand, no deliberate austerity, not even the threadbare untidiness of the don's room, with paper everywhere, and stones collected on odd beaches and brought home because they were interesting. If it had any character, it was that of the outgrown schoolroom – books, on shelves, all round the walls, not glassed in, a huge, square ugly desk in light wood, a wooden armchair, and a desk chair. There was a typewriter on the desk, and a jug of flowers, arranged by Caroline, on one of the book-cases. There was a large fireplace, and a sage green carpet, slightly silky, and nothing else remarkable but space – clear, uninhabited, sunlit space. The study was the centre of the house, and round what went on in it everything else was ordered – by Caroline, because she had decided that this was how her life should be, by the children because they had never supposed that it could be otherwise, by friends and visitors because they were almost always in awe of the idea of Henry Severell, and assumed that his needs must be different from and more pressing than those of others, a feeling which Caroline did her best to encourage. Whether Henry himself was aware of all the protecting and arranging that went on, whether he expected it or took it for granted or never noticed it at all, it was difficult to tell: he spent most of his time, most of the year, closed in the study, and what he did there was his own business. He was not a communicative man.

Caroline looked automatically for him where he always was, at his desk under the window, and felt a tiny flicker of apprehension when she located him, standing in the opposite corner, doing nothing, and looking as though he had been doing nothing for some time. He looked down on her, and blinked, but did not offer to say anything. Caroline looked back at the desk again, and saw that it was unusually littered – with books, with great piles of frayed manuscript, with boxfiles dusty and bulging with notes. She went across, and turned over one or two of the books. Bishop Berkeley's *Siris*, Boehme, Coleridge's *Notebooks, Aids to Reflection*, Henry More's *Conjectura Cabbalistica*, Dorothy Wordsworth's *Journal*. Then she turned back to Henry, and could not keep back the reproach, although she knew it would do no good.

'Did you have to start on all this again just now? Just when Oliver will be here?'

'Oliver?' Henry asked flatly, without showing any real interest, and without answering Caroline's question. He came back to the desk, rearranged the books Caroline had disturbed, and began to turn his pages of manuscript, smiling intently over them, but standing restlessly, Caroline noticed uneasily, as though at any moment he might plunge into the garden and disappear. She said with patience, 'You knew they had been asked for this week. I told you. You agreed that Margaret didn't look well. You promised to fetch them from the station this afternoon.'

'Did I?' said Henry, still turning papers, and smiling.

'They will be here in half an hour. You will have to hurry to be at the station in time.'

'Can't Anna go?'

'They won't want to see Anna,' Caroline explained as though this was self-evident. She was finding it difficult to concentrate on getting Henry to the station – she could not help being preoccupied by the unexpected recurrence of Coleridge and Wordsworth, and all that this entailed, just when it was most awkward. She examined her husband for any further signs of over-excitement, or wildness – he was now leaning over the desk and pencilling rapid notes on one of the odd pieces of scrap paper which were scattered there – and thought, as she always thought, how splendid he was, and then that she must try to keep it to Coleridge in the study, whatever happened, whilst the Cannings were there, and that Henry must be made to come to meals, and that this would all be very difficult. Henry became aware of her scrutiny at last, and swung away to the window, where he stood, looking out, his back to her. This was worse. She said miserably, 'Did something go wrong with the novel, then? It seemed to be going so well. I mean, you were working so hard. I thought it was nearly finished. I told Oliver – '

'I wish,' said Henry, surprisingly fiercely, 'that you – that people – wouldn't tell Oliver anything. He pries, he nibbles, he draws conclusions, he defines, on scraps of information no one with any real tact would try to make anything out of. He will ask questions all the time. I have to make an effort to ignore him. I can't think what he was invited for.'

'He has been very useful to you.'

'I could do without him.'

'And he is really quite devoted to you. You must admit that. He would do anything for you. You said once that he saw what you were getting at better than anyone. Didn't you? And then, Margaret looked so ill, and I'm sure bringing them here is the only way to make him give her a holiday this summer – he drives himself so hard, he doesn't notice what she needs.' Caroline, a sacrificially devoted wife herself, explained this perfectly practically without any hint of censure. Margaret must look after herself; men's work came first, but if it was possible to help her, she would. Henry looked put out. He said vaguely, 'I forgot, that's all. I'm very busy. And I do wish that man would learn not to ask questions.'

'It's only because he's so interested.'

'I should get on better if he kept quiet. He should have the sense to see that. And just at the moment – ' His gaze wandered back to the papers on his desk. 'Just at the moment I want to get this in order.' He always said that, too. 'I might finish it this time – it's surprising how exhilarating it is to do a little purely intellectual work, when one's been writing for some time – lots of fresh air and sunshine. And I'm really getting somewhere.'

Caroline was genuinely distressed now. She said unwisely, 'But you never do get anywhere. You just make more and more notes. And then – oh well, you know as well as I do what happens then. It's been years, now – '

'It needs years – '

'And just at the moment it really will be difficult if you go off into one of these – moods – you must see that. With Oliver here – who only comes to see you. Can't you manage to finish the novel first?'

'I'll finish that,' Henry said, obviously retreating from the conversation entirely, and no longer ready to explain himself or his intentions. 'That's all right. That can wait, it'll do it good.' He repeated, distantly, patiently, 'I've just seen the way to get this in order,' and sat down at the desk, sifting what looked like the most recent set of notes, and dismissing the whole issue entirely. Caroline considered him with exasperation – when he was writing the novels she would guard him from any disturbance, would alter meals, would entertain and placate people like Oliver Canning, who were useful, as well as deserving, Caroline thought, a real gratitude for their devotion to Henry. But she had been dubious some years ago when he had begun on his *Analysis of the English Romantic Movement* and was now entirely sceptical: it was not his kind of work, it never seemed to be any nearer completion, he was unsettled and difficult when occupied with it – less distant and more aggressive than when he was writing novels – and it was, moreover, almost always only a prelude to fits of really strange behaviour which she feared because they were quite out of her range. And Henry, normally a mild man, was surprisingly touchy about the *Analysis* – any criticism of it made him angry to the point of rudeness. And Oliver Canning – in Caroline's opinion, rightly – would be bound to criticize. She looked at her watch again, and then at Henry, and the lapse of time over the argument made her momentarily panic-stricken about her ability to deal with any of this.

'Please, Henry, at least don't miss the train. They rely on being met: I told them you were coming: it's important to them, whatever you think.'

Surprisingly, he gave in. He stood up, smiled with a sudden huge gentleness, and looked about for his jacket, which she found hastily, and helped him into, handing him the car-keys from the desk.

'There's just time, if you hurry. Besides, it's almost certain to be late. It's very good of you.'

'I know,' said Henry, still warmly. He added, 'If that man treats me again with the proprietary air of a don with a good undergraduate who's produced a first-class paper entirely through his help and advice, I shall tip him out on the side of the road and leave him there. No, don't worry, I'll get there. I'll be back before you've had time to worry. And then you can take over and make them feel at home and I'll get back to work. That's fair.'

'Yes,' said Caroline, more hopefully. He seemed at least willing now, and thoroughly aware of what was going on. Perhaps it would be all right, after all. Perhaps they could last the fortnight. Perhaps Coleridge, and whatever he did to Henry could be kept at bay. She felt confident enough to begin to plan, tentatively, how it could be done, considering Henry as though he was a chess piece, and so intent on her problem that she did not catch the amusement with which he noticed her look. It was not easy, in any case, to catch his precise expressions. The first impression of him was overwhelming – he was an enormous man, well over six feet tall, broad shouldered, with strong, wide hands, and a huge head, covered with a very thick, springing crop of prematurely white hair, which merged into an equally live, almost patriarchal beard. This had been grown originally to cover scars left by the war, but had the effect now of a deliberate flamboyance, of a pose, aesthetically entirely satisfactory, it had to be admitted, as the successful literary giant – if the idea of posing had not entailed the idea of fraud, which few people would have accused him of. He was successful, and he was generally considered to be one of the few living giants. He looked like a cross between God, Alfred Lord Tennyson, and Blake's Job, respectable, odd, and powerful all at once. But if all the hair made an immediate impact, it made it difficult to tell more about him. The mobile features seemed to retreat; his eyes, under the exuberant silver eyebrows, were pale and shy, retiring until they seemed almost empty; his mouth, hidden amongst fronds of hair, suggested gentleness, and very little else. He could smile with tremendous kindness from time to time, but there was a curious reticence about him, a lack of presence, a lack of openness, which caused people meeting him to feel obscurely cheated – an impression which they usually had strongly on a first meeting, and later dismissed as unreasonable, remembering it only intermittently.

Caroline was so used to looking at him that she saw both that he was splendid, and that his shirt collar was dirty, and more vaguely that he seemed at ease now, and would almost certainly get as far as the railway station efficiently, and come back. She repeated, 'It *is* good of you,' shepherded him out of the door, and stood for a few moments on the step until she heard the car starting up in the garage. Then she went back into the drawing room, to sit in the window and watch for their arrival. She allowed herself a satisfied smile — what she could do, at least for the time being, had been done. The rest was outside her province.

A moment or so later Anna, who had also heard the car start in the garage, came cautiously down the stairs and stood for a moment in the hall, listening to the silence of the house. She was seventeen, the elder of the Severell children by five years, and had always been much the less prepossessing, a fact of which she was aggressively aware. She was small for her age apparently, and thin, with pronounced hollows above the bones at the base of her neck; she suffered, nevertheless, from that late adolescent padding of flesh which cannot be called fat, or even puppy fat, but contributes a certain squareness to the whole appearance of girls of a certain age, adds a heaviness to the cheeks and chin, makes the waist less marked, and the ankles thicker than they may later be, and suggests even in those who carry themselves well, a certain inevitable clumsiness. Anna did not carry herself well most of the time — on horseback and occupied she had grace, but otherwise she slouched, as though attempting to conceal an over prominent bust, which was not necessary. She was dressed, as usual, in a shapeless Aertex shirt, which had been her school hockey shirt, and boys' heavy jeans, held somewhere between the waist and the hips by an old Girl Guides' belt. She wore no shoes, and her feet, wrists and throat were a deep coffee brown: it was a good summer and she had been out most of the time. Her hair, straight and dark and fine, was like Caroline's but suffered from Anna's indecision over whether or not she was growing it. It had been cropped by regulation at school — a precaution, it was to be assumed, even in that highly expensive establishment for young ladies, against nits — and now it hung, half-way between long and short and bunched irritatingly in her shirt collar. She had Caroline's large dark eyes, and Caroline's narrow nose, but her mouth where

10

Caroline's was wide and generous was prim and round, and was pursed in an expression of habitual vague disapproval. She looked younger than seventeen, and was aware of this too.

She was, at the moment, intent on getting out of the house and hidden before the visitors arrived. She knew that Caroline would have liked her to appear, in a clean dress with her hair pinned back, on the doorstep to greet them, and she had magnified this piece of ordinary politeness into a kind of elaborate social torture contrived by her mother to humiliate her – her dresses, left over from school, were so shapeless, she would be put at such a disadvantage, and her mother knew it. Jeremy would be there, in a clean shirt with his hair brushed, smiling with just the right amount of diffident charm, and that made it worse. It was all right for Jeremy to take part in a family tableau as one of the children, he was young enough, he could carry it off, but for her it was a mockery, it made her even less certain of who she was, and her presence must be embarrassing not only to herself but to the Cannings and everyone else. She was annoyed, with part of herself, that so small an incident should seem so overwhelmingly important, and she could with the same part of herself entirely understand her father's accusation that she was humourless, but the rest of her knew quite certainly that it was important, vastly important, that something would be destroyed if she did not get away and hide.

It was not that she disliked the Cannings. Indeed, in different ways she approved of both of them. Oliver had always been sharply polite to her and had otherwise left her alone, for which she was grateful. Margaret possessed a bright beauty which Anna on the occasion of their last visit had worshipped and envied. She was also happy, in an obvious, wholehearted, exhilarating way which Anna had not believed was possible until she had seen it, and had tried clumsily to share in a way that must have been as upsetting for Margaret as it had become for her. Margaret had been kind to Anna – had tried to talk to her about clothes, about school, about her future, as though she was really interested in Anna's views on these things. Anna had not had any views to offer in recompense for all this attention and had responded only with a slavish, pink-faced, clumsy devotion, a belated schoolgirl crush, over which, remembering it

11

now, she blushed and wriggled again. Margaret was so elegant, she was all golden and perfumed and swept down to breakfast to fling her arms round Oliver's neck with a vigour which no one else Anna knew would have permitted themselves. She would say 'I *like* that, that's *splendid*' and leave for a moment amongst those who were listening the feeling that everything was equally likeable, equally splendid, if only one could achieve the initial enthusiasm to come at it as Margaret did. She would have been sympathetic to Anna's doubts and troubles, Anna supposed, but they were alien to her, they were things she must always have known how to avoid and Anna was ashamed.

It was not as likely as Anna supposed that Margaret had been embarrassed by her behaviour. She had then, as she intended to do now, sulked and hidden, and neither her devotion nor her embarrassment had been very obtrusive. Anna herself was not very obtrusive. And perhaps, if she got out of sight before the car came back, everything could really be avoided. If she came in again at dinner time she could, she thought optimistically, be legitimately silent over her food.

She peered cautiously into the kitchen, just in case Caroline might be there, although she knew her well enough to be fairly certain that she was waiting in the drawing room window by now. Then she went through, and out through the kitchen door into the back garden, under the ash tree and onto the terrace. Out there the heat was solid and stepping into it was like stepping into something thicker and slower than air, a hot bath. Anna pulled her shirt tail out over her jeans and shook it so that the air spread, almost cool for the moment, round her body. She gave a little wriggle of pleasure: she could stand any amount of heat, and had always been able to. This she was proud of – it was one of the few things she had in common with her distant and largely unknown father.

She jumped down the three feet from the terrace onto the back lawn; this was one of her rituals, she never went down by the steps, always leaped from this corner so that the earth was worn bare in one patch, which annoyed the gardener. Then she looked back cautiously and saw that she had been seen.

Her brother, in a spotless white shirt and his school tie, leaned

12

over his bedroom window-sill and called to her in a round boy's voice, 'Anna! Where're you going?'

'Down the garden,' Anna said, driving her hands into her pockets and looking back at him darkly over one hunched shoulder. Jeremy's voice rose anxiously – he was as compulsively sociable as Anna was solitary, but she was not clever enough to see that, and knew merely that he was well-behaved and generally liked where she was not.

'But they'll be here any minute. You know they will. Honestly, Anna, it's *rude* – '

'I don't care. Nor do Oliver and Margaret I should think. Don't fuss.'

'You know Mummy's been looking for you. She was calling you all over the house. Gosh, I don't think you care what *anybody* feels.'

'Nobody cares what I feel,' Anna retorted, and was ashamed of the childishness of this as soon as it was said. She tried to recover herself and said mockingly, 'Don't create,' in the voice of a maid they had once had whose favourite saying this had been: for some reason it always drove Jeremy into a frenzy.

It did now. Jeremy was always, unsupported, less strong than Anna, who had ever liked him and had, since he could walk, avoided any contact with him with a quiet and complete desperation. Like everyone else, he was uncertain of how she fitted in or what to expect of her – now, suddenly visited by an imagined picture of how she might behave if forced to be present at the welcoming, he was not at all sure that she was not better at the bottom of the garden. He said miserably, 'Well, *I* don't care what you do,' pouted slightly and looked vaguely away over her head at the hills beyond. Jeremy had never been one for prolonging a difficult situation, or fighting a losing battle. Anna saw that he had given up, said, not very hopefully, 'And you might have the decency not to go and tell them where I've gone,' and set out again for the orchard, quivering with rage and self-pity. It was horrible to dislike one's family so much.

The orchard was reached through a gate in the fence at the other end of the garden. It was well kept, but not tidy, and very cool and green after the dryness under the sun. Anna dodged between the trees to the far end where there was the messy

13

corner common to all gardens, the place for bonfires, the carefully built compost heaps, piles of canes and old flowerpots, all collected against the high beech hedge, beyond which was the country – lanes, cornfields and low rolling hills. In this corner they had a hut – neither a summer house nor a toolshed but something in between, made of planks and tarpaulin with a wide window onto 'the view' which had been put in at Henry's suggestion. This window was against a gap in the hedge and looked out through it. From the orchard side it was impossible to tell whether anyone was in the hut or not, and Anna had a latch on the inside.

It had been designed as a place to play in for both children once Jeremy was old enough to take an interest in it. Before that it had been for Anna to play house in, which she hadn't done, very much, and there were still the child-sized shelves and benches and cupboards which had been put in for her. They had never played there together – Jeremy had taken it over first as a fort and then as a workshop, and at those times Anna, who had always used it quite simply as a hiding-place, had not gone near it. But lately Jeremy had spent most of his time out of doors, playing tennis and cricket and badminton and above all riding, and Anna had come back. She had been very secret about it, did not go there very often when there was any chance of a real search being put out for her, and had been careful not to shift any of the signs of Jeremy's last occupation – tools in boxes, unsuccessful pieces of carpentry, woodshavings, nails – so that anyone looking in quickly would have seen no sign of her habitation. She did not know what they thought she did down the garden and suspected they thought she left it altogether and went out into the country. So the hut was safe so far, and she could be still there. Anywhere would do; she had no real urge to go further afield.

Once inside, with the latch closed, she spent some time wondering what to do next, thinking that she could sit in the sun if she didn't have to hide, or that she could have got right out and gone to the stables if there had not been a chance of meeting people there whom she had decided not to meet. It had become, as usual, a matter of getting through time until bedtime, of letting the day run through itself somehow without allowing

14

herself to upset herself too much by thinking about intangibles like sex, or her own future, or why she was alive at all. She had become quite adept at not thinking of these things – sometimes she could not remember having thought of anything for some hours together – but as she got older it became more difficult. She saw that this was perhaps inevitable but did not like it. She could not imagine being able to deal with things in any other way.

Having spent some time tucking her shirt back into her jeans and then letting it out again she fetched out from a cardboard box at the back of a large drawer which had once held Jeremy's screwdrivers the exercise book and ball-point pen with which she believed spasmodically that she was writing a novel. It was to be expected that she would want to write. People who met her, knowing that she was Henry's daughter, assumed it, and it was certainly true that at school she had shown no interest in, or aptitude for, anything but the Arts subjects, particularly English. She had been good enough at those for it to be assumed that she would go to the University and read English, at least before the trouble with the school, after which she had left under a cloud. It was still assumed that this was what she would do, but nothing was done about it. Anna did no work, and expressed no interest in applying to colleges or preparing for examinations; Caroline, discouraged by her own lack of knowledge about universities, Anna's unhelpfulness, and the need not to disturb Henry, had done little more than reproach her from time to time, and feel that she must tackle the situation before Anna would have been due to go back to school in the autumn. It was so tiresome, she would say; the school would have arranged it all for them if there had not been all this awkwardness, and really Anna seemed to care so little about anything at the moment that it was probably a waste of time to arrange anything until she knew better what she wanted. There was no real hurry – she could always stay at home until she found out.

Anna turned the pages vaguely, looking at what she had written. From time to time she took intense pleasure in writing, in the act of putting pen to paper, but this never lasted for more than a sentence or at most a paragraph at a time. So that all she had in her notebook was a series of flat mnemonics –

15

phrases, 'light like knives', 'we are all alone' and half a poem. 'Why trees were green once Was of course yourself' – all ordinary enough, but intensely important to her, because she had only just first met them, had only just, for the first time, taken possession of them by writing them down. And the proposed novel, in so far as it had any plot, or life, or impetus, was a string of the same jaded literary mnemonics – the Heathcliff hero whose wickedness Anna, possibly unusually naive for her years, had only just realized the attractiveness of, the heroine, a little timid, a little self-willed, with her face 'framed in a bell of' metallic hair – alternately copper, bronze, silver, whatever Anna pleased – and the worn mixed metaphor really suggested to Anna a new and startling beauty.

But nevertheless, however real and possibly valuable the pleasure Anna might derive from the largely inactive, largely fantastic reconstruction of such a tale, she could not indulge herself, as it is probable most other clever girls of her age could quite profitably have done, with vague dreams of literary fame in the future, caused by some written product entirely different from what she was now amusing herself with, resulting from a labour of writing which at this stage she was, properly, not only not willing to embark on, but not capable of. Day-dreaming and indulgence in stock emotions might well quite simply have been Anna's way to writing, had she been left to herself. But in this area, of course, she was not left to herself. There was Henry Severell. It was likely enough – though not certain – Anna often reflected, that it was almost entirely because of him that it was writing, and writing novels, which so occupied her meditations. That in itself was not an encouraging thought – it made it so much more difficult for her to see her way clearly, or to see who she was, or what she wanted, in her own right. But when it came to the writing itself he was crushing. He presented a standard that it was already impossible for her to attain; he sat in his study, for long hours, and wrote and wrote (he had the tremendous productivity, at the least, of genius) with a slow, satisfied smile under his beard which Anna knew she could never emulate. She could see how it was, in fact, and she could not attain it, and watching Henry drained her dreams of their force. And therefore she could not know, or see clearly enough

16

to wonder, how much force they might have had; she shouldn't have been needing to think *about* them, but there it was, and sooner or later, whenever she began to think in that direction, she came up against Henry.

This was particularly true at home; at school, distance had given her a certain freedom to work in; so that now she merely turned her notebook over once or twice before putting it aside and climbing up onto the bench to lean up against the hot glass of the window and stare out at the fields. She had learned to short-circuit the thought of Henry before she got there, to stop thinking automatically before she reached anything troubling, and now she spent some time feeling the glass, and stirring the dust in the corners, before coming round to considering anything else.

There hadn't, until lately, been very much else. Anna was embedded in that section of the English middle classes which prolongs childhood deep into late adolescence. The deb. or the shopgirl would by Anna's age have had social lives and love affairs of their own to brood over, but Anna still spent her time either with other girls in a girls' boarding school in the country, where her nearest contact with any other form of life was the nostalgic tattle after lights of those more advanced than herself, or at home, again in the country, where she was still officially a child, on a school holiday, and where such entertainment as was provided for her was holiday entertainment for children – tennis, riding, picnics, family parties – with a vista of packing hockey sticks, knee-socks and woolly gloves back into her trunk at the end of a recognizably limited period of pure amusement of this kind.

She had always been outwardly placid and had been possessed of an incredible capacity for living in the present. Being a child had, on the whole, bored her; she had not wanted to be one, and had not wanted what children want. She spent a wartime childhood in a solitary way, living at first alone with her mother in the large house at Darton, and later with her maternal grandparents in the Derbyshire vicarage, sharing a governess with the three daughters of a local bishop. She cared very little for these children, and less for the governess, an intensely Christian woman who spent most of her time encouraging the children

17

to read the Bible and make paper models of Jael and Sisera, David and Goliath, or the crucifixion; Anna's saints and patriarchs, owing to an inbred clumsiness, were more monstrous than Goliath himself, and their monstrosity was what chiefly struck her on looking back at her early schooling; no Homer, no discoveries, no excitement, no golden land, nothing else. Caroline in those days, subdued by the presence of her own parents, and by Henry's absence – Henry had been in a Japanese prison camp in Burma – was difficult to love and perhaps too ready to assume that Anna was content because she always seemed more or less occupied, and did not have fits of hysteria, temper tantrums, asthma, or any of the other troubles which assailed children she knew.

And Anna herself acquiesced, more or less, not unhappily. There had grown in her from as far back as she could remember a sense that she was, as it were, in cold storage, that she was waiting for a sign, for a signal of release, for some event following which she would be able to move into violent action, to be, and to do, and to understand what she was for. It was all there, in the future, it was all possible; what she had now was so insignificant partly by contrast. In the very early days she identified this event with Henry's return from Burma; when he did return, and changed nothing, leaving her still a child and occupied with nothing, it was pushed further into the future. Childhood is so large an area, and seems interminable, so that all that had been possible had been to wait quietly, from day to day, like a prisoner whose life sentence, although he knows that he may be released eventually if he behaves well and does not die first, seems to surround him completely, to cut him off from any future and any brightness there may be. Anna had known, at times almost passionately, that there must be an end to this life which was only eating and sleeping and playing, and, knowing it, had for most of the time put it out of her mind with an extraordinary calm, and had eaten, and slept, and played as though she were a child completely, with a deliberation that amounted to the carrying out of a ritual.

The torments of physical adolescence, which came upon her later than is usual, took her entirely by surprise. She was suddenly clutched by too much energy, by wild fits of bodily anguish during which she was driven to occupy herself by banging her head rhythmically against a wall, to bite her hands, or at the least to go for long miserable walks which left her more tense, and apparently more straining, than she had been when she set out. She went about with her hands clenched until the nails marked her palms, and her teeth set unconsciously together so that she noticed that her jaw ached with the effort, and still could not relax it. Things became suddenly beautiful, intolerably beautiful, and she intolerably aware of them: she found herself, despite herself, driven to tears by the intense green she saw, looking up through the apple trees at the summer sky, unable to reduce the profusion of the gold-edged crossing twigs and the overlapping, deepening, glittering rounds of the leaves against that uncompromising midsummer blue to any order that she could comprehend. Her senses were assailed that summer, everything was disproportionate – the feel of damp grass, the smell of wet earth, even the odd patterns of the light shining on her mother's polished tables, distressed her altogether. It was all too much, and yet it was not final; it was as though something had grabbed her and flung her wildly about, however she protested, and yet would never shake her quite into submission: the times of wild excitement and distress always alternated with times of extreme dullness, where she could hardly summon strength to creep out of the house into the garden, or strength when she was out there, to lift her hands from her sides or her eyes from her path in front of her to notice the trees or the hills and sky beyond. And so she endured; she was capable of enduring because the strain of laziness deep in her allowed for this uproar as it had allowed for the boredom of childhood. She believed she would ride this storm as she had ridden the calm, and this exasperated her curiously – why, if she could endure, if she could arrive at her event, which was not yet, must she be subjected to so much embarrassment? It was not real, even the immediate agony was only momentarily complete, and that was the worst thing.

Finally, some weeks through her enforcedly extra long holiday, she had fallen in love. His name was Michael Farne, and he had kissed her unexpectedly one afternoon in the stables, belonging to a certain John Ellis, where he kept his horse and where Anna and Jeremy went to ride. Until that time she had not noticed him particularly, although she had envied him his horse, a huge black hunter which won prizes in the open jumping throughout the county. He was large, blond, square-shouldered and pleasant. He had just come down from Cambridge, where he had taken a Third in History, and was waiting to be called into the Navy. This was all that Anna knew about him, and all that she had dared to attempt to find out. Once she had decided she was in love with him she did not know what to do with his presence. She could not meet his eye, or speak to him, or offer him any encouragement. He called, once or twice, casually, at the Severells' house, and was offered tea by a puzzled Caroline. He took Anna to the cinema once, too, and held her hand all the way through, whilst Anna shivered, and suffered, and waited with awful longing for the moment when she could relive all this for herself, alone in bed at night. In the end, discouraged possibly by her silence, and by the apparently cold and defiant gaze she had turned on him, he had not come back.

Anna made no attempt to find out why – partly because she had never been in the habit of doing anything about anything, and partly because it was not until he had gone, and she was not preoccupied with what to say to him next, that she came to see how much she loved him. She did go to the stables, once or twice, to stare at him mutely and desperately across the yard, but she did not cross to him, or address him, only looked, as though she was intent on learning him off; his clothes, his face, the ways his bones fitted, the shape of his haunches in his breeches, the silver bleached line of shaved hair above his ear. He glanced at her curiously once or twice, and she hunched her shoulders, drawing miserably into herself, hoping not to be seen. There was nothing provocative about her, only this intense, painful stare. Michael did not come over.

Once she was sure he would not, she dropped into love like a stone into water, and submerged tracelessly and altogether. She spent her time constructing conversations and embraces which had never taken place and were not likely to; she dreamed of Michael, naturally and obsessively, night after night: she imagined, when out walking, that he was about to appear around every next corner. She found, curiously, that although bad at drawing, she could produce a recognizable likeness of him, and filled page after page of her notebooks with the same square, blond, slightly smiling face, or the same solid body, set lightly on its feet in every conceivable and inconceivable posture. He became a way of seeing, a way of possessing by incantation the things seen which had so distressed her. She would look up at the branches and say 'Michael, Michael, Michael', confusing the one intense feeling in the other, reducing the earlier loose distress into something comprehensible because it was love, which was expected, and could be mastered at least to the extent of being named.

This was in some sense an advance. The nastiness was that deep down Anna knew it was an advance and knew why, and despised herself for it. Something in her withdrew cautiously from this love, preparing already for when it should end and no longer be enough. It was a coldness, a wariness, a holding back. Anna did not like it, and ignored it as far as possible, and yet rested lazily on it since it was her last strength.

But now, for the moment, Michael was a way to a first tentative sense of power. She relaxed on her bench and considered the cornfields through the blurred and dusty glass, seeing the lanes across his imaged face and his hair in all the reticulated gold of the corn, and she had a first faint, wary sense of having her place in the world, a way of taking possession of the bright things seen, and she was elated and afraid.

TWO

THE TRAIN FROM London to Darton was a stopping train with no corridor, and high, benched uncomfortable seats without arm-rests. The Cannings had a compartment to themselves and sat in one corner of it facing each other. Oliver was working. He had opened his briefcase, and surrounded himself with papers, the moment they were settled, and now he read, and scribbled, and tapped his teeth with his pen, altogether closed in. Margaret watched him. In her lap her gloved hands were crossed over a copy of the *Listener*, which she had bought because it had a picture of Henry, a commentary on a dramatized reading of one of his novels on the Third Programme, and a letter from Oliver, pointing out mistakes that had been made in the reading. Underneath the *Listener* she was hiding one of the glossier cheap women's magazines, which she had bought from the station bookstall when it became apparent that Oliver was not going to talk to her during the journey. She was ashamed of this now, and had not opened it, had tried to pretend she hadn't got it, although she was almost certain that Oliver had seen her buy it. She had always been addicted to these magazines, seeing them, she believed, as an alien but comfortable world, full of bright little hints for improving one's 'home' or appearance, which she never followed but knew her way about in altogether, and stories and letters which managed at the same time to make love a glamorous and uncomplicated and energetic passion, and to cast some of this glamour and energy into the ordinariness of secretaries and suburbs and bachelor girls in London flats. Margaret herself was not ordinary in this sense, but nevertheless her interest had not, perhaps, entirely the quality of amused looking in that she attributed to it. She believed in love, and the power of love to invigorate and transform and illuminate, in love as a last resort from dullness, and derived genuine comfort from the stories, with their endings so final and certain, cast as she was on a shore where things were strange and dry, and both love and dullness wore forms so alien and complicated that she could not always distinguish one from the other or recognize either for what it was until too late.

Oliver, she had discovered, believed the reading of such papers to be positively morally wrong. She had continued to read them for some time after her marriage, and he had said nothing to her; she had discovered what he felt quite accidentally, by overhearing a speech he was making to one of his friends about the students at the training college for women where he worked, one of his fierce, absolute little speeches,

22

which frightened both her and the students. 'One has *never* time to read that kind of stuff,' he said. 'One has so short a life, and there is always something one could be reading that would add to one's knowledge, or give one some insight into things.' Oliver's friend had acquiesced, as he had been expected to do, as a matter of course, and Margaret had received another of the small shocks she was always open to, living with Oliver: she had never managed to learn in time which things carried this tremendous moral importance, and now and then she went, as she saw it, badly wrong.

Now, having looked at the photograph of Henry and taken pride in Oliver's name, solid and undeniable at the bottom of his letter, she did not want to read any further in the *Listener*. She had heard Oliver talk it all over, before. She turned instead to watching Oliver write, and to looking out of the window anticipating Darton, her spirits rising with every further rattle and plunge of the train.

The Cannings were an odd couple; everyone thought so, including Margaret herself, who used to brood over their oddity from time to time with feelings that ranged from a kind of illicit excitement, a feeling of freedom from anything she had known, to a completely bewildered sense of having lost her bearings, and having let herself in for coping with something she would never be competent to understand. She liked this too, most of the time; she had always approached even the least likely relationship with zest, as though if she applied herself entirely to it something supremely important must emerge. Sometimes it did. Sometimes, on the other hand, people suspected her, in her innocence, of trying to get round them, of wanting vaguely to get something out of them, although what, beyond a quite straightforward personal contact, that something might be these people never stopped to ask, and would have found no answer if they had. It was probably partly her look which gave that impression; she had the well-ordered classical beauty, with not a hair out of place, that always seems a little remote; there was something languorous and elegant in her from which one does not normally expect the first advances. She was tall – a good six inches taller than Oliver – and rose blonde, with a gold skin and large yellow-brown eyes. She wore her hair long, having the theory that what men liked was hair, as long as it was good hair, and that too much arrangement only distracted them from it. Like many real blondes, she was never quite sure that what she had was not slightly vulgar, and believed she would have liked to be black-haired and dark-skinned and mysterious; this did not stop her understanding and exploiting her blondeness to the full.

Oliver was a little man, and had the little man's way of sitting with his shoulders stiff, his back straight, and his head pointing slightly upwards; he had the little man's compact command over his own body, too, and sat drawn together in a way that made him look even littler, like a small animal, a field vole, a water rat, which can shrink itself through holes one would never dream of putting it through. His head was large for his body, long and thin and pointed, his nose and mouth sharpened, his eyebrows cornered at the top. His skin was pale, and looked as though it would mark easily; his hair, black, and wispy, was short back and sides, but grew to a widow's peak on his forehead and straggled a little across the top of his head in one or two long locks which occasionally fell into his eyes. He had little, useless-looking hands and feet, the bones so slender that it seemed possible to crush his hand on shaking it. From the way he gripped his pen it was apparent that there was more strength in them than that; there was a determined, wiry precision; it was even possible for him to write legibly on a train. Margaret watched him, as she had always done, with a certain basic excitement. He was that kind of man – usually a little man – in whom almost all women can immediately sense great sexual energy, very near the surface, very controlled and directed.

Nobody, when they had married, had predicted it, or been able immediately to explain it. They had been married five years now, and had met, the summer before their marriage, in Cambridge, where Oliver, a post-war graduate, had been finishing a Ph.D. thesis, and applying for Fellowships. He had been an old student; born in 1922 he had been called into the army in 1940, and had gone up to Cambridge in 1946, taken his degree in 1949, and had spent the next three years writing his doctoral thesis. Margaret, five years younger, felt in many ways a generation younger when she met him – this was partly because she was herself, at twenty-three, slightly older in fact than the young men she came to visit, although nobody noticed it.

She looked out of the window at cornfields and allotments which glowed, even the grimiest of them, in that sun, like glimpses, constantly whisked in and out of sight, of the summer holiday in the country to which she was at last being carried, full ears of corn, tall lupins, dusty-blue scabious, sweet peas and bachelors' buttons, hot pink and gold, so much sharper and clearer than the dying sparks and the grit which the train cast on them, and then down at her own lap again and met the small blurred newsprint eyes of Henry Severell. The Cannings' life lately had not been easy and the thought of Henry was to Margaret a promise not only of physical comfort and rest which they both, she thought, needed, but of a larger space for living, for understanding how they were living, which she thought they needed even more. It would be good for Oliver, she thought, to be able to talk daily with a man with a mind like that; she did not specify in what way she thought it would be good, but she knew it would be. Henry Severell was after all a genius, they said; he saw some things more clearly than other people, and was preoccupied with larger issues than those they were struggling with. She hoped vaguely that some of all this might rub off on Oliver, and for that matter on herself: it was like first communion, like first saying 'I love you', it was time to reflect and make contact with the depths.

He looked up, frowning, to ask, 'Where are we?'

'Darton, next stop,' said Margaret. 'It can only be ten minutes.'

'I suppose Henry will be late,' Oliver said, packing papers into his briefcase. 'Do I look tidy?'

'Beautiful,' said Margaret, meaning it.

Oliver looked suspiciously at her, and stood up to comb his hair, very carefully, in the railway mirror.

The train came into Darton Station. Oliver removed his spectacles, with a click, from his nose to his pocket, and began to lift suitcases from the rack. Margaret hung dangerously from a half-open door, gripping her hat and surveying the platform.

Henry was there, striding amongst milk churns sparkling with sun, mopping his face with his handkerchief. He had nearly been late. Margaret thought, Henry was there, it was going to be all right, with a hugely disproportionate feeling of relief, stumbled to the platform as the train jerked to a halt and began to run, noisily on high heels, towards him. People turned to stare as she came up to him, throwing herself against him, and burying her face in his solid shoulder.

'Henry,' she said. 'Henry, oh, Henry. Dear Henry, what a wonderful day. Oh, Henry, how good to see you!'

'And you,' said Henry. 'I was rather afraid I was going to be late.'

Oliver came up with the suitcases, a line of sweat already along his lip.

'Hullo, Oliver,' said Henry. 'Give me those.' He disengaged himself from Margaret's embrace, took the suitcases, put them down to shake Oliver's hand, gathered them up again and set off towards the ticket barrier with his guests hurrying behind him. The ticket collector said, 'Good afternoon, Mr Severell,' and enquired after Jeremy, whose departures for school were made into charming social occasions by Jeremy's polite questions about the station master's wife, and the difficulty of formulating the summer time table. Henry replied that Jeremy was healthy, and turned back half-way across the car park to shout that he had taken a First in the junior open jumping at Aruncester show. The ticket collector roared back his congratulations whilst Henry pushed Oliver and the suitcases into the back of the car, Margaret into the front, and started with a jerk.

'They like you here,' Margaret said to him.

'They like Jeremy,' Henry said. 'He'll wear himself out, getting people to love him.'

'But if they *do* – ' Margaret began. Henry did not take her up, and sank into a silence which seemed quite natural to him and so determined that neither of the Cannings broke it until they reached the house. Margaret was content to relax and enjoy her coming; Oliver, on the other hand, sat bolt upright on the back seat, pressing his hands into the leather, and studying Henry's erratic driving with an apparently growing concern.

When they turned into the drive, breaking into the stillness

26

of the garden with a crunch and spurt of gravel, Margaret saw
Caroline on the doorstep, one hand on Jeremy's shoulder, and
prepared with pleasure for the ceremonial of arrival. Henry
opened her door for her, and she came out into the sun, shaking
her skirts free and smiling at the roses; Caroline and Jeremy
came down from the steps to meet them in the path; for a
moment she put her face against Caroline's cool cheek; and
they they were telling each other that the weather could not
have been better, that the journey had been very easy, meaning,
Margaret thought with joy, that they understood this talk, they
could do it, they knew where they were. She could have hugged
Caroline, except that that would have been out of order, and
would have spoiled it.

Jeremy came up and held out his hand to her, and told her,
slightly husky with shyness, how much he had been looking
forward to her coming. Margaret smiled vaguely at him. He
was a very beautiful child, although she had assumed boys
didn't like to be told so, dark like Caroline and Anna, with
high cheek-bones, and clear eyes under unusually long lashes,
and a skin so smooth and glowing that she nearly put out a
finger to touch it. She assumed he would really dislike that, and
may have been right, although he had already begun to encourage older boys at school who felt the same desire – with nothing
more than a gentle smile, it was true. Jeremy simply liked to be
liked. He said now, 'May I take your hat, Aunt Margaret, and
your bag?' and Margaret was pleased again to be so accepted
by all of them. It had been Caroline's idea that Oliver and
Margaret should be uncle and aunt to her children – a procedure
she followed with most of her fairly regular adult guests. This
amused Oliver, delighted Margaret, and gave full scope to
Jeremy for the intimate use of first names which was to be such
an asset to him in his later life. Anna called them nothing at all
when she could manage this, and otherwise alternated clumsily
and unmethodically between Mr Canning, Uncle Oliver, and
plain Oliver, depending on her mood, and her current theory
as to how much Oliver disliked her.

Caroline took Margaret upstairs to her rose and silver room,
and showed her drawers, towels, cupboards, smiled when Margaret admired her flowers, and then sat down in a friendly way

27

on the edge of the bed to wait until Margaret should be ready to go down to tea. This was a sign of intimacy, that she should wait like a girl with a school friend, rather than leaving Margaret politely alone, and Margaret took it as such, but neither of them spoke, Margaret because she did not want to spoil this silent friendliness, this moment of calm communion which she felt was between them, and Caroline because she was suddenly extremely angry with Anna, and found it, for a moment, all she could do not to burst out with some exclamation of fury and disappointment.

She was not given to questioning herself, but even so she had lately wondered why she was so often reduced to trembling with rage over all Anna's small misdemeanours. She had been one of those clean little girls who had cried when put down on her first beach because the sand was dirty, and now felt a positive nausea at the sight of Anna's shirt collars, or her grimy bare feet, trailing up the stairs. When she wanted Anna, as she did now, she thought, her underclothes sticking to her with heat and crossness, Anna was away sulking somewhere, and never thought of welcoming visitors, taking them off Henry's hands, or carrying tea-trays. When she did not want Anna, she was sure to fall over her, stretched full length and grubby on the drawing-room carpet, involved in some private agony which she imposed upon Caroline without any intention of allowing her to share it or alleviate it, as Jeremy might have done. Her shoulders, folded in grief, were hunched over every meal table, however little she said, so that Caroline felt that she was some evil spirit who had taken possession of the life she had arranged round her husband and her house, and was brooding over it, was weighing on it, would never leave it.

She had been prepared to feel, and suppress, some small annoyance over the growing up of another woman in her house, but Anna could hardly be called a woman, she had no idea of anything, Caroline thought more and more wildly, no will and no intentions, she would never go away, and she, Caroline, was growing older and would hardly manage to get rid of Anna in time to enjoy what she had spent so long building before she would become tired and restricted herself. She was never so much a mother that she did not still dream of a privacy which excluded children and left her as young as she chose to be; this had intensified with the onset of the menopause. Anna would not go unless someone made her; it was time all the talk about universities was brought to something, one way or the other. She resolved to speak to Oliver about it. He would know, and was efficient; he would find out whether it was any use thinking of sending Anna to any university. This would have the added advantage of not troubling Henry. Having made a decision brought her a little peace, although she still felt sick at the prospect of Anna's appearance at dinner, in jeans doubtless, with unwashed hands and unbrushed hair. She said, rather proud of herself for having sat still and unruffled through all this distress:

'I think it's hotter today than ever, don't you?'

'Terribly hot,' said Margaret, 'but so much fresher here than in London, one doesn't mind so much.' She had washed her hands and face and was now sitting at the dressing table, brushing out her hair; when she was in someone else's house she always took advantage of spare room cleanness and neatness to attend to herself in a more leisurely and thorough way than at home; she was on show, to herself as well as to others, and liked to watch her face in strange mirrors and play to herself the fine lady that all little girls pretend to be and all women still imagine to be somewhere either in the future or some other surroundings, whose possibility is suddenly glimpsed again in places bare of personal associations, spare room, cloakrooms in restaurants, mirrors across the table at public dinners. She turned quickly to Caroline, gathering her warm hair between the brush and her hand, coiling it gently and stabbing it with long, bronze coloured pins. She did not really need to look at it. 'You've no idea,' she said, 'how much coming here means to me. After even so much of this kind of summer in London, to be really in the country, really resting. Heaven!'

'I thought you seemed a little tired, when we last met.'

'I have been very tired,' Margaret burst out. 'It hasn't been easy lately. I –' She stifled a confessional impulse; it would not do to break the peace so soon, it might not be necessary, and she was not sure how Caroline would take anything of that kind. She went on, 'I don't stand heat well –' and turned back

29

to the mirror, brushing mascara into her lashes, and colour into her lips, turning a dark pencil once or twice on a beauty spot at the corner of her mouth. Her face sloped this way and that, stretched and contracted as she treated it, all planes in all directions, and then suddenly slipped into place again as she took out a tissue and blotted her lipstick. She gave herself a long look, enjoying herself, and was gathered together, made up. Caroline looked at her incuriously. She had long ago passed the age where confidences were usual or desirable, and from feeling that talk of clothes and children and housekeeping was a useful and civilized clue to the woman beneath the talk, she had come to be genuinely more interested in clothes and children and housekeeping. She registered Margaret's trouble and skirted it, and said gently, 'If you're ready . . .'

Margaret stood up and ran over to the window, to look out and establish her position in the place. She looked down into the garden, and over it to the fruit trees, and beyond them to the hills. It was all still shining with heat. Beneath her, Henry and Oliver were crossing the lawn towards the orchard, Henry striding, and Oliver, just behind him, hunching his shoulders to counterbalance the weight of an imaginary gown, clenching his fists in the small of his back. Margaret almost called down to them to ask if they would wait, if she could come with them, and then thought better of it. Oliver would like to be alone with Henry. It was something, after all, to be walking intimately with Henry Severell in his own orchard. Margaret turned to Caroline.

'I'm quite ready,' she said. 'For anything at all, here.'

In the garden, Anna heard their progress between the trees, and shrank into herself on her bench, peering out with one eye between two boards so that as they came nearer they crossed her line of vision once or twice, first her father, with his head huge among the branches, then Oliver, almost scurrying after him, small and black. 'So they're here,' she said to herself, clasping her hands round her knees, motionless, 'and Oliver's after him already.' Protecting Henry from questions was bred in her, and she had seen the two of them together before. 'Not that it's anything to do with me,' she finished to herself, and heard their voices clear through the orchard.

'Nice,' said Oliver, 'to have this on one's doorstep.' They had come now to the hedge and were standing over the gate, not far from Anna, looking out into the cornfield, beyond which were a few trees, hawthorn and birch, and beyond that the rise of the first hill, warm green and russet with bracken, grey with the odd, uncovered stone.

'Is any of it yours?'

'Not beyond the garden.'

'You always wear such an air of the landowner, I'd thought all this was yours, too. Why should I have thought that?'

'I don't know,' said Henry, who did know.

'A pocket of England as it used to be,' said Oliver, 'before subtopia got it, before concrete and corrugated iron and diesel fumes, before London and Birmingham and Manchester started putting out feelers towards each other and spreading smoke further than that. You're a lucky man.' Henry stirred with something which was possibly irritation.

'It's terrible now,' Oliver went on, as Henry said nothing, 'when I come to the country, when I see real grass and trees, I don't believe in it, I imagine it's all a show specially put on and preserved for my benefit, you know, like ancient monuments – filled up with period chairs fetched from everywhere else to make the house look lived in again – as it never *was*, not with *those* chairs. I think they've put a tree here and corn there, and let some water run across the corner of the picture, so I can have a bit of everything and see what country used to be. But all so permitted, so contrived. Don't you find that? I'm sure now, if I walked out of your bottom of the garden frame, I'd find something quite horrid before I went very far. Oh, I know it's all here, but I don't believe in it, it's not relevant.'

'You would find something quite horrid. They're putting up asbestos pig sheds in rows, in the field just down the road. Very subtopian pigsheds. I don't know if you mind subtopia for pigs.'

Oliver laughed, small and sharp. After a time he said, 'No, but don't you feel, sometimes, that this is a bit thin, now, you must know what I mean – that it's not what's important now? Doesn't it make you feel guilty? Don't you think you should go out and come to grips with the horror?'

'Come to grips?' asked Henry, in his slow, singing voice. 'Do

31

you mean describe, or condemn, or both? No, I can't say I do. And I wouldn't know how else to come to grips. I'm not going to live in it, or near it. I don't have to. Why should I?'

'Because it's real. Because it's urgent.'

'I find this real and urgent enough,' Henry muttered into his beard. He looked away from Oliver, and down at his own hands side by side on the top of his gate, large and clumsy and very passive. His face became vacant; this was because he was angry that Oliver, with his concern, should act as the forerunner of his condemned subtopia, imposing it where it was not, talking limits into land Henry lived in, and found, easily, limitless. Oliver seemed aware, if not of his anger, of a certain constraint; he was silent for a moment, and then began again, coming round at his companion another way.

'I suppose all this,' he said, sticking doggedly for some reason to the scene in front of them, 'must seem a bit comfortable to you now, after your war in the jungle, and so forth. I always find the south a bit tame, myself, even, coming from where I do – I expect the land to be all rocks and heather, and sharp edges, and ups and downs, you know. The south's a bit rounded off, for me. A bit too finished.'

'I haven't much sense of proportion,' Henry said oddly. He moved slightly, twisting his head down and then up, to ease his neck muscles, so that Anna saw his face for a moment, the eyes, then the mouth, open and drawn tight, then the flash of the beard. Like a cross horse, she thought. Oliver should learn not to tackle him so, like a newspaperman; anyone can see he doesn't like it.

'Ah,' said Oliver. He waited a moment, then said, 'Now I've annoyed you; why?'

Henry laughed. 'I suppose because you bring so much with you. All the problems of urban sprawl, the north against the south, mining villages in Derbyshire, jungles in Burma – oh, yes, and my work – you go on driving that round and round. Why can't you just look at it, and leave it alone? I like looking at that hill.'

'We all bring so much with us. We can't help it.'

'That's all right,' said Henry, making a flattening motion with one of his hands. 'But let it lie, let it lie.'

32

'It's not in me,' said Oliver, with mock sorrow. 'It's not the way I go on. It may work for you. Only I am full of care, and I don't stare, I think.'

He sounded a little patronizing and a little defensive. Then he came closer to Henry, and said, very fiercely, 'And you think too. Why else do you write novels and not lyrics? When shall we see the next novel?' Henry swung away from him.

'I don't know. I'm doing a little academic work.'

'On what?'

'Oh – Coleridge – ' said Henry unwillingly, thinking that it was a curious intimacy, between a writer and his intelligent reader. There was so much less space either for privacy or for discovery than there should be. He and Oliver had been so explicit on paper; he about his world and Oliver about his intelligent reading of that world; they knew, in this one area, more than most men ever knew about each other, so that to talk was ridiculous. And yet, as men, they had no touch. Oliver made a series of experimental holes with his screw-driver mind, and he, Henry, did as best he could. He did not like to be researched into in the flesh. He wished he had not said as much as he had about what he was doing. He gathered himself together and expended his energies on retreat, staring at his hands on the gate until he was conscious of nothing but them, the lines on the knuckles, the rough, flaking paint on the wood under them, the short hairs, that stood up and shone along his wrists. '*I can look at a knot in a piece of wood till I am frightened at it*,' Blake said. Henry could look at anything until he was lost and saw, and heard, nothing beyond it. The shadow of leaves on his right hand was peculiarly satisfactory, small rounds and long dashes; on his left, in the sun, the sweat glittered slightly in the pores. His hands grew and glowed at him; he felt slightly dizzy; from a long way away Oliver's patient voice repeated firmly, 'And Anna? Where is Anna?'

That was a safe question; it was conversation, not interrogation, nor exploration. He said, 'I don't know. She's been moody lately. She's in love.'

'Happily?'

'Naturally not.'

'I'm sorry,' said Oliver dryly. 'I suppose she goes back to school shortly?'

'No, she was – we were asked to remove her. She ran away from school, you know, last term. Not in this direction.'

'Who enticed her? Where did she go?'

'I don't know,' said Henry. It was apparent that the idea that she might have gone to someone else was new to him. 'I don't know, she doesn't seem to want to say. We don't interfere.'

'You should find out. What will she do now?'

Henry looked vague, and began to move away from the gate. 'Nobody seems to know. I believe she's quite clever. The school seemed to think so, before all this trouble.'

'Isn't it time,' said Oliver professionally, 'she was making her mind up?'

Anna saw them for a moment and then heard them weaving back as they had come, between the trees, one behind the other. They said something indistinguishable and then Henry's voice reached her for a moment, 'She'll grow out of it,' and then she heard the creak, very small, of the gate into the garden. Grow out of it, she thought. Of course I'll grow out of it. I'm growing out of it now, that's what hurts. I'm growing out of everything, all the time, too quickly. One gets sore. Of course, she thought, hating her father now, too, for betraying her so casually, so carelessly; of course, I'm silly. I know I'm silly, I know I'll grow out of it. But meanwhile, until I'm not silly, there's nothing. One is trapped in one's own silliness, quite as much as in love. Probably more.

And they had broken her mood, obtruded things she was deliberately not thinking of, her future and, worse, her abortive attempt to escape, which she would have preferred to forget altogether. She had left quietly one Sunday morning whilst the other girls were putting on their Sunday hats for church and had taken the train north as far as the nearest large city, which was York. Here she went out into the city to look at it; there was nothing she could do that day, it was Sunday, nothing was ever done on a Sunday. She climbed up onto the walls, with her suitcase knocking against her knees, and walked briskly round them, looking out brightly at roofs and sloping grass ramparts. Just not to be at school was a release, to be doing something on her own, alone, was to be light and singing.

But in the evening she began walking from hotel to hotel, hesitating at every front door, afraid to go in. She felt that inside, under bright lights, porters and receptionists would immediately see that she was in some way a fraud. They would know she was out without leave from somewhere where she should have been shut up, and they would find out from her where it was, and make telephone calls. She walked a long way in this indecision, and in the end, when it was already dark, she came back to the station and sat on her suitcase, staring miserably at the bulk of the Station Hotel. She was very tired and there was a fine rain falling. Looking back at this time from the garden Anna told herself that she had had no reason to be afraid, no reason at all, that she had behaved extremely stupidly – and nevertheless she shuddered, remembering the heavy street, and the cold gas lamps, the sudden grim and oppressive northernness of the city that had been by day so lightly poised, and carved, and clean.

Finally she walked into the first house she came to – a small Victorian tenement house, painted an uneven chocolate-brown, with narrow, dirty windows and a hand-painted notice in red ink. Bed and Breakfast, 10/6. Her room was horrid – a sloping attic with frosted glass in the window, and grey, limp curtains and sheets which seemed slightly greasy to the touch. The bed was cast iron and rattled. There was no mirror, only a huge wash hand stand with a bowl of water, filmed over with dust. She felt suddenly and finally trapped – when she pushed up the window with a great deal of effort to look at the sky, she was confronted by a blank wall and a dark window. Once up, the window would not close again, and the draught sucked directly across the bed. Anna slept badly.

And then, failure set in. Looking back, Anna could still not understand it, and jibbed, so painful was the remembering, as trying to do so. She hadn't known, when she got there, quite what she meant to do, but there seemed, from the garden, to have been so many things. She could have got a job. She could have sat, alternatively, in the Minster, which was beautiful, and have thought out what she wanted. She could have worked all

35

day and written the novel at night. But she had gone to the cinema, afternoon and evening, sitting in the red warmth in the cheapest seats, sometimes seeing the whole programme through twice. At first she had been filling a putative 'waiting time' and later she could not think of anything else to do. When she had visited all the cinemas, and her money was running out, she packed her suitcase, paid the landlady and spent her last shillings on a ticket back to school. She had been quite calm over all this at the time, as though mesmerized by her daily routine, cold breakfast, cold early lunch, the cinema, supper, the cinema and cold bed, into thinking not that this course of action was inevitable, it was nothing as forceful as that, but that all her actions had no weight and no importance, that she was living in a vacuum, and might as well do any one thing as any other. It had been a running down, an unwinding, and when her mind was moving slowly enough, she saw, in blinkers, no road except the one back to school. So, with this curious calmness, she went back.

When she arrived late at night, she was hustled crossly into the san., isolated, and allowed to speak to no one. In a day's time, Henry appeared and told her she was to go and pack her trunk, they were going home, now. Anna, who had spent her period of isolation sitting on the bed and looking out of the window, had not got up when he came in; now she looked up at him and said, 'Why? When'm I coming back?'

'You aren't,' Henry said. 'I've been asked to remove you.'

'Why?'

'They say they can't do anything with you, and you don't participate in the life of the school in the slightest. They think they've failed with you, and you'd be better in some other kind of place.'

'They seem to have said a lot.'

'They have. They've been on the telephone every day for the last week. At great length.'

Anna put her hand to her mouth; this counted very badly as disturbing Henry's work. She said sulkily, 'I don't see why they don't leave me alone.'

'The police were out after you, you know.'

Anna digested this and was silent. Outside the san. there was

36

the sound of tennis balls, plucking against taut strings; Henry seemed to listen, and count for a moment. Then he said, in his vaguest voice, looking up out of the high window at the summer sky or the dangling blind cord, 'Well, where did you go, and why?'

Anna could only see his beard, and chin, turned away from her. She said, 'I went north. It was all right. You can see I've not come to any harm. There's no need to fuss.'

She was conscious of a desire that Henry should hammer at her with questions, should find out for her why she had gone, and what she had wanted, and why it had been so peculiarly nasty, but he said nothing more, neither then nor later.

She saw that this was meant as a delicacy, a respect for her privacy, and was grateful. At least, she believed she was grateful; underneath the gratitude there was a feeling that this very delicacy was a casting off, and that she would have been happier if her parent had not left her alone with the responsibility of knowing what had happened.

She sat for some time exploring, in spite of herself, the York back streets over again, and wishing that there was not such a paucity of other things to think about instead. It became very slightly cooler. Then she heard steps in the orchard, and, as they came closer, smelt, faintly, the bitterness of cheap cigarette smoke. Someone tried the door, which opened as far as the latch, a hook on a ring, would let it.

'Anna,' said Oliver, 'let me in.'

Anna sat still, and said nothing.

'I can open it myself, of course,' he said, and curled two thin fingers, stained dull yellow with nicotine, round the door and under the latch. Anna shrank into her corner and watched him come in. He closed the door behind him, and brushed his hands together, the cigarette hanging for a moment, incongruously, from his mouth corner. Then he put up his fingers again and took it, and the momentary look he had had of street corner gangsterhood vanished altogether.

'Well?' he said. Anna remained curled on her bench and looked at him defiantly over her knees. She repeated after him, 'Well?' and did not move.

'I knew you were here, of course. What are you doing?'

'Nothing in particular.'

'All afternoon? I don't like the idea that you should find it necessary to hide from us, particularly if you're not otherwise occupied with anything. I shouldn't think it's politic, either. Your mother's looking all over for you, and she's not getting any more reconciled. Why don't you come in to tea?'

'I don't want to,' said Anna. She added, unwillingly, exposing herself, 'It's not as though it made any real difference to anyone whether I was there or not.'

'Ah, I see,' said Oliver, as though she had offered him an important confidence. He seemed to think that she had given him the right to settle in; at least, he drew forward one of Jeremy's boxes from the wall, dusted it, and sat on it, facing her.

'Even if that's so, there's something to be said for managing people in their own terms. You get more out of them that way. For instance, why don't you do something about your hair? Surely it's better to be able to see? And do you always wear those trousers?'

'I don't see that it matters what I look like,' Anna said, stung. 'I'm comfortable.'

'One should always be some sort of presence to the world. All this messiness – so ordinary – such a *usual* protest. I should have thought you could do better than jeans and shagginess if you did want to be against things.'

'I just want,' said Anna, sliding hastily down the bench, and standing with her back against it, ready to escape – 'I just want to be left alone. If you don't mind.'

'No one can be.' Anna moved towards the door, and Oliver put out a hand to stop her. 'No, wait. You should be glad that I'm paying so much attention to you. Now, tell me, what do you mean to do with yourself?'

'Wash my hands and go in to tea, like a good girl.'

'Don't be silly. I mean, what are you going to do next? With your life?'

'I don't know – '

'Any ideas?'

'No – I – I shall think. There's plenty of time. Something'll turn up.'

'That's a phrase I intensely dislike. How old are you? Eighteen? It's time you thought. For instance, if you don't do something soon, university'll be out of the question, and that's all sorts of paths closed to you. Already. I gather you're bright.'

'At some things.'

'That's enough. I'll look into it for you.'

'I don't think I want – '

'We'll try and find out what you do want.'

'Please,' Anna cried, 'leave me alone.'

'You've been left alone too much. I should have thought that was obvious.' His voice changed; he said, much more gently, 'Why did you run away from school?' Now that the question had been asked, Anna found it intolerable.

'It isn't your business. It's nothing to do with you. I don't know why I did. Please '

'You should have been asked before – '

'And don't criticize us. Nobody should have mentioned it to you at all, don't you see. *It's nothing to do with you.*'

'Anna – ' said Oliver. But she had brushed past him, and was moving through the trees, her own feet so heavy on her ears that she thought he was behind her. But when she came up to the gate and clutched it, and looked back, he was standing stiffly by the hut, expressionless, both hands rather awkwardly in his pockets. So she went on into the house, and washed her hands for tea.

THREE

THE FIRST WEEK of their visit passed uneventfully enough, partly at least because it was too hot for any of them to want to do more than sit in the garden, or walk to and from the village along the back lanes, amongst the dust and hawthorn. They all had a sense that it should be a quiet time, a time for doing nothing and taking stock, too hot to make any effort, yet.

Jeremy alone was energetic; he was at that age; later they all remembered him as an essential part of the good weather and holiday feeling. He was always in and out, hunting partners for tennis or badminton, someone to ride with him or watch him jump or to cycle with him to the open-air swimming pool ten miles away. He was reaching the gawky age; his legs and arms were growing long and spindly, and his voice was very slightly uncertain, but he managed to transform all this, too, into his own precise grace – he was beautifully brown, like an oiled athlete, and never still, so that they always seemed to remember him, moving purposefully and at some distance, his beautiful face shining with excitement and complete attention, his limbs clear and patterned against the sun.

For Margaret he was a symbol of the Severells' ordered life. For Anna he was the extreme example of the oppressive emptiness of summer at home, but that was not his fault. It was unlikely that Anna would ever – except as a masochistic exercise in deliberate justice – see anything in Jeremy's favour.

Caroline, on the other hand, was made entirely happy by him. Everything was going very well, better than she could have expected, but there were flaws in a great many of her patterns that might suddenly become apparent. Only the weather and Jeremy were perfect, and she rested on them; she felt that she and God together had stage-managed this display of how things could be, if everyone would innocently enjoy what was provided, and not ask too much. She supposed it would never be the same again – Jeremy could hardly, since he was to start at public school in the autumn, be so unspoiled next year – but she refused to look into that future. She would, whatever happened, always have this to remember.

It was Jeremy himself who came at last to equate this summer with his innocence, in retrospect, and long after the others had all come to see it as something potentially bad, the beginning of the trouble, he, detached from their affairs, continued to look back to it as a perfect time, and twelve as a perfect age, which was possibly not good for him. In the September he went back to school and was seduced; an event which he told himself was perfectly usual, to be taken in his stride, but one which nevertheless led him into a continued attempt to please, or deceive or placate other people, at much closer quarters than he had been used to. This he did not like, quite apart from its incalculable effect on his future; he resented the fact that now he was expected to partake of quarrels and jealousies as well as admiration. He would never, he felt rightly, be free again.

Anna found herself, admittedly, in a different way from what she had expected, an essential part of Caroline's plans for entertaining the visitors without either disturbing Henry or allowing his dangerous state of mind — which persisted — to become obtrusive. The first evening, after she had been sent to bed, Caroline had a little talk with Oliver, and found him very understanding and ready to meet her more than half-way. Together they perused Anna's school reports, neatly filed by Caroline since Anna was eleven, and considered Anna's Advanced Level marks, which had arrived a week or so ago, and in which Anna had shown no interest. They were surprisingly good. 'No reason there for her running away,' said Oliver cheerfully. Caroline looked at him repressively; she had consulted him about Anna's future — Anna's failings she preferred to keep to herself. Oliver had expressed a desire to see some of Anna's work, so Caroline had taken him out to the garage, where Anna had left her school books, all anyhow, at the bottom of her trunk. There, in the thick summer evening he had read through her schoolwork — essays, poems, romantic girlish compositions — pressing his lips together over them, and shaking his head wisely, whilst Caroline hovered behind him and grieved over the mess Anna had made of her trunk, letting mud from her hockey boots, and jam, and soapflakes escape indiscriminately into it and collect on the books at the bottom.

'A nice little mind,' he said finally. 'A nice little mind. Not very original, but you can't expect that, at this stage. I should think we might get her into Oxford, or Cambridge, with a bit of pushing. If you think that's the right thing.'

'I don't know what would be the right thing. There seems to be nothing she's interested in.'

'A bit of hard work will likely make her mind up, one way

or the other. I'll give her a few lessons, whilst I'm here, if you like.'

Caroline expressed gratitude, very sincerely. The arrangement had the excellence of keeping Oliver, largely, from any vigorous questioning of Henry, as well as disposing of Anna, both now, and hopefully for the next three years.

The next day there was a scene when Anna, informed of her future, became wild about Oliver's invasion of her private papers, and burst into tears. Caroline said, 'Well, if you don't want people to look at them, you shouldn't leave them lying about, should you?' and went away to write for entrance forms to the Oxford and Cambridge colleges recommended by Oliver. Oliver said, 'Look, Anna, I sympathize even if it was me that did it. But all the same, I think you'd be best to try doing things my way for the next few days. I shan't be here for long, after all. Now stop crying, and get a pen and some paper, and we'll find out what you know, and what you're interested in, and what you've got to learn.'

Anna had every intention of refusing to co-operate, but Caroline arranged a card table and two canvas chairs for them on the back lawn, in the half-shadow of the edge of the orchard, and Oliver asked her, patiently, a series of questions and constructed out of her monosyllabic answers a reading list, a syllabus, essay subjects, points for discussion. 'We shall do very well,' he said, and Anna, ready to be despondent, found that this was true. He was a very good teacher and she was intelligent enough to be provoked by him; together they hunted through Henry's books and sent off for others; they spent most of the day working at their table, and in the evenings Oliver drove Anna to write so much that she was no longer self-conscious about writing, but only anxious to produce something in time, which was what he intended. If she sometimes told herself angrily that she had been forced into all this before she had had time to think, she supposed too that she might as well be doing this as anything else, it committed her to nothing, and it was, in spite of Oliver's prickliness, curiously comforting to have anyone at all so exclusively interested in what she thought or could do. Moreover, it was nice to be placed; to be asked at dinner 'How's it going?' and have an answer anyone could understand; she was someone. Someone who didn't fit her sense of herself at all corners, admittedly, but that perhaps was something she had no right to mind about, perhaps it was only youth which made one hope to be seen for oneself – who, after all, was not very likeable – all at once. Anna had a horror of being typically young. So she worked, for some days, not unhappily.

Margaret had been so determined to enjoy herself that it was unjust that she should suffer as she did from the heat, but it was unfortunately true that a more usual English summer would have suited her much better. She protected herself with oils and lotions, Ambre Solaire, lanoline and large hats, but even so her skin cracked and flaked, and her hair came out and became brittle at the ends. She was slowed down by the heat, saw everything fuzzy at the edges, and had a feeling that she was constantly distracted from the importances around her by some physical discomfort or other – burns on her shoulders, eyestrain, rubbed ankles under sandal straps in the heat.

She dealt gallantly enough with these irritations, and told Caroline several times that this was the happiest summer of her marriage, but she felt she was missing something, and later went over and over the whole time in her mind, imparting significance at last to most of the conversations and incidents which had taken place, and to several which had not. One thing was certain. Oliver was happy, and the Severells had accepted him entirely. He was even relaxed enough to explain to Margaret, after they had retired, his theories about the deficiencies in Anna's upbringing, and not to complain when she came and sat with him for a few moments during the lessons, when she was not helping Caroline in the kitchen. She could not help being a little jealous of the trouble he was taking over the development of Anna's mind, where he had never found it necessary to pay any attention to her own, but she cured this by taking a part in the refurbishing of Anna on her own account. She made her one or two presents of lipsticks and stockings and one day, when it was slightly cooler and when Oliver had given Anna the afternoon off – 'to digest George Eliot' – she consulted Caroline and drove Anna into the market town to buy her a grey striped skirt in silky cotton, two shirts, some mascara, and a straight, cream coloured, sophisticated little dress, which Anna carried home herself, put in the wardrobe, and never wore.

There was also, of course, Henry. Henry was not behaving well, although perhaps only Caroline, watching him apprehensively, and exerting great self-control over not confiding her anxiety to anyone else, was constantly aware of this. It was not the sun which troubled him. He liked sun, responded to heat like a salamander, or any other cold-blooded creature, moving and walking more violently as the temperature increased. He had often thought of moving to the Mediterranean, or to Mexico, he would say, if it were not so obvious that Caroline could be happy nowhere but in England. Nor was it the Cannings, although it was certain that he found their presence an irritant – when Caroline asked, tentatively, if he would mind if their stay was extended, Oliver was being so much help with Anna, he said, 'What does it matter?' glared at her, and swung wildly into the study.

Inside the study, paper was piling up untidily; he had begun to sleep very little, and would leap out of bed in the middle of the night, to make monosyllabic notes on the backs of envelopes on his chest of drawers or in his pockets. All these, too, found their way into the study, and lay in groups across the carpet and over the desk. Nobody touched anything, that was understood. He was once or twice very rude to Oliver, who mistakenly asked what he was doing; Caroline had to explain that he was under great stress, he did most of his 'creative' work in the summer, and this year it was proving difficult. Oliver said that he understood, of course, but Caroline felt that he would have respected Henry more if he could have behaved normally at meals; anyone would.

Not, Caroline came to know, that he was working, even on the *Analysis of Romanticism*, for much of the time. His restlessness increased out of all proportion, and he became obviously odd. He would stand up, silently, in the middle of meals, and rush into the garden; he rarely answered when spoken to, and was seen, once or twice, climbing up and down the stairs, five and six times, three steps at a time, soundlessly, looking as though he needed some much more violent physical activity. From the garden the others could see him, for increasing lengths

44

of time, striding up and down the terrace outside his study, his shirt sleeves rolled above his elbows, his hair like a white fire in the sun. Occasionally he made uneasy sallies into the garden, skirting the tutorial card table at a distance, and staring so intently at the two dark faces bent over it that they could not tell whether he saw them, or through them, or nothing. 'Genius at work,' Oliver murmured once, dryly, as the huge figure turned and disappeared rapidly into the study. Anna was embarrassed for him; whatever he was, it was certainly in bad taste to look so flamboyantly like the poet in the grip of the divine madness – and, she thought, considering his usual gentleness, it was not even true. He was giving Oliver the wrong impression, and she did not know how to set about removing it.

One morning, when the air had been so long saturated with heat and light that it had seemed impossible that it should become brighter, or more burning, Caroline came in from her inspection of the garden and the greenhouses to tell Margaret, who was waiting for her in the kitchen, that it was two degrees hotter than yesterday, the highest yet that summer. Margaret said that she could hardly believe it, and sighed. Caroline betrayed for the first time a certain sense of strain.

'One begins to wait, in spite of oneself,' she said. 'Of course, one knows it's all so unlikely, one shouldn't wish away a day of it, one should merely bask and bask. But – I suppose one is so English – one can't help saying to oneself that it *must* break, that today or tomorrow there will be a thunderstorm, which I hate, and everything will be levelled, and another branch will surely break off the acacia. It's a bit silly worrying, when there's no sign of it, but I do, and there it is.'

'It does seem very heavy,' Margaret said. It was not one of her good days, and the news that it was to be hotter than ever made it no better. Oliver, who had been, whilst they stayed there, quite remarkably loving and excitable – 'Come here, Maggie,' he would say night after night, and grin, 'while we needn't huddle under blankets' – had last night been distracted and turned away from her; so that morning Margaret was prey again to all the pricks and anxieties she had come with. Love exposes one so, she thought, one is so dependent on it, and maybe one will never be intimate enough not to care if anything

– she didn't specify – goes a bit wrong. I can see one *could* be, she thought vaguely.

'And the garden needs rain,' Caroline went on. 'Jeremy has been very good with the sprinkler, and you and I have carried enough cans of water, goodness knows, but it'll have been a losing battle if it doesn't rain soon . . .' She faded into silence, and for some moments they were both peacefully busy with dishes, and the preparation of lunch. Then Caroline said idly, 'I expect it would be better for you if it were cooler, too. You still don't look very well. I meant to give you a complete rest, but we don't seem to have done you as much good as I'd hoped.'

'Oh, you have,' Margaret protested, feeling herself more unwell and worn as she said it. 'Really. Just being here doing things like – like cooking and cleaning and oh, how can I say?' Her voice rose, almost strident, 'I'll explain – in London, I go about doing this and that, pushing a carpet sweeper, arranging cushions, and it all seems so trivial, I think I shall go on doing this until I'm *dead*, and what shall I have been?'

'I think of it as an art of living,' Caroline said, 'and somebody must do these things.'

'I know,' Margaret agreed hurriedly. 'Here it is like that, I've noticed. That's why I – I mean, here it's *for* someone. Henry, and Anna, and Jeremy, here it's real, because it's for them – but if it's not wanted, and one still has to spend one's life on it – ? You know,' she said, the whole thing rising at her from where she hid and nurtured it, 'sometimes I think Oliver would have been better off if he'd not got married at all – he doesn't seem to want – ' she hesitated – 'to *know* anyone at all – '

She had said too much, too loudly, she saw, as Caroline regarded her silently, a slight crease of concern between her brows. She finished, limply – 'I'm terrified of going back to London.'

For a moment they faced each other across Caroline's scrubbed white table, Margaret with her whole face, pitiful and vulnerable, taut in an appeal which she had not the strength to deny. What Caroline thought it was impossible to tell; she stood for some time, her hands pressed into the table, quite quietly, then she lifted her head, possibly to speak, and Henry, coming in behind her, cut short the conversation which had never begun

46

and caught for himself over his wife's shoulder the full force of Margaret's desperate look. 'I knew that – ' he thought to himself with satisfaction. 'I wonder precisely what – ?' He put the thought away for later, only half-consciously, and coughed. Margaret made a half-successful attempt to collect herself – she drew into herself, pulling her arms nervously round herself under her breasts, pushing her shoulders out over them, drawing her face into further creases as though covering hastily what had been indecently exposed. But her gaze remained in all its urgency fixed on Henry's face.

'What do you want?' said Caroline.

'Nothing,' said Henry. 'In particular.' He shifted his weight from one foot to the other, and then reached up, hooked his hands onto the ledge above the door, and stretched. Margaret watched him, fascinated. The movement elongated him incredibly – he seemed suddenly, in his bright white shirt, several sizes too large for the room, which was spacious as kitchens go, and unusually airy. He might pull it apart, just pull it apart, she thought fleetingly. Caroline began to separate eggs, cracking them into unbelievably even halves, sliding the gold, round and elastic, from shell to shell, whilst the white hung, heavy, translucent, in thick sheets, and blobbed suddenly into her basin. Caroline sliced it off with the edge of the shell, knocked the next egg against the basin, and said severely, 'You ate no breakfast.'

'Didn't want it.'

Caroline was silent for a moment, probing the egg shells with her fingers, breaking, separating. Then she transferred the whites of the eggs to a rosebudded meat dish and slapped at them tidily, with a palette knife.

'I'm making you lemon meringue,' she said, 'for lunch.'

Henry hung crucified from the door ledge and did not reply. He wondered what precise horror Margaret had been about to communicate, and studied her for a moment as he might have studied a plant that was drooping for no apparent reason. Margaret could not bear his look; she decided he knew everything and could see everything – his resemblance to the church god of her childhood was remarkable – and was offering her an infinite wisdom which she wasn't capable of accepting. She

47

thought, how important Henry makes everything, and turned her gaze to the rising peaks of foam on Caroline's plate. Something is going to happen, she thought, and was carried away in anticipation. Henry was so splendid, whatever happened must be splendid too.

Henry began to walk round the kitchen, looking into cupboards, turning over spoons, banging against a stool. Caroline asked, 'Please, if you don't want anything, go away? You're so distracting – '

Henry went round the table again and ended at the back door, his hand on the latch.

'Where are you going?' said Caroline, so sharply that Margaret looked at her in surprise.

'Out,' said Henry. 'You know.'

'Lunch,' said Caroline imperiously, but with an undertone of defeat, 'will be at one.'

'Don't wait for me,' he said very vaguely, 'I might not – '

'Please take a hat, at least – '

'I haven't got one,' Henry said, opening the door fully so that the heat advanced into the room. 'I lost it. Don't you remember?'

'You'll get sunstroke.'

'I know,' said Henry. He edged his large form round the door. 'I know.' The door closed behind him.

Caroline sat down at the table and put her head in her hands. Margaret stood in silence for a moment and then asked, 'Where has he gone?'

'I don't know,' said Caroline. She stood up and began to put her pie together. 'It's not the first time. He just goes off. I've given up interfering. He seems to need it. Sometimes it's only a day or two. The worst time it was four and a half weeks. He's always exhausted when he comes home. One can't help worrying – he – he isn't quite himself at these times. And it can be so inconvenient for everyone else. I'm sorry it happened whilst you were here. If he has really gone, that is.' She thought, crossly, it will mean finding a tactful way of telling Oliver and the more I satisfy Oliver the angrier Henry will be when he finds out what I've told him when he gets back. He doesn't think of these things. She finished, 'I may be quite wrong, of course. He may turn up quite naturally for lunch, or for tea, perhaps. We'll have to wait and see.'

But they both knew that Henry would not come back, for lunch or for tea. For some time they contemplated him, imagining him something monstrous, hardly human, in retreat towards something towards which they had neither the power nor the wish to follow him. They were unsettled – a masculine imperative had stalked across their horizon and opened up distances they found daunting, let in an air they shivered at. But they both collected themselves well enough, quite soon, and went back to their doings as though Henry's shadow had cast even on the rejected lemon pie an extra significance.

Caroline thought of how she must cope with Oliver, slowly taking pleasure in her imagined approaches, and at a greater distance of what she would say to Henry, and how she would arrange for him when he came back. Whilst Margaret was suddenly released into a whole new way of looking; to see Oliver in terms of Henry's passage through to the unknown was to have quite a different perspective from Oliver's friends' wives' disapproval of her for not holding him, and him for the way in which he neglected to inform her of where he was going, and when, let alone why. Caroline had said, 'He seems to need it,' and did not, as far as she could see, feel herself rejected on that account.

So they cut radishes into roses, and tomatoes into water lilies, and arranged them carefully on ice. Henry did not come back to lunch, and the roses were eaten, except for the stalks, and the ice melted over lunch in the garden into a puddle slightly pink with tomato juice. There would be more to do, however, tomorrow. As Caroline had said, someone must do these things. Or so it was assumed.

In the garden, Oliver said, 'I like that skirt. And the lipstick. And your hair like that. I'm glad to see I didn't offend you enough for you to stick to the jeans out of perversity.'

Anna thought, I wish he didn't think he had to *talk* about it all the same, smoothed her hands over the stripes, and said flatly, 'Aunt Margaret gave it to me. It's nice isn't it? I expect mother got onto her. I expect she said, "Can't *you* take Anna into town and make her buy some decent clothes? She won't listen to her mother, but she might listen to you. She admires you." ' The reproduction of Caroline's inflections was exact, the more because Anna added no comment, no intonation of her own.

Oliver asked 'And do you?'

'Do I what?'

'Admire my wife?'

'Of course I do.' Anna looked up at him, surprised, through her newly blackened eyelashes, and pursed her newly pink mouth. 'Anybody would. She understands such a lot. It's just the right skirt. I think it looks like somebody's skirt and not somebody's daughter's skirt, you know, not chosen for somebody, not off a shelf saying age group fourteen to seventeen, or Teen styles or anything else awful or girlish.'

'It looks like you,' Oliver said with heavy gallantry.

Anna grinned at him. 'Oh no it doesn't, it looks good and anonymous, that's why I like it. I'd hate to be conspicuous.'

'Why?'

'Oh, because – '

'When you go to Cambridge, I expect you'll think differently. Most of the girls there seem to be very conspicuous. They get spoiled, I'm afraid.'

'Perhaps I might,' Anna agreed, without enthusiasm. 'But I shan't get in, so it's not worth bothering.'

'You should, if you try. You're quite clever enough. Not *that* clever, of course – the dons won't fall on your neck, and say, "Please accept a major scholarship, Miss Severell." But you should manage a place, if you behave sensibly. Besides, you're Henry Severell's daughter.'

'That's nice for me,' said Anna, 'that that should make a difference.'

Oliver was prevented from replying by the arrival of Henry himself, who came rapidly across the lawn and stood over them slightly flushed, balanced enormously on his toes as though he was about to set off at a lumbering run for the orchard. Oliver lit a cigarette and Anna bent her head to stare at the ice cube filming slowly into her glass of thick, sugary, home-made lemonade. Henry's mood impressed itself slowly, on Anna at least. There was general unease; partly because they had been caught out considering Henry as a problem and here he was, large and human, partly because it became more and more apparent that Henry was alive with some urgency which he was going to make no attempt to communicate. He said, once or twice, 'Well – ' and once, 'I see you're busy?' and looked fiercely down on Anna, who would not meet his eyes. Oliver said, 'We're getting along quite well; Anna has a very good mind. I'm very pleased.'

'Good,' said Henry absently, not attending. Anna was annoyed to see Oliver ruffled on her behalf; anyone with a little tact could have seen that it was not the moment to present anything to Henry, it wasn't fair to judge him – or by implication, herself, and what she could usually rely on him to care about – by his present mood. He was so much more than usually elsewhere. It shone on him.

'I think you must arrange more teaching for Anna after I've left,' Oliver went on. 'She still needs guidance and someone to read essays, that's natural. You could advertise for a tutor, unless you know anyone. Do you?'

Henry blinked at him, studied him for a moment with infinite arrogance and then slid his eyes away again, to the hills over the hedge.

'Excuse me,' he said. 'I think I must go. Please excuse me.'

Oliver offered to speak again, and Anna kicked his shin, sharply, under the table. Oliver swallowed, leaned down, and mumbled.

Anna said in her mind: go if you're going, don't stand here and drive me mad. Henry, as though suddenly released by what had been holding him over them, broke away and strode, nearly at a run, through the trees and out, and onto the hill at the other side, looking splendid, magnificent, hair and beard and shirt shining, and also slightly silly, with a touch of the large man hurrying for the bus. This last cut him off from them more finally than his splendour could have done alone; he looked very lonely, very much an object, as he began to climb up amongst bracken on the other side.

'God, he moves fast,' said Oliver, and for some time they were both still, watching him. Then Oliver said, 'What was all that about? Have you done something to annoy him?'

'Of course not. It's not like that at all.'

'What was wrong with him, then?'

'Nothing,' said Anna.

'He was upset,' Oliver persisted. 'Where did he go?'

'How should I know?' Anna cried, angry. She could see the white light of his hair still, bobbing and gleaming into the distance, cold and bright amongst all the soft gold and rust of the bracken, and she was overcome with her own limitations; it was terrible not to know, to have no idea what he went for, what he thought; she wept to herself, I would give anything to be like that, if I knew what like that was. How can one sit here, just the same, when there's anyone alive who finds anything as tremendously important as he finds climbing that hill?

She said repressively, 'He gets like this. He just goes off. We've given up paying any attention any more.' She managed to convey that to pay any attention was in slightly bad taste. She said, 'I expect he wants to get away and think.' Think, she told herself, was a poor word for it, whatever it was, but how could one find a better, when one knew so little, could follow him in imagination only far enough to stick fast at a consciousness of one's own inability to follow further? The patch of white that was Henry glittered on a ridge for a moment, and then seemed to rise into the air, before plunging into a dip out of sight. Oliver, disconcertingly, picked up her thought, standing up uneasily and staring after Henry, as though he too found it fleetingly irksome and inadequate to be still here.

'I wonder what about? Or for that matter, how. I find it daunting, don't you, to read his things and think that *never* now, however hard I tried, could I ever produce anything like that – not only because one hasn't his command of language, but because one hasn't the experience, one doesn't know where he starts from, except by guessing from what he writes. It's nowhere I've ever been. I'm not sure it's a legitimate place for most people to go, or to be preoccupied with. But one can't keep away from it, or at least I can't. It's the fascination of what's alien, I suppose – there's lots of good stuff written that I don't find alien – stuff one hasn't produced oneself, but quite easily might have, you know. Stuff one takes possession of when one's reading it, and feels one has a right to criticize the direction of, with authority, if it goes wrong. But not him. I have a constant struggle to read him, and I always feel he's battered me into agreement. I accept his view *because he knows*, not because I know. And I tease myself sometimes with wondering how he gets it, what sort of processes. He doesn't give much away, does he? How does he work?'

'I don't know,' said Anna. Something in her voice caught Oliver's attention; he turned back from the hill, and looked at her closely.

'You don't seem to like to talk about him,' he said sharply.

'I haven't really got anything to tell you about him.'

'There's no need to give me the unwanted newspaper reporter treatment,' Oliver said. 'I don't want "Henry Severell – the Inside Story. By his Daughter". I want to know what you think.'

'That's the same thing, really, isn't it? Anyway, I don't, very much.'

'Which means you do, all the time, and aren't going to be caught admitting it,' Oliver finished, friendly and accusing. Anna was washed by a wave of that useless anger which catches us when someone makes what appears to be a profound psychological criticism of us, which, although we have considered it carefully and objectively ourselves, and believe it, in what seems a balanced way, to be untrue as it is stated, we cannot protest against, since the protest must only confirm the critic's belief in his own perspicacity. Besides, she had been asked too often about Henry already. It was an unfortunate truth that at the point when people thought they knew her more than superficially – girls at school, the English mistress, even, once, surprisingly, Michael – they asked her about Henry. And me, she thought, who am I?

Oliver said, 'I can see it can't be very pleasant for you, living under his shadow. Great men are always hard on the next generation. And genius is unfortunately very selfish; I suppose you're so organized round him that you don't have much time to see who you are or where you are yourself. It's not the sort of thing he'd notice, I'm afraid.'

'I'm away at school,' Anna pointed out wearily, 'a lot of the time. And I don't want to be noticed, any more than I am. I'm all right.'

53

'You didn't seem to like school very much, either, did you? I've been thinking about this since I came here, and it seems to me you don't see – or don't want to see – the dangers. You've got to be honest with yourself, more than most people, or you'll just be submerged. And that'd be a waste.'

Anna winced, and said nothing.

'There's your father. Not a normal father – how often does he talk to you, or take you out, or notice your clothes? And at the same time he pursues a way of life that's impossible for most people, and as far as I can see enjoys it more than most people enjoy most lives – well, you're not going to be like that, let's face it, and it seems to me you'd better cut away from it or you'll never find what you can be like. No, don't argue with me, yet – '

'I was going to say, he does – he did – talk to me.'

'I know you must believe that. I haven't seen him, while I've been here. Then there's your mother. She thinks he comes first. She thinks you should think so, too. He's a trust. Isn't it so? And she doesn't like you.' Anna winced again; Oliver had a habit of making short statements as though they were absolute truths and excluded any other view of things, which she thought must be wrong, things were surely more complex than that. And yet, perhaps she was so put out, just because they were the best approximate truths. At that moment it seemed obvious – and wounding – that her mother simply disliked her. It was just that one didn't think about these things because – like all other girls – one wanted things normal, parents who didn't stand out, but automatically cared for one, like anyone else's. Why does he want to do this to me? she asked herself, in pain.

'I don't know why she doesn't like you,' the thin voice went on. 'You do your best to annoy her but I'm not sure which is cause and which effect, and I keep an open mind. Anyway, you've less defences, and suffer more. Your brother seems to have his own means of getting loved in this barren situation; that may be his weakness yet, I don't know. I'm not concerned with him at the moment. Now, unfortunately, you're financially so situated that you don't *have to* get out, ever, in any way. There's nothing to stop you just rotting here, in this garden, admiring genius for the rest of your life, is there? Ostensibly waiting to get married, I suppose. I think highly enough of you to think you can make more of yourself than just a wife, in any case. If only you showed any sign of wanting to.'

Anna stirred in her chair.

'What is it?'

'I think you make – clearer issues of things – than there are. I don't really feel like – like you think I feel.' Oddly, what most stung was Oliver's conviction that she would never be like Henry, would always be second rate, for that was what it came to. It was not so certain, there was her event still in the future, there were things she could be – under Henry's shadow or not – that were not so dry, and grindingly achieved as what Oliver seemed to be thinking of. She was aware of more than he thought, but the awareness was difficult enough to hold on to, with Oliver as he was, looking intently into her face.

He asked, 'Do you read his novels?'

'Of course,' said Anna, watching him note the discomfort she could not conceal. She had in fact read Henry's novels, each of them, once and no more, as quickly as possible, partly out of a feeling which Oliver would presumably have understood, that in some way to study them too closely would be to submerge. And she had had, until very recently, the child's irrational fear that the parent may be exposing himself, making a fool of himself in public. And lastly, which was presumably behind Oliver's asking, she was clever enough, and perhaps enough like Henry, to distinguish some of his raw material in what he made of it, and she did not like the idea of having a father who was in secret so detached, so merciless a watching intelligence. If it was in one's mind, it made it impossible to approach him naturally as a father. But it was not, she thought against Oliver, very often in her mind, she had deliberately forsworn close acquaintance with the work, whereas she had lived with the man – since he came back from the war – long enough to be able to ignore the writer in the father, surely? It was not as though Henry saw himself in any way as a great man. He was mild and gentle, and friendly, when not preoccupied. Oliver himself brought out the worst in him, but one could hardly say that; it would be rude.

'The important thing is to be honest with yourself. You

mustn't deal with being neglected by pretending you're not –
you can *mind* as much as you like, but you mustn't for a
moment pretend that things are going to be any different,
because they aren't. There are other standards besides his, and
you've got to set your own, within your own limits. And you
mustn't expect anything of him – beyond the start he's given
you, and his company isn't all bad, enough of it must be a
stimulus I wouldn't go without – but you mustn't expect what
he can't give, interest in what you can do, or even natural
curiosity. Most children are their parents' future, but he's his
own, and it puts you out of place. But you mustn't mind –
you're Anna, not Henry Severell's daughter. And you must live
your life.'

Anna could find nothing to say except a reiterated protest
that it wasn't true. Henry was better to her than that.

She said, 'You frighten me.'

'I will do, because you've refused to think. But you must
think soon and you'll see I'm right. Do you try to write?'

'No.'

'Good.'

'But what must I do?' Anna asked, mesmerized by Oliver's
fierce face, and the harsh little lecturing voice, into accepting
his view for a moment absolutely.

'At the moment, get into university. Then you'll be with other
people who know what the real world is like and are making
choices like the one you'll have to make. Just break away, then
you'll know.'

Anna bent her head over her books.

'I don't like the idea of just abandoning everything. I don't
think one can, as simply as that.'

'Oh yes, one can. If one tries. Now this morning, I thought
we'd cope with Matthew Arnold. . . .'

Henry came over the hill into the sun. The descent was steeper
than the ascent had been; the valley was rounded, on the upper
slopes bracken and some stones, in the bowl trees, mostly beech,
a quick leaping river, divided again and again by large boulders,
crossed in one place by a wooden bridge with a handrail, and,

on the other side of the trees, slopes of thick gorse bushes, butter yellow, and more bracken. There was a boy on the bridge watching the water. He was camping with a friend, in the next valley, and had quarrelled with him, as two people alone on holiday together are apt to do, so he was watching the water rather sulkily, wishing he had something better to do, or that he had not come at all. The first edge of the bowl was almost vertical, ten feet or so of rock, tufted with wiry grass. Henry appeared on the top so rapidly and so suddenly that the boy had hardly time to take him in, a huge figure with flailing arms against the sky, before he was over. The boy made an involuntary movement to warn him – which at that distance was useless – of the drop. But unlike the philosopher, Henry was not swallowed for presumption; he came down, on a difficult stone, on one foot, balanced all his huge weight on it for a moment, swinging his arms wildly with all the power in them to keep a balance which it suddenly seemed impossible he should lose, took off in a huge leap, and was down the hill again like some enormous animal, an ancient white bull, in full charge.

He had his head down like the bull, and, with the curling mass of his beard and hair obscuring his face from this angle altogether, presented something of the same solid, blind, purposeful front. His speed, or some earlier gesture, had whipped up his hair into two great curved peaks, not unlike horns, which added to the illusion, and the whole of him, silver hair and white garment – his shirt was outside his trousers now, like a tabard – shone in some strange way, with a white glitter, as though he was giving off a concentrated light of his own and not merely the refracted light of the still sun over the hill.

What unnerved the boy was the directness of his progress. As he had come over the hill, so he continued, in a straight line, going over the hillocks, and through gorse bushes, clattering stones out of his way down the hillside. As he came down, in what seemed only a few moments, but must, even at Henry's speed, have been much longer, towards the river, the boy moved aside altogether, pressing himself against a tree for protection. He felt sick with unreasonable fear; either the man would come near him, or he would break his neck in the river, which was here quite wide. It was not full – the summer had been too dry – so the channel between its banks was unusually deep, and the stones were sharp, and glossy with bright olive green moss. Henry came down, still even in the shadow, shining, ignored the bridge, stepped, wide and lightly, one stride into the river, and one, from the same foot on the slimy stone, apparently effortless stride up onto the far bank, shook himself and went on out into the sun again and up onto the further hill.

The boy looked involuntarily up the valley towards where Henry had come from, to see what had been driving him, but the valley was clear and empty under the sun, and nothing monstrous, nor even human, appeared on the skyline. So he turned back to Henry and watched him make his way, with no diminution of speed, towards the next ridge.

Henry was afraid of the thing towards which he was driving himself; it was partly that he was driving, not only that he was driven. In a sense, now, he knew enough about his present state of mind to be able to predict what would be the outcome of his walking. In a sense, too, he could control it, and knew why he must walk as he did, and how far he could go. But more powerfully, it was all new every time he set out, it was all to be learned, to be undergone again, and from his present, still fairly rational state, it seemed terrible. He would, quite consciously, have liked to be able to abandon the whole undertaking and go quietly home to his work, but what came first was to walk, it did not matter how far, to walk until he was exhausted, and at that time he felt himself inexhaustible.

What he called, liking the precise medical metaphor, his attacks of vision, had come upon him very gradually, only becoming really nasty when he was about Anna's age. At first it had been only an inexplicable attentiveness, a tightening of sight, a thing seen suddenly and remembered as a visual touchstone, a tree like a branched and burning candlestick, with flame upon flame of leaping green light. But once, in the main street of the small county town where he had lived as a boy, the thing had shaken and changed him, and the pattern had been set. There had been first the visual insistence – hard outlines, the lines on the pavement suddenly slicing and dangerous, the salmon pinks and dull brick reds of the housefronts suddenly thickened and glaring to the point of suffocation. There had been no pleasure in seeing, then, largely he thought, now, because he did not know what was happening, and fought it, was most unhelpfully afraid. After the sight changed, there had been as now a sudden bewildering access of strength pumped up from inside him, so that, as now, he had lengthened his stride, and pushed things, which, in this case on the crowded market street, happened to be people – out of his way, thinking in confusion that he could like Samson rip up the gas lamps by their roots to part them more effectively.

Over the years, he had learned to come to terms with these attacks. He recognized the symptoms earlier – noticed a quickening of sight he could not have been alive to when younger; light in his own green glass paperweight had warned him this time, weeks ago, it had been dangerously beautiful, disproportionately important. When it came to him, now, he had to stop writing in the end, he could not attend to anything as long drawn out and demanding as that; he went back to his study of the visionaries, finding all their sentences, all their descriptions of the indescribable, equally, in some curious way, an inspiration and an invitation. Later, when he was an artist again, he found parts of Blake banal and some of Coleridge's notes meaningless, but at the time everything connected, all meanings were a network, and his coming experience the master-knot. He thought a great deal about this, having accepted it almost immediately as the most important area of his life. He knew already before the war that his visionary moments were a direct source of power and that his only way to make a statement as high and as demanding was to write a very violent, stylized action, remote on the whole from the way most people lived, most of the time, which should rarefy, or concentrate what he knew to the bright intensity with which he knew it. But before the war he had not quite known how; the prison camp had taught him that.

He never, curiously, attempted to write anything other than novels – it may have been that his extreme shyness needed the distance of the dramatic form before he could speak at all. His thought formed itself around whole men, whole actions; it was epic; his own solitary experiences were not, and he always knew it, raw material.

On leaving Cambridge he wrote a countryman's novel, after Hardy, not unsuccessfully, published it, and then found a way out which for a time satisfied him, and wrote elegantly, very much in the manner of the early E. M. Forster, parables on the power of the earth, using the comparatively neutral machinery, which had now, at least for most of his readers, only a literary life – peasants, dryads, Apollo, Dionysus, Pan. But his work, though now admired, was in a strait jacket, it was bursting at the seams, and he was conscious of it.

It was from the land that his strength came, but at that time he could not cope with England as a setting or a symbol. He admired, but could not share, the Bloomsbury novelists' far-away, gentlemanly, aeroplane view of their country and its society, as some kind of an informing presence. He was not, in spite of Oliver's view of him, enough of a gentleman to find any inherent value in it; he did not want to write about a society, and yet found it difficult to extricate himself from it. This was behind his move to Japan, where he taught English in a university, and wrote his Japanese novels, a study of the exile of a general to a rocky island, the story confined entirely to his struggle for survival, one or two bold fables about the spiritual discipline of the monks and soldiers, studies of crises, not of conscience, but of consciousness.

He came back to England before the war, and was sent East again by the army, because of his knowledge of Japanese; this was not much use to them as it turned out, since he was almost immediately taken prisoner. He survived imprisonment better than most – he was very strong – and now never mentioned what he had experienced. But he had learned something; it was after that that he wrote the two novels that drew Oliver's attention to him; war epics that Oliver did not hesitate to call works of art and tragic.

He had always had a curious, geometrical visual memory, whole areas of things seen fined down to one visual symbol. Now, as he came up through the hundreds of bright yellow lights of the gorse, he saw, superimposed on the dignified English sun, which sailed like a dignified English angel, splendid

60

and calm and powerful on the clear blue, that other angrier copper circle, dancing furiously on a sky so petrol-dark with heat that it seemed stormy where it was not, and saw both as the orifice of a cone, in the centre of which he walked, here on crushed bracken and crumbled turf, there, delirious with dysentery, backwards and forwards in the beam of the sun's searchlight, across the terra cotta dust of the compound. And to see them together was to strengthen both. He walked more and more quickly, using all his body. If he kept still at this time, or tried to look, it would all be too much for him.

He came over the next hill, and down into a further valley; here there was a road, and a high, pale stone wall, the boundary of someone's large estate. It was getting later, but there were still hills in the distance, which still shone.

He took the road for a short way; it was tar spread and was alive in the heat, seething and bursting here and there, with every now and then a little hiss, where a bubble rose, rounded, burst, and sank again. Where the dust was not on the tar, at the edges off the road, this was lined and crossed with light, which moved with it, like pale little snakes along its molten surface. Henry didn't like the road; it reminded him irritatingly, in spite of its emptiness, of Oliver's view of his world as a picture, sandwiched into a frame of man-made tidinesses, which wouldn't do, and besides, walking was too easy, the only battle was with the sucking of the tar. So he crossed, put one hand up to the top of the wall, jumped, hung for a moment from one arm, and pulled himself up slowly, straddled the wall for a moment, and was down in a ride, with empty country in front for miles, and a gentle slope, and more hills in the distance, towards which he set out, through bracken and turf, and clumps of trees. He flexed himself to see if the climb had tired him at all apparently it had not. But there was sweat on his hair and beard, and his shirt was damp and less bright than it had been; there was less of him in some way, already, than when he had set out.

When evening came altogether he was miles away, and unrecognizable. There had been water in his way, more than a pond, less than a lake, through which he had gone, wading across most of the way, half swimming for a short time in the middle, having a struggle at the far end with long clinging green weeds, which wrapped themselves round him and were dragged up from the water bottom sucking and protesting, bringing with them clouds of fine black mud, so that now he was streaked with green slime, and stained, hands, beard, shirt, trousers, unevenly black, green, grey, the black coating cracking as it dried along his fingers and wrists. His progress was very audible, but he was less visible, almost, except for the white top of his head, as though he had deliberately camouflaged himself. He had looked back at the water, across whose flat, white, reflecting surface the ribbons and arrows of his track were spreading and disappearing, slipping against reeds and making an infinitesimal sound as they rolled and died. As he looked, the sun died from it, so that the white mirror grew dark and deep, and suddenly very cold; the sky went blue and deeper blue and then dusky grey. Henry came into a land which had been laid waste – the bracken was broken and tangled, the ground was flat, torn up, pitted here and there and heaped into unnatural piles of raw, orange grey, clay earth, crossed again and again by huge machine tracks. It was forestry that had been done there, he saw – great boles of trees lay all at angles to each other, very dead, their roots, bushed and dried, hanging sadly in air, their length ending abruptly in a pyramid of sawn, clear wood, coming to a point, like bloodless amputated wounds. Things were still growing on them, thick moss, grey and yellow, and bright green lichens, picking up the first light of the moon already, which was nevertheless, in that devastation, a cold light. Perspective deserted him; the rifts and furrows in these dead skins opened at him like pits; he began to run, in his wet shoes, wildly, between them – these he could not go over – afraid now in earnest not of this dark, but of another. The worst thing, he had always known, would be if the vision went black on him, if outlines shouted at him, not with importance, not with something that was too much for him, but with the other thing, the knowledge of nothing, which was always present enough, a warning, just over the edge of the height he constantly walked.

But he came to a track between high banks, on whose top there were tall trees, standing black, but with the moon on their leaves, and at the end of the track he was suddenly in fields in moonlight, fields heavy with hay, smelling warm even in the cold night, fields soft green, and pale gold surrounded by trees.

Henry went along, in the shadows, and the hay moved, in the light, in the square of open land, this way and that, falling heavily against itself and sighing, changing colour from grey, to straw, to gold, to glass as it swayed. He had the illusion that there were walkers with him, who went directly across the bright land, pearl grey figures, who strode taller than men, and gave off their own soft light. They went ahead of him; he could not count them; and rose over a hedge; he climbed a gate and found himself in much more open country, walking on bright spikes of stubble, amongst corn that had been already harvested, and they marched ahead of him, in line, between the stooks, leaving, it seemed, trails and threads of white light like nets over the heads of corn, or like snail tracks, wherever they had passed or touched.

Henry went after them, walking steadily, calmer now the sun was off him, feeling himself very peaceful, in a dream. He was a grotesque figure, if there had been anyone to see, with his thick white cap of hair, and rivulets of mud drying spikily over the rest of him, and green weed caught in his trousers, taking its watery bright colour momentarily under the moon. He thought, amongst the sheaves, which in some lights were almost bodiless, cages for light, of Joseph; the stars were up now, like lights off metal. How arrogant it was, and how organized, he thought, and how he would hate to be placed in that way, with the sun and the moon and the stars and the clear sheaves flopping down so submissively, so politely in front of him. What a responsibility, what an impediment, to have the world so neatly pointing out one's position in relation to other people. Joseph was always right, too, the baker, the butler, Pharaoh, his family, Potiphar's wife, the sun and the moon and the sheaves, they all meant what he said, and pointed his moral, and showed that his way was best. Maybe one could find out that kind of thing, if that kind of thing was what one wanted to find out. Henry gave up thinking about Joseph; prophecy was not his country;

63

he liked the sheaves as they were, leaning away from him, holding their own shapes, their own tension, giving off their own light, nothing to do with him. It was more likely that he would lie down by them and never get up again than that they would come out of their shapes in the field and flop in front of his human path. If they did, he would be, quite intolerably, not alone. And would therefore not know; he would be too busy.

The land was flatter now, uplands, airy; there was a lump of a hill on his right, covered with beautifully compact little round bushes, rich amber, touched red by the moon, but the moon poured a path in front of him, along the stubble, and he went that way, the impulse to climb having left him for the time. Behind him, he left a trail of black dust: he could not begin to predict, still, how much longer he must go on.

FOUR

IN THE HOUSE, Henry's absence informed the holiday feeling; it was tiresome of him to go, Caroline felt, if only because everybody immediately began to wait and watch for him to come back; people brushed past the windows more slowly, looked up at the hill behind the garden, if they lunched there, once too often. She herself preferred, although troubled about his physical safety, to treat these absences as business trips, from which he would bring back, in due course, material for one or two more novels. She wished she could have persuaded others to behave with as much restraint. Particularly Anna, who, when her father had been gone two or three days, became extraordinarily difficult, did not turn up to some of Oliver's lessons, and replied to questions about her work with the statement that it was all a joke, they were making fools of themselves to think that anything academic could be made of her, and that anyway she saw no point in it. Oliver too became tight-lipped, and carried with him an atmosphere of unspoken criticism.

Once at dinner he said, 'I must say, you take all this very calmly, how do you know he hasn't broken his neck?' and Caroline was only saved from the embarrassment of defending herself by Anna, who cried, 'Leave him *alone*, you make us all so much smaller by criticizing,' burst into tears and rushed from the table. Caroline apologized to Oliver for Anna's bad taste, and was saved from the unpleasantness of mentioning his own.

She took the opportunity of clearing up Henry's study, or at least of dusting everything, sweeping the floor, and moving as little as possible. When he came home, he was very unlikely to want all this paper, that was one blessing. Then she began on all the other work that had been forgotten, laying in food, cleaning things, moving things, so that when Henry came back she would have all her time free for coping with whatever he had done to himself. There were cans of liquid fertilizer which they bought at a discount from John Ellis, who owned the stables; no one had collected those before Henry went; she thought now that it would be something for Anna to do, since she was being difficult, and went out into the garden to find her.

Anna was with Oliver at the table, which was encouraging, but as Caroline crossed the grass she heard him ask three questions, and wait for an answer after each which was not forthcoming, so she saw that Anna was, nevertheless, still being difficult.

She came up to them, and said, 'I don't want to break into anything, if you're busy, Anna, but if you had time it would be a great help if you would go and get those cans from Ellis – you know the ones I mean. Ellis will know if you don't.'

Oliver said, 'Anna seems a little jaded, it'll do her good to take time off.'

Anna said, 'I don't want to go. I'm sorry.'

'Anna.'

'Someone else might like to.'

'I'll go, of course,' said Oliver firmly. 'And Anna will come with me. Don't be silly, Anna.'

'I don't want to go,' Anna repeated. Caroline stood by, dangling the car key, which she had brought out for Anna. Something in her was annoyed that this stranger should so firmly have taken charge of her own child, but she saw that the outcome would be what she intended; they would both go. Oliver gave one of his by now familiar sidelong glances at the hill over which Henry had vanished.

'Why?' he asked. 'Why don't you?' Anna wriggled under his glance, afraid that if he looked long enough he might find out why, said, stupidly, 'It's too hot,' and burst out, with that disproportionate childish fury that had been growing in her lately, 'I wonder when I shall ever be able to call my life my own.'

'The answer to that is never, and if you aren't old enough by now to know it, you ought to be. I suppose I ought to have been teaching adolescents long enough by now to be ready for these childish fits of petulance, but I can't say I like it, and I don't see why I should put up with it. Why won't you come? Give me a reason, is there someone you don't want to see? A reason's a reason, I can recognize a reason well enough, I hope I'm not unfair. Tell me why.'

'I don't see why I have to come, if you're going anyway.'

'Because I don't know where to go, because a change of surroundings will be good for you, because if I leave you, you'll brood, and because you can tell me any thoughts you may have on the relationship between literature and morals on the way. Those are all reasons.' He stood up, and took the car key from Caroline. 'Come along, Anna.'

Anna stood up and followed him, without looking at her mother, who said, 'It shouldn't take long,' and stood expressionless, in the middle of the lawn, watching them make their way to the garage. She felt, in fact, uneasy, as though someone were managing her affairs from inside, for her; at that moment, her feeling for Oliver crystallized into dislike.

In the car Oliver said, 'There, I told you she doesn't like you, she doesn't care at all what I say to you, does she?'

'I expect she thinks you're right.'

'That doesn't alter it, and she ought to mind my telling you. Imagine, if you were Jeremy.'

'Why do you keep on about it?' Anna cried. 'What are you trying to do?'

66

'Make your mind up,' Oliver said, changed gears violently, and swore. 'Make you see. Where do I go now?'

'Left.'

'Good. He still isn't back. Aren't you worried, any of you?'

'No.'

'I wonder why not. It seems to be a family habit, this running away. I don't like it. Was that what it was? Were you emulating him?'

'Asking like that,' Anna said, as rudely as she could, 'over and over again, isn't the way to find out. I thought that was obvious by now. Take the right here, it's a cart track. What about literature and morals then?' She was often, now, driven into asking questions about her work, on her own initiative, only to avoid Oliver's other sharp 'psychological' questions about why she had run away, what she would do, all the rest.

John Ellis's farm, and stables, were at the end of a long narrow track. Anna pointed this out to Oliver and said, 'It's up there. You can park on the verge here. Then you walk.'

Oliver pulled in obediently, then leaned out of his window, and peered between the hedges.

He said, 'I can get the car up there.'

'I know you can. The tractor goes up. The point is, they don't like the cars going up because of the horses and because there's no room if the tractor or the horse-box happens to be coming down.'

Anna would in fact have driven up herself, if she had been alone, since she was not strong enough to carry the cans back down the track, but now she repeated, 'They don't like it,' and climbed out of the car before anything else could be said. Oliver sat for a moment with the engine running, drumming his fingers, and then shut it off, and followed her.

The track ran slightly uphill, narrow between high hawthorn hedges which were hung with long strands and tangles of hay from carts which had passed, and dangled with twigs, broken by the lurching passage of the tractor. The ground was deeply rutted by wheels on each side, trimmed and grassed over in the middle, and the baked mud in the ruts was marked by countless hoofs. There was a smell of dust, and a smell of drying grass. Anna, who knew this track so well that she remembered every

67

curve and puddle accurately in her dreams, began to walk rapidly in the ruts, watching the dust collect and settle in the pores between her sandalled toes. She had her father's turn of speed, and thrust her head forward and down in his way. She did not wait for Oliver to come up to her at first, and was now aware that he was some distance behind her.

'We are not racing, you know,' the small voice came after a time behind her. Anna swung round on a tuft of grass.

'Am I going too fast for you? I'm sorry.'

Oliver in his black townsman's shoes walked up to her and said rather breathlessly, 'I like to look about, that's all. You Severells swallow up the land so, walking's a battle. Why the hurry?'

'I didn't think I was hurrying. I expect I walk fast naturally. It's uncomfortable not to go at one's own speed, I think.'

'Of course,' said Oliver. 'Do you think we might compromise? I'd like to arrive in some order.' He looked at her steadily, and said, putting her in the wrong, but nevertheless apologizing, 'I'm sorry you had to come out, when you didn't want to.'

'That doesn't matter.' She surveyed him from her small eminence. He was very hot, almost steaming; his face shone, his clothes were too thick for the weather and he seemed uncomfortable inside them. It was the first time she had seen him really at a disadvantage, and she could afford to feel friendly. Oliver held out his hand, she took it, and allowed him to help her down; when they arrived together at the stable gate, she was still holding it.

The stable yard was large, and paved, with bright green moss growing between the stones, and docks tall beside the water-trough. It was surrounded by a brick wall, faded to a soft crumbling dark colour that bore no relation to newer tomato-sauce coloured bricks, which was topped by tombstone like slabs of grey-green stone. Anna and Oliver looked in between high gateposts, each carrying a ball of the same stone, like the heads of massive chessmen. Across the yard from them were the looseboxes, the paint on them dark blue, old and faded, but not untidy. It was all very sunlit and empty; the only sound was the occasional movement of a horse in one of the boxes, with the scrape of metal on stone.

Tied to a ring beside the mounting-block in the far wall to their left was a huge black gelding, a good 16 hh., heavy and powerful, but now dropping his head, half asleep. Anna, seeing him, twisted her hand away and walked into the yard. Oliver, his hands clasped behind his back like Napoleon, came after.

'Nice place,' he said. 'Some horses live better than many men, don't you think? Maybe that's right, of course, but it's a thought at least, isn't it? Eight to a room the size of one of those looseboxes, in London. I've seen for myself. The main room of the house I was born in wasn't much better.'

Anna wondered vaguely when and why he had taken to slum visiting; there was so much of him one knew nothing about; and thought, he was hardly here before he had made it uncomfortable, the world topsy-turvy, one's values intolerable.

'Well, what would you do?' she mocked distantly, knowing he could have no exact answer, only a consciousness to prick with.

'Shoot the horses,' he said so that Anna could only just see that it was a joke. 'Start with what's concrete, at the bottom.' She watched him enjoy her horror. He said, conversationally, 'Seems to be no one here.' He stood, stockily, in the middle of the yard, and looked around himself. 'That's a nice animal. Not that I know anything about horses.'

'That's the Wizard,' Anna told him, taking a step towards the horse and then moving away again. 'He wins in point to points; he jumps too, but he's unreliable, he has a nasty temper.'

'Do you ride it?'

'No, at least I did once, but I got scraped off under a tree. I'm not strong enough to hold him.'

Oliver laughed loudly, as though this was very funny indeed. He showed no disposition to move away from the middle of the yard. His laugh sounded very clear off the stone; the horse rolled an eye at him, and Anna became panicky.

She said, 'Mr Ellis'll be in the saddle-room,' and had to restrain herself from tugging at his coat. 'Unless he's away. Shall we go and look? I expect we'd better hurry – '

'Severells again,' said Oliver, following her however. 'Rushing me, hurrying about. You don't remember, I'm not used to the scene, I like to take it in, I don't see many horses where I come from. The Great English Past, concentrated to – '

'Please!' Anna said. They stooped under a door at the right end of the row of looseboxes, and were in the saddle-room, which at first sight seemed uninhabited. That was all right, Anna was flooded with relief, if *he* were there one could not for a moment not notice. But her hands were trembling; that was bad. It did no good . . .

John Ellis was in fact asleep in one corner; a small man, with a leather face in a deep leather armchair, with his short legs in their breeches crossed neatly above the level of his head, and resting on the glass case which contained the ribbons, the rosettes, and the cups. Around him, like a liana jungle, the dark bridles dangled from the ceiling, smelling of leather soap and wax, bits and chains glinting amongst them, and plaited thongs of hunting crops snaking between them. John Ellis snored, no more than the whisper of a whistle.

This world of stables had been the only one of Anna's childhood rituals into which she had ever hoped to enter completely. She had felt love for the horses, animals so good to touch, and so beautiful, who kept silence and expected nothing, unlike human beings. It had been, for once, much more than knowing that this was the sort of thing that at her age it was necessary for her to be interested in. She had touched saddle soap and sponge with the reverence of the novice for the implements of his new ceremonial, and had learned the horseman's esoteric vocabulary with the fervour of the initiate for the language of the mysteries. But, of course, she reflected now, as the old feeling of wonder and wistfulness crept over her with the dark smell of the saddle-room, she had never managed it, she had never belonged. The observance of a ritual is not adequate to ensure belonging until it has ceased to be observed to be a ritual, studied from the outside; it must be accepted, absorbed, worked out from, and that she had never achieved; this was worse with horsemanship than with many other more deliberately aesthetic rituals, since it was based so much on practicals, on common sense and healthiness. The whole ethos of the pony books with their emphasis on the tomboy, their bludgeoning mockery of sentiment and sensibility, was against her.

And she was such a watcher, she was so conscious of little rituals, the whole unreal performances of nursery tea and school prayers, that here, where she would have been thankful to take what she could, she was against herself. Her conscious pleasure in the act as she ran her hands down the bridles, adjusted a buckle, sifted quantities of oats and bran between her fingers, had damned her. She set herself impossible standards; she thought it wrong to be conscious of enjoying pure speed in the show-ring – she felt, from the talk she heard, that she must think only of the jump ahead, and the possible prize at the end. But the practical note, in conversation, eluded her, and although she rode well, and tremendously enjoyed other people's references to colic, and splints and spavins, she could never, partly because she was so anxiously enjoying them, follow them up. John Ellis thought she rode well, and had often asked her to show his horses for him, but he treated her unconsciously as someone from another world who amused herself by playing with his. Anna wanted him to respect her for doing her job – a child who rides for pleasure is one who has a whole existence of different pleasures, or one for whom some other pursuit is the important life, and who finds riding a pleasant relaxation. Anna as a child had had no pleasures – she had thought this out and was sure it was really true – but she had had no life either, and therefore no right to look on. But there it was; lately, since she had been avoiding the stables because Jeremy was there now so much, and because of Michael, it was less important.

Anna knelt on the tiled floor beside John Ellis and touched him timidly on the knee. He woke easily, without starting, and gave a creased little smile.

'Mr Ellis – I'm sorry to disturb you – '

'Anna Severell. Well, well, Anna Severell. I was beginning to think you'd deserted us. Why haven't you been in? We've seen a lot of young Jeremy – he's shaping very nicely – but you've been missed. Something better to do, maybe?'

Anna smiled up at him. He was one of the very few people whom she thought she liked, without reservations.

'They've been making me work for some exams. You know how it is.'

'In midsummer? What kind of exams, then?'

'Oh, it doesn't matter, let's not talk about it.'

'You look well enough on it. Very pretty, if I may say so.'

Anna blinked at him, surprised; she remembered that she had never been to see him in anything but jodhpurs, and would have thought it bad form to come in a skirt, if she had had time to think, but the compliment was so unusual that she was flattered, and taken aback.

'It's not only been myself that's missed you, either. Young Michael Farne's in nearly every day, now, and he usually asks after you. "Where's Anna?" he says. "Why's she not been down?"'

'Michael – ' said Anna, slowly, transparently. 'Michael – does he really?'

'Every day – ' he insisted, enjoying himself. 'He says, "I can't understand what's got her." I must tell him, it's these exams. I suppose he might like to know about that.'

Anna put her head down, so that her hair swung across her face, to hide it, and clenched her hands in her lap. There was a dry little cough amongst the hanging leather, and she became aware of Oliver, quiet and stiff behind her.

'Oh,' she said, 'I'm sorry. I forgot altogether.'

'Not at all,' said Oliver, advancing.

'Mr Ellis, this is my – this is – this is Mr Canning, who is staying with us. We came for those cans.'

Ellis took his feet down, wiped his hands on his breeches, and offered one to Oliver.

'How do you do? I didn't see you there, at all. Sorry to be rude.'

'Not at all,' said Oliver.

'I'll have to get those cans down from the house. It's not too far. If you'd not mind helping – '

'Not at – ' said Oliver.

'I'll help,' said Anna. 'It's my fault, we should've let you know we were coming, it was silly of us.'

'No, you won't. Too heavy for you. You stay here, and if anyone comes, tell them to wait. Two of us is quite enough. This way please, Mr . . . ?'

Anna followed them into the yard and watched them out through the gate behind the stables. The house and farm buildings were some distance away. Anna stood alone in the yard for a moment, looking across at the Wizard, and then went back into the saddle-room and fetched his brush. She began to work on him slowly, pressing her face against his side, smelling his warm smell, moving her hands, one with the brush, one naked against him, in little circular movements over his haunches and flanks. The horse, who was used to her, and enjoyed being groomed, pushed at her once with his nose, and then stood squarely relaxed, nearly leaning against her. Little by little the hot sun, and the warm smell of the animal and the rhythmic movement overcame her; she relaxed, and dreamed, and closed her eyes. She was awakened by the horse, who suddenly pulled away from her, and gave a little ruttle of sound.

Opening her eyes again into the sun, she could barely see; the yard, smoke dark like a negative, tilted this way and that through concentric turning circles of black and flame. The familiar figure stepped jauntily across the square, gold head erect on the gold neck, rising out of the blue shirt. Michael, real Michael, invested with all the summer and all her dreams. The light settled as she looked, and the yard became again an ordered square pool of pale sunlight. She found herself out of breath, stepped back, put the brush down on the mounting-block and after a moment's hesitation swung herself up beside it. She felt safer sitting down.

Michael held out his large golden hand to the horse, who bent and pushed happily at it, with soft lips.

'Hello, Anna,' he said. 'Long time no see.'

'I was brushing him. I hope you didn't mind.' Her voice was weak, would hardly hold to the end of the sentence. And inside, her stomach turned and jumped.

'Good for him. He likes it. Sensual old brute.' Michael slapped his neck, and the horse moved sideways twitching his skin with pleasure. There was a long silence; Anna began involuntarily to work out the pattern of how she would remember this meeting.

Michael said, 'It seems a long time – '

'Yes, yes it does.'

'I never seem to see you about, now.'

'No.'

'I don't know why – '

It was part of Anna's peculiar code that things – important things, like Michael kissing her – must never be mentioned, must be assumed never to have happened. One must behave as usual; this may well have been what he found daunting. If pressed for a reason she would have said that it would not have been fair to force him to remember what he would almost certainly rather forget, but this was not the root of it, the root of it, the will to forget, was in herself, although its cause was maybe impossible to hunt out.

She said now, hastily, 'I've had to work, they've decided I ought to do these stupid exams. And we've had visitors, for a long time now. And things, you know.'

'Yes,' said Michael. He said, 'What I wondered was – you know, you used to be here all the time. And now you don't come. So I wondered if it was anything to do with me.'

'Oh, no,' said Anna hastily. Michael scrutinized her, wrinkling his broad brow.

'You're a funny girl. I don't understand you. I've been thinking about you,' he explained.

'Oh.'

'And – ' he elaborated magnificently, 'I can't make you out. One never knows where one is, with you.'

'Oh,' said Anna again, seeing suddenly that he was being brave with her.

'If – if I've upset you, or anything, you mustn't not come here because of me. I mean – a chap can't help wondering whether you're avoiding one – or anything. I'd rather you didn't, that is. If – '

Anna said nothing because she was trying to catch up on herself. It had been an essential part of her picture that Michael should have been carefree, self-assured, even slightly cruel; he was easiest to admire like that. She did not quite know what to do with his anxiety; it was encouraging, but it diminished him in some way. She gave him back the upper hand, as far as she could, and said, 'No, no, you don't understand. I was only afraid you didn't want to see me any more.'

'But *why*?' Michael almost shouted.

'Well, I thought – ' Anna hesitated.

74

Michael smiled suddenly, beautifully, and put his arm round her shoulder.

'Then it's all right. Isn't it? It's all been about nothing, surely? What a waste of good weather. And you'll come back, now?'

'Yes,' said Anna, 'I want to.'

'I've missed you,' Michael said simply but so certainly and with so honest, so happy, so hopeful a smile that Anna's doubts suddenly dropped away, and she began, tentatively, to see a further ritual that might be acted out. It might be possible to be a girl, with a boy friend, like any other. She could imagine being entirely absorbed in walking, and riding with Michael, for days together. And this afternoon he was so pleased to see her, that the usual impossibility of ever *talking* to him foolish and remote. There was a lot to say, there was an ease, it was so much better after all than admiration from a distance. It was real, whatever real was. The word stirred an echo of another voice, but she shut it off without recognizing it. Michael said, 'Do you know, I've never seen you not in jeans before? You look rather nice. Sort of faraway, but nice.'

'It's because of the visitors,' Anna said, deprecating. She twisted her fingers selfconsciously in her hair.

'It's not bad, to be feminine, whatever for,' Michael said, settling himself beside her on the block and drawing her towards him. There was a silence; the next thing was the embrace; Anna waited, intolerably conscious of Michael so large and golden, and her blood hummed.

'Anna – ' said Michael, leaning over her.

'Anna,' said Oliver. 'Are you ready? It's time we went home.'

'I see you found each other,' said John Ellis, behind him, quickly. Anna thought crossly, it *isn't* your home, and Michael jumped hastily down from the mounting-block.

'Uncle Oliver, this is Michael Farne. Michael, my uncle, Mr Canning.'

'Ah, yes,' said Oliver, like a real uncle with a small boy who needs encouraging. 'I've heard a lot about you.' Which was not even true, Anna thought, staring at her knees and hiding miserably behind her hair. She wished Oliver would at least collect his cans and go quickly back to Darton, now that he was here. But he showed no hurry; he stood with an interested look on his pointed face, and waited, expectant, for Michael to say something. Michael was hideously embarrassed; he was, though Anna didn't know enough men to be able to generalize, the kind who is put out entirely by being seen to be serious, or display emotions, in public. Now he blushed, a dull, hot red, under the gold surface of his skin; the colour was very beautiful, but Anna was not disposed to look at it in that way.

'You ride a lot here, I take it?' Oliver said, and then, 'What else do you do? How do you spend your life? I'm curious.' Michael answered, already apologizing; Oliver proceeded with his catechism as though he was interviewing a scholarship candidate who had never had, and should have known he had never had, a chance of an award.

His degree, what use would it be? Did he think he had any right to live on the land and pursue – sports – of this kind effectively at other people's expense? Why had he gone to university at all, Oliver was professionally interested, he must excuse the question. Wouldn't he – if he wanted to breed horses – have been better at an agricultural college? Had he got anything out of his history, then? There were answers to these questions, but Michael was not the man to find them, and Oliver's tone as he asked them delivered his judgment in advance. Anna only listened to the beginning of the conversation. She sat in an agony of rage and embarrassment, hating, not Oliver for his rudeness but Michael for his inability to stand up for himself, for his rapid disintegration into a very young man with an unsteady voice. This was a little unkind of her; it was surely in Michael's favour that he should be sensitive to Oliver's standards or, however dimly, troubled by the injustices Oliver saw. The kind of young man Oliver was really getting at would have been quite impervious to such criticism and would have dealt with a god-like impatience with Oliver himself, so obviously not a part of any world that 'mattered'. Except that there was a disproportionate intensity of feeling to the whole exchange – Oliver was putting so much more of himself than was apparently necessary into his biting little questions that it would have taken a very strong man not to feel himself, in Michael's place, in the dock. But Anna was at the age where dignity – her own or her friends' – is of paramount importance;

Michael was so 'right', this was what had made her so certain of love in the first place. And now, as he searched with a troubled smile for reasons for courses of action she didn't see why he should give reasons for, or murmured, 'Oh, I do agree really, I do see your point,' she kept still and made no movement to show that she had heard anything. Already she was thinking, what shall I do now?

It was Ellis who put an end to the interrogation which seemed to Oliver to have limitless possibilities. Ellis had decided with unusual vehemence during the short walk between the house and stables that Oliver Canning was an extremely unpleasant little man, and now to see him, strutting like a fighting cock and tearing feathers from Michael Farne, who was a nice boy, and kind, only in order to impress Anna Severell, for that was how he saw it, made him mad. He said, 'Excuse me – I've a lot to do, and I'll do it better with these cans out of the way, if you don't mind.'

Anna slid off the block, with relief.

'My best wishes to your parents, Anna, and young Jeremy.'

'Yes,' said Anna. 'Thank you.' Her face was sullen and withdrawn again. Oliver picked up his cans, and set out towards the gate.

'Thank you,' he said shortly, obviously accepting Ellis's dislike and finding it proper, making no move to overcome it. Michael said, 'Let me help with those. I'm going anyway.'

'Thank you,' said Oliver. 'That will be kind. Only we must hurry.'

'Come back and see us,' Ellis said to Anna, aware of her constraint, and anxious to dispel it.

'Thank you,' Anna said. 'I'd like to come. I've these exams, you know how one gets pushed about. But I'd like to.' They both saw that she did not mean to come.

'Hurry,' said Oliver from the gate, and turned it. Anna hung about in the yard, whilst Michael saddled his horse, and then they set out together, Michael leading the horse with one hand and carrying the heavy can with the other, Anna loitering deliberately, dragging her feet in the dust. Michael laughed uneasily.

'He's fierce, your uncle. Made me feel terrible. One doesn't like people to think one's really worthless, you know. Why did he – ?'

'You shouldn't let him,' Anna said savagely.

'Oh, I don't know. One has to admire him. I suppose he might be right in a sort of way. Don't you think?'

'No,' said Anna. 'I don't. Let's not talk about him, shall we?'

'You aren't worried about anything?'

'No,' said Anna, in Oliver's clipped voice. 'Why should I be?'

When they reached the car, Oliver had already stowed his can, and was leaning against the bonnet, watching them. He said, 'You seem to be less anxious to hurry in this direction, Anna,' and took Michael's can to push it into the boot. 'Thank you,' he said. 'Get in, Anna.'

Anna stood beside the horse and looked steadily at Michael, a little forbidding, showing nothing of her desperation that he should do the right thing, and restore what had been. Michael hesitated a moment, and then put his foot in the stirrup, and swung up into the saddle. The horse plunged, shied towards the hedge, and dug at the earth, with one curved hoof, delicately.

'He's restive,' said Michael.

'Anna . . .' said Oliver.

'Anna . . .' said Michael. 'I'll see you, won't I?' Anna clenched her fists and stared dumbly at him. He said, 'I'll expect you. I'm here most days now.' In the saddle, he had regained all his beauty and strength; he sat easily, whilst the horse shifted and snorted, like a gold St George. Anna, looking up at him, was dazzled by the sun behind him, so that it seemed concentrated into flames around his head, and his face danced against it, a shifting, empty circle, framed with light. He said, through his halo, 'I'd better be off.'

'Michael – '

'I'll see you, Anna.'

'Yes,' said Anna, desolate, and Michael touched the horse with his heels, and turned to smile as they leaped forward, black and golden, with the air parting round them. Anna stepped automatically out into the cloud of dust they left.

'Michael,' she said. 'Oh Michael, Michael, Michael – ' Behind her the dry voice said, 'You're making what my mother would have called an exhibition of yourself, I suppose you realize that.'

Anna turned on him. 'And what do you think you are doing?'
'That's enough,' said Oliver. 'Get into the car.'

Henry was still walking. He moved very slowly now, automatically, lightly, the division of his senses and the sense of his own identity disintegrating from moment to moment. He was in the last stages of exhaustion, and very dirty. In the odd moments when he was conscious of his body at all, it seemed to him attenuated, brittle, entirely weightless. He was walking along the top of a curving ridge; when he came to the end, he was suddenly over a wide harvest land. He stood and swayed for a moment, and nearly fell; then he gathered himself to look.

The corn was all colours, field after field, from red gold to parchment, to a white wheat – Capelle-Desprez, Henry's memory murmured – like spears of glass. The barley was necked, in the fields near him, the awn was down, the whiskers pointing into the earth, and across the plain, on the side of another round ridge, a field of oats had been tangled by the wind, and strange troughs of shadow moved amongst the bright paleness of it, as it swayed, with its own weight, this way and that. For a moment he stared at a field of yellow mustard, sharp and painful, throwing light at his eyes until he was dizzy with it; when he looked back at the corn the yellow glare superimposed itself on the glossy waves so that they were at once clear and ablaze. Light began to move, lines of poppies were nooses of fire, rushing upwards out of the ground. He began to move again with it, running awkwardly down the hill into the burning harvest; trees and bushes flamed, slid past him, hissed in the heat and crashed behind him; he could hear the air burning with an angry singing. He had the feeling that both he himself and the bushes were struggling hopelessly to hold their shape in the crushing brilliance of the live air, in danger of collapsing like tin cans in which a vacuum has been created, under its battery. He saw the whole turning bowl of light which was the valley held into shape, dangerously, tenuously, by cords of light drawn from the corn, the angry, magnificently dark trees, the hedges, flecked with little bursts of intense white, and himself, straining to breaking point against the glittering ropes, in a balance that could hardly endure any longer.

And still the light poured, heavy, and white, and hot, into the valley before him and collected, molten and seething, on the corn beneath him; he could hear it thundering into the silence; and still he had to see, so that his cone was now an hourglass funnel, opening both ways, and the wide light all pressed and weighed in the point of intersection which was himself, and the gold figures, hieratic, with gold faces and swords of flame, walked in the sea of corn in ordered patterns, like reapers; he recognized them from before, and he knew that he had come to the end. They burst like dragon's teeth men, one by one, from the bright land; he knew they were not tangible, nor presences, nor differentiated one from the other; they were a way of seeing, when too much light was accumulated to see unshaped, without being struck blind. To see like this was to be alive, he knew, before everything was conflagration, and he crumpled and rolled on to the edge of the fields, whilst, very slow, very still, his inner eye opened on cool, wide, white plains, in which he rested.

'Anna – '
    'Yes?'
    'You're very angry, now. Why?'
    'You know why I am.'
    'I assume I've offended against your canons of good taste. I'm not sorry.'
    'I can see that. I don't think there's any point in talking about it. It would count as being rude to grown-ups. You've taken two wrong turnings' – she thought she must point this out since she had at last been driven into speaking – 'and I want to get home. Take a right next, we may hit the road again.'
    'I wish you wouldn't lean forward and grip the car. It's distracting.'
    'I'm sorry,' said Anna, not relaxing. There was a silence. The car bumped and spat, and there was a smell of burning rubber. Oliver sat stiffly behind the wheel, stared ahead of him, and frowned. He seemed determined to discuss the episode: Anna

wondered whether he made situations only because he then so much enjoyed dealing with them, overcoming them, arranging. If so, it was rather expensive from her own point of view. She said nothing; that was easiest as well as probably most effective. After a time Oliver began again, 'I suppose you think it was terribly simple minded and *earnest* of me to intrude large social questions into your happy afternoon with the horsey young man?'

'I'm trying *not* to think.'

'That's irresponsible, you'd better. For myself, I can't help knowing that there is one clever, innocent, unsophisticated boy from a grammar school who's been deprived of a whole life because your friend had the money, or the schooling and the initial intelligence, to ensure that he could spend his socially obligatory three years doing nothing gracefully in an educational institution.

'I suppose you think that's all very obvious and can't be helped. I don't see it that way. I don't mean them to get away with it.'

'How do you know that he – that Michael – isn't intelligent, then?'

'Well, is he?'

Anna did not reply. 'You see,' said Oliver. He went on, 'I know them, I've taught them. Nice jolly puppies, with no pretensions to brains, normally very friendly, sorry they can't produce essays that will interest me, but never mind, it's easier for me not to have to make an effort to understand anything. Once a year they get horribly drunk over some boat that bumped some boat – I may be without humour, I persist in thinking that childish – and they systematically destroy the room of some outsider who can't run, or went to the wrong school, or works a bit too obviously for a First. I suppose you'll say they'll grow out of it, but some of us do better and don't grow into it. Again, I may not see the joke, I'm an outsider myself, but I call that irresponsible and wicked. I suppose you may say this doesn't happen any more, but it does, I've seen it, we've heard all this before, but that doesn't do away with it, on the contrary. And when I meet it, I don't pretend to like it. One must be honest.'

'You don't have to be . . . unpleasant.'

'I don't have to cover up, or lie by implication.'

'Michael is my friend – he never tried to be anything but nice to you. He's *my* friend – he's not a symbol, he's not a way of life, he's himself. And he's nothing to do with you. Why can't you leave me alone?'

'And you – ' said Oliver savagely. 'Where do you think you're going? Have you tried to think?' He imitated her. 'Michael, Michael, Michael – where do you think that will get you? What do you think he's got to give that will add anything to you? An intelligent girl with a future and a responsibility to try to understand yourself – and the world – soberly – what do you think you've got in common with that dead way of living? Oh my God . . . can't you *see* yourself married to him, hunt balls and county dinner parties, church on Sunday, inherited Nanny, hampers at pony shows, tweed skirts, talk about dogs and horses, and Conservative women, hanging and flogging – ? Look, this is the truth, you just *can't* shut yourself into that, it's insuperable, it isn't real, it's a substitute for life, I mean it, real human beings just don't happen where your friend is. And you've got to try, damn you.'

'I don't think that's the point – '

'Of course you don't. And it isn't entirely. Shall I tell you what it is? It isn't an accident, is it, that that young man is just the kind of young man your mother would like to imagine her daughter married to? I say her daughter, I don't suppose she thinks in terms of you – what's wrong, and you must accept it, is that neither of them have noticed or approved of you for so long that you don't know where you are. But you must believe me, this rather pathetic attempt to fit yourself into a picture where your mother might be able to approve of you won't make it any better and it'll ruin your own chances of anything worthwhile. In the end you've only yourself to account to.'

Anna felt battered; she said weakly, 'You always take things much too far.' And Oliver retorted, 'And you persist in refusing to look beyond your nose.'

'All this psychological explaining . . . I don't . . .'

'But it's right, isn't it?'

'I don't *know*,' Anna wailed. 'It doesn't seem like that to me.'

She thought how like Oliver it was to insist on thinking of her being married to Michael; she had not got as far as thinking of marriage at all, that was in a future, with the event she was waiting for, far too far away to affect her. What mattered about Michael Oliver had left out entirely, his gentleness, his beautiful body, the way he was part of the sun and the summer and not having to think ahead. And it was cruel of him to suggest that he thought Michael might please Caroline, from whose disapproval Anna, she believed, had seen him partly as an escape route. The suggestion, once planted, was difficult to uproot; how horrid, Anna thought, if it was even half-way true.

'You're always telling me what *not* to do. But what shall I *do* then?'

'I've told you. Leave home, find out what you can honestly make of yourself — school-teacher, librarian, secretary — and be that. On your own ground. One thing's sure, you'll not be anything if you just sit about and wait and breathe your father's rarefied air. A ghost, a shadow; I'm not exaggerating.'

'But if I want to be here?'

'You don't look to me as though you do.'

Anna cast about for what was disproportionate in all this, and said slowly, 'I can't see why you mind so much. Why do you go on so? I still can't see why you had to be *so* nasty to Michael.'

'Because I like you, I suppose.'

'Yes, but why?'

'I told you, I've come to like you. That's enough. I get personally angry.'

Anna had provoked him to this, and she took a pleasure, both malicious and innocent, in his agitation; she liked to feel, simply, that she had power enough to have caused it. She had not the slightest idea what to do next and certainly no desire to provoke him further, and she was extremely angry with him, but there was a certain pride of possession in her as she looked secretly across at his set face, bright with sweat, and slightly pink. She had done it, and this, she thought in her innocence, gave her a hold over him.

*

Henry rolled over and sat up. This took him some time. He was hardly used to his body, and bruises and cuts and grazes of which, before, he had been altogether unaware, were now stiffening and very painful. It was strange how he could not remember, already, what he had seen or how he had been, except that he knew, as he always knew, how unnecessary it had been to be afraid – fear had nothing to do with so absolute a loss of time and excitement. He propped himself carefully on his hands in the dust, and looked up at the sun, the same sun, but no longer blazing, swimming it seemed to him, infinitely remote, through depth after depth of an air clear, substantial, lucid as water. He was extremely happy, he thought – and added, being capable again of deliberation, how we have murdered our superlatives, how can we now, at the edges of experience like this, find adequate words to replace extremely, intolerably, perfectly, infinitely? One must find a language new and washed clean, and the things it is necessary to say require these superlatives. He was becoming a craftsman again, and took pleasure in that too; he thought of his desk and the novel he had been writing, and the thought of the words on the paper warmed him, and excited him so that he smiled involuntarily.

But he was in no hurry. He sat for some time, still considering the sun, remarking how earlier it had drawn everything into its own Phaethon career across the heavens and was now still and solitary; mildly, distantly alight, but nothing to do with anything else. More than anything, quite basically, he was surprised at the human capacity for reflecting – a nice metaphorical, Platonic touch, he thought, still considering the sun, if I were sure that the metaphor didn't distort a little what I mean, didn't draw too close a connection between myself and that, which is far too much a fact to be for me any symbol of consciousness, or intelligence, or power, in myself, without losing something of its own certain solidity, there deep in the sky. Metaphysics fascinated him, religious symbolism even more – his visionary times gained a tremendous life from his knowledge of Platonic ideas of the intellectual meanings of sun, and light, or Coleridge's complex ideas of the reflective nature of the moon's light and minds like the moon. He became angry only when these figures were translated into assurances and the leap was made into faith, of one kind or another; intimations of immortality, the assurance that there was a creative mind behind the universe. These detracted; he had no need of immortality, he could not get beyond the fact of where he was.

He would never, he thought, get over looking up there at the light and *knowing* that he was looking up there. He was so constantly, so consistently surprised to think, here is a man seeing and knowing – if not precisely *what* – that he is seeing. He imagined his death as a progress into a more and more lucent inactivity – or at least, at these times he did. He had other moods, but that summer they had become less frequent, and he was even beginning to wonder if he had established a way of life which was both possible, satisfactory and peculiarly valuable.

An arrowhead of tiny black birds came, direct, whirring beneath him and the sun, and distracted him; they glittered white for a moment as they wheeled, and soared on into emptiness. Henry stood up as though they were a signal. Round him, the corn was all milky, and melting, the cars formless, the edges lapping into air, and there was an illusory sound of water far away, breaking softly. Henry said to himself, Beulah, the delectable mountains, of course, and saw almost immediately that the curious haziness of everything was due to his own extreme fatigue. 'It will be tiresome,' he said aloud, enunciating clearly in the empty humming silence of the cornfields, 'if I have made myself really ill this time. I shall have to see. If I walk I shall find out.'

He went along the edge of the field, shambling in the dust, lurching every now and then, falling once entirely, into the corn. It was an agonizingly slow progress. Henry was so intent on the next few inches that everything narrowed to them. What he did, he did entirely. As he walked, the cuts on his feet and legs began to bleed again. The pain was excruciating.

Oliver was all wound up, Anna thought. She was sure by now that he was losing the way on purpose, only to be able to lecture her longer. She was doing her best not to listen to him, but he spoke on, explaining to her 'reality' as he saw it, commitment, the society she might not like but with which she must come to terms, her own terms, 'if you are to do anything meaningful at all'. Lawrence had left England, Anna pointed out, having by now ascertained the importance of Lawrence in relation to these themes. Lawrence, Oliver retorted, had been a great man, and a prophet, whereas she, Anna, was a moderately intelligent girl with, as far as he, Oliver, had discovered, no particular skills – and moreover Lawrence had written nothing really relevant after forgetting the society he knew.

'That's two contradictory points,' Anna said.

'Not at all. It's two points, both apply to him, that is not to you, not to me. What would we make of Mexico, anyway? I wouldn't feel I'd a right to ask anyone to give us the money to go. We've got to keep things running the way we can. I teach people reality. You set about finding out what you are. Never mind whose shadow you're under.'

'You tell me I'm someone with one hand and take it away with the other. That's what I can't bear.'

'What you can't face is finding out precisely what kind of someone. As long as you don't do anything you don't have to admit that there are some things you might be unable to do – '

'I *do*,' said Anna.

'No, you don't. You say to yourself, I'm young. I don't have to think yet, when I do I expect I'll be able to do this or that? Don't you? Isn't that how it is? But you're not *so* young. And it isn't true, at any time. Think how short your life is, and there's only one of it.' He was exalted.

'I *do*,' said Anna.

They turned a corner into a narrow lane: at one side a field, all stubble, early harvested, sloped steeply into them, hardly contained by a sparse hedge. Henry came, staggering and stumbling, in full view down the field; he fell once to his knees and righted himself, rushed suddenly down the last few yards, and through the hedge, unseeing, and crashed flat into the side of the car. Anna saw his eyes roll up as he put out his hands, clumsily, and went down in the road.

'Oliver,' she said. 'Oh, no. Oliver. It's father.'

'Don't touch me, damn you, when I'm driving,' Oliver said, trembling.

Anna removed her hands from his arm. She said, 'What shall we do? What, then?'

'Shut up,' said Oliver. He got down into the road and Anna followed him. They stood looking down on Henry, who lay spread on his back with his arms above him. He was grotesque: Anna's first feeling was one of furious embarrassment. His clothes were ripped, and hardly wrapped round him; the hair on his chest was matted with mud and spangled with slivers of bright straw dust; these shone too on his head, and his beard. His beard was horrid, blood had run into it in several places from scratches more or less deep, and had caked on it; there was still black river mud round his throat; his hair was twisted, damply, into horns and spikes, like the corkscrew rays of the conventional pictorial sun, but these were all colours, grey, green, straw, blood brown, earth black. His mouth was open and he breathed heavily through it. From one corner of it blood still ran slow and bright, into the grey dust which lay like a mask on his face. His face, owing to the caking down of the beard and hair, appeared surprisingly naked and surprisingly thin. He looked empty, lifeless altogether. His eyes, closed, were very deep in his head; now and then the lids twitched up, and showed an empty ball. There was a lot of him in the road, limp but solid, and lying at such an angle, the dusty feet together, that it seemed as though he had been broken across by a heavy blow at the base of the spine. Anna thought, for one terrible moment, that she was going to disgrace herself entirely by being sick.

'He's alive, anyway,' said Oliver.

'Yes,' said Anna.

'Which is something.'

'What shall we do?'

Neither of them could bring themselves to touch him. Oliver said, 'He looks as though he's been in a fight.'

'I don't know.'

'Or entirely at odds with the vegetation, which is unlikely. Though according to him, it's intractable, the vegetation.'

'What shall we *do*?'

'He looks as though he's come pretty well to grips with it,

whatever it was he went roaring out after. He looks as though it got the better of him, wouldn't you say?'

'Don't – '

'Well, what did happen then? Have you no curiosity? He looks as though he's been trying to do what a bulldozer could do much better for him. Now, if he'd gone out on a bulldozer – '

'Don't, stop it – '

'If he had, I'd understand. I can't get away from this feeling that all this struggling with the elements just won't wash any longer. We've got it under control – it's a lie to pretend we haven't.'

'*Please* don't go on. You don't seem to see. You don't seem to care. He may be very ill. Don't treat him as an *object* all the time.'

'He doesn't precisely encourage treating him any other way, does he? It's a kind of respect.'

'*Please*, Oliver – '

'All right. What shall we do then? We're a pretty ineffectual pair when it comes to it, aren't we? What do you advise? Moving him? Or do you think that might damage internal injuries? I really am trying to think. I wonder what he has been doing, though, so many days?'

Anna's lips trembled. At that moment Henry opened his eyes and gazed calmly up at them. He said, weakly, the civilized voice sounding odd enough amongst the scarecrow wildness of his face, 'Dear me, how convenient. How do you happen to be here? I was very much afraid I would not have got back alone.'

'Where did you go?' asked Oliver, staccato. Henry's eyelids flicked and closed again. Anna knelt down beside him and took his hand.

'Please,' she said. 'Are you all right? Can you get up? Will you come home? It's been horrible without you, will you come home, now?'

Henry, very faintly, returned the pressure of her hand. He said, 'Of course, just a moment and I'll be perfectly well.'

'How has this happened?' Oliver persisted.

'Can't you see,' Anna cried, 'he doesn't want to say? Anyway, what does it matter? And who do you think you are, to find out?'

88

'Don't be rude,' Oliver said, retreating unfairly into his adult privileges. Henry sat up, with more ease then any of them would have expected. Anna said, 'Let me help. There, lean on me. Now, if you can get into the car, just –'

'He doesn't need all that help,' Oliver said. Anna nevertheless helped Henry into the back seat of the car and propped him in one corner. Then she climbed in beside him and slammed the door. Oliver drove them home, very slowly, agonizingly slowly for Anna, and did not speak again. Nor did Henry, who leaned back into his corner, jerked like a skeleton with every bump of the car, and closed his eyes. Anna surveyed him covetously – she thought, I would like to do anything at all *as much as* he seems to have done whatever it was he was doing. He was rather terrible, so distant. It seemed suddenly, enormously important that he should be her ally, that he should support her in some way against Oliver's commonsense, or she was lost. There was an answer to what Oliver said and to what he did not say and Henry must know it. She was, after all, Henry's daughter. She edged closer to him, and looked up at him imploring. There was a slight smile on his mouth, visible since it was for once not covered by the beard, but he did not open his eyes.

The house, when they came back to it, was exactly the same, and Anna found the sight of it shocking and defeating. To go in there and wash her hands and eat supper would be an admission of ultimate defeat – by Oliver, or by Caroline? she was not even sure. Better to make a scene and keep everything still in a state of flux, however childish and silly. Better to do anything rather than drop, unprotesting, into yesterday's – or tomorrow's? – orders and restrictions. It was humiliating and it was frightening and she did not even know precisely what was so wrong. But Henry, if he could be brought to tell her, Henry back from goodness knew where, with the relics of goodness knew what strange knowledge adhering to him, the shreds of another brighter world, Henry would know.

They all three got out of the car in the drive, and looked at the house. No one was there to meet them. No one seemed to be there at all. Henry, who seemed much recovered, said abruptly,

'Must get cleaned up, before Caroline sees me,' and made off into the house. Oliver began, 'Well – ' in a tone of dry amusement, but Anna would not let him go on, she said. 'Don't say anything else to me, not just now – ' and went after Henry. 'I must speak to you,' said Oliver behind her, but she pretended not to hear.

She pushed open the door of her father's dressing room without knocking, and went in. He was sitting on the bed, his chin jutting forward, looking out of the window. He looked, she thought, rather pleased with himself, but not, not precisely, helpful.

'It's you,' he said, accepting her. 'Get me a sponge, will you, and I'll start on some of this.' Anne squeezed a sponge obediently under the hot tap and handed it to him: he began to wipe, rather ineffectually, at some of the dried blood; Anna went and leaned in the doorway, watching him. After a bit, she asked, for a beginning, 'Where did you go?'

'I don't know. I walked.'

'What did you do?'

'I don't know. I must have walked in a circle. I think I've a touch of sunstroke.'

'No, but do you feel *different*, now? What *difference* does it make? I want to know – '

Henry tilted his slow head sideways and considered her. He said, 'Don't you know?'

'I try to guess – ' Anna said in a rush. 'But, I don't know, no, I don't *know*. I want to ask you . . .'

'Well – ?' asked Henry, encouraging. Anna struggled dispiritedly to find out what she did, precisely, want to ask him. Henry felt a dismay which he tried very hard to hide. People, particularly the unfortunate Anna, were always at their most urgent just when he was exhausted, or preoccupied entirely with something of his own. His head was swimming now; he gave up the attempt on his beard, and leaned back carefully on to the bed; then he said, 'Go on, please,' in a voice which he hoped was non-committal, neither formidably parental nor yet artificially man to man. But it was an effort. If things had been different, if it had been some other time, he could have helped her more than that.

Anna ran furiously over beginnings in her mind, and rejected them one after the other. She could not touch on Michael; that was humiliating, and anyway Henry would not understand. She could not – because he was himself parental authority, it was his mandate which kept her inactive in the garden, if only by default – protest that she was in some way being kept from knowledge she should have. She was still not sure precisely what Oliver was advising her to do, but only of its general area. The area of 'life as it is lived', by most human beings, or at least most English ones, jobs and marriages and culture, town planning and the Obscene Publications Act, little magazines, science for the layman, the divorce rate, the birth rate, lung cancer, teenage crime, and the monotony of factories – Oliver had told her about all these and she had given them in her imagination a background which would have shocked him, the bed-sitter, the 'cocktail party', the boy meets girl in London of the women's magazine, innocently, because this was all she really knew about jobs, having never even begun to consider her schoolmistresses, who were creatures, in her eyes (and probably in Oliver's), isolated from life as irreparably as schoolgirls were.

So she could not say to Henry – 'Oliver says I must do such and such, why do I feel I must not, when I see he is right?' Besides the crux was not there; if it were not for Henry himself, there would be no real problem, nothing she could even begin to hold on to to set against Oliver. Or alternatively, without him, she would know it for herself, and not need to ask for a way out of Oliver's line-up. When one was six or seven, she thought, or twelve or thirteen even, one might not have liked only sitting in the garden, only taking things in, but remembered now all of it seemed valuable, because then there had been no alternative. She had thought then, as she did now, that she was getting through the days somehow. But it had been much more than that. It seemed, looking back, she thought in confusion, that she had had time to be herself and see how things were. But, like an expanding gas in a narrow jar, she grew, and remained confined in a little space, the same garden, the same school, the same girl, and something must blow up: Oliver was right there, she had been thinking so before he came, something must happen. But the something was — it was desperately to be hoped — nothing of his order. It was her event, her change, her sudden recognition of her proper activity after being necessarily passive for so long.

Because she *agreed* with Oliver, she had to, she began in a circle again, and he was right that being at home and not changing for years was bad for her, and he was right that most of Michael's likely ways and views were not tolerable. It was only that something else was going too, maybe a capacity to wait without anxiety and take what came, which was not heroic, but had been leading certainly to her event. Or had it? In this homer pen, this goldfish bowl, how could she know? But Henry knew, it was still on his face, no other face she had seen had ever been so peaceful and so live as his was now. He had found the third way, neither into the enclosure, nor out into Oliver's myriad concerns, but an extension, a development, of what she thought she had already.

Having reached the end of this by no means clear or exhaustive survey of her worry, she felt irrationally that she had already explained it to Henry, and that it was now there between them to be discussed. So she waited for him to speak. When he did not, she said, in a voice aggrieved and slightly petulant, 'I don't know what to do with myself.'

I have a genius for making myself sound insignificant, she told herself immediately.

Henry sat up again and rubbed at the back of his neck. He said, 'I think I must've wrenched something. Surprisingly tough, the human body.'

'Please!' said Anna sharply.

'I'm not not listening,' Henry assured her, probing the muscles at the back of his neck with careful fingers.

Anna said, 'I've had a ghastly day. I can't begin to tell you. I can't bear to go on like this. I don't *do* anything and nothing seems important — look, you ought to understand, I mean, really, *nothing seems important*, just think how trivial all the things I do are, carrying cans, laying the breakfast table, washing things, changing clothes, going on walks and coming back. Have you ever felt like that?'

'Yes,' said Henry. He felt he must say more, but tiredness

was lapping round him again, and his daughter's shrill, childish voice jarred on him. He made an effort and added 'At your age, I did. It often gets worse just before one finds something that is important.' An avuncular generalization, he thought guiltily. Anna ignored it, after a moment; it was what she wanted to hear, but had been said so perfunctorily and had indicated no direction.

She said, 'All right, it's my age. I tell you what, I *hate* adolescent novels, they're so boring. I tell you what, they're not interesting, they're not important, and neither am I, they're all about nothing, and so am I. People think muddles are interesting – anything at all, if it can be put on paper – but I don't. And I'm not. I wouldn't mind so much if – that is, I wish they hadn't set Oliver Canning on to me. He finds me so interesting I could scream. He keeps telling me why I've grown up' – she tortured herself – 'useless, and in unloveable, and purposeless and ineffectual . . . he keeps telling me what to do. And he keeps telling me why I don't. I can't bear much more, I'm warning you.'

'Why hasn't he gone home?'

'Because he's stayed to get me into University. Where I don't want to go. There doesn't seem much point, does there, if I don't have the slightest idea what I want to do with myself?'

'You must do something.'

'That sounds just like him!' Anna said desperately. Henry showed no sign of telling her what it was that he knew, and she had no skill to make him, apparently.

'I'm sorry. You mustn't listen too much to him. You've plenty of time . . . There is so much else – ' He could not rouse himself out of his weariness enough to tell her what there was, it was no good, he hardly saw her, half the time, at all. Her desperation hit him in little bursts, and could not stir him, and faded again. He felt bad. He was aware of what she wanted, well enough. But even if he was not tired, he was always desperately shy; there had been no habit of communication between them, or indeed between himself and anyone, about what he knew. So he lay on the bed, his arms dangling, and peered at her gently and apologetically under his wild and dirty eyebrows.

He said, timidly, 'Don't bother so much, Anna,' and she,

taking his timidity for dismissal or lack of interest, thought Oliver must be right after all, and began, noisily, with mounting violence, to weep, making the scene which was, as she had foreseen, her last resort from acquiescence. Henry lay still, drawn into himself, his face as beautifully expressionless amongst the wreckage of his patriarchal good looks as a sleeping child's, and, even overcast with the greyness of fatigue, potentially as vigorous. His limbs were all anyhow, as abandoned as a child's, one could see that he was taking pleasure simply in not moving them, in letting them be heavy and inert. And the mud and blood on his face looked sculpted at last, the carefully applied ceremonial paint of the medicine man. Anna stared at him, and wailed at him, at Oliver, at the strangeness of things, which up till now she had taken for granted. The noise she made attracted Caroline, who was passing on the landing with a pile of sheets in her arms, and came in now, busily, laid them on the chest of drawers and said, 'Henry!'

He opened his eyes, narrowly, and began to sit up.

'No, don't sit up, don't be silly, you may damage yourself. What have you been doing?' She expected no answer; things were in her hands, now; she went across and examined him carefully. 'Migraine?' she said, and fetched him codeine, and a glass of water. 'Anything else, besides dirt?' Henry shook his head. 'Have you had any food?' Henry shook his head again, deprecating. 'You don't deserve looking after. You'd better get to bed, I think. Take your clothes off.' She sat down abstractedly beside him, and began very gently to wipe his face with the sponge. 'My poor Henry,' she said, very lightly, asking to be allowed to care. Henry put his hand on hers and smiled at her. Anna, in the corner, began to weep again, making an ugly, raucous noise, breathless and importunate. Caroline turned on her.

'Ah, yes, you. What's the matter with you? What are you doing here? Why didn't you tell me he was back?'

'She's overwrought,' Henry said. 'Something's upset her.'

'Something has always upset her lately; I'm running out of patience with it. You might at least think, Anna, before you come and bother your father when he isn't well and needs to rest. Do you *ever* think about anyone else?'

Anna made a hopeless little gesture and stood stock still, and continued to weep, the tears running salt off her nose into her mouth corners, and down behind her cheeks into her neck.

'It's this sun,' said Caroline more kindly. 'And neither of you has any sense of proportion. You'd better go to bed, too, Anna. Take some of these, here's some water, and get to bed. I'll bring you both some supper, later.' She snapped down Henry's blind and his room became a dim, coffee-coloured tent. 'That's better.' The thought of Anna safe behind her door for the evening was very pleasant; as Anna showed still no sign of leaving she said again, 'Hurry now, I told you. Go to bed.' Henry said nothing. Anna looked at him desperately, and then stumbled out onto the landing and began to trail towards her own room. Caroline squeezed out the sponge again and set to work on his face, with extreme gentleness: she said, 'I'm glad you always come back. It's funny, I'm still frightened you might not.'

'Why?' asked Henry easily.

'Oh, there must be so many more interesting places you could go to, I sometimes think.'

'I don't know,' said Henry. Caroline's hand stopped over his face. He looked up, and saw that she was really anxious. He said, 'I don't mean to leave, you mustn't think that. I'd say if I did. I mean – I wouldn't go without you. You know what I mean, don't you?'

'Yes,' said Caroline, and began again to clean him, like someone cleaning moss from an effigy in a churchyard.

Outside Anna's door, as she had half feared, Oliver was waiting with his harrying look. Anna knew that her face was mottled and bulging with tears, and that Oliver would be able to work out his own not too inaccurate reasons for this. She hesitated, turned back indecisively towards Henry, then gathered herself, and went on, towards him. He began immediately:

'Please listen to me for a moment, Anna. I want you to understand. I don't think you're being quite fair.'

Anna licked up a tear. She said, 'I've been sent to bed. At least let me go there.'

Oliver looked as though he was thinking, in some general direction, 'I told you so,' but at least he did not say it. He was

95

in her way: she would have had to push past him to get at the handle of her door, and at that moment, wound up as she was, she was physically terrified of him; if she had had to touch him, with both of them so angry, she would have broken down completely. So she stood, and trembled, and faced him, very forlorn.

'I want to say, I didn't mean to hurt you, this afternoon. I'm sorry you think I'm interfering, I really only mean to help. I'm sorry if we have to quarrel. You're one of the last people I'd willingly hurt. I – '

'It doesn't matter, I can see you don't mean any harm. I think you make too much of things.'

'But you're half frightened I don't.'

Anna began to cry again. 'Don't keep *telling* me. If I've got to be adolescent, at least let me get on with it my own way.'

'It isn't just adolescence.'

'Stop *telling* me.'

'I'm sorry,' said Oliver, very red. I didn't mean to start again. I'm sorry. I didn't mean to say that at all. I meant to say – I know I go about it the wrong way – I'd like you to think I was there. I mean, that I care what happens to you. I thought you might like to know there was someone who really cared – but – '

'It's a funny kind of caring,' Anna said ungraciously; she was frightened by this new attempt at intimacy much more than by his earlier pontifications. It was harder to defend oneself against him in this position. She said, 'It's nice of you. But I really do think you think there's more wrong than there is.'

Oliver looked at his shoes, and said gloomily, as though he was trying to extract some residual comfort from the situation, 'I'm glad you find it possible to be honest with me, at any rate.'

Anna felt suddenly very mean. It was true what he said, he was trying to help, and it was kind of him to care, she had no right to reject him, or to hurt his feelings, which were obviously very susceptible, just because her own were hurt, partly over Michael it was true, but partly at least by her father about whom Oliver had been, it appeared, however hatefully, right, and for whom he was certainly not responsible. She said, 'I'm sorry. I'm just being nasty because everything's so muddled. I don't mean it. You've done a lot for me and I'm grateful, honestly . . .'

'Let's forget it, all of it,' said Oliver, brightening up immediately. He held out his hand. Anna could not bring herself to take it; it was still immensely important not to touch him, she knew that without thinking about it at all. She began, instead, to droop at him, deliberately playing for sympathy, hanging her head and leaning drunkenly against the doorpost. She said, 'I feel terrible. So tired. All the heat and all this fuss . . .'

Oliver became immediately, in his own way, solicitous.

'You look done in. Poor Anna. You'd better lie down and try to sleep. Very important to develop a capacity for rest.' He held the door open for her. 'Now, get along with you, go to bed and relax. We may well have been over-working you, you must take the evening off.'

Anna scurried past him before he could pat her shoulder, gave him a weak smile, and closed the door firmly on his sharp enquiring face. She was not sure that it had not entered his head to come after her and tuck her in. The idea crossed her mind that he had manœuvred her in such a way that she had to be grateful to him for opening her door and encouraging her to lie down, when it had been he who had prevented her in the first place. But, as she took off her clothes, and climbed in between the sheets, she was able to smile to herself with a new feminine indulgence over him. He was very tiresome, but what he said was true, he did care for her, he seemed to think she was worth caring about. And, however many reservations she might make about the direction of his caring it would be uncharitable not to accept it. She was so lonely, she thought, with a new access of self-pity, she couldn't afford to refuse anybody's interest. He thinks I'm someone, he thinks I'm too good to leave alone, she told herself, remembering his fury over her theoretical future as a country wife, and was almost amused. And he's a clever man, he should know, I'd better be nice to him, she thought further as she fell asleep.

The next day went on as usual. The day after that, Michael telephoned twice, but Anna put him off with vague, expressionless little promises about next week, if she wasn't working too hard. By that time they were all involved in preparations for the picnic.

FIVE

THE PICNIC AT St Anne Crane had been organized by Caroline as a regular family event, every summer, very soon after they came to Darton. She had to believe – being the woman she was – that 'a family must do things together', that 'children need both a father and a mother'. Since they had never gone away anywhere on a long holiday together, largely because Henry's best work was always done at home in the summer, she had insisted with unusual firmness that he must make a part of her picnic – this had thus become a ceremonial event, laden with ritual importances and anxiety that it should go well. St Anne Crane was some miles away, on the coast. It was the kind of little place, unspoiled and natural, that everyone dreams of finding and conceals the existence of jealously from friends and acquaintances. It was outside the usually acceptable radius for expeditions from Darton, and thus getting there required a long and arduous car journey, beginning, in order that the picnic should be as expansive as possible, very early in the morning, before any of them would normally have been up.

Caroline had arranged the picnic, this year, for the last day of the Cannings' visit; two years ago, she had decided, with reluctant realism, that family solidarity would be better maintained if there was some alien element in the party. Otherwise it was only too likely, whatever the ideal, that Henry would forget himself and wander away entirely, or that Anna would turn nasty and refuse to play with Jeremy; there had been one or two very unpleasant incidents already. This year she was quite glad that it had turned out as it had; it would keep the Cannings occupied and show them that an effort was being made to entertain them which went beyond board and lodging;

it would also give Henry, if he behaved, some chance to alleviate the bad impression he had made on Oliver without having to talk to him too much or too intensively; he could show him the Norman church which would be friendly and not taxing.

She had made a lot of the arrangements, with faith, whilst Henry was away. She had arranged the hiring of a second motor-car, and had hunted out the wicker picnic baskets, flasks and cutlery several days in advance; she had ordered food, and washed swimming things, packed canvas stools and checked the maps in the car. Now, on the day itself, she had only two worries – the usual one of the weather and when it would break, which was really, she told herself, slightly absurd by now, and Henry's health. The sky shone as blue and clear as ever – Caroline returned its serene stare across the breakfast table as she poured coffee and ladled kedgeree for a party roused early for the occasion. At the other end of the table, Henry looked well enough; his cuts were healing, he had spent two good nights and was eating a large breakfast. Jeremy, working busily through his second plateful of kedgeree, saw her look towards the window and said solicitously, 'I do hope the weather doesn't break. That would be awful, wouldn't it?'

'Oh, surely it won't,' said Margaret. 'Not just when it's important.'

'You have a touching faith in the weather's sympathy,' said her husband. 'However, in this case, I can't see it as likely that it will rain. Even taking the law of averages into account.'

'You are always laughing at me,' said Margaret.

'Not at all, I said it was touching and I'm touched. I mean it.'

'I can't eat kedgeree in this heat,' said Anna, pushing her chair back. 'May I get down?'

Caroline stiffened with automatic annoyance. Anna had come down late, in her old jeans, with her hair obviously uncombed and her face flushed. If she was in for another of those days it was really too much. Caroline said, as pleasantly as she could, 'You look feverish, dear. Are you sure you're quite well? Did you sleep?'

'Like a log. I don't think I'm feverish. I just don't like kedgeree.' She stood up and went out slamming the door.

Caroline said, 'Really, her manners.'

Margaret said, 'I don't think she does look very well.'

'She never does. It's hardly surprising. She thinks it beneath her dignity to take any care of herself. So someone else has to and there has to be a row about it.'

'Excuse me,' said Oliver, and went out, after Anna. Henry got up, as surreptitiously as his bulk allowed, and padded off towards his study. Caroline caught his sleeve.

'Henry! The second car. Who will collect it?'

'Oliver. And Anna, in our car. Give them something to do. Anna can drive back. What did she learn to drive for?' He went out, incontrovertibly. Caroline sighed. 'Everyone enjoys picnics, but no one seems to think they might need arranging. Anna is impossible. Do you think Oliver would mind?'

'I should think he'd be only too pleased.' Margaret hesitated. 'I really don't think Anna looks well.'

Caroline drew her mouth together. 'I expect I handle her badly. I'd like to see anyone else do any better, that's all. You wouldn't think anyone could show such a complete lack of interest in everything. And such a complete lack of comprehension about ordinary things – she's quite frighteningly stupid with pressure cookers, and Hoovers. And she'll have to cope with them some day, she's a woman, nobody'll cope for her. But she won't be interested. She can't manage *anything*. Not even school and everyone gets through that somehow, don't they? She ran away from school twice, I don't know if I told you, they expelled her in the end. I suppose it was a bit hard, but I can't say I blamed them. I suppose it's my fault – it's supposed to be, isn't it – but what I think sometimes is if you look at people they were *born* the way they are, really – I mean, all this putting it on to the parents leaves people with nothing that you could call *them*, does it? I can see my getting cross with her makes her no better, but what flummoxes me entirely is just that – that – that I feel she's nothing to do with me. Nothing to do with me. She repudiates me. That's what it is.'

Margaret said, 'Isn't it simply that it's time she left home? She's just not at an age where it's possible – for most people – to be at home. I know felt like that – I don't think there's anything unusual – '

100

'No,' said Caroline, who did not want to have to think there was anything unusual and may indeed have been right about that. 'In any case, I don't see where else she can go.'

'She could come to us for a bit. I'd have her willingly; she'd be company for me when Oliver's out and Oliver could go on coaching her. He thinks highly of her; it must be good for her to have someone so interested . . . that is, I mean, someone who knows of something she can do . . . Would you like that? I'll ask Oliver, I'll ask Anna herself, she might talk to me better, I might be able to find out what she does want . . .'

'I don't know,' Caroline said dubiously, trying to weigh the disadvantage of being further indebted to Oliver, against the advantage of having Anna out of the house and usefully employed. 'It might be too much for you. I'd have to ask Henry. We'll think . . .'

'Do,' said Margaret. 'And I'll ask Anna, tactfully, shall I?'

An hour later Caroline had them all together on the lawn and covered them with a counting look, whilst she ran over the inanimate objects which had been collected earlier.

'I really never thought I'd get you off. Now – the baskets are in the boot of our car. The rugs, the swimming things, the first-aid box, and Jeremy's cricket and Jeremy's frogman's things are in the hired car. There are maps in both; it will be best if Henry drives our car and Oliver follows in the hired car. Margaret and Anna had better go with Henry and Jeremy and I will go with Oliver, so that I can guide Oliver if Henry gets out of sight. I think that's all; the house is locked, is it, Henry? Have you all got hats?'

They all had, except Oliver, who did not mention this but looked the other way, deliberately vaguely; Anna, watching him, thought, he has to pretend he hasn't heard because even he can't face mother telling him to take a hat without giving in or excusing himself. Anna herself had been made to change, and now she and Jeremy looked oddly alike, in timeless grey shorts and white shirts and linen sunhats. They stood together, brown and long-legged, any country children on any country outing. Anna's hair was bunched up in her shirt collar, not yet long enough to fall free of it. She stood with her hands in her shorts' pockets, which were not intended for that; her stomach protruded and her shoulders sloped awkwardly back. Caroline said gently, 'I wish you would learn to stand more gracefully, Anna.' Anna shifted from, one foot to the other.

Margaret wore a cotton sundress, rose and white striped, with a full skirt and petticoats; over it she had a white piqué jacket, buttoned with tiny pearl buttons. She wore white strapped sandals with a little heel, and an enormous white cartwheel of a sun-hat tied with a rose ribbon under her chin. It was one of her feminine days – she had had decided on these clothes as proper for the occasion and rejected jeans and espadrilles. In her hand she carried a little leather case of lotions and protective creams. Oliver had told her – mockingly but with obvious pleasure – that she looked very nice. He liked female clothes, swinging skirts and low necks, hats and necklaces, whether they were fashionable or not. Caroline on the other hand frowned slightly over the probable fragility of the sandals – no good for scrambling over stones – and the impracticability of a froth of petticoats on a cliff edge. The childless, she thought, had no sense of the realities of life. Herself, she wore a blue and white printed linen dress and Clark's ladies' sandals, with a summer version of the Henry Heath gardening hat. Short sleeves, and no petticoat. She noticed that Oliver had no hat.

'Perhaps,' she said, attacking, 'you would like to borrow one of Henry's hats?'

'I don't think so, thank you. I've a thick skull, the sun doesn't affect me. Hats irritate me.'

Caroline flushed. 'The summer is exceptional and the sun by the sea is always brighter . . .'

'Let him be.' Henry by the car was buried as far as the bridge of his nose in an enormous panama which Caroline had once brought back in triumph from the Army and Navy stores, after Henry had protested that his head was too large for any hat he could purchase. 'Let him be. He's over twenty-one and no relation. I don't suppose he'll suffer. I was out without a hat and look at me. Perfectly fit.'

Caroline was effectively distracted. 'Are you sure? Are you really fit? Do you think you can drive? Perhaps Anna –'

102

'Don't fuss, my darling,' said Henry. 'I'm all right. I prefer to drive myself to my own destruction. I'd tell you if I wasn't all right.'

'I doubt that,' said Oliver, but this gratuitous piece of trouble-making passed unremarked.

The journey was long, and dusty and not very exciting. Anna sat behind Henry and Margaret and did not speak. She still believed firmly that to travel, even unhopefully, was almost certainly better than to arrive and was disturbed unpleasantly from her drowsiness when Henry swung the car over a last little rise – they had been climbing for some time – and they found themselves falling rapidly down a wide, cobbled main street, between high, railed pavements and higher houses, into the village of St Anne Crane. At the foot of the main hill was a square; Henry parked in it, and opened Margaret's door. It was very hot in the car, but Anna was gripped by lethargy. The air was clear, the sun washed the white square, and gulls called, but Anna felt that the effort of moving her body, of having to notice or move herself at all, would be altogether too much; she sat curled in the back seat and surveyed the place through the dusty glass of the window, whilst Henry strode around the square which was the end and centre of the village and explained it to Margaret. They seemed to be some way ahead of the others. Margaret tripped after him with quick little steps and exclamations of delight. Her skirts swung and flashed in the sun.

'This is all there is,' Henry said. 'This street and then the square, and the pubs, one on each side. The wall at the far end here is the sea wall – here.' Margaret came and stood beside him and leaned over the wall to stare down; there was a long drop, a steeply shelving beach, a landing stage with two or three fishing boats and to the right a tongue of cliff, enclosing the strip of shingle altogether. 'All the beach here is luckily inaccessible to traffic,' Henry went on, 'which is why it's been left alone, I suppose. And this stretch isn't particularly nice, anyway – the coves further along are where we picnic, and it takes a good walk and some scrambling to get down to them, though there are rudimentary staircases cut in the cliff in places.'

Margaret looked uneasily down at her shoes. 'It's a beautiful place,' she cried. 'You are really terribly clever to find places like this in these days. So utterly unspoiled.'

Anna caught the last part of this and winced at the word, without at first knowing why. It seemed suddenly a vulgarization and an intrusion, a word associated with the dishonesty of travel magazines who broadcast all secret places, sharing their 'unspoiledness' chattily with all their readers, and not only betray secrecy but in some way reduce all places to the same norm of unspoiled prettiness and 'scenery'. She doesn't *see* it, Anna thought savagely, she just cries out like a parrot, 'Unspoiled, unspoiled,' and then was angry with herself for snobbery – sharing, having to share, places, makes one angry in itself, unreasonably, and there was no reason to suppose that Margaret was not bad at words rather than at seeing, the two did not always go together, one hand no need to see vulgarly because one used vulgar words, probably. Henry was now leaning back with Margaret, and pointing out and up to where, although in the shadow of the George she could not see it, the little earthbound Norman church squatted on the hill.

Anna looked out at the pale and glittering strip of sea beyond the wall and wondered what she would most remember – the very real bodily pleasure she had taken in the St Anne picnic in the early days, as a child, in sand and sea and climbing, in the sound of gulls and water in which she had been, she thought first, absolutely involved, or the enormous social discomfort it now caused her. Looking at it through the car window distanced her, although she was there now, in the middle of it – it was all overlaid with dust and scratches, like an old film, to be assessed, an object. The empty square, patterned with jutting shadows where she was, white with sun towards the sea, was layered with mystery and importances for her – the mystery which comes from collecting and choosing between, or attempting not to choose between memories.

St Anne, where she had been first taken by Caroline on a conventional picnic, had been for years Anna's dreamed retreat and edge of freedom. It was the first place that she had recognized as beautiful – probably because she had been told it was beautiful – and now she carried with her as a touchstone the fined down image of all this emptiness and clarity, of the sudden, peculiarly poised rush of buildings to the edge of nothing and the horizon stretching beyond them, solid, shining metal blue, and the bodiless paler blue of the sky laid on it weightlessly. She remembered the heaviness and darkness of the little church and its damp smell. She remembered the smaller coves, and liked to sit lonely at the bottom of a funnel, enclosed, with high walls of chalk curving almost round her, but with the sky opening above and the sea bright through the gap.

Over the years she had polished these three images so that now they were bright and easily accessible; she had taken, in her way, possession of the place. But her feeling for it was essentially a thing of the past. Once, some time, she had found it violently beautiful, and now she found it so not because it hit her with the immediacy of that postulated moment in the past, but because it was weighted with the memory, and the nostalgia and the recreation of that moment. She suspected, dimly, that in fact the moment of knowledge had never occurred, that she had never, directly, completely, taken anything in, that what she now remembered was a whole series of half-realized impressions or even later imaginings, which had little to do with any vision at the time and were much less incompatible with her other memories – the continual frustration of Jeremy's presence, Caroline's insistence that she should enjoy herself, the heat and irritation of walking, scrambling, hurry to arrive and hurry to leave – than any such vision would have been. Perhaps the past as it really was, she thought, or this present, as it would be when it became the real past, were impossible to remember and not even very relevant. Perhaps one built oneself out of what one constructed of what one had seen, and perhaps what one had done, or really felt, were only important in so far as they affected this. Anna knew perfectly well what she meant by building herself – it was what she must do – what she could not find out was how. To build oneself, it was maybe more important to remember a whole vision, than actually to have one. Or maybe, on the other hand, to build on that was a lie. It was certain that to care for things seen was important, but how seen? If the way of seeing was artificial, a construct, what then? She thought. St Anne is beautiful for me now – or will be, even more, when I come to remembering, to

105

reflecting on now – but when I am honest I cannot remember having seen it as I have believed I saw it.

And one's memories, Anna thought, glowering out at her father and Margaret, as the breeze lifted Margaret's skirt and Margaret held it down with flat palms and laughed, one's memories won't hold together, as fast as one manages to gather one up another falls away, I can't manage to keep hold of how beautiful this is and how tiresome the family is both together, I am two people with regard to these two things, and yet they are both true and to build oneself one must take account of what is true, or what is built will crumble and crack apart. And one can't do anything if one is two people – one upright, clear-eyed, possessing a place, and one angry child. If I went away and lived my own life, she thought, I might manage to be everything I am, or have to be – and then I might see and not only remember having seen. The thought brought up with it Oliver, and the question of what his presence and his ideas would do to her picture of St Anne. And she was suddenly discouraged. Watching Henry coming back across the square with one hand under Margaret's elbow, and carrying his hat, she thought, and anyway, my own life that I keep thinking about, it's all a game of comforting myself, I shall find nothing important enough to see or to do. I might just as well go on like this.

Henry called to her, 'Anna. Won't you come out and look? It's a good day.' 'Anna!' said Margaret, as she crawled out into the air and drooped against the car. 'How can you bear not to come out? Oh, I do think you're lucky. This is so beautiful. Oliver will love it. It's incredible. I didn't know there still were quiet beautiful places like this. All this *air* – ' Her gesture managed to suggest that the air had been laid on specially by a benign landscape designer.

The other car came over the rise more smoothly than Henry had, with less rattle, more of a rubber bounce on the cobbles. Anna saw her mother's head inclined towards Oliver and wondered what those two would ever find to talk to each other about. When they drew up beside her they were both laughing.

'How pleasant,' said Oliver, jumping down neatly, slamming the door. 'How very pleasant.' He went round and with

106

exaggerated gallantry helped Caroline into the square. 'St Cecily in your *Poor Monster*, I take it, Henry? Rather Faulknerish, surprisingly, that one, I've always thought. Odd. I must look at this place carefully. It's obviously worthy of being looked at. But first we need a drink, don't you agree? It's a hot drive, I'm exhausted. We must sit on that wall and have a long drink, here are two pubs, don't you think that's a good idea?' He was ebullient, he was still, surreptitiously, laughing about something. Margaret, who had meant to run up to him and tell him how beautifully the place, now completed by his presence, struck her, was a little daunted; she moved closer to Henry. When Oliver was not there she always imagined what he would do if he were, and in this case she had seen him, infected by the sea air, kissing her casually, taking her hand, sharing his first impressions of it with her. But instead, he was shepherding Caroline, organizing. Anna drew circles with the tip of her sandal, and thought that today he was being very grown up. She meant something very precise by this, something to do with laughing with her mother.

Caroline said doubtfully, 'I don't know, Oliver. It takes us some time to find a place to lunch, we've always found . . . It's quite a distance.'

'Oh, I shouldn't worry,' said Oliver, cheerfully ignorant of the long cliff walk still before him, and the rush and effort attendant upon the Severell pursuit of the ideal picnic. 'I should think we'll manage. Don't fuss, it's bad for picnics. Anyway, I'm not moving another yard until I've had a drink. I've driven like a maniac and deserve something. Come along.' He settled Caroline on the sea wall. 'Sit there quietly. What will you drink?'

'Cider,' said Caroline meekly.

'Darling? And Anna?'

'The children like lemonade,' said Caroline. 'Schweppes, if they have it.' Oliver winked at Anna, an avuncular wink. Today she was back on Jeremy's side of the fence, it seemed they all had a tacit agreement about it. Yesterday she had wanted to stay there.

Oliver counted, 'Three lager, one cider, two lemonades. Will you help to carry, Henry?' They went off towards the George.

'You could always start unpacking the cars,' Caroline suggested to Anna. Anna, although out of the car now, was still suffering from the feeling, common to girls of her age and quite unappreciated by other people, that in her state of inexplicable exhaustion to move at all would make her faint, or be sick, or at least give her a violent headache. She trailed across to the boot of the car and unloaded picnic baskets.

Caroline pursed her lips. Anna came back to the now completed row on the wall and sat on the end of it, next to Jeremy, holding her unwanted lemonade and feeling very cut off and far away. Jeremy swayed to and fro on the wall, thinking his own thoughts. Anna was the only person towards whom he never felt any social duty. She would not be entertained and she was not entertaining. Next to him Margaret, with half an eye on Oliver, complimented Caroline vivaciously on St Anne and its unspoiledness and Caroline accepted her enthusiasm graciously, as though she were St Anne's builder. Beyond Caroline, Oliver was telling Henry exactly how Henry had used the sea symbolism in *Poor Monster*, and why the death on the beach in the sun was so effective. Henry, Anna could see, leaning dizzily back over the beach to watch them, was not listening. He had removed himself, he was staring out to sea and quite deliberately not listening. Anna realized that she had had Oliver's constant company for some time, now, and that tomorrow he was going. She would miss him, she knew suddenly, in spite of his tiresomeness.

'He treats me like *someone*,' she repeated to herself again. 'And not just part of a-a-thing – a set-piece – a-a-*concept*, like family photographs, or this silly row of us like birds on a wall.' She kicked viciously and half accidentally at Jeremy's bare, swinging, childish legs. Jeremy, who had been humming to himself, stopped, looked injured, and rubbed his shin ostentatiously. Anna leaned back further, bringing her feet up against Jeremy again – 'exercise his Honour Code,' she thought, as Jeremy, grimly silent, rubbed even harder – to see whether Oliver saw how much she was suffering. He had still not noticed that Henry was not listening, although Henry looked far too polite. Anna was angry with Henry. She thought, anyone can see Oliver minds so much what father thinks, it's dreadfully

108

selfish and disagreeable not to listen to him. Yesterday she would have thought that Henry was right, that he had no need to submit to interrogation, but today she was bathed in melancholy indignation on Oliver's behalf. He ignores us all, she thought; who does he think he is?

Caroline, cutting in neatly on the end of one of Margaret's sentences, raised her voice a tone and said, 'If the men carry the picnic baskets, and the children carry the rugs and the swimming things – ' She walked them all away briskly along the cliff path: Henry, then Oliver, then Margaret, Anna and Jeremy, with herself last, like a goose-herd. The path was rough and narrow, and wound along more or less the extreme edge of the cliff, touching it here and there where there had been a fall and the earth was bare and broken. On their left the sea shone, on their right the cliff grass stretched away, over lumps and hillocks, and whispered and whistled although there was little breeze. Margaret, who had no head for heights and whose shoes hurt her, began to feel sick. They turned a corner, to the left, and the path began to twist around the orifices of the coves; now and then Henry would stop and look over, and point out a flight of steps or a winding path, and Caroline would call, 'No, I don't think so, not quite yet, do you think?' and they would all move away again one after the other.

Anna, resting her chin on the high pile of rugs in her arms, and struggling with Jeremy's slipping stumps and bat, had nevertheless walked herself back into the long Severell stride, and was again travelling hopefully. She was submerged in her St Anne daydream, of herself retreated to a cottage on these cliffs, writing good novels and contemplating the water. She would have rooms with little windows and deep window seats, an untidy garden, and a white kitchen with a stone floor and an enormous refrigerator humming in it – the refrigerator somehow put the seal of reality on the whole thing. Henry would be dead, or removed to the Mediterranean or Mexico, and anyway she would write under a pseudonym, no one would know she was a Severell. She would have a table with a typewriter, in a window looking out in the direction of the sea, and she would work all morning and go for long walks in the afternoon, she would come and go when she wanted, no one would visit her unless invited, no one would interfere. She would have time on her side, then.

She walked through her garden, up and down her stairs, in and out of all her rooms – it was an exercise of the imagination familiar and efficacious by now; she stared happily and arrogantly out over the water, amalgamating her pleasure in it with her pleasure in her hypothetical writings so that the one became a specious guarantee of the other. The dark trumpets of the currents curved and widened around the rocks beneath her, streaks of a duller, more dangerous blue on the pale flat surface. Further out, a stray patch of wind whipped the water into a network of little weals. I shall remember this, she told herself, as though a promise was contained in simply seeing it. I shall remember, I knew I could . . .

She realized that Margaret had already addressed her, twice, by name, with some urgency.

'Anna – '

'Oh yes. I'm so sorry. I was dreaming.'

'How much – further – do we – have to go? My feet hurt – I put on the wrong shoes, so stupid – and I haven't much head for heights. Where do we stop?'

Anna caught up with Margaret on a widening of the path and made another grab at Jeremy's slithering cricket things. She wondered for a moment whether she should not just let the whole bundle slide away and be lost, and then decided that since her brother was immediately behind her this was not practicable. She answered Margaret's question companionably, with weary experience.

'Mother won't rest until we are well past the church.' They were now skirting the rise on which it stood. 'So that anyone who wants to come and look at it will have to walk all the way back. And there are people in that cove down there, look. We can't stop where there are people.'

'Why not?' asked Margaret, who liked people, and still hoped for some revelation, some momentous friendship, from every new meeting. The people below looked harmless enough; a couple on little canvas chairs, a gaggle of diminutive children, burned to a smooth chocolate colour around scarlet and peacock briefs, poking delicate feet at the frill of water. Margaret liked small children. Anna put her head up and looked at her in surprise.

'I don't know why not. It's a family party – I mean – we never do go where there are people.' She considered, 'I suppose it's a pity in a way – one sees enough of the family.'

'I was wondering,' Margaret said, 'what you'll do now? When Oliver's gone? I mean – who will teach you?'

'I expect they'll get a tutor. I don't really care very much, you know.'

Margaret persisted. 'Wouldn't you rather be somewhere else than at home? I know I would have, when I was your age. You need to live your own life – you know – manage your own money – go to your own parties – have your own friends – and come in when you please.'

'Yes,' said Anna non-committally.

'I wondered if you'd like to come and stay with us. Then Oliver could go on teaching you – I know he thinks that's very important – and I'd love to have you. We could do all sorts of things – I'd introduce you to people – it would be London after all – there'd be parties – and clothes to buy – and theatres – I'd enjoy it no end, and I wouldn't interfere, no more than Oliver thought good for your work.' She laughed uneasily; she had completely lost the feel of any contact with her audience, who said now, flatly, 'They wouldn't let me.'

Anna did not know why she was so sure. Her parents paid little attention to her, but she was certain that they would be automatically opposed to her leaving home unnecessarily. That was accepted on both sides, her place was there.

'I think they would. I asked your mother.' Anna peered at her over the cricket stumps with a start of interest.

'Did you? Do you think they . . . ? I'll tell you what though, he – Uncle Oliver – he wouldn't like it. What does he think, then? He's had enough of me by now, I should think.'

'You mustn't say that. He minds very much about you and he believes in you. I know that.' Anna had a fleeting vision of the Cannings, sitting up in bed together, intimately discussing her problems. She could see Margaret clearly enough, nesting in pillows, her thick hair let down all over, warm and concerned. Oliver in pyjamas, Oliver in any kind of undress was much more difficult. Oddly enough, this idea was very comforting after Oliver's exhortations – she didn't feel Margaret's interest as an intrusion at all, but as something human and a safeguard. Margaret's offer of clothes, and parties, and friends, of an interesting life with interesting people, made Oliver's world so much more habitable, and now, by contrast with her own, so attractive. Although, she thought, it was doubtful whether she could live with Oliver any longer and keep her reason. She said, 'It's nice of you, but I think I'd drive him mad in a week, I really do.'

'You must let him decide that,' Margaret said, generous on Oliver's behalf and solicitous for his comfort at once. She felt that so far she had done nothing to further any real contact with Anna; all that had been said was so ordinary, and Anna would not look at her. She wanted to show Anna that someone really understood, someone was on her side, and would do something practical about it, but she could not find words to get it over. And she became a little annoyed with Anna and suppressed the annoyance; she would have been even more annoyed to know that this was most people's usual reaction to Anna. She said, 'I envy you, you've got everything to come; you won't believe me, but you don't know how much I envy you.' Anna did look at her then, drawing her breath in sharply as though she was afraid, which she was, with the look of a suspicious colt. Margaret thought, you needn't look so scornful, people your age never realize how much they are to be envied until it's too late, but it's true, all the same. And Anna thought, everyone thinks I have something to come, I think it sometimes, but if I haven't – and I've never seen whatever is – how much worse it will be when I find out. She was nevertheless grateful to Margaret for her friendliness, which she sensed much better than Margaret gave her credit for. She was much more certainly grateful than she was to Oliver, but Margaret was quite unconscious of that.

Caroline called to Henry, who had suddenly begun to walk much faster, staring out to sea and giving the beach below only the most cursory examination.

'Henry! Why don't we stop here? this looks ideal – '

'He's not listening,' Anna said wisely to Margaret, as the

112

whole crocodile pulled up in some confusion and turned back on itself. Henry strode on, and Oliver ran after him and pulled him by the sleeve.

'I told you so,' said Anna. 'I can always tell.' She broke away from them suddenly and plunged down into the cove, running and sliding, bundle and all, down the steps cut in the cliff, and had dropped her burden, all anyhow, and was out at the sea mouth, surveying the water, before any of the rest of them had begun the descent. It was a good place – a wide shelf of sand, with rocks and pools at the foot of the cliff nearer the water. There was no one there, and the sun was on it. Margaret, who came down last, and insisted on being helped by Oliver, found time before the descent to say to him, 'I asked Anna to stay with us in London. I thought you could go on teaching her. I thought she needed to get away for a bit.'

'Did you?'

'I thought,' Margaret ran on happily, sharing Anna with Oliver, 'that what she really needs – you know – is to have a bit of a fling. A real boy-friend, a bit of dancing, late nights.' She laughed. 'Oh, I know her work comes first, but don't you think I'm right, too?'

'And you were going to provide it?'

'I thought I'd introduce her to a few people. I've not got about much lately, it'd be good for me – '

'I see. What did Anna say?'

Margaret laughed again. 'She was worried about you. She said she'd drive you mad in a week. I said you'd like to have her.'

'Did you?'

Margaret looked up at him, then, dubiously. 'I thought – as well – at the moment – it would do us good – maybe – to have someone else in the house – as well. Sometimes – when one has been getting on each other's nerves – '

'Oh,' said Oliver. He looked down to where Anna stood at the water's edge, the slight breeze lifting her hair away from her face, her legs long, planted apart, under her childish grey shorts. Margaret followed his look.

'She'll be quite pretty, in another few years. Don't you think so? I thought, if someone told her so now, it would make such a difference – '

'She'll find it out, quickly enough. I shouldn't worry.'

'She's so unsure . . . At her age, I knew so much more about life. I really think it's terrible, how little of anything these English middle class children get at – hockey, instead of dancing, and horses instead of human beings – '

'I agree with you, there – '

'And it is a good idea if we have her to stay?'

Oliver looked at Anna, and then said curtly, 'You're always too generous, you know. You want to take the world on single-handed. I don't think you'd make much difference to her and I've too much on my hands to go on coaching university entrance candidates. I think she's quite right, as a matter of fact. She'd drive me mad in a week. If you've committed us, of course . . .'

Margaret's mouth trembled, 'Oh no, of course I haven't – '

'I don't need to coach anyone, not even Henry Severell's daughter – '

'I know,' said Margaret. 'It wasn't that. I only thought – '

Caroline called up that they were ready to lunch if they came down. They made their way down the path; Caroline was saying, 'Come along, come along, we shall never eat if everyone doesn't give a hand. I think if we sit round this rock – in this patch of shade – like a table. We shan't have time to digest our food before bathing if we don't hurry a little.'

Caroline's picnics were always splendid and successful; never too much and never too little. They were packed and served, chilled and protected, in plastic boxes and plates of all shapes and sizes and clear colours, without depth; Caroline spread a cloth on her rock, and arranged everything, glowing palely on it. She was pleased with it, she even twitched the leaves of the lettuce and arranged a curl of endive round a sculpted tomato as though she was creating a flower arrangement.

'The new materials make this kind of thing so much easier,' she said. 'It's a modern miracle, I think. I can't imagine how I managed before there was all this. So light and clean and such pretty colours.'

Henry picked up a sky blue translucent beaker and bent it

114

across. 'It's slightly repulsive,' he said, examining it with his enormous fingers, 'I find. Like dead skin, or a false skin. No body. I imagine us living in a world of prettily coloured skin, and when we lose our tempers we shall have to learn to rip instead of smashing and that will require more deliberation and more skill as well as more strength and we shall be more hardened and nastier criminals. Anyone can smash a plate.'

'I don't see why you should want to destroy them,' Caroline said calmly. 'I think they are very nice.'

'So they are,' said Oliver. 'They're an advance, an improvement, they raise the standard of living and they are very pretty too – don't be so conventional.'

Henry grinned amongst his beard. 'I suppose I must confess now to the expected hankering for old things – pewter and horn spoons, and earthenware – solid things, that wear down gradually. Do you know what this stuff does when it's old? It doesn't grow thin and delicate, like horn. It gets fat and fluffy and peels off, like leprosy.'

'Oh, Henry,' Caroline said, laughing. Henry built up the idea with an extravagant gesture of the hands.

'Like some growth, some disease,' he insisted. 'Unnatural from beginning to end.'

'Natural, unnatural,' said Oliver, sitting cross-legged on the rug and leaning forward, his teeth bared, attacking like a terrier with a rat. 'I find your terminology very unhealthy, Henry. It's symptomatic of something in you that I find very distressing. A minor version of this William Morris crankiness, the golden age, beautiful mediævalism, the appeal to nature, whatever nature is. Isn't it natural for man to make plastics? How can we accept what you say if you want to persuade us to live in a world that doesn't, and can't exist.'

'I was talking about plastics,' Henry said, deprecating.

'You'll find, in the end, you can't afford to dismiss what is. Plastics are with us, they're a fact of life, you've got to take them into account, or you're weakened. You must make terms.'

'I was talking about plastics,' Henry repeated. 'I wasn't not talking about plastics. I wasn't ignoring them. I was saying what I feel, I don't like them.'

'You can't get out of it that way. You can't just dismiss them by not liking them. You can't get away from them.'

'I can,' said Henry, suddenly and disproportionately, magnificently angry. 'I can if we're talking about plastics. Have you no sense of scale? Some things are important and some are not, and some I care about and some I don't. I will not – do you understand? – I will not have you fasten on to everything I say and make an issue of it. It's intellectually dishonest. It isn't right to accuse me of all this – golden agery – it isn't relevant and what's more you know it isn't. You don't write anything as stupid as some of the things you say, and I won't have you sitting there and trying to provoke me into pronouncements. You won't get anything out of it. No help with my work, if that's what you're at. If you'd stop labelling before you looked you'd get further. Though I imagine you'd better give up labelling altogether if you're ever going to understand anything much. That's what I think.'

He sat and stared, with complete intellectual arrogance, hard at Oliver. Then he shook himself, like a large dog, and said, looking down, 'I've been used to thinking of myself as a friendly creature, but I won't be harassed.' He took up a leg of chicken – like a parody of a mediæval knight, Anna thought – bit off a large mouthful and chewed angrily. Oliver flushed, slowly, painfully, a dark reddish brown, and closed his eyes momentarily.

Caroline said, 'Henry, really,' in the voice of a mother whose child has been rude to a visitor, and must, whatever the rights and wrongs of the case, apologize under the law of hospitality. Oliver, recovering, muttered with an attempt at lightness, 'I should have said that was a pronouncement if ever there was one.'

Henry turned away from the picnic and the table and began to stare into sea. He was concentrating on the sound of it, the roar in it, barely submerged even on the mildest of days. Caroline saw that she had lost him, he would get up after lunch and go away, there was no help. She was very annoyed with Oliver, and to cover it turned to him and offered him more chicken.

*

116

Caroline wiped the dishes on paper tissues and packed them into the baskets. Jeremy leaned over her and embraced her. 'What shall we do now? What shall we do now? May we swim?'

'You must let your food settle.'

'Shall I play cricket?'

Caroline looked at Henry's face and then Oliver's, and Margaret's, and saw, not without some indignation, that it was no use trying to orient the party towards games on the sand with the children. They did not share her concept. She said, 'Anna will bowl to you.' Anna, who was unfortunately good enough with a cricket ball for Jeremy to consider it beneath his dignity to use her, had no choice. She said, ungraciously, 'I'm far too tired,' and wandered out towards the sea to help Jeremy fix his stumps in the damper, harder sand. She took off her shoes and threw the ball viciously at Jeremy, who missed it. The bails fell.

'That wasn't fair,' said Jeremy. 'I wasn't ready. You must give me another chance.'

Anna retrieved the ball and went, in a desultory manner, back to her own end of the pitch.

'And don't hit it out to sea,' she told him. 'Or I'll bash you with your own bat, and I won't play any more.'

'You'll have to, or mummy'll be upset.' This was irrefutable. Anna delivered the ball again, more gently. Jeremy twisted the bat and slapped the ball neatly into the sea.

'Not a bad shot,' he said. Anna walked after it, watching the water come up darkly in her footprints. The sea was cold, and smelled clean and good. Anna stood, calf-deep, waiting for the waves to carry the ball back to her, thinking of Margaret's offer and the endlessness of the water, and how remote and unreal it all was, especially herself, as she saw herself, a child playing on a beach. Change was always possible, and never imminent, one was neither what one was doing nor the person who watched the doing. The sea was calming, because there was so much of it, one looked out of oneself, away over it. It was odd how rarely one lifted one's head at the seaside and looked right out. One was always digging holes, or picnicking, or throwing balls. 'I don't believe in myself,' she said aloud. 'One day I must, but not now. I am certainly not a child on a beach.'

'Can't you get it, Anna?'

'Yes,' said Anna, bending down to retrieve the ball as it knocked against her leg.

'You're very slow.' He said importantly, 'I've got to practise pretty hard, old Bodger said I'd be really good – *really* good – if I kept at it. I might play for the school.'

'It matters to him,' Anna thought. 'He believes in himself, altogether.' She threw the wet ball at him, all anyhow.

'That was wide,' said Jeremy. 'You're losing your touch.'

Caroline smoothed out the rug, on the sand, in the sun, and sat down on it, leaning against a boulder. She had a little basket open in front of her from which she took a piece of clean white linen and a needle.

'I shall sit here,' she said, peacefully, 'and enjoy the sea air and do a little sewing. I shall embroider the tablecloth I promised Helen Ashley for a wedding present. I find I have very little time for embroidery these days. That's a pity. It's a very soothing occupation.'

She selected a skein of cornflower blue silk and smoothed it, lovingly.

Henry stood up, stretched, yawned, gathered himself together, and said, 'Oliver and Margaret ought to look at the church.' He peered down at them abstractedly, and began to edge away in the other direction.

'Would you like that, darling?' Margaret said.

'I'm too tired,' Oliver said. 'I'm terribly tired. I must sleep. I shall sleep at your feet, Caroline, and be soothed vicariously by your sewing.' He lay back, spreading his arms above his head, and closed his eyes. Henry moved further away.

'Henry,' said Caroline, not very hopefully, without looking up.

'I shall go for a walk myself,' Henry announced. 'A long walk.' He broke into a run and was up the cliff steps.

Margaret stood uneasily over Caroline and Oliver and wondered what to do. Caroline had all her skeins of silk pinned neatly to the lid of the sewing basket – only blue, but every possible shade of blue, from the palest periwinkle to the deepest midnight. She had stretched the linen over a hoop, and was

118

blocking in great petals of silk, enormous, full blown blue roses carefully shaded, stitch by stitch. Oliver's eyes were firmly closed and his face was still. Margaret, looking at the neat curl of his body and the way his shirt was pulled taut from his shoulders to his waist, was overcome by desire. She would have liked to crouch on the rug beside him and stroke him and caress him until he turned to her, but Caroline sat over him like a Victorian angel, blue and white, and in her shadow his sleep seemed innocent and remote. Margaret, as though caught out in an obscenity, found herself blushing, deeper and deeper, in the shadow of her hat, and then trembling. Afraid that Caroline might notice, she turned and walked quickly away, after Henry. At the bottom of the cliff path she looked back in time to see him roll and stretch and hump his body sleepily close to Caroline's ankles. It was suddenly imperative to get to Henry; she began to scrabble up the cliff side, clawing with fingers and toes, her ribboned hat pushed sideways on her head.

Henry walked fast and angrily for some time. He was ashamed to have been caught out in a burst of temper, aware that Caroline was cross with him and had hoped for something better, and profoundly thankful that the Cannings were leaving tomorrow. He was conscious that Oliver's public and persistent worrying of his books had affected his own attitude to them. Oliver's academically preaching tone, applied to things with which Henry was concerned, clarified them for him because it was alien to him. On the other hand Oliver's manner, Oliver's excesses, Oliver's weaknesses and the weaknesses of the school to which he belonged – chiefly, Henry thought, a kind of priggishness, a preaching from within an enclosure at one remove, irritated Henry to an absurd extent. He wished that he had never met Oliver. 'The man wastes my time and messes up my work,' he thought. 'I shall take days to get over this visit.'

He was a controlled man, usually, and had his own way of directing himself back from distractions to his main channel. Now, since there was a part of a chapter that he had meant to walk clear this afternoon before starting on it tomorrow, and because Oliver had scratched at his novel so that he found it difficult to concentrate, he began to sing. He had a strong voice, not unpleasant, resonant even, but little sense of pitch, so that his repertoire was confined almost entirely to hymns with obvious tunes, in which it was the incantatory repetition of words that he found pleasing. He lifted his head, contemplated the horizon, and began,

'Holy, holy, holy
Lord God Almighty
All the earth shall praise thy name
In earth and sky and sea.'

I have something wrong there, he told himself, there should not be that repetition of 'earth', it's clumsy. 'Land', on the other hand, would be worse, in that line – or do I only think so because I've sung 'earth' for so long? He went on, his voice clear, dropping over the sea,

'Holy, holy, holy
All the saints adore thee
Casting down their golden crowns,
Around the glassy sea.'

Lovely, long slow words, he thought; as a child he had trembled with pleasure over that verse, had had a vision, every time the boys around him piped it and the piano thumped it, of the rows of saints, stiff white pillars, crowned with gold, standing, raised, as in an amphitheatre, around a glittering, perfectly round bowl of ice, and slowly, measuredly, overarm, hurling down crown after crown to roll and clatter and slide and lie piled in the centre of it. This ice rink of a sea had been enclosed under a dome of glass; the weather, if it could be called weather, had been grey and cold – the scene had been beautiful, fascinating, but rather deathly, really. Henry repeated the verse, looked at the flat sea beneath him, and the light running liquid along its barely indicated ridges, and wondered why his sea had been so certainly indoors and so certainly ice; if he were seeing it now, he thought, they would throw down their crowns and dance in ecstasy, on emerald grass, at the edge of a bright humming, open, sea under a bright sun. He sang it again and noted that the old, rigid saints were still more powerful.

He changed key and began.

> *'My God, how wonderful thou art,*
> *Thy Majesty how bright*
> *How beautiful thy mercy seat*
> *In depths of burning light.'*

The tune swooped up and down. Henry exaggerated its curves, roaring with pleasure, smiling wildly over the sun and water as though he were part of them. In the midst of his pleasure, something slid into place, the pattern of the part of the chapter he had been looking for. He knew no more about precisely what he would write than he had known, but a shape, a pattern of relations had come to him – his imagination carried a diagram, a squat triangle, a long one on the same base reaching out, and when he sat down to write, the pattern would be available now, he could draw on it, spin from it.

'*In the depths of burning light,*' he repeated, negotiating a crack in the path, and became aware of steps behind him.

Margaret ran along the cliff path after him, zig-zag, stumbling here and there, clutching her hat. Henry increased his pace automatically for a moment and then turned reluctantly, filling the path, at bay. In her rose and white dress, with its floating bell of a skirt, and dancing ribbons, she swayed and blundered in her progress like a huge drunken butterfly, just born. When he turned, she waved, and called thinly, 'Henry, Henry,' through the sounds of the gulls and the sea, and then came up, stretching fluttering hands to him and gasping for breath.

'Henry, oh please take me with you, can you bear it?' She patted her skin with a moist ball of handkerchief. Inside the low neck of her dress her breast moved rapidly, dusky pink and shining with the sun and the hurrying. Henry felt her presence cut across his mood like a knife. He said mildly, 'By all means,' and began to walk again, moving unconsciously faster and faster.

'Were – you – going – far?' Margaret asked.

'I don't know.' He was aware that he was being ungracious. 'I like to get a look at the next village.'

'It's so much fresher up here,' Margaret offered. 'Much better than just sitting all afternoon.'

'Yes, indeed,' said Henry, striding. Margaret was silent for

121

some time, walking rapidly just behind him, taking little running steps from time to time as he moved away from her. At last she said, 'I've a fearful stitch, I'm sorry. Would you mind dreadfully if we sat down for a moment or two?'

Henry turned and looked at her blankly. 'Oh,' he said. 'Oh dear. Yes, of course, please sit down.' He indicated the grass at the edge of the path. Margaret sat down thankfully, with her back against a hillock. Henry lowered himself beside her, folded his arms, and studied the horizon. Margaret ran her fingers through the tufts of wiry grass and waited to see if he would say anything. He did not, so that after a moment she burst out, 'Henry – '

'Yes?'

'Can I talk to you, do you mind?'

'Please – ' said Henry non-committally.

'I just can't go on, any more. I've been trying not to face it, I can see that, for some time. But we've got to go tomorrow and I've got to admit it, Henry. I'm absolutely terrified of going back to London and being alone – with Oliver – again.'

'I know.'

Margaret looked up at him childishly, with a candour which invited intimacy, and said, 'Yes, you do know, don't you? I was sure you did. Tell me what to do.'

'I don't know that I can precisely *tell* you anything,' Henry said vaguely, not accepting the invitation.

Margaret was silent, for a moment, studying his averted face. There was little of him to see, the eye lost itself in the abundant hair, attention was dissipated by the curls and waves and fronds of the beard. The eyes, into which she tried to look, were lost like drowned pebbles behind the lashes and brows which sheltered them like vegetation in a pool. He was rather like the sea, Margaret thought, all the hair rippled like the water, and looked warm and soft, and alive, and endless, like the sea. She transmuted the softness of the hair to a gentleness in Henry and was encouraged; it was somehow easier to talk openly to something as dispersed, as mysterious, as apparently imperturbable as he appeared. She gathered herself and looked away from him again and twisted the tuft of grass under her hand, round and round, torturing it.

She began, 'Shall I tell you something? You know those advertisements for central heating – they're mostly for central heating, but some of them are for carpets – where you're looking into a room and the weather outside's usually nasty, and it's so warm to be inside? And there's a man in a chair with a paper and a woman knitting, and children piling bricks and it's all closed away and cared for – with a *thick* carpet, and lots of warm light – I don't mean the jolly ones, you know, where everything's bright yellow and red, and mum comes on in a frilly apron carrying Walls ice cream on a plate and everyone cheers. I mean the restrained ones, with good, comfortable, modern furniture – what Oliver calls bourgeois – it's funny, I know quite a bit about good china and antique furniture, but it's these super-ordinary chairs that turn my inside over – ' She thought a moment and went on, reflectively, 'Some of them are gas board, or maybe it's electricity. With a warm glow – '

Henry jerked himself out of a doze and wondered when would she ever come to the point, if there was one. He caught for a moment the full absurdity of these visionary gas fires and armchairs and carpets, here under the summer sun, above the empty sea, with a grasshopper whirring behind them and sea-pinks quivering, just on the other side of the hillock he leant against. He gave a little indeterminate snort and Margaret jumped, laid a hand on his arm and turned desperately to him. 'You do understand?'

'Yes,' said Henry.

'I wanted to be married, I wanted to have children, I wanted to be *with* someone and sit round a fire and talk?'

'Yes,' said Henry, 'and Oliver?'

'Oliver – ' Margaret began and stopped. 'People either understand about Oliver straight away or think I couldn't have married anyone worse. You do see? He takes life so seriously. He tries to make something of it. And then – you know – he's working class, he's out of a world where my sort of super-ordinary room is just what you want, and half of him wanted it too. You know, he's got a real working class mum, in one of those awful towns without any character in South Yorkshire. She doesn't like me, and when we go there he sides with her – he takes pleasure in washing up for her at me, and carrying

123

coal and saying there's nothing like mum's neck of mutton and tinned peas and dumpling and wet cabbage cooking, oh my God. He goes all homely and shirt sleeved in that nasty little tenement house. And I can *see* he wants what she'd want for him. That's why – I mean – and I love him, so much, I do love him. I live for him really.'

'And Oliver?' Henry repeated. Margaret looked away, and twisted more rapidly at the grass, so that the juice, even out of those dried spines, came moist from the bruises onto her fingers. She faltered. 'We've lost touch,' and Henry wondered whether this curious couple had had any touch to lose. He could find nothing to say to Margaret. He saw her, with a dispassionate finality, already doomed, her marriage, her reality, structures like the rooms she had worshipped on the bright pages, parodies, lies, houses on sand.

Margaret cried, 'Oliver does need me, he does, I know it, he's so insecure, quite as much as I need him. I don't know *where* I've gone wrong.' She flung herself against Henry, pushing her face into his neck, and wept hysterically. After a moment, Henry clasped his huge hands loosely across her back; he did not like tears and he did not like physical contact; but this, and not to talk, was what Margaret had come for, and the end was therefore in sight. He shifted himself, leaned back more comfortably, stared out over Margaret's heaving shoulders at the sea, and endured.

After a time Margaret gulped and sniffed, reared herself in his arms, and said, almost brightly, 'Life is so much more complicated than you think always, isn't it?'

Henry nodded.

'Oliver is missing so much. He can't live *only* for his work, can he?'

'No,' said Henry.

'It's easier to make allowances,' Margaret said, 'when you know you're right. But I have to talk it out, now and then – ' She seemed suddenly cheerful as though she had talked herself into quiescence. She hooked her hand suddenly round Henry's neck and aimed a kiss at his mouth.

'Dear, dear Henry,' she said. 'You are so good to me.'

Henry avoided the kiss instinctively, disengaged himself and stood up.

'I'm not good,' he said roughly. 'I've been little help, if any.' In some inexplicable way he felt endangered by Margaret, as though some of the ground on which he stood so proudly was being eroded just by her sharing it.

'You *are* good,' she protested now, coming nearer again. Henry offered his handkerchief. 'Your eyelashes have run,' he said. Margaret, distracted, wiped, and licked, and scrubbed, and pink rims appeared round her eyes. Henry stood back a step, onto the very edge of the cliff, and peered down, dizzily, onto a bed of bladderwrack, olive green, khaki, with patches of a glistening brown. The point where they were jutted seawards, and here the water sucked in and out of a channel, bubbled and coughed and came back again welling up each time a little higher in a pool amongst the weeds. Across the mouth of the channel a huge streamer of that smooth flat weed that is nearly translucent, like rubber, and like rubber a golden brown, floated and waved. Henry looked at it and tried to calm himself; he was angry over his lost chapter. He was overcome by an old sense of the precariousness of his own position, his own, ultimate loneliness, however shored up by Caroline's attentions.

One day, he thought, I might find I couldn't see, or couldn't write, and then I should be broken. He shivered momentarily, and his head turned. But nevertheless, to fall was really unthinkable, here in the sun, with the pattern he had just worked out available, however interrupted, for the future. He straightened himself, watched a gull turn, and passed a hand over his face. He felt obscurely guilty towards Margaret; he bowed, put an impersonal hand under her arm, and escorted her back towards the others.

Caroline was sewing steadily, but Oliver was nowhere in sight. Towards the sea, Jeremy was standing amongst a network of canals with a monarchical tilt to his head.

'He'll make an engineer,' Henry said, nodding towards him. When he thought about his son, which was not often, he was afraid that he might become a sportsman – a professional tennis player, an Olympic runner, something like that. There was something wrong with making a life out of a pastime, Henry would think, and then grin over the idea that many people might suppose that he himself did just that.

Margaret said, 'Where's Oliver?'

'He went swimming, with the children, since you seemed to have disappeared. Then he went up to look over the church.'

'He didn't wait for me.'

'He didn't know where you were,' Caroline said reasonably.

'Where's Anna?' Henry asked.

Caroline looked round her. 'She was here a moment ago. She was drying her hair.'

'Everyone wanders off,' Henry said, inanely. He caught Caroline's eye, and sat down on the rug. Caroline's look asked, very clearly, what was wrong and he did not mean to discuss it. He lay back and closed his eyes.

'The sun,' he said mendaciously, 'makes me so sleepy.'

Margaret was again left standing. 'I shall go and look for Oliver.'

'I shouldn't,' said Caroline. 'He's probably on his way back by now and it's such a hot climb. I should sit down and wait, with us.'

'But I haven't seen the church.'

Caroline looked as though she knew that Margaret was not interested in the church. She reiterated, 'I should wait.'

'I want to go and look for Oliver,' said Margaret, and set off, swaying on her inadequate sandals, in that direction.

She found the walk to the church even longer than she had expected and very tiring. The slight breeze there had been in the morning had faded; the air was dead and heavy, whilst the sea lay flat like a canvas, under which some strange current moved aimlessly, lifting it here and there. She wished suddenly and passionately for a holiday beach, with crowds, ice-creams, striped umbrellas, the odd gramophone. The Severells made her lonely. Their passion for privacy extended Oliver's withdrawal, gave him a right to close his eyes and ignore her. Down there, Caroline had even seemed to be protecting him. And Henry, however good, was so remote; he would not suffer with her, whatever he knew.

At the little gate at the foot of the flight of steps which led up to the church, someone was sitting, head curled into knees. Margaret came up and saw that it was Anna, in a black regulation woollen bathing suit, her fine hair blue-black and sparkling with salt, spread over her fingers, her body as smooth as a brown egg.

'Hullo,' said Anna. 'I'm drying out. You look hot.'

'I am. I can't stand much more.'

'Neither can I. I can't really face the climb up there. I shall just sit here till it's time to go home. Are you going to look for Uncle Oliver?'

'Yes,' said Margaret. 'Do you know if he's up there?'

'Oh, I think so. He said he would be.'

'Did you have a good afternoon?'

Anna spread her hands. 'Well, you know. It could have been worse. The swimming was all right.'

'I must go and look for Oliver. You're sure he's there?'

'Well,' said Anna, 'he hasn't come down.' She sat, immobile, and watched Margaret toil up round the hill to the church. It was a pity, she thought, that people who were designed to look calm and decorative should ever need to become hot and flustered. Margaret's going up there settled at least the question of whether she should do so herself, which was a relief. She had been divided, that afternoon, between a need to talk to Oliver about herself to prove that she did not belong with Jeremy and the old feeling that it was dangerous to talk to him, she was best left alone. They had all three gone into the water together – Oliver white and wiry, with a timid band of black hairs across his chest, somewhat improbable in trunks – and she had left Oliver to conduct a water battle with Jeremy and had swum away from them, out to sea, to turn on her back sideways in the trough of the waves, with nothing above her but the sky, glittering through the salt in her eyelashes, and the occasional swaying line of a rising wave. If he wants to come, he can, she had thought, and he had, as though summoned, swum up behind her, unnoticed since her ears were underwater, seized her by the hair and plunged her back and down. For some moments they had fought, quite seriously, thrashing and struggling in the spinning water, until, when Oliver had her by both wrists, she bent, frantically angry, bit at his hand and drew blood.

'Don't be vicious,' he said, releasing her, licking his hand.

'You started it.'

'It was a game.'

'I don't care, you hurt me.' They regarded each other, two trunks, sliced off at the waist. Oliver shrugged his shoulders.

'I'm going out now. I shall go and look at that church. Do you want to come?'

'I don't know.'

'If you do, come up after me. I'll expect you.' He turned and strutted away, out of the sea. He was wet, and his damped down hair exposed suddenly a bald patch on his crown, and his body was pale and insubstantial; but he was still, even screwing up his feet where he stepped on a pebble, jaunty. Anna sat back into the water, and made whirlpools with her hands. She thought, oh dear, he wants to be serious. He's always furtive when he's serious. I don't know if I want that. She had nevertheless followed him as far as the church gate; it had been the easiest thing to do. But she was glad that Margaret had settled it. They were to leave tomorrow and there would now be no more serious talking, nor anything else. Anna kicked at a stone, and felt irrationally triumphant, as though she had retreated of her own accord and with dignity from something unpredictable and possibly unmanageable.

Margaret stood in the church porch, to recover her breath. There were notices on a green board – the usual ones – a list of those responsible for the altar flowers, entry forms for the Women's Institute Jam Competition, a photograph of a negro child with yaws next to that picture of Christ in a wood with small animals and children, which Margaret had had in her bedroom until she married Oliver, who had picked it up, the night he moved in as her husband, and carried it down four flights of stairs to the dustbin. He had referred to her other favourite picture – Dali's *Christ of St John of the Cross* – as 'that obscenity'; Margaret never knew whether he had noticed that she had herself disposed of that, after the other, without, at that time, much regret. That had been when she was going to be a wife for Oliver, a willing tabula rasa, and had assumed that he would take pleasure in talking to her and forming her taste.

The heavy door swung inwards with unexpected ease. She almost fell down the three steps into the body of the church. She closed the door behind her carefully and listened to the silence between the arches. The air inside was cold and her movement seemed to have disturbed it — it came swinging at her, enveloping her. It was too dark to see very much; inside the church was as low and solid as the outside had been, the pillars were squat and the windows tiny. Margaret succumbed easily to atmosphere and was always hushed and reverent in a church, in an embarrassed, war memorial kind of way. But this church was so low and dark and thickly enclosing that reverence was very near fear.

Over on the other side, someone moved, softly. Oliver, perhaps, probably. Margaret took two steps into the darkness and the heel of her loose sandal clattered on the stone floor. The noise startled her and the movement on the other side ceased abruptly. She stopped again, to get her bearings. In the window over the altar, in crude reds and yellows, the mild, self-confident prim Christ of the children's picture sat on a crimson hassock with a lamb, whilst figures representing nurses and soldiers and Young Crusaders clutched at his skirts. It was partly the hot colour of what light there was that made the church seem so claustrophobic. She walked several more paces down the aisle, with her own echo tapping behind her, filling the building. There was another movement, to her right. She had the silly feeling that something was going to jump out at her, not Oliver, but something indeterminate and nasty that was playing hide and seek with her amongst the thick pillars. She went on, towards the altar, touching the corners of the pews for reassurance and for balance.

Under the altar rail was a carpet, which took away the sound of her presence and some of her fear; she walked, quite rapidly, round past the lectern towards the little chapel whose window glimmered vaguely to the right. She wondered how whoever was in there could keep so still for so long. She came to the screen which divided it from the rest of the church, put her hand against it, and peered in.

Oliver was standing quite still in front of the altar, his hands crossed before him, staring up at the window. Margaret was surprised by how much she had expected not to find him there.

'Oliver,' she said, in a church whisper.

'Hullo,' he said, without turning round. His voice was always quiet; there was no reason why he should have lowered it. 'I thought you might not come.'

'I wanted to. I wanted to talk to you.'

'Look at this window,' Oliver said. 'I like rose windows, this is a good one. How they had the effrontery to put in the twentieth-century anthropomorph over the altar when they already had this, I don't know. This is so durable, it's satisfying. So *ordered*, that's what I like — all those meanings, number symbolism, twelve apostles, twelve tribes, twelve months, look, all so formal, and so neatly tied up. Rosa mundi. Do you know about rose windows?'

'No,' said Margaret. She came and stood beside him and clasped his arm. 'Oliver, I want to talk to you. I never seem to be with you, now —'

'Margaret,' he said, turning round and blinking. 'Margaret. Did you have a good afternoon?'

Margaret said savagely. 'Don't. Don't talk to me like that. Don't ever use that tone of voice to me again.'

'I don't know what you mean.'

'You keep me at a distance, as though I was less of a person than anyone else. I can't stand any more. Please listen to me, *I can't stand any more.*'

'Do I?' said Oliver, as though paralysed.

'Don't pretend you don't know. Don't just slide away. Try and be with me, a moment —'

'It's something I'm not very good at —'

'You must, you must. We're *married*, Oliver, you've got to come in with me, and be married. I may not be as stupid as you think. Try it. Just look at me, and talk to me —'

Oliver's small mouth twitched. 'I wish you would not mind about me so much. I don't know how to deal with it.'

'Then you shouldn't have married me.'

'You knew what I was like and what I couldn't do, when you married me. Didn't you?'

'Marriage changes people.'

'Oh, yes,' said Oliver.

'Have you stopped loving me?'

Oliver backed away a few steps, little and cornered. He said, 'No, I don't stop loving as easily as that. I think you muddle things up. I should have said, I have had the capacity for making scenes left out of me. Whereas you need them. I prefer things unsaid, you like to go over them. It's not insurmountable.'

Margaret cried, 'But I'm so *lonely*,' and began, suddenly, involuntarily, to scream and weep, kneeling on the carpet and clutching Oliver's knees.

'Now, now,' said Oliver, stroking her head with a small quick hand. 'You've caught the sun. That's what it is. If I say, I didn't realize what I was taking on, you mustn't take it amiss. You seemed so self-possessed.'

'I did?'

'Yes, you did. I suppose it was partly the social difference. Don't look so upset, and stop crying. We shall contrive. We must. If only you could stop battering us. I mean to do my best.'

Margaret, comfortable at his feet, wept on.

'Look, it's that time of the month, too. You must *think*, Margaret, before upsetting yourself like this. Aren't I right? In another week you'll be quite different. You imagine things at these times.'

Margaret, unhappily, recognized the justice in this. She said, 'Talk to me, Oliver. Please, talk to me.'

'Of course. What about?'

'Anything. Your work. You. Anything, as long as you're talking to *me*.'

Oliver gathered her up and settled her in a chair, at the front of the chapel. He leaned over her, intent, his face curiously grim and gentle at once. He said, 'I didn't marry you only to talk to you,' a remark which Margaret found sinister only later, in retrospect. She was saying, weakly, 'Oh no, Oliver, not in a church,' when the air moved again and the heavy door behind

131

them swung open. Anna said clearly, 'Oliver — are you there? Mother says will you come now, they're packing.'

SIX

ONE, TWO, THREE, and miss the next one. Anna, in a white cotton nightgown, came down the small flight of stairs from her bedroom, counted steps and listened for the creak of a warped board. The darkness was large and mobile and she could feel its different textures — the way it hung like silk curtaining over the stairs, the way it was fine and furred over the carpet on the landing. She felt delicately for the fifth step with a bare foot and heard her own breathing, soft, regular, too quick. Everyone was withdrawn, half human, in their sleep behind the closed doors. Anna was glad of it; they left the house and herself to her.

When they had come home, that evening, no one had been very happy or wanted to talk very much. Margaret had complained of sunburn, Caroline had been sharp, even with Jeremy. Henry had said, 'Hush, I am thinking,' whenever he was addressed. There had been something antagonistic between them all, as there so often is between those who have been expected to enjoy themselves in each other's company. They had all gone to bed early. Anna licked her lips, and put her whole weight very carefully onto the last step. They were negligible now they were asleep. She imagined them all with delight, inert and solid under their sheets, their hair tangled over the hot faces pressed into the pillows. Their sleep gave her power over them, just because she was awake, and moving.

The weather was about to break, and Anna was waiting for it. She had been sitting up, watching the window, listening for the slightest sound, the slightest tremor, to mark the beginning of the storm. So far there had been nothing; the night was evenly black and undisturbed; but she knew it must come. It prickled on her skin, she had scented it already, it was a question of time only. Anna like storms. They excited her always, but this time it was worse than usual. It had been too long coming. In the end she could not sit still, and had come downstairs for a glass of water, needing movement and a change of place. She crept along corridors, feeling a prick of electricity even in the carpet under her feet, and came to the white closed door of the bathroom.

Inside, it was beautiful; so beautiful, that she made a little noise of excitement and had to look hurriedly behind her in case she had disturbed one of the sleepers. An earlier owner of the house had been wildly and uncharacteristically extravagant over the bathroom, had stripped and remade it along the glass and chromium lines of the chic furniture magazines of the late twenties. The old iron bath, on its lion's paws, which Caroline would much rather have had, now stood in one corner of the garden and Henry grew hydrangeas in it. Caroline felt that it would be somehow too much to put it back and decorate round it. She was nevertheless ashamed of the ostentatious costliness of what she had and annoyed because the bathroom made it, she had to hope, painfully obvious that their house was not the family heritage she liked to pretend to herself that it was.

But tonight, with the soft light from the summer moon leaning gently on the corner of the bath, propped triangularly like another pane of paler glass between the window and the floor, there was nothing garish about the bathroom at all; it was a drowned world, a sunken secret world, with pillars and planes of light shining gently in its corners and the odd brightness of a tap, or the sliver of light along the edge of the basin, winking like living creatures, strange fish suspended and swaying in the darkness. The shelves were a miracle of green and silver, shadow of transparent shadow, reflected and admitted, block geometry made ideal in light, under the brittle circular shadows of the glasses, which rested on them and through them. Shadows of light, Anna thought, thickness on thickness, all these textures of light, caught and held in glass, spirals and cones and pencil trellises, where the shadow of one shelf overlapped another. She crossed quietly to the basin; the water came out of the tap in little silver spearheads that danced in the glass like quicksilver and settled into a faintly swaying lucidity. Anna drank quickly – she was no longer, if she had ever been, really thirsty – and refilled the glass for the pleasure of watching the water. She carried it across to the window and held it so that light was directed and split through the water onto the floor of the bath. The circle of brightness opened like a flower, with crisp, spinning petals. She curled up in the wide windowsill and turned the glass lovingly, with outstretched arms. Nothing she had ever seen had been more exquisite, or more unreal. She felt balanced and complete, between all this trapped, plotted light and the approaching storm; she said to herself, turning the glass round and round, over and over again, not knowing herself quite what she meant, 'I can do something with this. Oh, I can do something with this, that matters.' It was all so extremely important and she would, any moment now, know clearly why.

Outside the trees sighed, and air ran across the garden. Now, she thought, now it is coming.

Oliver came in and had reached the washbasin before he saw her. He was very solid and woollen, in a black dressing-gown, and his feet were neat in pointed black leather slippers. He had carried his glass half-way to the tap when he caught sight of her, and Anna watched his face as he turned, in the mirror behind him, sharp and drained of colour.

'What are you doing here?' He did not start; only his hand, with the glass in it, was arrested.

'I came down for a drink. I'm waiting for the storm.'

There was a silence. Anna spun her glass and waited.

'Aren't you cold, in that thin dress?'

'No.'

Oliver finished pouring his water, in a matter of fact way, and came over to the windowsill. Anna moved into the corner, making room for him, and he sat beside her, sipping silently, looking intently across at her. He said, in the end, 'Do you intend to sit there all night?'

'Possibly. I can't sleep. It's more exciting down here.' Unthinkable to tell Oliver about the light.

'You seem remote, all white, amongst all this glass.' Anna crossed her arms over her breasts, and shivered.

'I thought I should see you, before I left. It seemed necessary. It's been a very inconclusive time we've had together.'

Anna, hunched into herself, said nothing.

'Are you afraid of me, Anna?'

'I don't think so. Why should I be?'

'You are still so uneasy with me. I should like to go away feeling that we were friends. I don't like to think I've handled things wrongly.'

'Things?'

'I should like to feel I've brought you a bit nearer reality.'

'Reality?'

'Reality. A combination of one's own limitations and, in some form or other, the eternal kitchen sink.' He laughed, shortly.

'It sounds grim,' said Anna. She twirled her glass, rocking the light in it. 'Sometimes,' she said carefully, 'I think perhaps I have no limitations.'

'And that is when you are most limited,' Oliver said.

'Don't, don't start again.'

'No, I wish I could have brought you to trust me more. It's odd, I have had a feeling, in spite of everything, that you're like me. You remind me of myself.'

'That's frightening,' Anna said, without rudeness. 'That's really frightening.'

There was another silence. Oliver cleared his throat, and smoothed his dressing-gown, whilst Anna, her eyes half closed, rocked backwards and forwards over her knees. The thunder poured into the silence like the tumbling of high towers, the crack of heavy stones and the dull rumbling of dust afterwards. The window behind them trembled, and Anna's hand tightened on her glass.

'It's come,' she said, whilst the sky shook. Oliver nodded, dryly. 'There ought to have been lightning.'

'There will be.'

They both turned to the window and watched. After a moment the lightning came, sheet after sheet, bright and metallic, splayed across the lawn and the orchard, so that the trees stood out against it sharp and black. After it, the darkness was thicker, softer and less loaded.

'Shift the lightning a little,' Anna said, 'and you don't recognize the world at all.'

'It's the same world,' Oliver said imperturbably. The lightning cracked again, a steady persistent flickering this time, and Anna, turning back from the sudden glare of its intrusion into her drowned world, found herself looking into Oliver's face, levelled by it into a white mask, with holes for eyes and blue slit mouth.

'Oh,' she said, 'I can't bear it.'

And then, as the thunder bore down upon them again, Oliver reached out for her and held her back by the hair, as he had done in the water, and she, after her first involuntary stiffening, clutched at his shoulders with sharp fingers and held out her mouth to him. No one had ever kissed her so thinly or so angrily before. Indeed the only other who had kissed her had been Michael, who was warm and comfortable, however exciting. Oliver's love-making was painful. Anna managed to draw a breath, and twisted away from him.

'Please –' she said, rather loudly.

'Hush,' said Oliver. He said stiffly, 'I'm sorry, of course, I didn't mean to do that.' He looked at her sideways and fiddled with the end of his dressing-gown cord.

Anna felt suddenly very grown up and began to laugh.

'What's funny?'

'You – and me – being so serious. Of course you meant to do that. You couldn't have gone home without. It's been coming all the time.'

'Anna –' said Oliver seriously. 'That's not why –'

'Oh, I know, that's not why. Don't look so worried. It doesn't matter, does it, it's just one of those things. It doesn't make any difference. You must be very careful, Oliver, kissing strange girls. Anyone less sensible than me might get very upset, or think you meant – something. That's what's supposed to happen. But I don't seem to mind.'

Oliver looked as though he found her hilarity in rather bad taste, and also as though he was a little hurt.

'It isn't important,' Anna said decisively. She stood up and reached for his hand. 'Let's go out. Into the garden, before it rains.'

'You'll catch cold.'

'No I shan't, I never do. I've got to get out, I shall suffocate in this house if I stay here any longer. Don't you feel it?'

'And with the lightning about, it may be very dangerous,' Oliver said. He followed her, nevertheless, down the stairs, through the kitchen, and out of the house.

'Do go in if you want to,' Anna said indifferently, tapping her bare toes on the cold grass. 'I just had to get out, don't you see? I mean, if I can be silly enough, I might get out, yet – '

'Out of what?'

'I don't know.' She paused, and giggled. 'You look so solid, standing there with your feet together. Pyjamas are so *flappy*.'

'How silly do you have to be?' Oliver demanded, with exaggerated impatience.

'I don't know. I don't know at all. I'll race you to the orchard.' She began to run, still laughing, across the dried grass.

'You little fool!' said Oliver. 'Come back.'

Anna went on running. After a moment, Oliver gathered up the skirts of his dressing-gown and ran after her, somewhat untidily. As they reached the orchard, the first rain rustled in the air.

'Listen,' said Anna. 'Now it'll all be clean – ' Oliver caught her up; she saw that he was shaking with anger and her assurance deserted her. Drops of rain sounded around them on the leaves, like snapped fingers. 'Come here,' he said. 'Come here, listen to me.' He made a grab at her and missed; she stood for a moment, breathing heavily, looking at him, half pleading with him, and then walked back towards him. 'Come here,' he repeated again and put a heavy arm across her shoulders. He began to kiss her, over and over again. Anna did not precisely like it. She was still curious, remained pliable, and kept still. She made no attempt to encourage or repel Oliver's one attempt at a more intimate embrace; he did not repeat it. She was clever enough to see that he was proving something to himself which he needed to prove, and she was not quite sure what it was. The rain at last seeped through the leaves and collected in a beaded mat on the shoulders of Oliver's dressing-gown and plastered Anna's hair to the back of her head until water ran down her neck. Anna thought, in a minute this will be over and I shall be able to work out what I think about it, and then, suddenly she was very cold and wet and shivering uncontrollably.

'Oliver,' she said. 'I'm cold. Please, can we go in now.'

Oliver shook the rain out of his hair and seemed to gather himself together. He said, 'I forgot myself, I'm sorry.'

'No, don't be, I've told you it doesn't matter, I don't *mind*. Only, I'm cold, I've got to go in.'

'You ought to mind, I think.'

'No,' said Anna. 'Neither of us minds really. There was nothing to do all summer. Let's not pretend. And anyway, I'm no good at minding things. I don't care if you make love to me, I – I like it, but I can't bear it if you try to make me think about it.'

Oliver wrinkled his brow, at a loss. He said, 'I don't like this not minding things – '

Anna said impatiently, 'You want your cake and eat it. Think yourself, for a change, where would you be if I *did* mind?'

'I'd manage. It'd work out.'

'Oh, yes, I expect, more talk. But I don't mind. So everything's all right.'

'I don't – '

'Please, Oliver, let me go in. Let me go in. I'm cold. I shall miss you, tomorrow.'

Oliver hesitated still, then took her hand and walked her into the house. At the foot of her stairs she leaned over and kissed him on the cheek.

'Goodbye, Oliver.'

'Goodbye.'

'It's all right, isn't it?'

'Yes,' said Oliver heavily. 'It's all right.' He looked suddenly very tired.

Margaret sat up and said, 'Oliver, darling, where have you *been*? It must be four o'clock, it's gone horribly cold and there you are, soaked to the skin. What have you been doing?'

'I've been out,' Oliver said, dropping his wet clothes one after the other on the floor. 'In the weather.' He climbed, cold and naked, into the bed. 'Let's pull up another blanket, for God's sake.'

'But, darling, *why?*'

'Just don't talk, please,' he said. He turned to her and studied her. 'You've never wanted to damage anyone, have you? Not consciously – '

'Damage?'

'It doesn't matter. I'm a Puritan at heart, did you know that?' Margaret looked puzzled. 'Never mind,' he said. 'Come close and warm me.' Margaret took him into her arms and put out the light. Almost immediately, she heard him snore.

Anna congratulated herself on her own sophistication in being quite unperturbed over having been passionately embraced by a married man and wrung her wet nightdress out of the window. Men are funny about sex, she told herself, as she climbed into bed. It doesn't matter to them as it does to women (everything one read told one this), it's just something they have to do, it doesn't *matter* to them. But they spend much more time having to do it and for some reason doing it means they have to prove they can make women mind and they are terrified one will mind and be a nuisance to them, and they are hurt and disappointed in one if one takes it as casually as they do. It's a funny pride they have, nothing one can recognize, quite mysterious, really. One has to learn about it, by experience. I'm learning all sorts, she told herself, I ought to be grateful to Oliver, really. She smiled to herself. 'Poor, old Oliver.' The sound of the rain on the roof accompanied her, comfortably, to sleep.

When they left in the morning, the drive was a slow river of yellow mud and loose gravel. Henry drove them to the station, with water slopping round the axles, and Caroline stood with the children, both of them, on the steps to wave.

'Come again,' she called, cordially, to the back of the car. 'Come again. We so enjoyed having you.'

They waved, misted, through the back window. Anna had dark rings round her eyes and the beginning of a cold. Caroline sent her to bed and told her that she must look after herself if she was to pass her exams.

Henry came back from the station and said, 'We got them off, just in time.'

'Oh, Henry,' Caroline said reproachfully. Then she smiled.

'I can get on, now,' Henry said, making for his study. 'People can be an awful nuisance, don't you think?'

The house closed around them, again, and the rain continued for five days. When it stopped, it was suddenly autumn.

PART TWO

SEVEN

NEXT YEAR, ANNA duly went up to Cambridge. Getting herself into Cambridge had not been easy for her, which, in spite of being able, to a degree, to say I told you so, annoyed her surprisingly. Her interviews went off not too badly. The worst moment was when someone asked her, in passing, a routine question: 'I suppose you were Head Girl?' and she answered, far too loudly, 'No, I wasn't, I was expelled.' 'We find a little experience of things outside school is often valuable,' her interlocutor murmured, and went on to other things. When they wrote to her and told her that they had unfortunately no room for her, but that she had been placed on the waiting list, she assumed that her exclusion was due to this indubitable sign of instability on her part. Later, after she had been offered the place refused by a series of young women who wanted to go to Oxford, or had emigrated to Australia, or had suddenly decided that they preferred immediate marriage to the academic life, she came to wonder. The prefects who had been interviewed with her were so much less in evidence, once she was up – or perhaps they had all changed – and Anna came to the conclusion that the dons thought as little of them as she did herself, and believed passionately in a quality they referred to as originality, and which turned out to be often enough, as far as she could observe, indistinguishable in practice from emotional instability and intellectual exhibitionism. They seemed – shy and solitary as most of them were – fascinated by extremes of student flamboyance, and Anna came to imagine that they had associated her breaking of school laws in some way with this, and that it had done her no harm, possibly some good. That was not all, of course.. 'Parts of your papers were abysmal, you know,' one of them told her later, 'and your French and Latin were shocking, but you had sparks, you had sparks, and you had a mind of your own which is the main thing, after all. And of course, it was likely you had the right background, though we do try not to take these things into account. Is your father working on anything at present?'

Margaret Canning wrote to congratulate Anna, on behalf of Oliver and herself, and enclosed a list of the names and addresses of friends whom they thought it might help Anna to know. Anna wrote back, too late and too curtly, thanked them for their congratulations, said she felt she would be in Cambridge on false pretences, and added, for Oliver's benefit, that she supposed they wouldn't have taken her if she hadn't been her father's child. She never called on the friends, partly out of laziness, partly because she was not sure whether the friends were Oliver's or Margaret's, and although Margaret's friends, if they took any notice of her, might be amusing, Oliver's would certainly be fierce, intimidating and a dreadful strain, which she had no intention of subjecting herself to. She did not see the Cannings again before going up. The summer visit was not repeated, and although Margaret still lunched and shopped with Caroline occasionally, and Oliver wrote to Henry from time to time, they did not cross Anna's path.

What she made of Cambridge was not apparent to anyone; neither to her parents, nor to those who taught her, nor to herself. She wrote essays, when these were expected, seeming to find it, as the dons certainly did, faintly surprising that anything as solid and committed as an essay, as opinions, in ink, on paper, should proceed from her and be detachable from her, to be criticized. These essays were precise, correct, unadventurous, and on the whole incontrovertible. She sat, thin and pale, with her head on one side, and Caroline's look of polite tea-party interest on her face, and listened to her supervisor's remarks about them but she was never to be provoked into saying anything further than she had already committed herself to; one of her tutors, who disliked her, came to the conclusion that she should never have been admitted. The other, more optimistic, continued to hope for some kind of mental tin-opener to present itself. Once she thought she had it, when she provoked in Anna an outburst of indignation over something contemptuous said about *Madame Bovary*. 'It's not dull, it's terrible,' Anna cried, but she was reading English, not French, and the incident was not repeated.

She was not friendless, as she had been at school; she had coffee with people, and went to parties; she attended the first nights of plays, and was seen in lectures and in libraries. But she was not remarkable and had no special skill, and this now began to matter, the elusive nature of her event in the future became tormenting, in a society of the clever, the extravagant, the ambitious. It would be nice to be really clever, she thought, the way it would have been nice to be really horsey, but as with the splints and spavins, the correct retort, the correct allusion, rarely came to her. And she saw that people thought her 'not worth the effort', and made less herself.

Caroline was not troubled about cleverness. Caroline saw the Universities as Zuleika Dobson had seen them; cities of young men, pleasant, eligible, likely to be successful young men. In Cambridge in particular there were ten men for every woman and Caroline reasoned that if Anna behaved even half sensibly – she had certainly grown prettier – she might well be suitably married at the end of her three years. If Anna, like almost any woman undergraduate, shared this view, it was only very vaguely, and not with any of Caroline's practical hopes. She supposed dimly that she ought to be in love, and in her own way cast about for someone to be in love with. Love, achieved, might even be the event she was awaiting. But not marriage; her view of love was still through the small end of the telescope; to be beautiful, it must be hopeless; if it looked, as Michael had, as though it might have been anything else, she took care to complicate it until it was safely impossible and remote again.

This took time. Eventually, after a series of experiments, and savoured failures, she arrived at Peter Hughes-Winterton.

Peter Hughes-Winterton stood in his doorway, waved the smoke away from his face and listened to the needle grate and slither on the last moan of the clarinet. He had meant this party to be quite different, had worked over it for weeks and now, three-quarters of its way over, it was like all other parties, dim, hot, airless and smoky, with people chattering in high squeals in his living room, or lying in untidy heaps in his darkened bedroom, and one or two couples advancing and retreating, twisting each other with closed eyes and sweat on their lips, by the record player in the window. Preparing the room before Hall, he had thought it all seemed new and glamorous, warm and a little bit out of this world, as a party should be. He had lit candles, tiers and branches of candles, silver candlesticks borrowed and begged from neighbours, from home, from the college, he had had them on all possible ledges and levels, all the walls, he had thought poetically, studded and scattered with little flames. He had bought crimson cloth and draped the room with curtaining, he had decorated with Victorian piles of wax fruit and piles of real fruit in the same style, he had commissioned several enormous, voluptuous drawings by a Pole with a genius for imitation Beardsley. There was a very special punch, in silver bowls with ornate ladles, made from a recipe which had been genuinely handed down in his own family from 1745. He had become quite excited, polishing the glasses, stirring the punch, arranging the gilt cords on his hangings for the last time before the guests arrived. He was practical enough to ensure that his candles and his tent of curtaining were in no danger of setting each other alight. He was rather proud of himself.

And then they had come, some in cavalry twill, some in jeans, with the usual indistinguishable girls in bunchy cocktail skirts and tarty little tops; they had brought their own records and had removed his minuet from his record player within minutes, to try out something new that had only just come out. They had rolled up his beautiful rugs – he supposed that was a relief, in a way – to make space for jiving, and they had gone into the bedroom, which he had put aside for coats, and were taking off more than coats. They had blown out some of his candles to make the necessary dark corners and had put some of them into bottles, in other corners, to light cigarettes from. They compared the drawings, in insistent, high-pitched, authoritative voices, with other décors executed by the same artist at other parties on other nights, so that they lost their mystery and became a conversation point like any other. They drank down the punch like anyone else's cheap wine cup, and said to him cheerfully as they passed him, 'Potent stuff, this of yours, Peter, very. We're getting rather high.' There was at least enough to drink, so that by any normal standards the party was a success. Peter was grateful for this, even in the midst of feeling let down.

He had made the party, as he had first conceived it, for Anna, whom he loved. He had hoped she might blossom in candlelight and good manners. He looked across the room for her and found her where he had left her, standing against the bedroom door, looking prim and lonely and quite obviously not liking the party now. She was wearing a dress – the high-necked, cream coloured linen one that Margaret Canning had bought for her – and her hair was now long enough to lie like a flat plate, curled round on the top of her head. She would have liked my party, Peter thought sadly, not being the man to call her so obvious dislike of the present party rudeness; he thought of it as honesty, which covers a multitude of social cruelties. He had gone to fetch her some brandy – 'I can't take any more cup,' she had said – and as he set out towards her his foot crunched on a broken glass.

Anna watched him approach and thought her face into a smile which did not manage to reach her mouth or eyes. She was, in fact, pleased to see him. He seemed, to Anna, one of the very few people she knew who seemed effortlessly able to *like* other people, or what he was doing. He liked being an undergraduate. He rowed, and talked, spoke rhetorically and not very well, but with obvious honesty, in the Union, and went out with the Trinity Foot Beagles. These things became him. They were what he had been born and bred for. His father, in fact, when he had been told he had a son, had imagined him a tall, blond, elegant undergraduate at his own college, had waited for the actualization of this, and had not thought beyond it; so that Peter, for him, was now ideal Peter. It was assumed that he would follow his father into the Foreign Office, but this was an assumption about a young man whose eternal present was the University, and neither Peter nor Sir Walter Hughes-Winterton had yet paused to think that there was only a year left of this present before it was all over, and he must apply himself to an examination that it was more unlikely he would pass than his father's generation could conceive.

Anna had met him first at the end of someone else's party,

where she had nearly fallen drunkenly down a staircase and had been saved by Peter's strong and unceremonious grip on her wrist. It was a silly incident, but she had been very frightened and very grateful, and carried with her a vision of Peter as very literally a pillar of strength, a salvation from the depths, blond, solid and confident above her and her slipping feet, which was never quite annihilated by the usual exaggerated female contempt for those who love, and expose themselves before they are loved.

Peter remained a protector, an opener of doors, a bringer of flowers, a provider of coats against the rain and cushions in punts, and Anna laughed at his punctiliousness, admired him for it and came to rely on it, all at once. She disliked his attempts to identify himself with what might be called the modern undergraduate, went once with him to a jazz band ball where he wore tight jeans and a scarlet shirt, sulked, and told him that that kind of thing just didn't suit him. She liked to hear him talk about hunting and rowing and even politics, and to leave the arts alone. This, Peter had decided, was because she resented the inevitable reference to her father which most literary conversation sooner or later produced, and he made a point of never mentioning Henry Severell. Peter was by no means a fool. He loved Anna because she was vulnerable and not vulgar, and attractive, and had he thought 'something in her', and because she needed, he thought, like most people, an enormous amount of kindness and attention, before she would unfold. He was waiting until he was indispensable. Anna, who was also not a fool, knew what he thought, and prodded her feelings occasionally to see whether he might not have become indispensable whilst she wasn't looking. So far, he had not, but she didn't want to have to do without him.

'Here's your brandy. Now, I must get my breath back.' Anna took the glass and looked into it. 'It's getting difficult to breathe at all,' she agreed.

'I didn't mean it to be this kind of party.'

'They're enjoying themselves,' Anna said kindly.

'I'm looking forward to your meeting my mother. She'll like you. Lots of character. Ideas of her own.'

'I don't expect she will like me.'

148

'Why ever not?'

'Mothers never do. I'm the kind of person people's mothers just don't like. Can't we go now? I've had too much drink and if I stand here any longer I shall just go to sleep.'

'I don't think I ought. I mean, it's my party, I ought to see them out – they might break something, or worse. I'm sorry, Anna –'

Anna drooped. Peter said, 'Let's go outside, anyway, and get some fresh air. Would you like that?' Anna nodded and Peter made a way for her, down the stairs and out into the court. The night was cold and Anna gasped and surfaced as though she had been flung into cold water. Peter was breathing heavily.

'Is that better?'

'Much,' said Anna, shivering. She swayed up against him, whether by accident or design neither of them were quite sure, and Peter pulled her firmly into his arms and kissed her.

'Oh, warm,' said Anna, classifying.

'Anna –'

'What is it?'

'Only I love you.'

'Hush,' said Anna quickly, feeling coldness and distance creeping over her as they always did with the importance in his voice.

'No, don't interrupt. I don't want you to say anything now, it's too soon. Only, when I'm in a position to, I'll ask you to marry me. Don't answer. I'll make you sure you want to, by then, don't worry.'

Anna still struggled with coldness, shrinking up like a touched snail.

'How?' she asked provocatively. Peter made no answer, only leaned over her, rubbed his warm face against hers over and over and murmured, not really to her, 'I love you, I love, I love you,' until in the end she said, experimentally, in a small, too clear voice, 'I love you too.' They would both have been so happy if it had been true, she thought.

There was something entirely comfortable about the solidness of his shoulder, and the warmth of his jacket and the strength of his hands. And something putting off, something ridiculous and distasteful about his heavy brooding face over hers. Sexual excitement, Anna had decided, did something horrible to men's faces, it made the skin heavier, they developed blubber mouths and staring, out-of-focus eyes, they grew all hot and damp and lined and stretched. She could see that if she was involved, she might not notice. But she had not been involved and she did notice, and resented what she was pleased to call their loss of humanity – whilst remaining, she considered, deploring it, herself all too human. She gave a twist of impatience, and said, 'Oh, please, can't we leave now? Can't we go? I do want to go – '

Peter hesitated, and then decided. 'Right, we'll go. To hell with them, for once. Look, wait only half a minute, I'll get your coat and our bags, you don't have to fight your way in again. Will you? Good. God, I love you, Anna.'

Anna knew from experience that to be slightly drunk inside the building was quite different from being slightly drunk outside it. She watched Peter turn and vanish into his staircase and wrapped her arms round herself. A wind had whipped up, which fluttered her skirts, chilled her knees, and got into her hair. Inside, lightheadedness and insecurity were comfortably cushioned. If one fell, one fell against someone else, or a piece of furniture. But out here, where the air thrust coldly through one's clothes and into one's flesh, there was no protection. The court was grey and bare and round, a wide gravel path circling a plot of untouched and untouchable grass. Anna shivered, felt her stomach turn and saw the path lurching elliptically round her and heaving up in serpent coils under her feet.

From Peter's window a strip of light hung like a banner, its pennant points split round the silhouette of an embracing couple, and the jangle and moan of the music dropped thinly down, until light and sound blunted themselves against the darkness. It looked warm and safe, and Anna, an unreasoning fright rising in her, nearly went after Peter. But she went instead over to the grass and sat down firmly on the edge of it. From there, the party took on all the colour and warmth of other people's firesides, seen dimly in their own light through half-closed curtains, or the party in the fairy story, where the poor child stands in the snow and sees the infinitely desired world from which she is shut out, the whirl of silks and velvets, the

150

glitter of chandeliers and flicker of candles, the glow of the wines in the glasses, the giant sugar roses on the cakes, oranges, lemons, grapes, flute, violin, bassoon, and all the rest of it. Anna had sympathized dreadfully with this child, all through her own childhood, and did still, but she was learning, she knew now, that it would not do – that the complete pleasure imagined from the outside had no counterpart inside, that peering through glass was a necessary part of it, at least for her, although others, perhaps Peter, might possess the world inside and enjoy it as it presented itself to be enjoyed.

She leaned backwards, and spread her hands in the cold, hard earth behind her, dropping her head out and down between her shoulders. The dark stone of the buildings rose in a circle round her, and the mist swirled and was blown in it, but above the pit of the walls the night sky was clear and luminous and the stars on it winked, and shrank, and sprang into life again with no apparent order or arrangement. She shook her head angrily at them, and they swooped and dived like pale brilliant fish on a swelling sea.

By dipping her head even further back she managed to trap one tiny point of light between the turreted corner of the gatehouse and the edge of the first roof. There, she told it, I've got you, I fix you, I know you, I shall remember you, I win. The bulk of the gatehouse building swayed gently and Anna's star was sucked into a funnel of darkness and disappeared. She was ready to weep with rage, jerked her head forward again so abruptly that she was nearly sick, and put it between her knees.

'I can't manage – ' she said, and saw that she was addressing a pointed pair of black shoes on the path in front of her. These, as she considered them, turned slowly and took a step towards her, then stopped again, close together, at attention. They were rather scuffed shoes, ornamented with a pattern of unlovely little sprays of intricate punch-holes.

'Rather rude,' she told them. 'Peering at other people's drunken distress.'

'I feel I should remind you that grass is college property, and that no one is allowed to be on it unless accompanied by a Fellow of the College. And even then, I should hope, not in those pernicious shoes.'

151

'Wait,' said Anna, looking up. 'I knew it,' she cried, with drunken triumph. 'Oliver. You would, of course. What are you doing here?'

'Visiting friends,' said Oliver, looking bird-like down at her with his hands crossed behind his back and his head on one side.'I do have friends in Cambridge.'

'I'm sure you do,' Anna said, soothing him, and added, 'I saw you once.' This had been on Magdalene Bridge, where Anna, advancing, had seen the dark figure between bursts of traffic, leaning over and looking into the water, and had quietly gone back the way she had come, not wishing to meet him. 'I ran away,' she said. 'Silly of me.'

People were leaving Peter's party unsteadily, clutching their coats around their throats, laughing and arguing, in twos and threes. Between them and Oliver there were fences of solid mist, set up, defined and limited by the light from the windows.

'They're, they're coming out. That's Peter's party, that I'm at, supposed to be. I'm waiting for Peter here, that's what I'm doing. He ought to have come by now. I can't think what's come over him, unless he's being sick. He looked rather sick,' she finished unfairly. Oliver looked down at her with disgust. She cried, 'I can see what you're thinking. Just like you. You'd make any party into an orgy. I don't suppose you were ever just happy.'

'Are you happy?' said Oliver. He held out an indisputable hand, and pulled her to her feet. 'I think I'll take you back with me to be sick if you have to, and have some black coffee to put you straight.'

'No, thank you. I told you, I'm waiting for Peter.'

'This Peter. Who is he?'

'He's called Peter Hughes-Winterton. He's nice. You wouldn't like him. I think I shall marry him – '

'Indeed.'

'Even if it would please my mother, which it will.'

'I see.'

Anna looked at him sharply. 'I wish I knew what you did think you could "see" in that tone of voice. Not that I care. When Peter comes, we are going to get in his car and drive to London. It's his birthday tomorrow, and I'm going to stay with

152

his parents and be vetted. So you see, it's all quite proper, and I don't need any help.'

Oliver stood for some time and then observed, 'He doesn't seem to be in any hurry.'

'I told you, he's probably sick. It was a pretty good party.'

'If he's as drunk as you imply, he's probably passed out. In the meantime, you are in danger of being locked into a men's college. Girls have been sent down for less. Moreover, if he's so drunk, I owe it to your father not to let you be driven to London by anyone in that condition. So you'd better come with me.'

'I don't want to.' Oliver began to quote accident rates and drunkenness figures, making his points in a dry grinding voice, with little stabs of the hands.

He said again, 'As a friend of your father's –' and Anna pushed confusedly at the wind in her skirts, resenting her own attempts to follow his arguments, and nevertheless, in her drunkenness, bothered by them.

'Whatever this Peter wants, he will want just as much tomorrow,' Oliver said, very firmly. Anna felt suddenly too tired to bother, too tired to wait, too tired to stay awake between Cambridge and London.

'It's utterly mean of me,' she said. 'But I always do what comes easiest. I think you're being bloody, Oliver, but I've not got strength to argue.'

'Good. Let us not try to find out who is to blame for what. We must hurry. Have you no coat?'

'Peter's got it.'

'You'd better have mine.' He was wearing a fawn raincoat, like a gunman in a thriller. Anna, as he wrapped it round her, felt furtively as though she was herself a criminal, slinking away from a crime committed, and was not really reassured by Oliver's look of approval. It turned out that he had a motor-car, hidden away in a back street.

'You never used to drive,' said Anna. It was an old car, a Ford Popular, high and square on little wheels, with uncertain doors and a stuffy smell, saturated with petrol.

'I do now,' he said. 'I rise in the world, slowly. An article here, a talk there, and I am in the motor-car-owning classes. Along with most of the rest of the populace.'

'How nice for Margaret,' said Anna, gritting her teeth as Oliver started the car, a single spluttering sound in the night emptiness of Cambridge streets. The movement changed the uneasiness of her stomach into a definite turmoil. At the beginning of Trumpington Street, in front of Corpus, she said, 'I'm sorry. You'll have to stop. I'm going to be sick.'

Oliver glared at her. 'Can't you wait?'

'No,' said Anna, and then, on a rising note, as he did not stop immediately, 'No, I tell you, I can't.' She struggled with the door and fell out onto the pavement as he drew up. She was very sick. Oliver sat back and watched her.

'How very unpleasant,' he said. 'Mind my raincoat, please. I can't afford another cleaner's bill and, whatever you say, they destroy the proofing. Can't you hurry? Someone might come.'

'Shut up,' said Anna, raising a haggard face from the gutter. 'You would make me come in your stuffy car, when you knew I was sick. Do you think I like it?'

'Quite easy to avoid it. I dislike drunken women. There's something basically repellent about it. My mother used to say, drunken women are an abomination. I've seen no reason to disbelieve her.'

'Oh, Christ,' Anna said, sitting down on the pavement. 'You do nag so, and always when I'm not up to it. I just want to go to bed. I've had enough.'

'It's your own fault – '

'Oliver – ' Anna screamed desperately. 'Please leave me alone.'

Oliver got out of the car and looked furtively up and down King's Parade to see whether a proctor or a policeman might emerge from a gate or an alley. He shook Anna violently by the shoulders and hauled her to her feet.

'Get in. I won't have you behaving like this in public. Get into that car,' he said, pushing, and slamming the door to prevent Anna falling out again. He came round and drove at a bouncing and careful thirty miles an hour out towards the Barton Road, with his passenger bunched against the door with rolling head and chattering teeth. After a time, she muttered, 'Where're we going – '

'Professor Ainger's house. He lends it to me.'

'Is Margaret there?'

'No,' said Oliver, opened his mouth, and shut it again.

'Are you here much?'

'I have a term off. I'm trying to write something. I use the library and talk to people.'

He turned into a pebbled drive, switched off the lights and let the car choke to death. The darkness pushed them suddenly very close together. Oliver said socially and stiffly, 'The Aingers are on an archaeological expedition. He was my Tutor. Incompetent, but kind. Still is kind.'

'Yes,' said Anna, struggling for some reason to get out of the car as though Oliver might attack her. 'I see.' Oliver got out himself and came round to open the door. He seemed irritated.

'What is the matter, girl? I won't bite. Pull yourself together.'

'I'm sorry,' Anna said, standing behind him on the door step and shivering whilst he hunted for the keyhole. 'I'm being an awful nuisance to you, I do see. You should have left me.'

'Nothing that coffee won't put right now,' said Oliver more cheerfully, finding the keyhole, and a switch which revealed a heavy Victorian cavern, flushed with deep salmon pink lights and furnished with several wild little mahogany tables, two enormous Chinese jars, protruding smoothly between them, and an involved coat, hat and umbrella stand, carved and beaded, with tortured and convoluted arms like Yggdrasil, on one of which Oliver, neatly, hung his mackintosh, retrieved from Anna.

'Goodness,' Anna said. 'Is it real?'

'Very. These houses were built by rich dons, to last, and furnished accordingly. The upper floors are let as flats, now, of course. There's a touch of the folly about this house. My bed – or rather, Ainger's bed – has curtains on brass rings. Cinnamon velvet. I find it soothing. It's the sort of middle class ostentatious comfort and showing off that my kind aims at, going in for this life, I suppose. Come in, come in and see.'

Anna came in. The room was red velvet and mahogany and leather and tapestry and lace, with a huge oil painting of a blasted heath in a gilt frame dominating one wall. There were two polar bears, trailing their two-dimensional flaps of furred skin behind their almost three-dimensional glassy-eyed heads. Oliver turned on more very pink silk lights. He waved at an embroidered screen in the hearth, which stood between two bamboo cylinders of pampas grass.

'You'll find the fire behind that. Warm yourself, whilst I provide the promised coffee.' Anna knelt down weakly and unearthed, from the deep fireplace, a single-barred electric fire. 'Stingy,' said Oliver, returning from the hall. 'Still, I find it does, if you sit right over it. What I came to say was, the bathroom's on the first floor, first on the left, if you need it again. I suppose you may. I think Mr Peter Whatever-his-name-is is as well rid of you as you are of him.'

'Possibly,' said Anna, struggling with the electric cord, which was wound neatly and impossibly round itself. 'Did you tie this up? It looks like you.'

'It's quite easy,' said Oliver, not offering to help. 'Once you've undone the first knot.' He disappeared again. Anna untied the first knot with hands that hardly seemed to belong to her, found the electric point behind an embossed brass coal bucket, switched on the fire and curled herself painfully in a leather armchair amongst a pile of fringed red velvet cushions. Oliver came back, with a Benares brass tray, two coronation mugs (Edward VII), a steaming kettle, a pewter sugar bowl, two apostle spoons and a large tin of Nescafé. These he put down on a pouffe in front of the hearth, and knelt before it in fur, mixing the powder at the bottom of the mugs with the inadequately short spoon.

'There. Hot, black. There isn't any milk, I find it's not worth getting it in. I hope you don't object to Nescafé. Some people, my wife, for instance, makes a great deal of fuss about it. I've never been able to tell the difference myself.'

'Oh, Oliver,' Anna protested, taking the burnt-smelling brew and sniffing it, hoping her stomach was resilient enough to take it on top of the punch and the brandy without disaster.

'I should think you'd better have several cups,' Oliver said generously, looking at her over his own mug, and smiling with sudden warmth. There was a long silence. Anna sipped her coffee heroically, to show willing, and because Oliver was so

156

obviously pleased to have been able to provide it. Surprisingly, it seemed to improve things, or something else did – the room became stable, and Anna began, drowsily, to relax. She plumped up the cushions, kicked off her shoes and dropped her head back. It occurred to her that in spite of the massive discomfort of the room, and the gloomy furniture, in spite of the thin red line of fire and the sharp, powdery Nescafé which had only heat to recommend it as a night-cap, in spite of fingers scalded in saving the spoon from submerging, in spite of the hangover, in spite of her background guilt over Peter, in spite, perhaps, of Oliver himself, she was for once wholly present, in that room, in some unthinking way, like an inhabitant of one of the houses she peered into in her imagination. She laughed, briefly.

'What is it? What are you thinking?'

'Only that I had forgotten how comfortable you can be. In spite of the nagging.'

'Thank you,' said Oliver. 'I seem to remember it wasn't so, last time we met.'

'I was younger, then. I wouldn't remember that, if I were you.'

There was another silence. Oliver began, conversationally, 'Well, how are you doing? How's Cambridge?'

'I don't like it,' Anna said briefly, after some thought.

'Why not?'

'It's a forcing house. You have to be able to do something, to make anything of it. And I can't.'

'You could work hard, at least.'

'Shall I tell you, I don't like literature? I – it seems to me – it's like a religion to them. They go to D. H. Lawrence like the Ten Commandments, to show them how to live. If I've got to be here, I'll tell you, I wish I did something pure and absolutely intellectual, like mathematics or crystallography. I was happier at home, when I didn't have to see everything in terms of someone else's seeing. Do you know what someone said to me at that party? He said, Are you a Lawrentian woman? Me. Who am I? I don't want to find out, in those terms. And I'll tell you a lot more, he didn't want to find out, either. Or he'd have asked differently.'

157

'You are very vehement, anyway,' said Oliver, leaning forward. 'More than I remember you.'

'More than I am usually. It's the drink.'

'Good, in that case. I'm not with you, of course, you know that. I believe in reading. It's necessary, if you don't happen to be a Lawrence, or a – a – a Lawrence, yourself, someone's got to see a bit further or a bit deeper, and we ought to be capable of learning, if not of finding out originally. Don't you agree? No, of course you don't. You can't. I ought to have seen that at first. You can't even begin to listen. What do you want to do?'

'I don't know.' She hesitated, and then went on, driven. 'But I don't want nothing. I want something, I want it badly. But I don't know what it is.'

Oliver burst out, 'You'd find out fast enough if you had to, wouldn't you? If you didn't have it all laid on, what I worked for, comfortable rooms, intelligent conversations, time to think, things like a water closet, and constant hot water and books on the shelves that you wouldn't begin to imagine yourself without, would you? You'd find out quickly enough what you were prepared to work for and what kind of work you were capable of doing. You've got time to wallow in criticisms and speculations. It's a pity you don't *need* a scholarship, or a First; you'd learn your Lawrence.'

'Oliver,' said Anna, 'I know. I do know.'

He turned to her more gently and pushed his hair back. 'I suppose you do. Listen, you're lying to yourself, you do know that? What was it you said? "I was happier at home, when I didn't have to see everything in terms of someone else's seeing." That's it, isn't it? But you know it's not true. You know we're not talking about Lawrence. Who did the seeing at home? Who's literature and the law and the Ten Commandments, whose authority and vision won't you take at second hand?' Anna waited. 'Henry Severell,' Oliver went on, too dramatically.

Anna began, very slowly, as though succumbing to a secret temptation. 'It was horrible when I got here. Everyone came round to see me, I got invitations from people I didn't even know. And when I got to their parties, they didn't say, This is Anna, they say, Come and meet Henry Severell's daughter. And they hint and hint – the good ones, particularly – that I might introduce him to them. How can I say he's too busy, he wouldn't like it – or if he would, I wouldn't want to know you any more. Not that they'd care what I want. They don't see me. I'm a walking apology. To be quite honest, being a Lawrentian woman was a kind of change.' She stopped, flushed, and finished, 'It's worse here, because here what he *does* is more important than it was at home, where what mattered was him having time to do it in.'

She looked across at Oliver, whose mouth twisted a moment, and felt suddenly how odd it was that a relationship, which had seemed ended or static, should take such leaps in periods of apparent lack of action. Here was Oliver, whose interest she had resented, whose view she had thought untrue, and here was she, having accepted in his absence what had troubled her, finding it easy, even a relief, even pleasant, to tell him a truth there was no one else to hear. An intimacy had grown, from that unpromising summer, that neither of them had, she thought, worked for.

He was saying now, 'What you must realize is that most of us are walking apologies. Not only you. We all want things first hand and have to be content with less. I used to think I could write,' Oliver went on. 'I used to think, if I couldn't, it wasn't worth my living. But I can't and I've learned to live with my own ordinariness, and do something useful with it. Those that can't, teach. And so on.'

Anna thought that this was the first thing he had said to her really from himself; rightly or wrongly, she did not put his sociological bumptiousness in this category. She did not quite know what to do with it, and so returned to her own problem.

'It's not, you know, that I feel I shall never do anything, or can't, or – It's that I don't know what to do. Possibly because I'm a woman.'

'What difference does that make?'

'Oh, I can always just get married. To Peter, for instance, if he'll really have me. That might use one up, one could put everything into someone else.'

'Not you,' said Oliver.

'What do you mean?'

159

'I mean you've no capacity for devotion. You're too selfish.'

'How do you know?' Anna cried.

'I recognize it,' said Oliver, with his *ex cathedra* certainty that always made Anna shiver. 'Because I'm the same. You'll find out. You'll find you'll never make out any guiding light beyond the very complicated day to day needs – and abilities – of Anna Severell. I know.'

'That's not true,' said Anna doubtfully.

'I think you'll find it is,' said Oliver decisively.

'But it's not what I want – ' Anna wailed, and was suddenly distracted by the sight of the clock. 'Oliver – oh my God – it's nearly one o'clock.'

'So I had supposed.'

'But college will be closed.'

'They won't be ringing up the police, will they?'

'No. I had an exeat, to go to London, with Peter. But . . .'

'In that case, obviously, you'd better stay here. You can have the Professor's bed and I'll sleep in here, on the sofa. It's bigger than many beds, it'll be no hardship. I should think you need some sleep.'

'I do,' said Anna, feeling suddenly very wide awake. There came over them that faintly conspiratorial self-conscious intimacy that comes over people who find themselves unexpectedly in the same house overnight, over the dinner guest who misses a train, borrows pyjamas, is allowed to observe the dirty pans and management behind his meal, the order of procession to the bathroom, who is promoted from formality to a temporary position in the domestic inner circle, behind drawn curtains and locked door. Anna took a curious pleasure in helping Oliver make up the bed on the sofa, in carrying pyjamas and shaving brush from bedroom to bathroom. 'It's rather exciting,' she said. 'It's rather unreally real. Like playing house, when one was little. Not a real house, therefore interesting.'

Oliver pushed her back into the shadows and drew the curtains carefully across the bedroom window. Anna, who liked to sleep with them open, frowned, and then understood.

'How cautious.'

'I was born cautious.'

'You were born all the tight little things.'

160

'They have been very useful. Would you hand me my hair brushes? I'll leave you my dressing-gown, you may need it. I'm sorry I can't offer you any clean pyjamas, or anything to sleep in.'

'Underwear will do. I'm not fussy.'

'Would you,' Oliver asked seriously, 'like a hot water bottle? I have one here.'

Anna began to giggle. 'This is very funny. Don't you think it is? Terribly funny, the last thing I expected, really.'

Oliver studied her suspiciously. 'I suppose so,' he said. 'I suppose it is.' He paused. 'I hope you have a good night!' He paused again. 'I intend to breakfast at eight.'

'You'll have to get me up,' Anna said. She gave an involuntary nervous grin. They stood for a moment looking at each other, and then, when each seemed to feel that the moment was growing too long, Oliver bowed, and Anna said, 'Good night, sleep well.'

Left alone she took off her dress and stockings, and hung them on a chair, washed her face in the basin and dried it on a handkerchief, turned back the bedcovers and sat down on the edge of the bed, feeling somehow cheated. She unpinned her hair, slowly, calculating, combed it through with her pocket comb, and then went over and stared at her own pale face in the mirror, in the half light from the bedside lamp. Most women can look like sirens in mirrors, unobserved and unabashed. Anna was rather excited by herself, arranged her hair in a careful disorder on forehead and shoulders, and posed, looking mysteriously under her eyelashes, from this angle and that. Then she swung away to wander aimlessly round the bedroom, looking into drawers, reading the backs of books – St Ignatius, *Prayers in Lent*, the *Screwtape Letters*. She ran her fingers along Oliver's initialled suitcases on a chair at the foot of the bed. This, inspected, proved to contain two collars, three ties, a copy of the *New Statesman*, half a bar of chocolate, a pair of underpants and a gown. Nothing he could conceivably want. I had better go to bed, Anna thought, stretching out her arms and pirouetting on one toe, I had really better go to bed. I shall feel bad in the morning, in any case. She sauntered back across the room to the wash-basin and stared at herself again.

161

The toothbrush – neon pink – that had been there all the time at last glowed into her vision. She picked it up reverently. It was Oliver's not the Professor's, who would have his with him in Asia Minor, it must be Oliver's in any case, it was still damp. He really can't do without his toothbrush, she told herself. She turned on her toe again, wrapped herself with a flourish in Oliver's crimson silky dressing-gown, and went out, bearing the toothbrush before her.

In the door to the drawing room she stopped, holding herself very upright, and waited. Oliver was sitting over the fire in his heavy black spectacles, with books on his knees and at his feet.

'Oliver, what are you doing?'

'Some work.'

'I thought you were tired. I thought you wanted to sleep.'

'I did,' said Oliver grimly. He did not look up. Anna held out the toothbrush.

'I found this. I thought you might need it.'

He looked up then, and Anna walked over, proudly on bare feet, into the narrow firelight. She gave an extra tug to the dressing-gown sash, so that the red silk was pulled, and twisted, very tightly round her.

'I didn't need it, it's my spare,' Oliver said, taking her in. 'Did your dentist never tell you you ought to let them rest one day between using?' Anna waited quietly. 'What do you want, Anna?'

'I don't know. I'm not sleepy. To talk, perhaps.'

'I see.' He closed his book deliberately. 'Why?' Anna did not answer, because there was no answer. Instead, she knelt down on the bearskin beside him and touched his knee. He was trembling.

'Oliver, you're nervous.'

'So would anyone be, in my position. What do you want?'

Anna put her head down over his knee.

'I wanted to know. I only wanted to know.'

Oliver lifted a handful of her hair, with a curiously light movement, and Anna knew that she had been right.

'I wanted to know, too,' he said, sounding almost amused, letting the hair run through his fingers to brush against her face. 'We are tossed together, from time to time – '

'Yes.'

'It all comes to seem relatively uncomplicated, somehow. Easy to follow.'

Anna moved closer and put her arms round his legs. 'It doesn't mean any more than just this,' she said obscurely but with growing confidence. 'Why did you really bring me here?'

'Why did you come?'

'Because it was easiest. I always do what's easiest. I came, because you expected me to, I'm an innocent.'

'Oh, no. You were never really innocent. Ignorant, maybe.' Like all his statements about her this had the curious flatness of absolute certainty, that made Anna believe immediately that he must be right.

She said, 'Neither are you.'

'I hope not,' Oliver said, and it crossed Anna's mind that they were rather ridiculously comforting each other, in case they might have been innocent. But this thought only flickered and was lost.

They were silent for some time, and then Anna laughed.

'What is it?'

'You know, that book of – was it Elinor Glyn's, love on a bearskin – '

'Rather nasty,' said Oliver.

'Militant decency?'

'No. Considerations of comfort. Bed would be better.' He looked at her primly and timidly. 'Are you coming?'

'Yes.'

Oliver held the door for her and laughed, and said, 'I wonder what your father would think,' but this was lost on Anna, who was suddenly and anticlimactically drowsy.

In the morning Anna, who had slept deeply, and dreamed that she was hiding in the orchard at Darton and being called in, more and more loudly and persistently, awoke to find Oliver not there. She was lying in a deep pit in the middle of Professor Ainger's feather mattress, with the sheets wrinkled messily round her, and her own brassière and briefs protruding from under the pillow. She thought, perhaps he has just left me

163

here and gone off, and then was involved in that particularly unpleasant panic which catches at those who wake in a strange house without a clock, and do not know whether they are inconveniently early or inconveniently late for breakfast, whether they are irritatedly awaited or will be properly called in due course. She sat up doubtfully and put on her underwear, which made her feel immediately more sordid and less abandoned.

Who would have thought, she reminisced, that Oliver had all that in him. And then, remembering how she had always been afraid of his intenseness and curled energy and small man's aggressiveness, she corrected herself, no, that's wrong, I would have thought it myself. She lay down again, her face in the stuffy pillow, and thought well, that's that. I can't wonder what that is like any more. A period had been set to what had been an ever-present curiosity, ever since she had known there was anything there to be curious about. She didn't think she missed the former state, the curiosity, but this was only the third real ending in her life; the other two had been her departure for school and her departure from school, and neither of these had been a prelude to anything that might have been called a real beginning. There was no reason to suppose that this would change anything either. Anna had sat in on conversation in college, where women she knew had swapped information about their reactions to their own deflorations, and had decided quite early that she herself was not one to whom anything of this kind would, in itself, make a tremendous difference. Things don't shatter me, she thought. And certainly not Oliver; that had been proved at the end of the summer. That was probably why she was here, because Oliver would not shatter her. There was a great deal to be said for having got over a hurdle of this kind without being put out; one was left free. Not that one did not mind at all, it was just silly to suppose that. One regretted the unknowing curiosity, already, surprisingly. I may come to mind a great deal, later, she told herself, but she was not really attending – later was not a word with any urgency in Anna's vocabulary, except when it referred to her event. Those who do not expect a revelation, a transformation, are rarely transformed; she had expected little, and was not, she decided, transformed at all, though she was certainly spending time thinking of it. What really needled was the uncertainty about when, or if, she was expected to breakfast.

She discovered that she had a hangover; a headache, a bad, prickling taste in the mouth, and an intolerable thirst. She clambered unsteadily out of the bed and was drinking messily from the cold tap, in cupped hands, swearing to herself, when Oliver, shaved and dressed, and with shining shoes, came in, closed the door behind him, and looked at her. He said, 'I have made breakfast.'

'I don't think I can face any.'

'I'd try, if I were you. You've got to get out of this house anyway in half an hour or so. I want to be in the library, and I don't intend to come back here again. So please hurry up and dress.'

'You should have woken me.'

'I thought you looked as though you needed the sleep,' Oliver said sharply, and handed her her petticoat, almost, Anna decided, averting his eyes. She dressed as quickly as she could, and tied her hair back; Oliver waited, tapped on the bedstead and handed her, silently, the shoes she had been hunting ineffectively under the bed. I am sure I should say something, Anna thought, I'm sure there should be apologies, or recriminations, or reassurances or something. We ought to want to know how the other feels. But I don't particularly – at any rate, not yet – and it's always so much easier not to say anything.

'I'm sorry there's nothing cooked,' Oliver said, breaking the silence as they came into the kitchen, a large dark room with a lost ceiling into which light came weakly through a limp floral plastic curtain. 'I don't bother, for myself. There's toast.'

'I hardly ever eat breakfast,' Anna assured him. 'And I couldn't this morning anyway.' She sat down at an incongruous little table with a crimson formica top, like crazy paving. 'May I open the curtain?'

'No,' said Oliver. 'There are neighbours.'

'My reputation will stand it.'

'It may, or it may not. Mine won't. When we've eaten breakfast, I shall leave the house, without you. You'd better wait half an hour. It makes it a bit less obvious.'

165

'Does it?' said Anna dubiously. 'It seems rather nasty.'

'Not necessarily, why? It's sensible.'

He hurried around the kitchen, making toast and mixing more Nescafé; he had the self-contained efficiency of the permanent bachelor, which cast an entirely new light on him for Anna, who wondered fleetingly what his breakfasts with Margaret were like, and then dismissed the thought. Margaret was none of her business, Margaret was Oliver's other more real life; what he did, on his own in this dim house, was nothing to do with Margaret, and not important. Except that if she, Anna, had not known that he was ultimately bound up in Margaret, none of this might have happened. However, she asked him, 'You enjoy being on your own, Oliver?'

'Not so much enjoy, as understand. I can get on with things, on my own. It's a human need, from time to time.' He looked down at his watch, stacked the toast in the toast rack and sat down at the table opposite her.

'Well,' he said. 'Do you know now what you wanted to know?'

'Some of it.'

'Good.' He said, very casually, 'What do we do next?' Anna stared at him, genuinely startled.

'Do? Next?'

Oliver tucked himself into his clothes, withdrawing. 'I'm sorry.'

'No,' said Anna. 'I didn't mean . . . I was listening . . . I just didn't know what kind of thing, you meant.'

'I shall be here next weekend, too. You could come – say, on Friday night, fairly late? You would tell no one, of course.' Anna caught up, too quickly to digest entirely this transformation of an episode into something more.

'Yes,' she said automatically.

'You must do what you really want, naturally.'

'No,' she said quickly. 'I'll come. I'd like to come. Yes, I'd like to come. If you promise not to nag – '

'I don't nag,' Oliver said, leaving Anna with a momentary feeling that she was still bargaining over something he had long ago bought.

'So that's settled,' said Oliver. 'Good. Good.'

EIGHT

IN THE AUTUMN, free from visitors, the sun, and his children, Henry Severell worked hardest. As a young man, he had walked houses in an agony of indecision and procrastination before ever setting pen to paper, so that sometimes he had barely written two or three sentences before dinner, and had then not liked those sentences, which were so disproportionate to the effort put into sitting down to write them and had as often as not crossed them out again. As a young man he had needed sleep, had gone to bed early to make love to Caroline, and had woken heavily and slowly, taking sometimes two hours over it, and several cups of coffee. But now he slept for a bare five hours a night, got up before dawn, or just with it, walked out into the garden and worked for two or three hours before Caroline, admiring and solicitous, brought his breakfast. He would write all morning, spend the afternoon walking, or gardening, and after dinner write again.

Henry gardening was a very different thing from the suburban Sunday gardener in shirtsleeves, Henry whirling a chopper or spreading manure, Henry with his huge hands measuring and sorting seeds, using his whole body in one small manœuvre, was to the Sunday gardener what the priest is to the part-time waiter, carrying biscuits and wine. Not that Henry would have liked to see it that way; he felt a sense of community with the Sunday gardeners, he liked to feel clearly human, wheeling pillars of plant pots in his barrow from one side of the garden to the other; he was aware that Oliver would have found him either sublime or ridiculous in his earthy – or less than earthy, since not peasant, not right down to it – ordinariness, and didn't much care what Oliver thought. This was the pattern of the autumn and winter – barring two or three days of collapse in early February when he would invariably retire to bed with 'flu, hot water bottles, an empty head and an evil temper, to be nursed by Caroline and to lie like a log in a great hairy dressing-gown, shifting himself unhappily, complaining of the heat or the cold, thinking of nothing.

On the morning when the second letter arrived, Henry was up at four-thirty having forgotten the first letter completely, and before he had lifted his body out of bed, he was gathering himself, concentrating, on what seemed an uninterrupted surge of excitement and interest, towards what he had yesterday been constructing. He looked down on Caroline, sleeping neatly on a frilled pillow, one long hand under her narrow cheek, her hair caught in the ruffled broderie anglaise collar of a Victorian nightgown. She looked tired in her sleep, there were lines round her eyes and mouth that he did not notice in the day; flesh ages so quickly, he thought, she is still comparatively young, and here is all this surface broken up, and won't ever mend. He bent down and kissed her, with a gentleness at which he had always been adept; she stirred, smiled and brushed him away with a hand.

He went downstairs and into the hall, where he opened the curtains to let in the grey light, too weak yet to reach the corners, where it seemed to be absorbed and defeated by a dark dust, and moved through, padding quietly into other grey rooms where everything was evanescent, immaterial, in this pale, thin morning light. Furniture and silver were dull, with no light to glow from their polish, they were ghostly presences only, carved refinements of a civilization that here for the moment could not raise itself to life. Henry himself alone had substantial presence, solid amongst his personal effects, like a member of the audience who had wandered by mistake onto an empty set for an elegant domestic comedy and feels that if he blunders in the wrong direction the whole construction – slats, rostra, painted hard-board doors opening on nowhere, wooden chandeliers hung from the lighting bars on string – will fall about his ears leaving nothing to see but the tiled, lavatorial back wall.

In his study was the flask of coffee Caroline always put out for him, and a bowl of chrysanthemums, on whose crisp, clawed points light and colour were already stirring, white and lemon, cream, butter and bronze, muted but increasing. Henry, though

168

he liked their crispness, and roundness, and the erect way the held themselves, was always uneasy with cut flowers; those were Caroline's art; he opened the window and went through into the garden.

He poked with a stick amongst the vegetables, shovelled some coke into the greenhouse boiler, and turned over several half shells of grapefruit, which were arranged regularly, smooth, acid yellow growths, like exotic fungi, amongst the knobbed and branching and disorderly sprouts; inside one of these he found three slugs, one huge black one, ribbed and glittering with silver slime, and two smaller ones, pearly and soft. He looked at them for some time, learning off the pattern of the ribbing, and the precise way the lower surface of the little ones shrank and frilled when they were touched. Then he put them and their yellow hutch absentmindedly back where he had found it. He was not very good at killing things, when it came to it. This was another thing about his 'imitation' earthiness which he knew Oliver would have despised and mocked. Oliver would also have said that if Henry was not going to kill the slugs he should further have put them where no one else would, and may well have been right.

Henry went into the greenhouse, tapped the thermometer, wandered up and down between the hothouse plants, in the heavy, musty tomato smell, and spent some time looking down into the trumpet of a gloxinia, one of the deepest black purple ones, until his consciousness switched and he was folded and furled in a deep purple, slightly furry umbrella, and thinking back and out about the lost Tyrian purple, the shells, the mourning robes, the thistle, so regularly palisadoed about with purple of the royal colour, and Aldous Huxley's remarks about the substitute visionary experience involved in the filming on wide screens of bright flowers quivering and unfurling; Henry liked these, they were a confirmation of his own lack of sense of proportion, they had tremendous power in the magnification, a nasturtium was yards and yards of yellow silk flame, the colour was a whole passion, and men might well learn to see violently and stay awake, through these. Caroline, on the other hand, thought them vulgar. She couldn't explain why, she had said, she just thought them vulgar. What she spoke in her careful

169

flower arrangements was a restrained language of small spaces, which Henry could only interpret intermittently and not in her terms. If Caroline had put his purple flower out on his desk she would have seen it, clearly shaped from some distance; she would never have let it for a moment swallow her. Henry put it down again, on a tray of others; it glowed at him for a moment, and then its power was retired, and it retreated. He ducked under something climbing and hanging, gathered a green tomato, and went out again, down into the orchard; the dew had been heavy and he left a trail of long dark crushed marks.

In the orchard the tall dying grasses brushed against him, wetting him. At the hedge, he paused and looked outside, over the field of stubble at the hill; as he watched, the sun came up behind it, the grey light wavered and thinned and began to shine, running along the stiff gold tubes of the stubble, catching a glitter here and there, and Henry saw that the whole of the field and the hedge where he was were alive and gently moving with the long bright filaments blown in the aerial dispersal of spiderlings. They were netted now, criss-cross, in the stubble, they were festooned and stretched from twig to twig of the hedge, giving it the insubstantial swaying brightness of a balloon about to take off. The dew was caught in bright drops on them, and as the new light swelled larger and more golden, they shone and glittered along every wet length of them so that everything was soft silver and gold; it was a field of light. Henry looked, quite passively, only looked; then he thought how many more times he was likely to see the sun come up and was possessed by such a happiness that he trembled for it. He turned and came back through the orchard, walking light and free, with a sense that the garden opened out from him on all sides into light; he had been possessed by this peace for so long now, that he thought of this as his condition, and rested on it.

He settled then at his desk, with his coffee, in the quiet house. He went though notebooks, settling his mind: he had never been able to cure himself of indiscriminate jottings, but it had taken him much longer to learn to read what he had jotted and he now made a point of it. He had meant from time to time to become organized, had bought filing cabinets and card indexes, but it was no good. The jottings proliferated outside the system, and the effort of organization seemed to have been expended once for all, on the structure of the work, which he had, it seemed, to carry in his head.

At that time he was revising, which he liked; he was a man who had to rewrite, seven or eight times, everything he wrote, and was happiest with the later versions, where he could see, and take pleasure in sharpening and improving, a shape. The earlier versions were too much like creating his own basic clay or metal to work with, and he wrote them with a sort of hatred. It seemed always too much, at that stage; a too heavy, brightly coloured mass which he could never hammer out thinly enough and he would struggle with this intractable first stuff for months, finding that what he wrote excluded what he had meant to write, and distorted what he would write next, and feeling all the time a nearly irresistible desire to get up, go away, postpone or abandon the whole business, so that every word was ground out only because he promised himself it was the last for that time . . . and yet, when he came to the end, he found he had been powerless to go and saw himself like Samson, at once tearing up pillars and at the same time, for a dizzily prolonged moment, putting out all his power to hold on his own shoulders the swaying structure which would, if it fell, engulf him with it. There was a time when he had almost had to let go, but not now – the moment grew longer and longer, the balance endured, and he was able to ignore, most of the time, his fear of failure of power.

So he revised, with the secret smile Anna so disliked, for some hours, and was pleased with what he did. When Caroline came in with his breakfast and the second letter, lying innocently beside his plate, he was too preoccupied to notice it, and only looked up at Caroline from a long distance, snorted and waved her to put the tray on his desk beside him. Caroline stood for some moments, out of curiosity, having recognized the handwriting, but Henry made no move to open the letter.

It was some time later that Henry reached out for his coffee and brushed against the letter. He opened it absentmindedly, and was then reminded by the thick deckled paper and the agitated sprawling writing of the first letter, which had come two days ago and which, he now saw guiltily, he had contrived to forget. He looked at the beginning of this one – 'Dearest Henry, *Please* write to me, *please* come, *please* understand – ' and put it down again. The letter brought a breath of sick air into his morning; he was reluctant to touch it. He thought for a moment and then spent some time searching through drawers and papers for the other letter, beginning in unlikely places and finding it at last in his letter rack. His coffee was cold. He could not bring himself to reread the first letter either, and put it therefore on top of the second, pressing the thick folds of both together with his green paperweight, keeping them down, burying them. For some time he stared out of his window, cupping his beard in one hand. Then he went through into the kitchen, where Caroline was rolling out pastry on a cool, rose-veined marble slab.

She was singing to herself, withdrawn. When alone she had a private life in which she sang Mozart at Glyndebourne; each morning, over the cooking or the dishes, she would re-enact her triumph, from the arrival of the elegant audience, to whose dresses she added a new rose, a new shawl, every day, to the final aria and rapt silence which followed it. She was not too pleased to be called back from her stage, and would not be interrupted in mid phrase. She motioned to Henry to be silent, and sang calmly and tunefully to the end of her passage, whilst he paced the kitchen from door to door, and then she made him a little inclination of the head, as though he should applaud, and said, 'Well, what is it?'

'I don't know. That is, I don't know if I ought to tell you.'

'Well?'

'Would you say I was kind?'

'Kind?' said Caroline. 'I wouldn't say you were cruel.' Henry looked at her sharply. 'Only not cruel? You mean, too lazy to do much harm, except perhaps by default. So, not a support to the weak, a shoulder to lean on, a very present help in trouble, the man to whom complete strangers offer their worries in trains – "Excuse me, sir, you'll understand, you've got a kind face"? – That's what they do say, but should they?'

'I wouldn't,' said Caroline with some firmness.

'Maybe it's only the size of my shoulders. Or the big soft woolly beard – '

172

'Like God the Father,' Caroline said, dabbing lard in little pearly knobs onto her creamy round of paste, turning this on the soft pink of the marble.

'But I'm not.'

'Oh no.'

'Then, why?'

'People think,' Caroline said carefully, 'that because you spend your time writing about people with insight or whatever the word is, that perhaps you care about them, or understand them – '

'But I don't?'

'Oh no,' said Caroline, looking up at him. 'It isn't at all the same, is it? It's a bit silly of them to think it is – I mean, they've only got to read your books to see that you're not even that kind of writer – you like crises, and things that blow up and moments of truth – you don't like *people*. You're never kind to your characters, or sympathize with them, or excuse them, and make them human.' She began to divide her paste, running over it with a fluted cutting wheel on a little handle, not looking up. She had, she thought, a shrewd idea of what was in the letter, but was reluctant to mention it until he did. She said carefully, 'If anyone is asking you to do anything you don't want to, you are not to. You haven't time, it isn't fair to ask you. People,' she went on, probing, 'won't grow up and accept life as it is. They can't cope with the fact that marriage can be boring, that it isn't all love and companionship, it can't be, not if a man is worth anything. They get bored, they say they aren't fulfilled and shout for help. They should learn to sacrifice themselves. Where would you be, for instance, if I was always trying to talk to you, or "fulfilling myself" instead of coping with the bank and the grocer and the telephone? I don't suppose I find these any more fulfilling than anyone else might. But they have to be dealt with.'

'Yes,' said Henry vaguely, irritated by this concept of sacrifice which had been obtruded before; he believed that it was not enough to live a life for someone else, and he didn't want to take Caroline's; he was nevertheless uncomfortably aware that he had accepted, so far, the sacrifice as it had been offered. He would not be answerable, he thought, for the burial of her talent, and was about to tell her so, distracted for a moment from his problem, until he saw that she was waiting for and looking beyond some such uncomprehending male reaction. He turned uneasily, not having found whatever reassurance he might have been looking for, and went back, finally, to read the second letter.

It was shorter than the first, but they were both very long. It was difficult for some time to see what they were about, or what he was asked to do. It was to be gathered that Oliver had left, or was about to leave Margaret, and that she was begging Henry to come to her, or to Oliver, and stop him. The anguish was apparent, the writing was driven and there was little punctuation. The letter assumed, as far as he could make out, that some promise of a terrible and intimate nature had passed between Margaret and himself on the cliff-top, during the picnic two summers ago. From various references to his own 'strong hands' and 'gentleness', he made out that Margaret believed that the incident had amounted to a love scene of some kind. It was not only this, however; the appeal was also to his eminence. 'You're the only human being he has any respect for,' recurred several times, and 'you're so much wiser and more understanding than the rest of us, you know what to do'. Interspersed with this were apparently pointless accounts of household tasks, carried out in solitude. 'Today I filled a bucket and washed the lavatory with a brush and put some Harpic in and then I emptied the bucket and polished the table, Oliver had split some bacon fat when he was last home, not that he ever stays long now, I forgot to buy any butter and have to eat margarine, not that Oliver would notice, he doesn't care what he eats at all, but one feels one is slipping, one ought to keep up, Henry, I want my life I want my life, I have a right to a life, if you don't come and tell me what to do I shall put an end to myself, I *mean that*, you might think I wouldn't because I'm scared of pain, well I am, but I've got some pills that just put you to sleep and kill you, Amytal, they're called, I saw a case in the newspapers, it isn't that I *want* to die, Henry, really I want a life, I want my life, I always used to think I had a life to live, but I've gone wrong and if you can't put me right no one can. I may as well die just for sheer tiredness, I *mean that*, I love

174

him so much but what good is love if it just turns back on you, I'm getting old, Henry, there are all sorts of things I shall never have again and I want my life before I'm dead, I want something to matter, today the milkman only left two pints and I'd expressly asked for three, I thought I could make a caramel creme for Oliver if by any chance he came back tonight but he hasn't and if you don't come I shall kill myself, when he does come anyway, he . . .' Here followed a detailed account of sexual sadistic practices attributed to Oliver.

Henry was alarmed. He did not know what to make of these references. Margaret was obviously confused in her mind about his behaviour and intentions. On the other hand, the descriptions were embarrassingly full and graphic. He did not know how well she could invent such things if she had not experienced them. Nor did he know how seriously to take the mention of suicide. That too was obviously thought out and had been brooded over; it was more than just a vague threat. Henry turned the pages of the letters over again and thought that they and Caroline's resignation came to a horrid whole in his mind. He did not like even this tentative identification of himself with Oliver, but it persisted and would not be shaken. He saw other people suddenly, life after life, occupied with margarine and the milkman, pastry and the telephone, elevating these from nothing into Christian sacrifice or causes for suicide and symbols of the failure of love, and he was ashamed and afraid. Caroline's attempt to dissuade him from ministering to what she had brought herself to consider Margaret's weakness gave him finally the impetus in the other direction. He must try and help, however unqualified. He would find it easier to work if he could dispose of these appeals from those who did not see what he saw. He hoped it was not only that.

He pulled the typewriter towards him, rolled in a sheet of paper, tapped out the address, the date, and Dear Margaret, rolled it out again and tore it up. Ink was after all friendlier. He wrote out a few painful sentences in a beautiful, character-less italic hand, saying that he did not know that there was anything he could do for her, but that he would come, if she wanted him to. He folded this letter without re-reading it, addressed the envelope and went back to Caroline.

'I'm walking down to the post. Have you anything?'

'Letters to the children, on my desk. You might write to Jeremy, Henry, he asks you to particularly.'

'He sells my signature to boys, that's why. I don't know where he gets this opportunism from. I did write to Anna two or three weeks ago, but she never answers.'

'I hope you've been sensible, Henry.'

'I think so,' said Henry evasively. 'One has to be charitable.' He went to her and said with difficulty, 'Caroline, I hope I haven't given you too bad a time.'

'I wouldn't want things any different.'

'But perhaps you ought to? I mean, I don't think it's right to live someone else's life – '

Caroline looked at him, puzzled, and then said with finality, 'What else could I have done?' She allowed Henry to embrace her, laughed with genuine contentment, and finished, 'Now don't you worry, you're no good at it, and it won't last.' She kissed him on the ear, and gave him a little push, out of the house. 'I'm as happy as most people, and you're happier, and had better stick to it. Now hurry, or you'll not get enough done before your lunch.'

Henry, without quite knowing why, was partially consoled.

NINE

MARGARET'S DAYS WERE very long. Oliver spent more of each week in Cambridge and less at home, staying perhaps one or two nights and leaving early like a businessman with umbrella and suitcase, in an aroma of toothpaste and shaving soap. Margaret would pursue him around the breakfast table on these occasions, asking him why he was leaving, what had gone wrong, begging him at least to look her in the face. Last time he had shouted, 'This is intolerable, that I should have to eat with you hanging over me, waiting to see whether I can

176

look you in the face. If you must know, I can't. And I don't want to.' He had gone out, slamming the door tidily, to his early train.

The days seemed longer as she spent less time on house and food, feeling that it was worthless when Oliver treated what he had done with love as an accusation levelled at him. Before she was married she had done these things as a training towards marriage, a labour of love on account. And she had dressed always for someone, the man of the moment, the husband of the future, and had never bought a dress or changed a hairstyle without calculating its effect on some other eyes, real or ideal. And now, with Oliver absent, in whom all these aspirations had finally settled and centred, she could not do as some other purer housewife and woman, such as Caroline might have done, take refuge in the thing itself. The carpet slippers before the fire, her own eyes and nose and mouth and skin, disappeared like the tree in the quad without the male eye on them, and Margaret was lost.

She did not go back to work because she had had no particular work, only stop-gap jobs, and could not summon up the energy to make the contacts which would open up these jobs again. Besides, she was not ready to admit in public that she was not fully occupied at home. She did not invite her friends round either. Most of them had been so annoyed by Oliver's manner in the early days that they would not visit without pressing invitations now. She had felt, rightly, that Oliver didn't want to see them, and had not, at the time, minded very much. So that now she would have been ashamed to call them back, and spent more and more of her days alone.

She got up later every morning, now; eleven, half past eleven, noon, and went to bed early to avoid the evening. She had learned to use sleep as a drug, to induce a torpor which calmed and slowed her. When she woke early with the sun, she told herself that she was very tired, and that if she got up there was nothing to do. Then she huddled under the blankets again, coaxing herself into a leaden sleep from which she woke some hours later, so hot and heavy and dizzy that her body ached and would not be turned, her eyes stung and would not be focused, and her mouth tasted of dry, furry mould. This sleep cost her so much effort that she could hardly drag herself about the house and always took a long rest in the afternoon, lying on the bed in her petticoat with the curtains drawn, to recover.

She ate little, and irregularly. She had come to rely more and more heavily on Bloody Marys. In the beginning there had been tomato juice with a dash of vodka, good for the figure, giving one a bit of a kick in the early morning. Now she had increased the number of drinks and the proportion of vodka; draining board and kitchen table were piled with empty tomato juice tins and dirty glasses. These she had always, so far, from a mixture of motives, managed to clear up every time she knew Oliver was coming home. But she was growing less enthusiastic and less ashamed.

That morning, she slapped into the kitchen barefoot in her housecoat, poured herself a Bloody Mary, drew back the curtains far enough to see that it was raining, drank down the first drink, poured herself a second, and slapped back into the living room to light a cigarette. It was nearly noon and felt like Sunday. Every day felt like Sunday now. Margaret smoked rapidly, standing uncertainly in the middle of the room, and wondered what to do. The curtains here, long, sunny yellow curtains with brave white daisies spread across them, were still drawn. They boxed in the room like a yellow tent and gave an illusion of warmth to the light. Margaret did not open them.

She lit the gas fire full blast, and turned on the wireless, which offered only a programme of French for schoolchildren. She put on a record of Ravel's *Bolero*, turned it up as loudly as possible, and decided to have a bath. She decided to have a bath most mornings now. It filled in the gap between getting up and the afternoon rest very nicely. But she could never decide easily, and always spent time wondering whether she could not find something better to do. Whilst she ran the bath she poured herself another Bloody Mary, and fetched the cigarettes and an ashtray which she balanced on a stool beside the bath. Then she turned the Ravel back to the beginning and the bath was ready.

When she slipped off her nightdress and housecoat and stepped down into the warm water she was immediately comforted. She sat for a moment, smoking with damp fingers, chewing on

178

shreds of wet tobacco, and ran the hot tap until the water slid up her body, warmly, round her breasts and into her armpits, so that she was almost floating. Then she took another mouthful of the drink and washed herself slowly and thoroughly. Although she had lost interest in her public face she had in recompense intense bouts of attention to personal cleanliness. She rubbed soap creamily all over her hands and body, brushed her face till it stung with a little round nylon brush, scrubbed her back with a long one, scraped her soft feet with a pumice stone and spent some time poking into every crevice, behind every nail, toe and finger with an orange stick. Then she shaved the hardly visible down carefully from under her arms and along her legs. When she got out she would spend time brushing her teeth, and even more brushing her hair, stroke after stroke for half an hour until it shone and crackled. Her body had become a thing to her to be cared for and admired. It was the residue, what was left. When she had finished the ritual of cleaning she lay back, resting her chin on the water, staring at her feet which protruded, side by side, pointed and gleaming with water between the bright taps. She watched where the water clung to the circles of her ankles like a skin peeling and thought, all the bits, the toes, and the solid bits one can see, and the vague bits underneath, all these bits are me. It is almost as though one might fall apart without the bath, as though all these lumps and circles might just float away from each other and not belong to one any more.

She lay suspended, studying herself, until her body began to chill at the water line. It was now afternoon. To judge from the small light that came through the frosted window and the pink frilled nylon curtain, it might have been any time. Margaret had no idea what time it was. She emerged reluctantly, shivering slightly, and rubbed herself until she blushed in patches all along her flanks and midriff. There were the toothbrushing and the hairbrushing to come, but she was already beginning to be afraid of deciding what to do after that.

'You really ought to get out,' she told herself aloud, peering down her back over one shoulder, patting the creases under her buttocks with her towel and dusting powder firmly over all the pink twisted expanse she could see. 'You really ought to get

179

out somewhere and do something. But I couldn't tell you what or where?'

And today, anyway, she thought, slipping her tingling body back into her housecoat, pink quilted and stained with tomato juice, today I am far too tired. I'll rest today, she told herself, as she told herself every day.

Teeth brushed, hair brushed, she was back in the curtained living room, with another Bloody Mary, some Twiglets and the Ravel again. Brushing might have been good for the hair's roots. It did not improve its appearance. It had been too often washed lately and rarely pinned up. It stood out round her shoulders, prickling with electricity, like the splayed ends of a large pale broom.

'What shall I do?' she asked herself, and lit another cigarette. 'I'll just sit and look at *Vogue*,' she answered herself, as she always answered herself, 'while I think.' She had taken to *Vogue* when the assurances and comfort of the central heating advertisements and the love stories of the lesser magazines had become intolerable mockery. *Vogue* responded to something in her present mood. It was full of things; it focused attention entirely on a delectable button, a daring sash; these things had an ingrown and sterile emphasis of their own. The masculine eye in the *Vogue* pictures lacked the cosiness of the husband or boyfriend with sweater and pipe in *Woman's Own*, who sniffed the Oxo or the new Paris scent offer with appreciation and humour.

The men in *Vogue* had enormous, remote eyes, and sneering mouths like the women, they fingered silks and held hats, focused on the things. There was a sort of jungle retreat for Margaret behind all the sophistication and glitter; something which called to her solitude in a house full of things.

Margaret opened the *Vogue* at the Beauty Guide. It was simple enough, three magnified pictures, an eye, seven inches long, a mouth, wide open, twenty-seven inches round, and a fingernail, five inches long. Each occupied a full page, bright and bold in a magnified background of salmon pale flesh. Most days Margaret might have flicked through the pages with an approving nod but today for some reason these pictures arrested her. Seen first and quickly, they had all the lit excitement of one's own mouth or eye, suddenly springing to life with paint in the mirror. They had the mystery, the exhilaration as Henry had seen it in the flower-films, of colours brighter than they are usually seen, the jewelled glitter of the mediaeval heaven. But Margaret looked too long, as one will sometimes look at a perfectly ordinary word until its spelling seems insane, and saw them too much, in too much detail. The eye was worst as it had as first been most satisfactory. The mouth and nail were less compelling and nastier. The mouth, a swollen pink round, with every crack of the skin magnified and glittering, seemed to her like what one of those almost animal fly-eating plants must be, moist and fleshy with a chocolate-coloured hole in the middle and three square wet teeth hanging below the upper lip. The fingernail, oval, rested on the fleshy pad on the finger and protruded over it. They had photographed the varnish being applied and the thick black hairs of the brush lay stickily on the fat pink slug, a molten lump settling slowly onto the nail, like a sweet half sucked.

The eye seemed at first more complex, more live. It lay, blue-grey, with gold spattered in the centre of the iris, between three rows of hairs curving right across the page. The brow was a half moon of scattered criss-cross black strokes like a child's scribbling, petering out. The lashes, the upper row obviously implemented by a false strip, were two fences of curled spikes. Again, the brush had been photographed in the act of applying the glitter, and it lay at an angle across the eyelid, pointed like a knife, on a half circle of bronze streaked and dotted with white. The pores shone with sweat. Margaret thought at first that this eye – a mild eye, a thoughtless eye – perturbed her because it stared emptily at her, and then she saw that she was afraid because it was dead. Its white, ever so slightly veined, was like the dead flesh of a hard egg, and the iris so beautifully lined and shaded had two dots of white in it where the light caught the eyeball, which seemed at first to shine as they should with light, and then as she looked at them, merely two dead, empty patches of paper. The defining edges insisted – the rim of the eye, the rim of the nail, the blob of raw flesh in the inner eye corner. The blacks were more cutting, the area of background flesh vaster and less connected. The mouth was

181

dead vegetable, the eye a dead hairy animal, the nail dead worm. Margaret experienced again, more violently, the sensation she had brushed in the bath, that she was falling apart, that bits of her were separate and falling irretrievably away. Nothing held, everything was a jumble of bright dead things. She was shaken, and began to sob and weep wildly, not, as she wept often in the afternoons, for the sake of almost comfortably having a good cry, but with real terror and an increasing lack of control.

Henry came in carefully, like a burglar, having rung the bell and had no answer. He stooped under door after door tracing the sobbing, found the right room and stood on the threshold.

'Margaret?' he said. Margaret looked up frantically – his voice was huge in the small room – took in the size of him, swamping the doorway, and began to scream with shock.

'Margaret?' he said again, timidly.

The screaming reached a crescendo, and Margaret gasped for lack of breath. He saw he must move, however reluctant, and went across the room to take her by the shoulders and shake her.

'Stop it,' he said. 'Stop it, do you hear?' Margaret screamed again, and choked, and Henry held her head still and slapped her sharply across a cheek, with the flat of his hand. Margaret stopped screaming, abruptly, and slumped against him. He held her uncomfortably, trying to push her back into the chair, with all her determined weight against him. Her naked legs protruded between his and her housecoat was open in places, showing rolls and slivers of flesh. Across the cheek he had hit, the pattern of his fingers rose darkly.

'Now,' he said. 'What is it?'

'I knew you'd come. I knew you would.'

'I'm sorry if I startled you. Tell me what's wrong.'

At this Margaret' body convulsed again, and her face puckered. She pushed the magazine towards him. 'I got frightened. Of this picture.' Henry took it and studied it. 'I've been too much by myself,' Margaret volunteered, in a normal voice. Henry closed the magazine and put it down on the table. 'It's silly to get frightened of a picture,' she finished.

'Not necessarily. There's something powerful about bright out of scale magnifications. I was thinking so the other day. We

182

see so little, ordinarily. Why has not a man a microscopic eye? For this plain reason, man is not a fly. But there are nevertheless ways and means of dying of a rose in aromatic pain, and now and then we come across them. I suppose you find the human body intolerable, presented like that? That's all right, it's understandable.' He went on, talking at random, and Margaret, lost in admiration, listened to a sentence and a half, and then gave up, and only thought how beautiful his voice was, how warm, how encouraging, like all those cheering broadcasts in the war.

Henry finished suddenly, 'Now let's have some light . . .' He drew the curtains and pushed open the window, letting in the cold, and a spatter of fine rain, and enough grey London light to make it possible for him to switch off the lamp at Margaret's side. He switched off the record player, took off his overcoat and dropped it on the sofa. 'That's better,' he said. He had been finding the smell of stale food and stagnant, overheated air unbearable. 'Now, why did you want me to come?'

Margaret, hunched in her chair, looked at him desperately with red and puffy eyes, and began to weep again.

Henry began to suspect that he had been summoned only to take her in his arms and soothe her. He felt a physical revulsion for her, as for most women, and felt he could deal better from the middle of the room. He stayed there, coughed, and repeated helplessly, 'Why did you want me to come?'

Margaret found it almost impossible to communicate anything to any man if there was no physical contact – confessions and appeals should be murmured against a shoulder, not spoken into space, to be judged coldly. She wept more wildly and Henry was in the end compelled to abandon his position, and approach. He knelt in front of her, clumsily, and took her face, all wet and slippery, in his hands. 'Now stop, please stop, don't cry like that. You're doing yourself no good.' He could not embrace her, and any moment now she would slop over into his arms entirely. Tears ran warm and damp down his fingers. 'If you can pull yourself together, we could go out for a drink – and dinner – and we could talk more calmly.'

Margaret gulped. 'I ought to have asked you. There's a drink in the kitchen. Would you like one?'

'No thank you. It would do you good to go out.'

'Yes,' said Margaret obediently. Her manner changed and became embarrassingly confidential. 'I feel all right now you've come. Just having you here makes everything more possible. I mean, just watching you looking at that picture made me see it could be interesting, and not nasty. The room seems bigger with you in it.'

'I opened the curtain . . .'

'You don't miss out on the big things, I like just to watch you thinking, things are important when you are thinking about them. I'm so frightened of being unimportant. I'm glad you're here.' She showed signs of coming closer again. Henry withdrew circumspectly and said, as he would have done to a child, 'Now go and get changed, and we'll go out.'

Margaret jumped up, pressed a kiss somewhere into his beard, and went out to change. She took some time over this. Henry wandered around her room getting his bearings, taking possession. It was very modern and restless.

The walls were all different colours, and the furniture had spiky metal legs. There was a little too much furniture – some of it had been Oliver's and had been moved in when they married. There were a great many books, shut away in bookcases behind glass. Margaret collected glass animals; blue horses and red dragons and white swans were scattered over all the available surfaces amongst dirty plates, tomato stained glasses, and overflowing ashtrays. There was a smell of over-ripe cheese, and bad pears. Henry turned back a cushion and found more dirty plates, and a box with a small layer of molten Camembert at the bottom of it; he wrinkled his face in disgust, and put back the cushion. There was a print of a Matisse still life over the hearth, and a row of scatter cushions on the cream sofa echoed its flat washes of colour, scarlet, and citron and peacock. The colours fought for attention, there were equally small amounts of all of them, nothing was particularly powerful or particularly subtle.

Henry disliked it all, instinctively, but occupied himself busily in learning it off. He was interested in Margaret's despair, its female intensity was a new idea to him, he thought he could use it and might write about it, some day. He dealt in facts, as a writer, not in talk; he would have been incapable of guessing at the tenor of Margaret's interior monologue, but he was intensely aware of her state, her final exhaustion. The colours of her room would be to him when he had remembered them like the little glass buoys fishermen float over lobster pots, surface signals from underneath which he could draw up and expose, when he chose, the whole beast in its cage, dark and mottled and gleaming, strangely shaped and struggling.

When he had gathered the room into his mind in some pattern, it ceased to trouble him. Even the smell receded into an interesting stage effect. He felt he had the place and the feeling in his power, now. He could hold it up in contrast to something else – he was not quite sure what, yet – and burst open the bright prison as he had seen it done on the stage, in a production of Ionesco's *Amédée*, where the box walls had risen, the furniture had trundled off, leaving the stage filled with nothing but a particularly warm and satisfying aquamarine light. He became quite excited, he would put it against some significant life, and break it down, that was what he would do. Some other woman, it must be, in a room full of air. . . .

The prisoner, at that point, returned into the prison. He was conscious, immediately and shamefully, that his plan had done nothing for her, that he had disposed of the prison for himself and left her precisely where she was. And then his knowledge was overlaid by the further certainty that what his art's arranging could not do for her, his presence did. She was freed, she was washed over with calm just to have him there, disposing of her predicament in his mind. She clung and clawed at his state of mind to keep from drowning. And as she looked up at him with complete trust, presenting herself for his approval, he felt that to take her trust was to be held under water himself, brought back again, partially at least, to a real presence in the prison. He shook himself, uneasily. He did not know how to behave.

It was apparent that he was expected to take her out to a very special drink and dinner. She had put on a bronze silk dress and tall, narrow bronze kid shoes, and wore a long rope of amber beads which bounced off her stomach. She had painted her face with great care; it was docile and inexpressive under

185

the thick covering she had put over her red eyes and burning cheek.

'You look very nice,' he said.

'Thank you. I don't get out much now, and I do like to.'

'I'm not really dressed for much myself,' Henry pointed out, barely disguising his crossness. He disliked large meals. They slowed him. Margaret's mouth trembled; she said, 'Oh dear, I hope I've not done anything wrong . . .' and gazed at him hopefully. It was obvious that she wanted to be seen with him. Caught between the fear of eating too much and the fear of Margaret's tears, Henry capitulated. He rang for a taxi, and they drove for some time aimlessly about London until it was time for an early meal. Margaret leaned her head heavily and passively on his shoulder in the taxi, and did not seem to want to speak.

He took her to a restaurant which was informally smart enough for neither his tweeds nor Margaret's dress to appear out of place, and which was well enough used by theatrical and literary persons to satisfy Margaret's sense of importance. He struggled with the menu to find something he could eat comfortably without impeding his next morning's work, and which would nevertheless not seem to Margaret to grudge the occasion. He ordered a bottle of wine and remembered that as an undergraduate he had dreamed of literary fame to be rewarded by dinners in such a restaurant, with such a beautiful woman. He smiled to himself, for here he was, neither bored nor blasé, nor disillusioned he hoped, but merely concerned exclusively with the connection between his stomach and his working routine.

Margaret seemed happy, even exalted. She clutched his arm ostentatiously when they came into the room, and peered around with a wide smile to remark how people noticed him and pointed him out to each other. She talked a great deal, leaning over and patting Henry's hand from time to time as she did so, throwing herself back in her chair when he spoke, and staring at him, worshipping, obviously not hearing a word he said. Her talk was almost all about Oliver and details of Oliver's personal habits which even Oliver would hardly have found interesting. The colour of a lampshade on the next table

186

reminded her of a silk tie Oliver had nearly bought some time ago in Bath and had decided against. Oliver did not like shellfish, they brought him out in great lumps in awkward places; once he had had to teach standing up for a week. When Henry spoke of something else, Margaret immediately followed his remark with Oliver's opinion, or probable opinion, of what he had said. Oliver thought the train services were very bad. Oliver thought that the rate of pay for university lecturers was scandalous. Was that man over there the one who had written the play about the T.B. Sanatorium? Oliver didn't think it was a good play; he didn't think death was either funny or dull; did Henry? She had a nervous trick of begging him earnestly to confirm views and information about which he knew nothing. 'Oliver's mother tried to stop him being educated, didn't she, Henry?' 'He can't work in the library all the time he's in Cambridge, can he, Henry?'

It was only over the coffee that she came in a roundabout way, to the request she had summoned him to hear. Would he, Henry, go to Cambridge and find out whether Oliver meant to come back? Would he find out what Oliver thought, why Oliver could no longer stay with her, or speak to her? Oliver would listen to Henry; Henry was the only person Oliver would listen to. She thought that Oliver was perfectly capable of carrying on as they were forever, but she was not. She meant what she had said; she thought of killing herself.

'Sometimes I think Oliver thinks you can't expect marriage to be any different from this. He thinks I'll settle to it. Well I won't, but I can't bring it home to him. You must, Henry, for me, you must . . .' She said loudly, so that several people turned to stare at her, 'Life ought to be better than this.' Henry believed her, and was for a moment completely involved in wanting to make it better for her. '*You're* all right,' she said. 'Please go and see Oliver for me.'

Henry promised, and immediately regretted it. He ascertained that Oliver had gone away over a week ago, leaving this time no indication of when he might return. He promised to go to Cambridge the next day – he had been more alarmed by Margaret than she seemed now to be herself, and felt strongly, once he had brought himself round to anything as unusual as taking steps about anything, that someone should bring home to Oliver his wife's precarious mental state, if nothing else. Besides, he had rarely been asked to do anything for anyone, and did not know how to refuse. Caroline usually did the refusing for him, and he had been so perturbed by the combination of her frustration and Margaret's that he felt, for a moment, that he had no right to let her do it any more. He adjusted his mind to the thought of seeing Oliver, which purely on his own account he did not want to do, and asked Margaret what she would like to do next.

She chose the cinema, 'It's so much more soothing than the theatre, isn't it, Henry?' They went to the last performance of an American musical, a form which Henry intensely disliked. He sat, bolt upright, conscious as he always was in places of entertainment that people were peering round his shoulders and over his hair, and were wondering audibly how anyone could be so large. He thought, as hero and heroine disappeared together under an arch of golden Technicolor clouds in a roar of celestial voices, that it could be argued that this was a debased version of his own method, gaudy, simple, larger than life and insistent, and this was perhaps why he disliked it. Margaret sat and wept softly, because it was comfortable to weep in cinemas; she slid her hand onto his knee, so that after a moment like a guilty schoolboy with a forward girl friend, he timidly covered it with his own. This completed his embarrassment; he sat miserably waiting for the end of the film, until it occurred to him that here at least he was under no obligation not to think of his work, and he began, furtively, to organize a sentence.

Afterwards, Margaret saw him off on the night train. It was not raining heavily, and steam and water were beaten back under the canopy and onto the edges of the platforms, rolling in tongues around barrows and passengers' legs, gritty with dirt. Henry and Margaret walked into this fog as they went down towards the front of the train; his beard and the hairy nap of his greatcoat seemed to merge with it; he lost substance. Henry coughed heavily. They were early for the train; he would have liked to get in and have it over with, but that was unthinkable. Margaret must have her goodbye.

She wore an evening coat she had had for years, made of

pale gold corded silk, and had unfurled her umbrella, also pale gold, before they came into the entrance hall, and had not put it down. She stood now, under this gold canopy which transmuted the anaemic station light so that her skin and coat were doubly gold, and the gloss glittered on her dress and shoes; she was an island of brightness in the dirt and hurry. She still had her hopeful look, as though Henry had only to decide to do so to change her life for her with a word or a gesture.

'I like the umbrella,' Henry said, for something to say. 'It was a birthday present from Oliver,' Margaret said evasively. Henry was aware that she was lying. He did not know why and decided that Oliver must have forgotten the birthday and the poor creature must have bought the umbrella herself from him. In fact it was not so bad: Oliver had simply given her money and told her to get herself something nice. The idea that her life must be a string of such lies exasperated him. It was a waste of consciousness, a waste of the possibilities of movement, to spend a whole human energy on such a fabrication. It was doubtless a waste of Oliver too. The man must have more in him than was necessary just to torment and evade this kind of love. He said hurriedly, and more urgently than he had said anything all evening, 'Look, why don't you just give up? Just let him go? Go away and do something else entirely? Something worthwhile. Start again.'

Margaret started violently, and her teeth began to chatter ridiculously. The umbrella above her wavered and trembled like a palm tree. She said at last, 'Do you – Henry – do you really think it's that bad? It isn't that bad, is it, Henry?'

He had not known she was still so rooted in spite of the way she had talked of Oliver all evening. He had not realized how singly she expected him to come back from seeing Oliver with a tale of nothing but a perfectly simple misunderstanding easy to clear up. Anything else was beyond what she had power to think possible. She said, 'It isn't really that bad, Henry,' pleading.

He persisted, 'Have you ever thought of doing anything else?'

'What would I do? There isn't anything I want to do. Is there, Henry? I don't want anything else.'

'You could remarry.'

'No . . .' she said, coming closer to him. 'No, no, that's not what you'd do yourself, is it? I don't want anything else. I want Oliver. I want . . .' Henry retreated, and thought he must undo the damage he had done before the train left. He said clumsily, 'I'm sorry. I only meant, think about it. I can't really say anything until I've seen Oliver.'

'No . . .' said Margaret on a sigh of relief. 'You're a good man. He'll take it, from you. It'll be all right.'

The announcer began to explain, patient, metallic, hurriedly, 'The train about to leave from Platform . . .'

'I must go.'

'Yes,' said Margaret. She scrambled into his arms, kissing his face, dropping the umbrella like an open flower over his shoulder.

'You're so good, so good, I rely on you. I'd have killed myself if you hadn't come.' She screwed at his coat collar with her free hand and said in a voice unrecognizably savage, 'I mean that, I mean that, I'd have killed myself.'

Henry murmured something reassuring, patted her shoulder, backed a few steps, and climbed with a rush into the train. He peered out of the window at her, pathetic in her bright clothes and pool of light, with the tongues of steam reaching out to choke and the dead light from the vault, grey like dishwater, dropping down to drown. He thought as the train moved out, and she waved her bright arm into the steam, that there was no necessity about her state; she might just as easily have married someone more equable, who would like her food, and admire her clothes, and have had children early, and her view of life would have held for her lifetime, very likely. He would not have liked to be, as perhaps for the time he was, in Oliver's place. Nevertheless anger with Oliver was stirring in him. Oliver had taken all this on. Oliver should be made to see what he had done. Or, if he had seen, to acknowledge responsibility, and undo it. This was a most unusual line of thought for Henry, but it held him for some miles.

Margaret waited and waved until the train disappeared. She thought she felt good; she had done the right thing, sending for Henry, he had made things all right again and would, having power over Oliver, fetch Oliver back and force him into the mould he should be in. But the doubt his last appeal had left with her could not be disposed of yet. He had said, why not give up? He had not meant it, he hadn't really thought things had come to that, he knew perfectly well that everything she was and had been would become a lie if she gave up now, he didn't want to reduce her to nothing.

But he had said it. Soon she would work out why, would silt over the pain in her mind like the grit at the centre of the pearl, would smooth it until it ceased to bother. She went uncertainly back along the platform, annoyed that her last memory of Henry should be adulterated in this way, and remembered the dirt in the flat, the unwashed glasses, the old cheese, the cigarette stubs. They were worse, seen from here in clean clothes, than they were when she was actually in amongst them. What warmth Henry had left with her wavered. She cast about for consolation, and found the imagined Oliver of their first few weeks together. She stopped and watched him, little and dark, stepping briskly across the station to meet her; she built him out of the shadow of the magazine kiosk, now closed, where it fell across the moving tea barrow; he emerged under the clock, now substantial, and kissed her face.

'You're late,' she said lovingly. 'I'm not, I couldn't be,' he retorted, and proved it to her. He said, 'You're always so beautiful. I'm glad I gave you that umbrella, even Henry Severell liked it, you see.'

'You have such good taste,' she told him, moving across the station, turning her head to chatter vivaciously to him over her shoulder. Several people turned to stare at her; she ignored them; she had long ago given up talking to Oliver only in her head; that was not real enough; she had told herself that people didn't really notice in the street, they were too occupied with themselves. It was therefore axiomatic that those who looked were looking at something other than her. 'I do love you, Oliver,' she said. 'When we get home, we'll go straight to bed, won't we, I've had a hard day. I'm tired. It was nice seeing Henry, but it's better now you've come.'

'I don't want to share you,' Oliver said. 'Even with him.' Margaret nodded approvingly. She said, 'He's a man I could have loved, if I hadn't had you, all the same,' hushed him

191

with a finger, managed to engage a taxi, and continued the conversation about how they would spend the night whilst she was driven through the wet streets. Sometimes the situation got out of control, and at night, in bed, Oliver tormented her. She became apprehensive now, as they neared the house, and, after paying the taxi, and climbing the dark stairs, she turned with the key in the lock and pleaded, 'Be nice to me, Oliver, tonight, won't you? Be nice . . .' 'I'll be nice,' he said, following her into the cold hall, looking over her shoulder into the dark bedroom. Faintly the smell of old food rose to meet them. 'Don't clean up,' he said, 'I don't mind, we'll do it tomorrow. Let's get to bed.' 'Promise you'll be nice,' she said, shivering as she dropped the bronze dress onto the floor, on top of a pile of others. 'Of course, I'll be nice,' he said. But it was early, yet.

TEN

THE GREY WEATHER continued, and Henry went to Cambridge. He came out of the station into a fine drizzle, and found a long queue waiting for the taxis, of undergraduates, debutantes and girl friends up for the weekend, brandishing umbrellas, clutching hat boxes, chattering. He felt a distaste for their youth and urgency and would not join them. He was afraid, too, that one of them might recognize him and try to talk to him. To take the bus was out of question. There was not really room for him inside one; he banged about, fell over people's feet, hit his head on the hanging bars, took up more than his share of a seat and became suffocated and unpopular. So he set off, hatless and without an umbrella, to walk through the grim and dirty part of Cambridge that leads from the station, thinking that this neutrally unpleasant weather and grime that could have been any English town were letting him easily into something he knew he was not going to like. He did not allow himself to think about Oliver Canning. The more he did that

192

the more distasteful the whole expedition, and more than just this expedition, seemed to him.

He was incapable of not striding, nevertheless. He came too quickly to Christ's and crossed the road into Petty Cury. Here unease took complete possession of him. He suspected that it attacked most of those who came back, whether three weeks, or, as he did, thirty-five years after going down.

Nostalgia was the response Cambridge seemed to evoke even from those who lived there, perhaps because their stay was so short that the end was in sight at the moment of beginning. But if his own unease could be called nostalgia, it was tainted. It was a constricting, sickening feeling. This was not the first time he had returned, but it was the first when he had been back alone. On other occasions there had been Caroline, who relied on him to behave as she saw him. Or, when once or twice he had come to give literary talks, there had been an admiring and talkative reception committee who waited for him to prophesy. Here was a place where he wondered whether he would not be better not to be alone.

He went, for no particular reason, except that he remembered it as a beaten track, up through King's, and down through Trinity, and out onto the Backs, where he sat on a damp seat facing Trinity Library and the wedding cake on the top of John's, and watched the rain frill the surface of the river and drop off the willows. It was heavier now. It was appropriate. He sat hunched up, looking at the water and avoiding the eyes of the passers-by, in case any of them might have been Oliver Canning.

He had been an insignificant undergraduate, large, timid, not apparently bright, and yet conscious, superbly, that he was capable of something enormous, and constantly tormenting himself over whether this consciousness was wishful thinking or not. People found him, as far as he knew, amiable enough, but he intensely disliked himself. His college was not fashionable, and he had never known the men it was considered desirable to know. But he wanted intensely to. He wanted to be remarkable for his wit and his waistcoats, to give parties with plovers' eggs and to go to bed with beautiful women and be known to have gone to bed with them.

He shifted himself on the seat, sweeping its covering of tiny drops into one bright swash, and was hot under his tweeds with distress over the women he had not embraced, the lordly young men who had never slapped him on the shoulder nor addressed him familiarly, the singing and dancing he had heard on the next staircase and to which he had not been invited. And what had he instead? he thought, in an access of adolescent misery. Reverence, a pedestal, like D. H. Lawrence. Well, Lawrence was dead and he had never known him. He might as well have been dead himself here. These young men might speak his name religiously, but they wouldn't slap him on the shoulder and ask him to come round and have a drink. That was something he had irrevocably not had.

They went past him in twos and threes, their hoods down over their faces, yellow, fawn, grey and blue. It was the depth of the duffle coat days, and these pacing figures with their heads turned down against the rain gave the illusion of a return to monasticism. He felt powerless; casting about for something to do which would save him both from his own uncomfortable memories and from what was worse, an attempt to come to grips with Oliver Canning, he suddenly remembered Anna, and was ashamed that he should have forgotten her. He supposed that she might know these young men, might even take part in whatever was the present fashionable substitute for plovers' egg lunches and champagne trains. He had really not the slightest idea how she lived, here; the thought of her substantially doing anything at all was difficult to entertain. He stood up, and set out towards her college.

Here he had the usual masculine difficulty with porters, directions and long red tiled corridors which seemed to lead to nowhere inhabited. In his day one had not visited here, except to attend a chaperoned tea party if one happened to be related to one of the young ladies, which he had not been. He had thought it was splendid for the women to be allowed to be there, and had paid no further attention to them. They had not been, in those days, the kind he would have wanted or been able to sleep with, and would not have made him remarkable had he been seen with them. Now, he went in for the first time with a group of hooded boys who hurried purposefully past him, sure where they were going, and disappeared into odd turnings and staircases. Henry stopped and bent to the porter's window, his shoulders bulging behind him.

'Excuse me. Miss Severell, Miss Anna Severell. How can I find her?' The porter gave him complex directions, to which Henry, as one does, once one has got as far as being directed, did not listen.

'Are you Miss Severell's father, Sir?'

'Yes,' said Henry, stiffening.

'One of the friendliest of our young ladies,' said the porter. Henry was sure he lied.

The corridors seemed interminable. Henry went too far, came back on himself, climbed several staircases and came down again, hearing shrill female voices behind closed doors and his own heavy masculine tread on tiles and lino and a hush in each room as he passed. At the end of a corridor he desperately opened a door and collided with a wild girl in a quilted dressing-gown, heavy breasts loose under it, towel and sponge bag over her arm, streaming wet hair over her shoulders and down her back. She smelt of steam and shampoo. She seemed quite unperturbed, even grinned at him between pink polished cheeks, but Henry, remembering the young ladies of his own day, backed wildly across the corridor, banged his spine on a doorknob, turned to read the name on the door and found that it was his daughter's. He knocked loudly. There was no immediate answer, but he could feel the silence in the room, weighed and inhabited. He knocked again. Anna opened the door a few inches with her hand against it inside, as though she was prepared to slam it again. She did not look as Henry had expected her to look. He could not have said what it was that he expected, but he had had some sense of a space to be filled by Anna, his daughter, and this suspicious stranger was not her.

'Oh,' she said. 'It's you.' She asked shrilly, nervously, 'What have you come for?'

'To see you. May I come in?'

Anna still held the door and stared at him, and for a moment he thought she was searching for courage to close it in his face. But she opened it wider, and stood aside for him, and let him in to the little, high-roofed box of a room, where he stood dripping rain on the carpet, stiff with shyness.

'Give me your coat. I'll put it in the bathroom.' She took it from him and put it on a hanger and carried it out, motioning him to sit down. He took the only armchair, a little, dumpy Victorian thing, round with a calico frill, which he dwarfed. He waited. Anna came back with a towel.

'Your hair's soaked. Shall I rub it for you?'

'Please.'

'I'll put the tea on first. I'm afraid I've only got one or two stale biscuits. I don't have many vistors.'

'I don't mind about tea.'

'Ah, but I want to make it for you. I like the idea of you being a visitor.'

She knelt in the hearth and turned on the gas ring. She was wearing a black woollen shirt and tight trousers; her spine stood out like a knife and her hips were sharp.

'You've got very thin, Anna.'

'I know. Don't tell Mummy, that's all.' She put on the kettle. 'Now,' she said. 'Your hair. Mummy'd have a fit if she saw you now, wouldn't she?'

She took the towel, stood behind him, and rubbed the wet mass of his hair vigorously between her hands until it stood up in peaks all over. Then she rubbed the back of his neck and the sides above the ears, around and around, until his head tingled. She said nothing as she worked on him, and Henry said nothing either, only looked at his knees and waited. When she had finished she smoothed his head, rested her hand for a moment on it, and went back to the kettle in the hearth.

She became busy with tea, sniffed the half pint bottle of milk to see if it was sour, wiped out the cups with a tea-towel, and prised open the biscuit tin.

All the light came from one of the twisted wrought-iron lamps peculiar to Cambridge women's colleges, which stood on a pile of books and trailed a thick flex across the floor and up to the ceiling. The light was very weak; the red glow of the fire on Anna's cheek and hair was stronger. Outside the rain spattered and rattled on the window, and the sky sagged, slate grey. It was one of those autumnal Cambridge afternoons on which he had, in his day, toasted innumerable crumpets on a coal fire and felt cosy.

Anna's room was not cosy. It seemed that it had not changed since she moved in; there were the haircord carpet, the tidy bed with its college bedspread, green with buff flowers on, curtains to match the bedspread, desk cupboard, coffin chest, book-case with a few library books. Nothing of Anna's. She means to leave no mark, he thought. Anna brought his tea, and knelt to display before him milk and sugar and spoon, plate and biscuits, with a submissive feminine gesture that made him stir with a sudden exasperation. He had been impinged upon and accused so much during the last few days by female preoccupations with the little things, the details of servitude. It was all wrong that Anna, already, should have begun to take up the same gestures. She bowed her head and shuffled back on her knees into the hearth corner where she sat, bent over, gripping her knees in her arms. He had no idea how to begin to speak to her. She, for her part, stared into the fire for some time and then obviously gathered herself together, and burst out abruptly, 'Now, let's have it. What have you come for, really. Who sent you?'

'No one sent me. Why should they?'

'Oh, I don't know. It just seems a bit unlikely.'

'I'm sorry,' he brought out painfully, 'I only wanted to see you, I seem to have come at a bad time.'

'How do you mean?'

'What's wrong with you, Anna? You are so uneasy.'

'Am I?' said Anna, turning away. 'I suppose I'm just surprised. I didn't expect you.' There was a silence. Henry turned his head to look out of the window, although there was nothing to see but the thickening sky. When he moved, Anna looked up at him cautiously, trying to assess his unexpected concern for her. When he brought his head down again, and met her eye, she said, forced to it, 'Are you sure no one sent you?'

'No, I told you not. I wish you'd – ' He broke off and examined her as though, she thought, he had never seen her before. Then he looked away, and there was another silence. What Anna's thoughts were, Henry did not know. His own were confused, and largely distasteful. He studied his daughter's brooding face, the dropped eyelids, the lips drawn together, secretively, and the tension in the clasped hands round her knees. A certainty grew in him that he was up against something now, to which the disturbance of the past few days had inexorably been leading him, whatever their appearances might have been. It hurt him, who had been so unresponsive to those other claims, that Anna should sit there, making no attempt to touch him, hiding herself. He moved angrily on the dumpy chair and Anna jerked herself uncurled.

'I'm sorry, I'm not paying attention. More tea?'

'No. I don't want any more tea. Leave the tea alone. What are you going to do with yourself, Anna?'

'What do you mean?'

'You know what I mean. What kind of a life do you mean to live? What are you going to make of yourself?'

'I haven't the slightest idea,' Anna said, with an attempt at lightness. 'I don't have to make up my mind yet, do I?'

'Please, don't try to evade me.'

Anna stood up, and walked away from him, over to the corner with the bed, so that he had to twist himself to see her. She said, 'Don't get all concerned about me. I can't cope. I honestly think one has to consider oneself responsible for one's own life, don't you, one has to think of it in terms of what one can do with oneself, or one will never get round to doing anything? It would make it a lot worse for me if I thought you were going to get worried about me. I should feel responsible for you too and that would be terrible. You've always been good, that way – left me alone, not nagged or lectured me, I've been grateful. So leave me alone now. Please.'

Henry, who had used much the same argument to himself over Caroline, that one was responsible for oneself, was now quite sure that this was perverse and wrong. He said, roughly and with love, 'You're my daughter. I do care what happens to you. So I mean to sort this out. Why are you unhappy? Is there something else you want to do?'

'No – ' Anna said suddenly, it seemed to him, accepting his concern. 'I don't want anything. I don't want anything at all. That's half the trouble. And of course I'm unhappy. I can't remember being anything else for as long as I can remember. I get used to it. I suppose most people are unhappy.'

'No – '

'Oh, not people like you, who have something important to do, that they can do, and get on with it. But most of us . . .'

'Don't,' said Henry, feeling that she was setting him apart again, refusing him the right to care, telling him that she was unhappy because it was accepted that he was not interested. 'Sit down. I want to talk to you.' He told her carefully, as he would have told the kind of friend he had not had, how he had been at her age, in Cambridge. He told her about the women and the poor degree he had ended with, and how he had been so nervous that he had shouted and spat in supervisions. He wondered whether she would feel that he was lecturing her, offering her himself as an example of someone who had made good, to be imitated. He was sure that this was not why he was telling her – he was telling her quite largely for his own sake, he liked watching her take in and understand what he said. He ended, 'What I mean is, I was awful, I was a silly great clumsy young man. And I was sure I could do something. Sure I could do something enormous. Bursting at the seams with it. But I couldn't start, I'd nothing to say and no idea how to say it. Only this energy, burning me up. Like putting cold hands in front of a fire in winter. Bone pains.'

Anna was silent. He said, 'Do I sound stuffy and preaching? I don't mean to.'

'That's all right,' said Anna, weighing something obviously in her mind. He had thought that to talk about himself might be a guarantee of good faith, of a willingness to step in deep here, a guarantee he needed himself as much she could. But once it was done he remembered all the times when other people's confidences had reduced entirely in him the desire to communicate anything in return. So often, communication was only possible to establish in one direction. Now, remembering his own father, and his own tolerant wish to protect him from himself, and his feelings for his son, he thought he had made a mistake with Anna, that she would have trusted him more if he had continued quiet and not attempted to be human. But he had wanted to tell her he was human. He felt they both ought to know.

Anna was bewildered so much by the wish she sensed in him to know her, or to be known, to establish some communication, that she forgot for the time the reasons she had had to be afraid of his coming. Perhaps if there had been more contact between them in the past she would have been more simply embarrassed than she now was; it would have been worse if there had been any form of parent–child contact to discard. As it was, she was simply ready to love him, and to tell him what only he would accept; she had been waiting long enough to do so, in one sense. So she said eagerly, falling over the words, as he turned to her, surprised and pleased, 'Oh yes, you know, that's how one feels – how I feel, too. Not only unhappy, not *necessarily*, unhappy, that's what makes it so bad. A lot of the time I feel as though I could live life tremendously – as though if I could find just the one *thing*, the event that would happen, all these little annoying bits of life would fall into place, and become important. Because I would be so sure I'd make them bright just by looking at them. I can see you know. I've watched you working, I've watched you just going about, I know *you* know. But I seem to get no nearer, and sometimes I think I'd better get down to something more obviously possible – my own limitations and the kitchen sink – or I'll have had worse than nothing.'

'It's a question simply of the best way of finding it,' said Henry, with a roar of triumph that lifted Anna's head so that for a moment they smiled steadily at each other. He said, 'You're all right, that's all right, everything's all right as long as that's what you feel. You can be as unhappy as you like, now, as long as you go on waiting and don't give in. Pay no attention to the kitchen sink. Why should you? You must never believe things can be no better. You must put yourself in the way of finding what you can do. That's all. Now how?'

'I don't know.'

'But you will know.' He hesitated. 'You're like me, you know. Whether you like it or not. You're my daughter.'

Anna studied him with a gentleness that was not his, but Caroline's. A sceptical, female gentleness. She saw that he had been carried away by a picture of her, having inherited his power, advancing further along his path, and she was touched by a faith in her which she had never hoped to see. But she had thought more about it than he had, and was more aware than he was of the difference there was between his power, and whatever she had inherited from him. She feared that she lacked his bodily strength, that she was not his size, that she could not be prodigal of power as he was, but must husband her resources or be easily exhausted, even when she had found out how to use them. This was partly because she was a woman; also because she was a woman she was constantly tempted as he would never have been, to give up, to rest on someone else's endeavour, to expend her energy 'usefully' at the kitchen sink. And this, she thought, made it harder to go on looking for ways to go forward, when one had to fight against the temptation – socially approved – to stay where one was. She thought, he doesn't really know, with a certain scorn. But the warmth of his hope for her was stronger. She said,

'Anything I've wanted to do has been what you do. I haven't had much chance to want anything else, perhaps. I wish I was a mathematician. But again, perhaps I am like you, perhaps I have inherited something? I am a bit cowardly about finding out. I do want to write a lot of the time; but I can't start, when you're there, doing things so well. How can I tell what I really want?'

Henry was silent.

'Perhaps I'm just too young to know.' Or perhaps, she thought, I tell myself I'm too young, to avoid having to decide.

Henry said, 'I think you should do something now. I think you can't wait any longer. If you want to start writing, you must write. What are you getting out of Cambridge?'

'Nothing,' said Anna too quickly.

'I thought not. I never thought you'd make a scholar of any kind.' Anna thought, you might have said so at the time, letting them force me through those exams, letting them torment me. But she kept quiet. Henry said, 'Ancient spells were supposed to lose their power if you put water between yourself and the place where the spell was cast, or the witch who cast it. If you want to give up here, I'm prepared to support you. Why don't you go away – from me, from people who know me, from all these books, the whole thing? I'll give you a sum of money and ask no questions – you could go to Mexico or somewhere, and

201

write something, or do whatever else you pleased. And don't say that a change of scene doesn't change the heart, or the problem, that's a facile defeatism, if it doesn't change things, it makes it possible for you to change them yourself. I should know. If I were you I'd take as little as possible and just move into the sun. But you must choose.'

Henry wanted very badly to discover a precise help he could offer to Anna; talk was not enough, he must do something for her, give her something to hold. Now, they both sat, watching the fire, and the imagined, alien sun he had conjured up in the little room glowed between them, round, burnishing, something first conceived, that they could have touched the smooth bright sides of. But this grew, as they considered it, and expanded and burst into light, so that they had opened to them within it a bright airy country under a clear sky. Their pictures were more or less the same, expanses of shifting sand, stylized mountains, blue-grey in the distance, little white houses inside whose thick walls shade was cool and welcome. Neither of them wanted to imagine anything more precise; to the urban English a hot sun and wide spaces are mystery and freedom enough.

Outside, it was nearly dark, the window was misted blue-black, the colour of a sloe berry. Henry, brooding on the bright sun, studied his daughter's face in the dim light of the gas fire and looked for a sign that she was stirred. Anna thought of cactus flowers, crimson and white, bursting mysteriously open in the heat, amongst the fur and spines, on their knobbed pillars in the sand. I should like to see things like that, she thought. And to be alone. Why not escape? One did not after all believe any more that God had put one in one's present station as part of his pattern for the best of all possible worlds. Why not fly in the face of this bureaucratic deity, why not take what was offered, what one could get, gather up one's roots – if one had any – and move into the sun? Why should I stay here, she thought, and know so little, about so little?

She said, 'I hadn't thought of anything like that. One always thought one could move after one knew – but –'

'One must try to know –'

'Oh, I know. I – it seems unbearably exciting. Just to go. Would you really?'

'I promise,' said Henry.

'I think I'm glad you came.'

Henry flung himself happily back in his chair, which creaked and protested. He was warm with achievement. He had found an answer for Anna, he had helped, he had made contact. And before he had had time to possess any of his achievements, he made his mistake.

He thought he could say anything to Anna, now; he wanted, having begun to talk, to talk on, to tell her how he saw things, to confirm in her the power to see things his way that he had decided she possessed.

He said, 'I've been thinking about waste, lately: about the way most people spend their lives – or at least, most of their time – on little actions that at the best leave them no more of a human being than when they set out on them and at worst bring them a bit nearer to the machine. You know; there are men who work machines that put tops on bottles – I know miserably little about it – and women who type out stuff they don't understand day after day – it's the building of it into an importance that's wrong, not the doing, it's the pride taken in these littlenesses that add nothing to a man. Do you know what I mean, Anna?

'Take Margaret Canning. I came to Cambridge partly because she asked me to. That marriage seems to be crumbling fairly rapidly, but she won't face it, because she believes in it – in that sort of way – so I'm to see Oliver. Not my kind of job at all. I keep putting it off. Now she was a woman with a great deal of life in her – and some natural instinct for how to live under all the beliefs she's come to have. I went to see her in their flat, and one could see it had failed, all the cleaning and eating left undone. In an odd way I admire her for admitting defeat. She was messy and the place was dirty, and everything smelt. But she won't let go of the principle, that horrid little man, who must be the husband. I'm getting to see him as a symbol – a sort of black destructive hole into which everything gets sucked, and churned out again, dead and masticated and labelled for future reference, my books and Margaret's sexual energy – and love.'

He thought he sounded a little strident – he had not realized until he began to speak, how much he hated Oliver. Hatred was not something he usually needed to feel. He thought he could have coped with Oliver if Oliver had written against him. It was the absorption and appropriation of his own work into Oliver's scheme of things which so ground on him. He could not disentangle his feelings about Oliver on his own account from his feeling on Margaret's, and thought he would tell this too, to Anna, and ask her advice. He began again.

'And she will tell me about their sex life – all sorts of elaborate sadisms . . .'

'Don't,' said Anna. 'Stop. Please, stop that.'

She got up, and ran blindly over to the door. But she did not go out, only put the palms of her hands and her face against the door and began after a moment to move her head rhythmically from side to side, sliding along the panels, bumping over and over the central strut. Henry listened to this bump, bump, bump of his daughter's head, and watched her thin shoulders working. It came to him that he knew what she was going to tell him, but he waited with an apprehension every bit as sick as ignorance would have been, for the telling.

'No,' she said, between the bump and her own tight breathing. 'No, no, no. Go away, now. Get out. I should've know better. It was a ghastly mistake, you coming. Please go away, now.'

She could only think that she must somehow get through the time which was still left before she could finally get Henry to go away. He must go away some time, he could not stay and this could not go on for ever. She had believed when he came that someone had told him about Oliver, and had not been able to imagine what he could say or do – accusations and reproaches were so far outside his range. She thought now, Henry saw, catching up on and understanding her earlier fears, that he did know, and had known all along; that his offer of movement was a bribe to give up Oliver; that he had been manipulating her like a child which must be humoured out of a wrongdoing for which its wise parents prefer not to hold it responsible.

'Anna –'

'No, it's no good, it's no good, just go away.'

Neither of them had any wish to embark upon the scene

which had to ensue before he could, in fact, go away. Earlier that afternoon, he might even have been shamed into leaving at that point, and then wondering why. But now he could only think that Anna was something to him that he did not want to lose; that he should have been able, as all parents think they should have been able, to prevent her from suffering this, that he loved her, and she was to be like him. So he stood up, and took a step towards her.

'How can I go? Anna – '

'Don't touch me.' She turned round and faced him then, staring out of the window over his head. He had thought he would be relieved if the head banging stopped, but he was not.

'Can't you see, there's no point in your talking? That there's nothing you can do?'

'You're my daughter.'

'Ah yes, but he, Oliver, he thinks I'm like him. And he's more right than you are, and I shouldn't forget it. It's all right for you to talk about meaninglessness and dreariness, as though you'd just discovered them. They may horrify you quite genuinely, but you – you're not involved in them, you're interested in them because they're a new fact. I bet you even think you could write about Margaret. Or me, I suppose? Well maybe you could, maybe that makes it exciting. You know what you are, you're the man with ten talents, you get busy, and make another ten. Christ was pretty clever, he knew who did the burying, the man with one. He hadn't got enough to get started on, poor thing. But I can't see it that way, I have to think what to do, it means me.'

'I don't believe that.'

'Oh, at the moment, maybe, you see me as your daughter, you think I can do – something. But there's not been much evidence of it. I ought to have known better. It's no good talking to you. You're as much good as the Blessed Damozel, leaning out of heaven along the golden bar, and weeping for us. You'd better stay in your heaven and weep.'

'Don't, Anna.'

'And I should have thought,' Anna said, 'that you could have afforded not to – hate him so much. How can you judge him? How can you say anything about him reading your books? You publish them, don't you? It isn't his fault if he has to get things at second hand – or mine – if all the glory we can get is reflected glory? Some people have to be readers and followers. Oh, he knows how I feel, he does know, though I pretended for long enough that he didn't. He knows what I'm like and what it's like to be like that. I ought to trust him. That's why I – love him.'

'I didn't know.'

'You didn't want to know.'

'You didn't think all this a moment ago.'

But Anna had swung wildly into the other of her two moods, the imaged sun was shrunk and dead and powerless. She said roughly, 'If I didn't ought to have. It's true. When you started saying that about him I saw – I belong with him. Not with you. I can never see things your way.'

Henry hesitated. Both of them saw clearly that conventional anger, or remonstrance, were quite out of his power; Anna even seemed to take some pleasure in watching him struggle. He said eventually, 'There is Margaret. I promised her I would see Oliver. I must see him, I think.'

'Oh, no, don't, don't, don't do that. That would be terrible. I can't think what she can be thinking of. You are the last person. I can't think what can be wrong with her. I should have thought she was all right. It would be terrible if you talked to him. He'd be nasty – much nastier than I'm being. He'd enjoy telling you there was nothing you could do, that you'd no right to tell me to do anything – you know why, you can imagine what he'd say. Please – look, please – just go home, and forget all about it. Please.'

'How can I? You're my daughter – '

'I don't know what difference that makes any more. I don't know anything. Please, leave me alone. Please, let me try and think.'

'I want to help,' Henry said, but with a gesture of defeat. He began to move towards the door. 'I shall try and see Oliver,' he said. 'I feel I must. That's all I can say. But, Anna – '

'Yes.'

'When all this is clearer – if you want me – or if you want

206

to go away – I will help. I want to help. You must promise to come to me.'

'I will, if I want help.' Anna began to cry. 'But I shan't, I know I shan't. Now, go.'

Henry got himself round the door somehow; there was a last slight anticlimactic contact when he had to return and ask Anna to extricate his damp coat from the bathroom for him. It took some time to find his way out of the building.

Upstairs Anna stood for a moment just inside the door, wondering whether it would do any good to have a good cry. She thought not, on the whole; she saw herself from somewhere outside herself, pointlessly silly, standing there, staring into the night, and snorting with indignation or strain. Heroics of any kind she found embarrassing when alone; she was a poor audience for herself, and always had been. So she dried up the remaining tears, breathed deeply, and began to clear up the tea things, washing and drying the cups, something she normally never did until just before they were needed again. She was to have gone to Oliver that night. That's something I won't do now, she told herself. Let father go, if he will interfere. Then we'll see what happens. She felt better, once Henry had left, as she had known she would; events were always more comfortable once they began to revolve at some distance from her, once her connection with them was remote and speculative, with a door in between. She could face what had been done with some solidness. It was doing, undergoing, that she did not like. And now any further doing was out of her hands, for the time, which was what she required.

Henry had so disliked the last scene, she thought, that he would hardly come back for more. She had been surprised that he had been prepared to sustain such involvement for as long as he had: she didn't suppose it could last much longer. Henry was out of the way now. But there was Oliver.

And there was also, it seemed, Margaret.

She had accepted, immediately and without question, Henry's picture of Margaret. But any thought of Margaret distressed or put out had never entered her head, before. Her thinking about Margaret had been confined to thinking about the attitude she herself would have taken in Margaret's position. She had assumed that Margaret, securely and happily married to an Oliver who had little connection with the Oliver she herself slept with, would have cared very little, as she was sure she herself would have cared very little, what he did when he was away from her. It was ironic that the only person to have been entirely convinced by Margaret's married face was Anna, who had watched her at Darton, kissing Oliver all over the face at the breakfast table, folding her arms suddenly round his neck from behind, kneeling gracefully at his feet to consult him about the shopping or the train timetable, bringing him back silly little presents from the village every time she went, and had seen in all this a glow of love, a real intimacy, an inherent brightness of spirit and body which she had associated unthinkingly, and uncritically, with the state of live satisfaction she had already recognized in Henry, and had stored in her mind as a touchstone for life, a state of living to some end which it was possible to recognize if not share. She could not quite, now, associate Oliver with this state, but that had only added a necessary mystery; a love like that changed a man, changed Oliver, to being capable of sharing it. And she supposed it axiomatic that to be completely in love, and certain, like Margaret, brought a kind of satisfaction which would say something along the lines of 'I don't care what you do provided you don't think you have to hide it from me. I'm sure nothing can matter to you as much as I do, and that's enough.'

Besides, everything she did herself, since it was not what she was looking for, was so unreal to her that she could not imagine its having any essential effect on anyone else. Any particular moment of action had a certain importance, because it was what was happening, and nothing else was happening. But it could have no repercussions, no extension in time, no effect on other people – her time had not yet come, and she was no one to be reckoned with. She believed Oliver sheltered sometimes in her lack of interest, her sense of unreality, because he shared it and could not sustain, knowing the shadows so well, a life continually in the sun. But she was for him, she supposed, as he was for her, only a temporary refuge from the search for the sun, or their own limitations, and Margaret should possibly even be grateful that he had this place to hide, and did not have to take out on her his need for this Limbo, this no life.

So now, if Henry was right, if Margaret had 'admitted defeat', where was she? And where was Oliver?

If Margaret was defeated, what had she, Anna, done to defeat her? And if Oliver was not happily married to Margaret, did he give, and take, as little in his affair with Anna as she had believed – and so hoped, and needed? She thought, I can't bear it to get important, I can't, I won't be responsible for Margaret. Or Oliver. Or Oliver.

She had told Henry she loved Oliver. That had been the wrong word; if there had been one thing that she had need to be certain of, it was that she did not 'love' Oliver. She had used the word out of a kind of prudery, due to her reluctance to bring out in front of her father, and an imagined Caroline, any other word which might conjure up any more precise picture of sexual relations. As a child, she had refused to imagine the possibility of her parents having sexual intercourse together. They just didn't, in her child's world, for long after she had known for a fact that they must. And now, as she had refused to imagine them, they must refuse to imagine her, they must be incapable of picturing her ever, undressed, in the act. It was indecent, and ugly. So she could not say to Henry, affair, sleep with, go to bed with; only love, the child's word, the honourable vague word which covered everything from Anna Karenina through Cinderella to *Woman's Own*.

And Oliver? She could see him so well, when Henry came. He so enjoyed precise discussion, elaborate classification, situations, scenes. The trap was closing.

All I can do is sit still.

And Oliver? She wished suddenly that she could after all go to him and tell him what Henry had said, how her mind was turning on itself. Perhaps there was a sympathetic word-magic about the word she had used; it seemed in retrospect that they had been so happy since that first night; they had done everything so well, and so carelessly. Oliver was so amused a lover, he would explain things in his precise little voice which made everything ridiculously more exciting; I was happy in bed with him, she thought, like riding horses. It had turned out to be something she could do. And they had talked; when they had exhausted the subject of Anna's future, and agreed tacitly to avoid the subject of Henry, they had talked about all sorts of things over baked beans in Professor Ainger's kitchen – nothing close to Anna, but things she found she liked to have views on; not English literature but things it was possible to talk about for ever without being touched by: abortion, capital punishment, the public schools' reform, Christianity; Anna had never had any feelings about things before, it had been an education, taking her out of herself, reducing, for both of them, the world of art and the world of love and the sun to manageable proportions. People like us need things, she thought, and things need us. I shall miss you Oliver, horribly.

He would be sitting in the kitchen now, waiting for her. He had a fine charcoal grey sweater with a V neck, that she liked to put her face against; he would have his tins of beans and Nescafé out on the table ready for her, and his sharp little face would be drawn together, waiting. His mouth, so thin, could move and change its shape as gently as it looked hard and set; whenever he heard a sound he would look up apprehensively and harden the whole area of his face round his mouth into a beak, to protect himself from being seen. And if she had come, he would have smiled, his special, eager opening smile that she supposed Henry had never seen.

Henry . . . Henry was impossible, he was just not possible, that was all.

But she was going to let things go their own way and not interfere. She wrapped her arms round herself, and imagined Oliver's shoulder blades, sharp and hard under the fine grey wool, and his ridiculously narrow waist under her hands, and his own hands, small and certain – Perhaps to do nothing was to betray him?

All the same, she was just going to sit still. She looked out of the window for a time and found that after all she was going to need to cry.

ELEVEN

AFTER SEEING ANNA, Henry walked up and down in the drizzle, lecturing himself, he told himself without amusement, like a third-rate serious novel, on having gone against life, on having neglected for an imaginary glory, for dead words, for man-made ideas, for second-hand experience – he lumped all these disparate things as cheerfully together as the novel he posited – having neglected for these, life, the tug in the blood, that was, for the two had become ridiculously inextricable, his own frustrated undergraduate self who had slept with no one and had never got drunk, and Anna his daughter, who had certainly not not slept with anyone, but who had so little sense of life or direction that she had come only to an affair with a desiccated middle-aged critic whose wife, moreover, said he was a mental and not only a mental sadist. Part of the trouble was that he was so upset that he had quite forgotten what he had been writing, and could not have summoned life or concentration enough to plan another paragraph; he saw his work now as he occasionally saw a novel the moment he had finished it – a grotesque parody of life, a string of words, selecting and obscuring facts to suit himself. And dead, dead, dead. He had a vision of himself in his study, a dedicated and misguided Casaubon, and saw the procession of lives that he told himself his touch had withered – Caroline whom he had allowed to think that teacups – for him – were enough; Margaret, whom he had thought arrogantly to solve by re-arranging on paper; Anna, who had gone pale in his shadow, and poked blindly about in no direction, a plant in a cellar.

The next morning he walked up through rain to the University library. This had been built since his time and he had not been near it before. He thought it extraordinarily ugly, with its tremendous, disproportionate mock Assyrian tower, its rows of laboratory windows, and inside the revolving door its curving staircases like a timidly ostentatious town hall, its heavy glass doors covered with gilt and brass curlicues quite irrelevant to the slightly clinical atmosphere that was the only really positive thing about it. He bolted up the staircase knitting his brow like an intent and absent-minded don, stumbling over the top step through his effort to meet no one's eye, in case he should be asked for a ticket, a fee, a gown, an explanation of his business – he had no idea of how the place worked, and he didn't want to know. He went ahead through three sets of glass doors, still looking at no one, and found himself in a large, grey metal and battleship room that seemed to be the main reading room. He realized that it was no longer any good not looking at anything. He must start trying to find Oliver. So he strolled around the room, on tiptoe, rolling heavily since he wasn't used to controlling his own bulk on the balls of his feet, not, at least, with eyes on him. He peered between the rows of desks and saw rows of similar people, in gowns, hunched over books, hundreds of worried or sleepy faces, most of them very young, one or two ecstatic. None of them seemed to be Oliver, but he hadn't courage to approach closely enough to make certain. He was cross with himself when he got out; he shouldn't have needed to be afraid of being spoken to, only because the room was silent and he didn't want to find what he was looking for. He put it down as another unpleasantness, on Oliver's account.

In the catalogue room he peered at a plan of the building without seeing it. Then he wandered vaguely along silent corridors, between metal book-stacks, up and down in little lifts. He saw that at any other time he might have liked this part of the library; the glass windows made a whole light wall to the stacks, and people sat in ones and twos at little tables against the glass and could look out, between thoughts, into air and branches. In the end, in the basement he lost his temper, snapped himself back into the lift, ground the machinery into action, and returned to the main floor. At the other end of a corridor was a notice: Anderson Room. Well, he would look in there, and if he couldn't find him, that was the end. He could go home.

He strode into the room, keeping his head turned well away from those at the desk, and therefore, having to set off fairly briskly towards the end of the room. The reading room had been too large to be more than hushed; the Anderson room, smaller, brighter, more airy, with wider tables and more space between the heavy armchairs, was tented in silence. The inhabitants seemed predominantly aged and accepting. There was a curious, uneven musical tinkle in the room. Henry finally tracked it down to the plastic knobs on the ends of the blind cords which were like little pale green bells and swayed, even on that airless day, one after the other against the glass. The only other sounds were the movement of pages and the rasping breathing of one or two old men. Here was the centre, Henry felt, of the pyramid. Here was the inner chamber where the dead thing all this had been built to glorify was preserved to be interpreted by future scholars or devastated by vandals.

It is not easy to pick out one from a series of bent heads all turning their crowns. Henry scrutinized them all, could not see Oliver, and decided to do his duty, after peering into the ultimate alcove, by coming back down the other side before crossing to the door. He was nearly through and was walking more confidently, breathing more easily, when Oliver spoke from under him, from one corner of the table near him.

'Are you looking for someone, Henry?'

He had been easy to miss, hunched in his chair behind the incongruously lurid neon cover of an American novel, and his own very heavy dark-rimmed spectacles. He smiled, thinly, and did not stand up.

'For you,' Henry whispered. The silence decided his tone for him; he sounded very gentle, very friendly, under his breath. He had an irrational feeling that Oliver had laid a trap for him, had hidden himself on the corner of this table and thought with amusement of him, Henry, hunting him all over the building, clambering in and out of lifts, growing apprehensive and wild. Next to Oliver a very old man with a yellowing beard cut in a spade shape, a hearing aid, a pair of convex, bulbous spectacles and an ivory handled reading glass picked out fragments of papyrus from a box at his side and scrutinized them, using his thickened fingers with infinite delicacy. He spoke the words to himself soundlessly and wrote them down with a gold pencil, hanging from somewhere inside his clothes on a long gold chain. He paid no attention, not the movement of a muscle, to either

213

Henry or Oliver. He had a look of complete, finished attention, a look of discovery, of travelling over golden lands, which distracted Henry, who saw him two ways at once, as an echo of his own absorption in his study, live and active, and as an appropriate inhabitant of this house of squandered effort, a waster of a dying mind on dead words. He was the Saint seeing the central life by looking through the glass and not at it; he was a grotesque gnome, a parody of a human being, who would give to life in the end phosphorus and carbon and nothing more.

Oliver continued to look at Henry over the edge of his book; he made no move to stand up, or help Henry to begin to talk to him. Henry hovered enormously, and whispered, almost lovingly into the silence, 'I want to talk to you for a few moments if you can spare the time.'

'Perhaps,' said Oliver, moving his head up fractionally and smiling slightly more widely, 'you'll let me buy you a cup of coffee in the tea room. There's not likely to be a crowd yet.'

Henry wanted suddenly to pick Oliver up under the arms like a baby and drag him out of the room; he wanted to bang about, to knock Oliver on the book-cases, scatter a few teeth, bruise that smooth, pointed, pale little face and smear a bit of real blood across all the piles of books and papers. He saw himself holding the little man by the feet and sweeping books from tables with his head, in a great whirling arc. Samson again, he thought. In amongst the Philistines. But Samson with his hair trimmed by civilization – or women – or both.

'Well,' said Oliver, a little more sharply, twitching his shoulders slightly.

'That'll do,' said Henry. Oliver smiled again. 'Just a moment,' he said. He screwed the cap onto his pen, began to blot his papers, one after the other, and then clipped them one after the other into a folder. Then he creased a piece of paper in eight, deliberately tore off a strip, laid it in his book to mark the page, closed the book, and placed it neatly on the folder. Then he took off his spectacles, clipped them together, fetched out his spectacle case, snapped them into it, and put it back in his pocket. All this took some time. Henry hung over him, huge and conspicuous. As they walked away together Henry saw the old man spread himself slightly over the patch of table cleared

214

by Oliver. He had a look of even greater self-possession and pleasure.

Oliver led the way down to the tea room, pulled out a chair for Henry at a table near the glass door into the courtyard, and fetched two cups of coffee without saying more than 'Sugar?' He looks like a bank clerk, Henry thought rudely, scuttling about in a tidy dark suit, slightly too generously cut, too deep at the instep, with his hair clipped very neat and short over the ears. Not at all like a scholar, much too businesslike and organized, and without any of the traditional flamboyance. Not surprising, Henry told himself wildly and unjustly, that this kind reduce reading to counting how many times a man uses the word red, or pink, or sin. Tallies and accounts, that's it, he told himself, and saw his unfairness clearly for a moment. What has happened to me? he asked himself.

'No good going outside,' said Oliver, 'in the rain. It can be pleasant in summer. You mustn't smoke in here of course.'

Outside was a small square courtyard with a patch of grass in the middle, sloping slightly upwards to a bare magnolia bush in a bare circle of earth. The brick and glass towered up on all sides. It was bleak, ugly, not Cambridge. Oliver seemed at home. He said, 'Must apologize for the coffee,' and receded into silence, leaving Henry to make all the running. Henry suspected that this amused him and looked suspiciously at him, but Oliver studied the surface of his coffee, and would not meet his eye.

Henry had not been able to think what he would say to Oliver but had supposed that something would present itself when the time came to speak; he found now that he had nothing at all to say, and no way of saying it, and was not likely to find any. He said hopefully, 'You'll know why I want to see you.'

'No,' said Oliver, into his cup. Henry paused and then brought out abruptly, 'I promised Margaret I would. I went to see her. She wrote to me.'

'Indeed?' said Oliver, but his head came up and Henry saw that this had surprised him. He would have said more, but could think of nothing to say about Margaret that did not sound pious or silly; indeed he found it hard to remember Margaret at all, or how things had seemed to her, since he had

215

his mind full of Anna. So he said, 'But I don't know what to say to Margaret now.'

'Indeed?'

'Since I've seen Anna.'

'Indeed?' said Oliver for the third time. Henry swallowed his coffee in one gulp and shouted, 'You know what Anna told me.'

'Hush,' said Oliver quickly, automatically, schoolmasterly. He said, 'Yes. I know.'

'So you see why I had to talk to you.'

'No, I don't. I don't know what you think you can do. You might just as well have kept out.'

This was what Anna had said. Henry looked into his cup, which was empty, and then began, clumsily, 'Anna is my daughter. She's under age. I want something good for her. A life. She can do something. Even you can't pretend you're helping her.'

'I think I am.'

'Oh, Christ,' said Henry, too loudly again. He said, 'What about Margaret?'

'My affair, not yours.'

'I don't see that, if she had to turn to me to save her sanity. And it's come to that, by God. And whatever she may be, Anna's my affair. She's my daughter.'

'Just discovered that, have you? It isn't much use your pretending you can horsewhip me and drag her home and incarcerate her, is it? It's out of character, you wouldn't really know how, or think you had any right, would you? And if you did get her home, you'd shut her in her bedroom and forget all about her again, your duty done, wouldn't you? Don't you honestly think she might be better with me? I care for her you know. She's not just a pretty girl. I want to help her.'

Henry sat silent, feeling exposed, already defeated. Oliver said, 'Is that all?'

'No,' said Henry. 'What I have to say is – you must see – I don't think you should involve Anna – not Anna – in – your feelings about me.'

'I don't see,' said Oliver very sharply. He put down his cup in his saucer, sat very upright, and began to drum with his finger on the edge of the table. 'I don't see that at all. Please explain.'

'Oh,' said Henry wearily. 'What do you want me to say? I don't know what you've told Anna – something about selfish genius, something about having too much expected of her because she's my daughter, something about cutting loose from me – some of all that's sense, I've told her so myself. I want to give her some money and let her go where she likes and fend for herself a bit.'

'Does she want that?'

'I don't know.'

'Escape's no answer. She must face facts.'

'But not your facts, not your way. I don't even know if you know how irresponsible you're being. How can I explain? I've always felt – right from the beginning – something in your attitude to me – or my books, I think both – a kind of grabbing, a pulling down – a hatred.'

'A standard love-hate relationship?' asked Oliver with edgy mockery.

'Yes,' said Henry, without irony. He tried to ignore Oliver, and his own wish to batter Oliver on the paving stones outside, and to present things dispassionately as he saw them. He noticed his own voice take on its remote Olympian tone, and he noticed that this, at last, irritated Oliver.

'I've always hated your reviews. Thought what I'd written was less good than I'd thought it was, when you'd been at it. Forgotten what I felt like when I wrote it, or whether what I'd written meant what you said it did, or something more or less, or different. Thought you were trying to take possession of me – I mean, of what I wrote – you know, like processed Gruyère cheese, mash it all up, put artificial holes in, cut it in neat squares, put plastic round, say there, I've examined it, it's what I told you, it's been through my hands, it's Gruyère all right. Gruyère? What do you know about it? Same with my life – you don't approve, imitation country gent and all that, I know what you think, all a bit pathetic – well, you make it so by coming and looking at it with your processing eye. And by God, you will come, won't you? You will share? You won't just stay away from what you dislike?'

'Well, if I let you get at me, that's my fault. I ought to be able to look after myself. I don't know why it should be me you want to get at.'

Oliver stirred; there was a tone of the old mild arrogance in this that seemed to anger him; he said hotly, 'Well, ask yourself why, ask yourself, show some interest in someone else.'

Henry went on heavily, 'But when it comes to Anna, that's different. I don't even know if you're doing it consciously. If you are, if you want to know, you've succeeded. You've got at me. I can't bear to think of you – taking possession – of her too, of Anna, and telling her she's got to be – like you. That's what you've told her, she said. That's not true, she'll come to see that if she's allowed to, if she's in a position to. But what I want to say is have you thought what it will mean to her when she works out why you're doing this? I mean, if she comes to think that this is a second-hand love affair because of me, just as everything else she's had has been – according to you too, remember – because of me. Don't you see even if – even if you did care for her – it wouldn't do, you're too much involved in what she's got to get out of? She's an intelligent girl she'll work it out in the end. And then what will she have had?'

'She's an intelligent girl,' Oliver repeated. 'Has it occurred to you she may have worked all that out already? And not mind?'

'I don't mind think so. In any case, she's wasting time she won't have again. And if she does know – how you feel about me – it doesn't dispose of the effect of your feelings about me on her. Does it?'

Oliver stood up, put his small hands on the table in front of him and addressed Henry in a harsh, low voice that startled Henry although he had meant to make him angry. Later he remembered the hands, one turned each way, out from the other, the pointed fingertips yellow with the pressure Oliver was putting on them, and then, half-way down the nail, flushed dull purple. And those thin little bones looking ready to splinter if any more pressure were applied.

'Perhaps we might both have found your country gentleman's horsewhip more satisfying in the end? Who do you think you are? All of us like dead albatrosses tumbling out of the sky to be hung round your neck as evidence of your spiritual progress?

My wife – Margaret – what's she to do with you? Why do you suppose I should enjoy your paddling about in my family affairs any more than you enjoy me in yours? I suppose you think the fact that you're not really interested, have no real motive, no need, gives you a right to meddle? Well, it doesn't. I don't see that you're any less irresponsible because you don't care, than you accuse me of being because I do. Margaret thinks you're a wise man, I suppose? She'd better think again. And you think I am only capable of loving where it concerns you, where I can get at you, to use your own elegant phrase – '

'Anna is my daughter.'

'Anna,' Oliver bore down, 'is Anna. Herself. Anna. She has her way to make, let her make it.'

'You let her, that's what I ask.'

'Will you let me finish? I don't know why you've suddenly started going all over jelly when Anna's mentioned, and rolling your fine eye, and promising to do this and that for her. I'd have thought it was a bit late. And if you think I'm not in a position to help her, how much less are you? Fons et origo, you are, by your own account. But you aren't God and you'd better remember it.'

'At least I've faith in her.'

'Since when? And haven't I? Perhaps a more realistic faith at that.'

'Reality's what you make of yourself.'

'It's what you're allowed to make of yourself. Have you any more to say?'

'I still consider myself responsible for Anna.'

'And me. And my wife if she wants. Why not? But what are you going to do? What can you do?'

'I don't know,' said Henry honestly. 'I shall have to think.'

'I'll leave you to it then,' said Oliver. 'And I don't advise you to order Anna to come home. She won't, and what's more she won't speak to you again if you do. And I must warn you, I've no intention of helping you at all, myself. You must save yourself – or us – your own way. If you can find time to remember that was what you were going to do.'

That was a final speech, Henry thought; he'll go now.

'Good morning,' said Oliver.

'Good morning,' said Henry slowly. Oliver turned and pushed his way out of the tea room, now filling rapidly with trailing gowns and a hum of voices.

He could not sit any longer, rose suddenly and violently, leaving his coffee untouched, ran to the desk in the entrance lobby and commanded 'Call me a taxi' with such desperate authority that no one stopped to explain that this was not a customary service, and a taxi was duly called. Henry waited on the steps until it came, a huge, black, hearselike vehicle, flattening muddy puddles into spray. He said, 'To the station, please,' and could not explain what train he was trying to catch; any train in almost any direction would have done; it was only to get away. He sat, tall and solid, a solitary mourner, clutching the silk ball and cord, and swaying from side to side as the taxi, its driver infected by some of Henry's urgency, rushed ponderously down Trumpington Street, jerking round cyclists, its radio cackling. A small dark man stepped out into the road and Henry for a moment felt a thrill in imagining the car proceeding over him, toppling him like a peg and leaving him flat and finished in the road behind it. So easy, so easy to destroy; only a hairsbreadth between this civilized truce and a real dead man in a gutter.

He paid the taxi-driver outside the station. The rain fell heavier and heavier, but without force to rain itself out. He believed it might rain forever, or for weeks anyway; at the moment it was absolutely damping to him, a real limitation, it was he who was getting wet.

There was a train in ten minutes; this was his usual luck reasserting itself; he felt obscurely guilty on account of it and wasn't sure whether the omen was good or bad.

TWELVE

ANNA HEARD NOTHING from Oliver after her failure to turn up in the Barton Road on the night when Henry was in Cambridge. At first she expected to hear nothing. She was absorbed in the sense that things were happening at some distance from her, and that if she only kept quite still and did nothing, things would continue to happen without her, which was what she wanted. But after a fortnight or so she became rather irritably curious. It was mean of Oliver, she felt, to make no attempt to let her know what had happened, or what was happening, or when the confrontation, if there was to be one, would take place. It was an indrawn, inactive curiosity, nevertheless.

She was expecting what she, like most women, called the curse, and was one of those who, despite the assurances of modern medical pamphlets, suffered badly from it. At school she had several times fainted dramatically in prayers, which had increased her unpopularity with those in charge, since for some reason one fainting fit in a crowd of girls almost invariably triggers off others, and the ranks of gym-slipped figures had then swayed like saplings in a storm, with here and there a crash on the polished boards of the hall. Anna still always spent the first few days of the curse curled up on hands and knees on the floor, swaying from side to side with pain and wishing she were dead. But this was always quite exciting and led to a period where some activity seemed possible.

It was the week before the curse, this week, she thought vaguely, not having really counted, that was to be dreaded. It was a lifeless week, a heavy, miserable week, a week of grief and pressure and hopelessness whose cause Anna usually managed to work out, and which she knew, rationally, would pass as it must with time; she was nevertheless always completely submerged by it. It was something to do with blood pressure on the brain, she had read somewhere, or with accumulation of fluid in the body. She had read too that most crimes committed by women – and not only crimes but driving offences and accidents – were committed during this miserable week. And once she had been lectured passionately by a woman don on the injustice of this man's world where a woman might have to sit an examination on which her future depended in this lifeless week. It was the sort of thing that would interest Oliver, that, Anna told herself; except that he would probably say with some justice that if women were subject to fits of despondency and unbalance of this kind every four weeks it was maybe right to employ men before them. No one will employ me, anyway, she thought; it won't make much difference when I sit an exam, what week it is.

She felt extraordinarily tired, and brooded over Oliver, Margaret, Henry and Mexico with a vague distaste for all of them; they were against her, in some undefined way, all of them, and they were best disposed of by keeping away from them and assuming they were not quite real. She was so tired that she told herself she was not very well, and ought to keep still; she spent her time in her room, only going out occasionally to have meals in Hall, or to look at the pigeonhole in which, if it ever came, she would find Oliver's letter. She wondered idly how many other people in this intensely active society spent all their time sitting submerged in one room, and was sorry for them. Mostly she did just sit. Not reading, not thinking, just sitting on the end of the bed and staring out at the College garden, at the trees, and the lawns which must have been so enthusiastically walked about on by the earlier generations of young women in boaters and long serge skirts, and looked now as though they must have been empty ever since. Anna stared and stared, waiting for something to happen – the curse, Oliver's letter, her event, or at least the next meal.

It was a curious period of her life to which she later looked back with incomprehension. The sky was heavy, an opaque slate grey for days on end, and her body was heavy, and she had reached what everyone would surely consider a crisis; and all she could do was stare, until even those heavy November skies took on a luminousness, a sort of ponderous, unrelated significance. Each bird mattered; a line of starlings, like fluttering dull rags falling, and then, as they gathered themselves, stretched and climbed, iridescent blue-green; the odd gunmetal pigeon, turning with a streak of brightness on its neck, against a gunmetal sky; they were omens, or rather they were ominous, it made some indefinable difference to have watched and seen them.

She tucked her legs under her, and let her hands rest on her crossed ankles so that she was squat and heavy, a broad-based triangle, watched for a morning or an afternoon, and then when the gong boomed, uncurled herself and went down to meals. She thought once, if I go on like this they'll find out, and send me down, and that'll fix it, but this idea came from somewhere very far away, not connected to her or what she was doing. She was so much not there that it was inconceivable that anyone should notice her; she could sit and sit and sit, and no one ever came, no one knew, no one cared, no one was in a position to care. She had the idea that it was like waiting to be born; pressure and incapacity, and inactivity, and a sense of complete ignorance combined with an almost entirely physical certainty that something momentous was in the offing, but could hardly come, because it was inconceivable. Like death, for that matter, of which she was afraid, because she could imagine the point of time before it. The thing itself, the complete change of circumstances, she could not imagine.

Finally, one weekend, when it was likely, although she had inspected the box every day for a week and a half before, finding only two messages from Peter Hughes-Winterton which she had put away unread, the letter from Oliver came. It was brief and unsigned. 'Why have I heard nothing from you? I shall be in the usual place tonight if you want to come.'

Anna was sure immediately that she did not want to go. It would be a terrible trouble, Oliver would ask questions, she would have to argue. He would expect an attitude, and she had not got one.

The thought of Oliver had brought a restlessness into her mood from time to time; she had missed him, dreamed about him occasionally, saved up for him the importance of the line of blown starlings as though it was something he could be told, as though the importance could be communicated outside her room, beyond herself. Sometimes she had thought, loving him, I am seeing this cloud or that tree for him, for Oliver, that is its meaning. And sometimes it had been to betray the object, to reduce it to these human terms. Love was not necessary to vision. Nor Oliver to love, it seemed suddenly; to remember him and need him seemed much more desirable than to walk out of the College and actually to confront him. He would bring up things. Henry, Margaret; irrelevant things.

Nevertheless, she put on a jacket at about seven that evening and went out. If she did not sign out, it was unlikely that she would be missed if she didn't come back; that at least had always worked before. Cambridge was cold and sloppy, and out towards the edges of the town, badly lit. Anna walked rapidly round the puddles, clutching the furry collar of her jacket around her throat. She knew this walk by heart, was mesmerized by it, had learned off every bush and gatepost, and would pace it in imagination as a substitute for counting sheep, to put herself to sleep at night. She had been forbidden to ride a bicycle. Oliver had pointed out sensibly that one might be recognized if she left it out in the drive. When she came, the house was dark, so that she wondered for a moment whether Oliver was, after all, not there. She tried the door, which they left open by arrangement; it opened; she walked in as she always did. The house was still dark, but there was a sound in the kitchen. Anna made her way, blindly and confidently, between the vases and tables to the back of the house. Oliver was sitting at the kitchen table, under the thin, greyish light, his head in his hands and a blue plastic shopping bag in front of him.

Anna said, 'Hullo.'

'Hullo,' said Oliver, without lifting his head. 'You're late. I thought you weren't coming.'

'I did, you can see.'

'Yes,' said Oliver, and for a moment they were both silent.

'Shall I take off my jacket?'

'If you're staying.'

Anna hung her jacket over a chair, crossed the room and switched on the electric bowl fire which they stood on top of the Aingers' Aga range – it was not worth lighting the Aga for

Oliver's weekends. The copper glowed red after a moment; Anna leaned over it, her back to Oliver, and warmed her hands.

'It's ghastly cold. Why hadn't you put the fire on?'

Oliver didn't answer. After some time, he said, 'What have you been doing with yourself?'

'Nothing. Really nothing. Just sitting in my room.'

'Working for a change?'

'No. Just sitting.'

'Wasting some other girl's chance of a good education. Why didn't you write to me?'

'I didn't think of it.'

'No, you wouldn't. Why didn't you think of explaining why you didn't come, last time? What did you expect me to think?'

'Oliver, don't. I knew you were going to make an issue of it. I can't bear it if you start nagging. Really. I wish I hadn't come.'

'I only want to know why you didn't come, last time. You must see that.'

'You know why I didn't. My father came. He said he . . . I didn't know what was happening.'

'So you took no steps to find out?'

'No.'

'That's like you. Is there anything you would exert yourself about? Or maybe it's just me – just my affairs – just my . . . that you don't feel obliged to bother about?'

'Oliver – you know I care. I do care. Look, here I am. I just didn't know what was happening, that's all. But here I am – can't we just be like we used to be? And not talk about it?'

'In a moment,' said Oliver doggedly. 'He came to see me, you know.'

Anna said nothing.

'He was rather unpleasant, I thought. I told him he'd no right to interfere. I told him you'd do what you pleased, whatever he said. I told him he wasn't in a position to tell you what to do.'

'Well?'

'He had nothing to say. As I expected.'

'Well, that's all right, isn't it?' said Anna. She felt that it was very far from all right; that Henry could not be dismissed in so cavalier a fashion; that he had a right to be heard, and his way of looking was not yet proved wrong. And that Henry was nothing Oliver should be allowed so easily to despise or pull down. But she was very weary, she would do what came.

'It's all right if you think it is,' Oliver said. 'When you didn't come I didn't know what you did think.'

Anna did not think anything formulated enough to communicate. She said, 'I'm hungry. Can we eat? Let's not make a scene, please, let's not.'

Oliver pushed the blue shopping bag across the table in her direction.

'You'll have to come to grips with things some time,' he said. Anna ignored this. She opened the shopping bag and found a tin of luncheon meat, a tin of baked beans, a sliced white loaf, a packet of margarine, a tin of peaches and two bottles of beer. Oliver had what amounted to a moral belief that in order to eat simply one must eat nastily, as his mother had done, as everyone had had to do in the war. Anna had tried on previous occasions to explain to him that an unsliced loaf could be fresher, that things could be done with eggs or cheese and potatoes, that were impossible with luncheon meat, that the extra few pence spent on butter made a great difference, that you could buy a whole ripe melon for the price of a tin of gluey peaches, that food could be a pleasure. At these times Caroline came out strongly in her. Oliver would retort illogically that he had never seen any point in making a fuss about food, and add that he had never been able to tell the difference between butter and margarine anyway, and what was more, didn't believe that she could with her eyes shut.

Anna gave up arguing when she worked out that this everyday food was a way of keeping her in her place as a Severell, and of emphasizing Oliver's own natural place. It was one of his social quirks, that was all, and better ignored. Today the thought of the grainy texture and artificial metallic taste of the luncheon meat made her feel sick, but she turned out the contents of the tin of beans – a basic food that she did like – into a pan, and stirred them over the gas without speaking. Oliver put out the meat, and brought plates and forks, and in a moment they were sitting, as usual, one each side of the scarlet formica, with the hot tomato sauce slopped on the cold chunks of meat,

226

and a piece of bread and margarine on the table top beside them.

Oliver said, 'I can't think what he'd got himself all worked up about. He's never shown any signs of caring what happened to you before, has he?'

'Well – '

'And now he wants to give you some money and send you away, he says. Or something like that. As though anyone couldn't see that the things you must face are here. And now.'

'I didn't know.'

'He can't avoid things that way.'

'Oliver, you're nagging again. You're . . .'

'Do you know what he told me? He seems to think that I – that you – that all this is my way of what he calls getting at him. A – a kind of revenge on him. For being a great writer I suppose. I can't see any other meaning in it.'

'Well, it's a feeling we all have, isn't it? That he's an injustice of some kind? That no one has a right to be so sure . . .'

'Anna. Now, look, tell me – you don't think there's anything in this? This revenge?'

'No,' said Anna wearily. She didn't want to have to feel anything about anything. She pushed away her plate and said, 'I can't eat this meat, Oliver, I just can't. I don't feel very well, I'm sorry.'

'You must tell me what you think.'

Anna, from a great distance, tried very hard. 'No one does anything only for one reason ever, do they? I mean, both you and I are drawn together partly because we're frightened of him, or discouraged by him, or something like him. For comfort, I've always thought that. But it's silly to think that's the only reason, or the most important. If I thought you were only getting at him through me, because I'm his daughter, I wouldn't come here. Obviously I wouldn't. Would I?'

'I was really put out. Such a pettiness . . .'

'Don't.' Anna was herself, in spite of the reasonable tone she was managing quite nicely, put out by Oliver's revelation of Henry's view of the affair. She was aware that Oliver was forcing the issue, making her decide to come down, deliberately and publicly, on his side. She knew that Henry was partially

227

right, and thought she knew that he was in a larger sense wrong. But she was hurt that he could think so little of her that he could believe her so easy for Oliver to take in. And above all, weary of having to work out other people's feelings in relation to herself. It was best, even if one knew it was not true, to be able to act as though no one thought about her when she was not there. She said:

'I expect it seems quite reasonable to him. I mean, you do attack him rather, don't you? And he wouldn't understand us – you and me – how could he? I mean, you've got Margaret, it's not as though ... You can't expect him to understand anyone needed comfort. He doesn't need it. All right, he's wrong, but do we have to worry about him?'

She knew that she herself would have to worry, at some later time. But not now, not now. If Oliver went on talking about Henry, they would work themselves into just the scene she would do anything to avoid. Oliver pushed his last little block of meat into his mouth and chewed it with obvious enjoyment. Then he pointed his fork at Anna and began again.

'I admire his work. I can't help it. I admire it more than anything else being written. I have to. But that's no reason for what he suggests, and no reason for him to dictate my actions –'

'He's not dictating yours, it's mine, isn't it, he cares about?' This was meant to annoy. It did.

Oliver said, 'I had hoped the two were interchangeable, here.'

'Oliver, you're nagging again, terribly. You've got to stop, I can't stand it. I can't stand it. Please stop going on and on about him – he's gone home and he's probably busy writing away and not thinking about us at all, and that's an end of it. I'd never come here again if I thought we were just going to go on and on discussing him. It's just what you ought to think would be very bad for me.' She said urgently, in another voice, 'Besides, I'm going to be ill. It's that foul luncheon meat. I wish you'd buy something else.'

Oliver opened his mouth to say something, but had no time to get it out before Anna was violently sick. She just managed to reach the sink. Oliver watched her for a moment, closed his mouth, and then asked very sharply, 'What's wrong?'

'I don't know.' Anna ran the taps, both of them full on. 'A

228

worried tummy. Worry takes me that way. I'm sorry to be so disgusting, it seems to happen when I'm with you, doesn't it? I feel better for it, if that consoles you.'

Oliver looked as though it didn't much. He said, The Aingers left a bottle of whiskey. Would that be good or bad?'

'Good, I think. Either that, or it'll finish me off. Do you think we ought to take their whiskey?'

'I'll replace it.'

Anna was not sure that he would, but could not care. Oliver, distracted from Henry, became very gentle; he shepherded her into the drawing room and settled her in a chair. 'Just keep still,' he said, with practical firmness. 'You look terrible.' He bent and kissed her for the first time that evening – an undemanding, reassuring kiss which made Anna suddenly want to weep with gratitude. He could be so good, she thought, as he went out again, so comfortable. The room was back with her, familiar now. For years after she had forgotten Oliver, she imagined, these things, red velvet and bearskins, pampas grass and Benares brass, cylindrical cushions and Chinese jars would knot in her midriff, disturb her, claim extra attention, put her on her guard. She thought, he has done this at least to me more or less permanently. And then, if this is all he has done I suppose I am lucky.

Oliver returned with whiskey, hot water and tumblers. He poured Anna what seemed to her a very strong drink, and then, after some thought, an even stronger one for himself. He sat down in the chair opposite her and said, 'I don't like you to look like that, Anna; I feel it's my fault.'

The harrying tone had gone; he leaned back on the chair, unusually relaxed, his face, as it always was at these times, less fine-drawn, older, kinder. Anna took a gulp of whiskey. Once it was inside her she was not sure it was a good thing. She took another, hopefully.

'Drink it slowly,' Oliver said. 'It's not medicine, it's good whiskey. I do hope you are happy, Anna. I hope I've made things better for you. I meant to, whatever he may think.'

'I feel distant from things,' Anna said, describing the happiness she had, and meaning that she felt distant from Oliver too. She was not sure if he had heard her; he was lying back in the chair, his face turned to the ceiling, his eyes closed. She took another mouthful of whiskey, studied him, and felt a prick of desire for him in her distance. Since she had known him she had learned to recognize a female version of the male undressing look, which masqueraded most often as an absentminded stare or an especially intent friendly smile – always a furtive excitement under some look that denied it. Anna began to think that she had done right to come. She might gain a peace from sleeping next to Oliver tonight, a real peace. He was now so much the only human being she trusted; indeed, in many ways, the only human being she knew. How impoverished I am, she thought. But not bitterly. If they could sit together like this all evening, she would have as much as she wanted or could manage. She would be comforted.

Oliver sat up abruptly and said, 'But we've got to talk. Haven't we? We've got to come to some decision about what to do next. We can't go on pretending that this is just a temporary entanglement, can we? We must say where we stand?'

'Oliver,' said Anna, sitting up. 'Oh, don't – '

'If we're going to go on seeing each other, we must know on what terms. I saw that when he came. It's been my fault. I've pretended to be looking after you, and pushing you around, and I've said nothing about myself. I'm not very good at talking about myself. I'm afraid of being snubbed. I've never been able to afford to lay myself open to being hurt. But it isn't fair to you – oh, and let's be honest, it's impossible for me, any longer – to pretend that I'm not – involved. I don't want to go on in this hole and corner way. I want to be with you, Anna, openly.'

In Henry's face, Anna thought, and clutched desperately at the arms of her chair, so that her nails scratched and slipped on the leather. She said, 'Oliver, please, don't.'

'You've been very good, you've never said anything about my being married, you've been remarkably accepting. Remarkably. But I've no right to expect you to go on indefinitely – not when we're both deeply involved. As we are. Both of us.'

'You don't have to – '

'Listen to me, Anna. I want to tell you about Margaret. For my sake. I want you to know what I'm like.'

'No,' said Anna. 'No, don't. I don't want to know.'

'He spoke to you about her.'

'Yes. But it doesn't make any difference. It can't. Oh, please – '

'You must listen to me, too, Anna.' said Oliver leaning forward and bearing down. 'I need you to listen. I want you to share.'

'No,' cried Anna frantically, standing up and retreating into the window. 'I said I don't want to know, I don't want to know, I don't want to care. It's nothing to do with me.'

'I see,' said Oliver. The dry sharpness crept back into his voice. 'I suppose I partly knew you'd take that line. I hoped you might have grown out of it. May I just ask, what did you think about me and Margaret, then? I suppose you must have thought a little? Or did you just assume we were happily married thank you, and that you were just an extra amusement, for my spare time, my weekends off?'

'Yes,' said Anna, since that was what she had thought.

'And you thought that was satisfactory? You thought I thought that was satisfactory?'

'Yes,' said Anna flatly. She saw Oliver's face and added, 'Oh, I know you're very puritanical, but you're very contradictory too. Aren't you?'

Oliver demanded loudly, 'Then what do you want?'

'I told you,' said Anna, still flatly. 'Comfort. A resting place. Someone – you – to talk to. Not to have to worry about people's feelings all the time. No more. I'm sorry.'

Oliver was silent for a long time, presumably digesting this; Anna could not look at him to see. Then he said wearily, 'Well, what shall we do?'

'Just go on?' said Anna doubtfully. She was aware that she had hurt him, and could not summon up the strength to do anything about it. It had never been her place to comfort him, and she didn't know how to begin; besides being uncertain whether she wanted to.

'Well – '

Anna went over to him and sat at his feet. She said, 'It seems to spoil things to think about them,' and, 'I'm sorry. I feel so ill, I can't think, I don't know what's the matter.'

This was the right move; it allowed Oliver to escape the

impasse by being kind and practical to her; they managed to spend what was left of the evening more or less peacefully, discussing the Sunday papers, and other neutral things.

Anna was aware that they both hoped that a solution, or at least a wiping out of what had passed, could be achieved in bed. They went to bed early. Anna managed to be privately sick again in the lavatory before going into the bedroom. She lost the whiskey and retched on an empty stomach for a moment or two until tears came to her eyes. She swallowed finally on the bitter taste left by the whiskey as though it was an injustice Oliver had done her. She was beginning to think that she had been attacked by food poisoning or an ulcer; practical worries about her health were another inheritance from Caroline that were just beginning to be apparent in her. She found a thermometer in the bathroom cupboard and took her temperature; it was just slightly above normal. I must keep an eye on it, she told herself quite in Caroline's manner, and went through into the bedroom where Oliver was already sitting bolt upright and naked on one edge of the enormous concave mattress.

'I never know what women find to do in bathrooms,' he observed precisely, whilst Anna undressed. They were beyond romantic modesty and the saving up of nakedness for the ultimate moment, but they were not the kind that romps, or laughs, or admires or discusses each other's body. Anna clambered up onto the bed beside him, and realized that whatever saving grace there might have been in passion, she could not face it. When Oliver made a move towards her she said with unintentional sharpness. 'Please be gentle, I feel bad,' and Oliver stiffened for a moment, and then was, silently and with some grace, very gentle. Afterwards they lay quietly with Anna curled against Oliver, her head on his shoulder. In the beginning, Anna had assumed that it was possible to sleep like this, but Oliver, disillusioned by other experience, always shifted her carefully and turned away from her, into himself, to sleep. He did this early tonight, and Anna, feeling that she had come to the end of something, slept almost immediately herself.

She woke quite suddenly, several hours later, feeling weighted and suffocated, tried for five minutes to pretend that she was not awake and to sink back into sleep, and then struggled out from under the hump of bedclothes onto the pillow. Oliver's head, turned away, was a furry black space beside her; beyond him, she could see the luminous circle of figures on his alarm clock. It was three o'clock. Anna decided that she felt now not so much ill as overcome. It was dark and stuffy, and the pressure inside her was so great that it seemed the curse must come at any moment now; something sharp and precise tugged like a plucked string in her belly and was decidedly unpleasant. She saw quickly that she would not be able to sleep again – there was nothing worse, she thought, hating Oliver for his unconcerned withdrawal, than having insomnia when one was sharing a bed with someone who could sleep and would be disturbed if one tossed about too much, or put the light on to read. She sat up cautiously and looked down on him, and despair swept over her. It was the black, angry despair of curse pressure; she realized this, and yet believed as she always did, that there was no reason to suppose that what she saw in these moments of lucid misery was any further from an ultimate truth because it took up only one week out of four. It made so much more impression on her, after all, than whatever occurred in those three other relatively placid weeks. She felt that she had come to nothing, utterly to nothing, that she had not lived one moment of her life, and probably would not. It was so powerful that it felt like a final revelation.

She remembered what she had felt when Henry left her, and thought that she had been right; this was too much for her, too much was expected of her, unless she moved quickly she would find that she had been radically affected, even changed, by Oliver, and nothing could be further than that from whatever she was waiting for. Oliver was not being helpful; he was beginning to talk too much. I won't come to my event, she told herself, with the mind of someone who had been involved with Oliver Canning. I shouldn't be fit. I must save myself.

She slipped out of bed carefully and began to dress in the dark, automatically and with surprising speed. It was the small clatter she made amongst the things on the dressing table, seeking blindly for her comb, that woke Oliver. She heard him stir and feel for her; then he said, 'Anna,' switched on the lamp and sat up.

Anna blinked at him, found the comb, and began to coil her hair round her head, feeling composed and unreal.

'What are you doing?'

'I'm going,' Anna said, applying hair pins.

'Why?'

'I can't sleep. I can't stand it any more. I don't want to go on with this any more. I'm going back.'

'Why?'

'Because,' said Anna finally, 'it's the only thing to do.'

Her absolute certainty of this seemed to convey itself to Oliver; he did not speak for some time, and then said, 'It seems a bit silly to start a scene at this time. I'll drive you back and you can think it over.'

'I don't want a scene, now or ever. I only want to go. And I don't have to think it over; I know. And it's no good driving me back because College doesn't open until breakfast time.'

'Hadn't you better wait, in that case, until you can get in? You're not very well.'

'No,' Anna persisted. 'I've got to go now.'

She looked at him, curious about what he might do. Now she was dressed, his naked trunk protruding above the sheets seemed ridiculous and faintly obscene. The room was heavy with slept in bedclothes and the warmth of sleep. Anna half hoped, as she had hoped earlier with Henry after running away from school, that he would now ask the right question, say the right thing, break her stubborn silence which she had neither power nor inclination to break herself. She was very conscious that if it had been any other week she would never have got so far; but it seemed both right and final. And still, she was curious about what Oliver would do.

He began to speak, then changed his mind and drew his face into its beak.

'Well, if you must,' he said, 'go. I don't want to have to think at this time of night. I'm too tired.'

He is like me, Anna thought with a last curious onslaught of love, as she realized he had no more to say. She could not think of a way to say goodbye, so she left silently, turning on the threshold to look at Oliver, who was lying down again, with the bedclothes pulled around his neck.

'Your coat's in the kitchen, remember,' he said. Anna thought, it's funny, he won't ever know how much I do love him, how I dream about him. She closed the door behind her. Oliver rearranged the pillows, pulled the blankets closer, turned from one side to the other and back, and then slept.

THIRTEEN

AT NIGHT, OWING to the neon lighting along the Queen's Road, the sky above Cambridge flickers with burnt orange and rust and copper, not bright, but dully transparent over the black, as one imagines the outskirts of hell. For miles up the air seems to burn gloomily, but beyond this smouldering curtain there is usually a strip of genuine deep purple night. This firelight is cold; it drains faces of colour and makes eyes no more than glittering balls like glass marbles. It reduces most colours to a decayed purplish green, although certain transmuted ones stand out – a vicious lemon-white made from buttercup, an artificial limeade colour made from clear blue. Black is rusty, edges and features sharper, shadows harder and more frozen. It is a cruel light, a destroyer, and terrible that it is cheap enough to be thought necessary.

Anna came out into it with hours to kill; even if she went back to College she would have to climb in, and she had never bothered to find the places where the railings could be scaled, or make the acquaintance of anyone with a ground floor window. The rain had stopped, surprisingly, and the night was clearer but laden. She walked aimlessly for some time down into the red, towards the Queen's Road, walking off Oliver. Cambridge dies at midnight, and was now quite dead; it seemed not so much asleep as entirely uninhabited. Anna went down West Road, past the dark hulk of the University Library, skirted Queen's and set off into the town, along Silver Street. On Silver Street Bridge she stopped and leaned over, clinging to the stone parapet, suddenly giddy. The night was very cold and so was the stone; she shivered at the touch of it. There was no one about, and it felt as though there never would be. Anna walked from one side of the bridge to the other, peering down into the water, thinking she would stand there and make out what had happened to her, what she would do. To be out at all at this time and in this place gave rise to a kind of self-conscious expectancy; times out of step like this were what one remembered, one was more aware of things because they were unusual.

Over the Queen's side of the bridge the water was very dark, and the river fairly narrow. A solitary punt floated, half into the shadow under the bridge, and the willows, bare against the glowing sky, brushed on the water, their trailing branches blowing together with a just audible dry clatter.

Over the other side, the river widened into the mill pond, and across the pond was the mill bridge where people perched in summer with mugs of Merrydown cider and blue cheese sandwiches. Under this bridge the water fell steeply, with frothed white curls on the edges and a smooth green slide of it, containing streamers of air, in the centre; the bubbles spread and broke in circles where the fall met the mass of the pond. To the left, below Anna, a pub had a little yard with one or two garden seats on the edge of the river. This was still lit, from high up, and the light reached out slightly, over the water, defining the arched shadows of the Silver Street bridge. This was a white light, and a kind white light; it touched paving stones and bridge softly, and brought out in the water currents of an earthy brown and a curiously vivid olive green. To Anna's right, the pond widened and shallowed, lost itself amongst tunnels of low, damp bushes, and ran, at the edge of Anna's landscape, into a deep silent pool. And beyond, tenting it all, wherever she looked up, the mist of orange light, limiting enough to make one imagine it tangible, possible to brush away and disperse.

Over this orange, reflecting and containing it, long pale clouds were moving, torn and elongated by the wind, multiplying quite rapidly and disclosing through ragged gaps now and then a blob of concentrated light that must have been the moon. The wind came up on the water, hurrying the surface, fetching up the edges of little currents over long weeds into sudden white lines. A large dark green bottle came down from the direction of the mill bridge, bobbing like a shadow, turning on itself in little circles, half submerged, suddenly glowing and glittering emerald in the light from the Anchor courtyard. Anna watched it under the bridge, even leaned over to follow it. As it went out of sight her attention came sharply into focus on the whole scene – as it had in the bathroom at Darton, and more uncertainly on the College lawn, the night of Peter's party.

She thought, this is going to be important, this is one of the times when I can see, and held herself for it, still and gathered to meet it; it became easier to recognize times of this kind as one grew older, times when one was conscious of moving forwards to the event, towards a time when one could act from oneself and from knowledge of oneself, times when to be motionless and to see clearly was the deepest and most violent kind of action. This will change me, Anna thought, and waited for the sense of valuable loneliness she had known after Peter's party; the warning and exhilarating hint that she could do anything, anything at all, and that here, to be caught if she could catch it, was the clue to how to begin.

The weather had been changing imperceptibly; the stirring in the weight of the night Anna had put down to her own internal pressures and had tried to ignore. But now the lightning began; white lightning, flickering amongst the farther trees and through the veil of rusty light, sheets of it jumping into being, there for a moment and gone again. It was low; the scalloped edges of it were below the level of the red light, which again was below the clouds and the dark night. Everything came at her with the lightning, everything insisted, bridges, surface of water, fall, trees, light from the pub, all of them bright and defined and holding their shapes against the force of the light, quivering against Anna's sight. I must put all of myself into seeing, she told herself, holding herself to meet it; I must know what it is, this time.

She remembered something she had once read: 'The earth still pulls at us because it is not ourselves – it is still the source for our moments of glory and our sense of brilliance; the visionary experience is still a real thing. But we have lost our certainty of God and, therefore, faced with this power which is not ourselves, we find it loose and violent. We are afraid. It is an odd paradox that in a world which we see no longer anthropocentric or anthropomorphic, a world where things are themselves to be seen, and studied, and known, our religious interests, our crises of the soul, have become more narrowly and exclusively human. The humanist morality, personal love, deep relationships, honesty, is arguably our most complete way now of arranging ourselves to meet life. But at time when we are alone with what is not human, we are terribly unprovided.'

It took Anna a moment to remember that her father had written it (it was from a preface he had written to a special edition of one of his earlier books). She was too used to denying any precise knowledge of his work. He saw things constantly' violent, Anna thought, he saw all the time, and this was where what he wrote had a power, a savagery, that Forster and Virginia Woolf were unaware of or could not communicate; he saw what was overwhelming, he was with Wordsworth and Coleridge, he had found a way of being alive, alone. She was looking, into this leaping light, for what he would have seen.

And then the cutting edge of the vision melted, the mill race no longer sliced her whole landscape but was only a fall of water, the lightning was no longer the defining limit of a world to understand, but merely an aimless flickering, the horizon eased and expanded and settled and ceased to insist, and Anna knew that whatever it was was over, and that she was very cold and alone. And that she had not been stirred out of herself, she had been moved only as far as a secondhand reflection, in a literary manner, in Oliver's manner, on a piece of prose (secondhand, reflective prose at that) about an experience that in its real, far, unimaginable depth belonged properly to her father. She was still small, and self-contained and watching, and the possible glory was gone.

She curled her arms for a pillow on the stone and put her head down onto them, closing her eyes. I don't think I am going to know, she thought, I think I am just going to go on as I am. I can't make it. I shall never make it.

She could not get further than that, to anything more coherent. The desolation was chilling. She began to shiver violently, and thought that this wild sense of loss would fade, she would become mildly hopeful again, and believe from time to time that nothing had been changed. But now, it was a truth, there would be no event, no transforming knowledge, and now, later, this moment of certainty would be there to remember when she thought about what she would know or not know; it would cast a shadow on things always now. She would always know it might recur. She repeated, looking out sideways over her arms at the dead water, getting used to it, 'I can't do it. I am not going to know. I am going to have to go on just as I am. I shall not change.'

FOURTEEN

SOME WEEKS LATER, about the time when Anna should have come home for the Christmas vacation, Henry had a letter from her. Caroline brought it with his breakfast, like Margaret's letters; she had not opened it, since it was addressed only to Henry. This was not usual; Anna wrote very rarely and when she did produced a schoolgirl scrawl with thank-yous for cakes and biscuits and shorthand accounts of largely fictitious social activities in answer to her other's repeated requests for news. Caroline continued to send food parcels and a weekly account of all the family's small doings to Anna at Cambridge as she had done to Anna at school. The difference was that at school Anna had been expected to write to her parents every Sunday afternoon, and had complied. Caroline thought it delicate not to mention this extraordinary letter of Henry's before he did. She handed it to him, and left him, thinking that Anna had probably, inconsiderately, decided to come home without giving her enough time to change the butcher's order, or buy more breakfast cereal.

Henry knew the letter must contain something nasty, but he opened it with a kind of relief; he had spent his time since he

239

came back from Cambridge feeling that he must act, must find an answer, must do something about Anna, and had not been able, as Oliver had predicted, to think at all what this something might be. But he had nevertheless tormented himself, and now hoped the letter, however unpleasant, might jolt him into action of some kind, might indicate a direction.

'My dear father,' Anna wrote, 'I don't want to tell you anything, I don't want ever to have to try to communicate anything again, but there are some things I'd be grateful if you could do for me, if you can bear to, so I shall have to explain a certain amount. I want to get married as soon as possible to Peter Hughes-Winterton. We want it soon, his mother says not until he goes down (this summer). We're still arguing that one out. If you could get it into *The Times* and the *Telegraph*, or whatever, I'd be grateful. I'd like a Registry Office in a hurry to get it over, but I'm afraid it will be orange blossom and champagne and a cousin who's a Bishop to please Lady Hughes-Winterton. I hope you think that's funny. I suppose I'll have to come home to get married, but I'm staying with the Hughes-Wintertons over Christmas and I don't want to have to come home again. I can't face you – I really mean, I can just about go on, if I don't have to face you. You know why, don't you? I write now partly because of *The Times* and keeping Lady Hughes-Winterton quiet and happy about that, and partly because if anyone can stop Mummy making a fuss and wanting me home and trying to inspect Peter, etc., you can. You do see? If we – Peter and I – win, we can get married in the New Year and live in digs until Peter gets his degree (which no one but Lady Hughes-Winterton thinks will be a good one anyway so no need to feel guilty about that).

'I ought to stop there, really, and let you think what you like. But in a sense you deserve an explanation (a back-hander that, I know) and if I don't tell you, you might be clever in all the wrong directions. Or try to say something to me, and I don't want you to do that, above all not that. I don't suppose anybody else's father could say nothing, but there's a chance you might.

'What happened was, I found out I was pregnant. I was a bit silly not to guess earlier, really. Except it seemed in such bad taste, and one knew so many people who did all sorts of things and managed not to be. And I went into a blind panic and couldn't cope, and saw I would never manage without someone to arrange things for me, like Mummy used to. Things seem to happen to me even when I don't do anything at all, life seems like that. So I went to Peter and said help, which is just what he loves. No, I'm not wickedly letting him think it's his, or anything like that, I just told him all about it, he's worked out a lovely psychological explanation of how Oliver and everything – my instability – all goes back to you, and parental neglect, and inferiority (me) and all that. He may even be right. He says I need to be loved and looked after, and I think I do – at least, I'm happy in a sort of way, letting him love me, and he obviously thinks I might never have married him if I hadn't got into such an awful mess and broken down completely, and I might not at that. I don't know why he wants me, but that's his business. It's nice somebody does. I mean to be so good to him, really I do.

'What I want is an abortion. I know of lots of people who seem to have managed them – and it must be easy to arrange one if I can only get away to London from Lady Hughes-Winterton's eagle eye. But Peter is all full of respect for life, and says no, let it be born, and adopted, unless we keep it – there's going to be a ghastly muddle, can't you see – I mean, how can it be adopted, Lady Hughes-Winterton must notice its presence before then – I think Peter's rather splendid, but I'd better win this argument or we'll never be able to begin to be married at all, will we? And I mean to try. I mean, Peter can't keep it up at that pitch, even I can see.

'This letter is getting too long after all, isn't it, in spite of my not wanting to tell you things? Perhaps you think Mexico would still be better. It would, if I were you, absolutely it would. But I'm not you, I've not got the power, I've not got – you know, what I've not got – so I shall just go on and do what Mummy would like and marry Peter. And be a human being. Wife, and so on. You can tell Mummy what you like. I'm nastily leaving it to you. You know what she can take, I never had been able to, I don't think she can take anything from me. You would tell her how unutterably suitable Peter is, just what she wanted.

'I must stop writing. It does no good. If things were different

I'd like to talk to you – about the way life traps one, the way things decided themselves by default – but I can't talk to you and go on, you ask too much. Peter gives me a warmth, a real warmth, that's worth something. Isn't it? Don't answer more than you have to, just fix things for me. And love, really, love, Anna.'

Henry sat for some time with the letter spread in front of him, taking it in. It was nasty, but not in the way he had expected, in so far as he had known what he expected. He was too involved to work out what mattered most immediately to him, which was Anna's attitude to himself; he could read the letter both ways, as a final gesture to his interest in her, or as a plea to him to disregard her bravado, her practical tone, to overbear her distance and fetch her home to himself. She wants me to know, he thought. She wants me to know what has happened to her. Or perhaps she only wants to write it down for someone to read, and thinks I'm the most harmless reader, because whatever I think of her marrying this boy, or getting rid of this baby, I shan't interfere. Probably she's regretting having written so much already. She is sure enough that she doesn't want to see me; that we have nothing to say to each other. We never have had. Perhaps I should keep out. Or perhaps she wants me to assert that there is something to say. But what?

He had so little experience of people wanting things from him. He had made enough mess of Margaret.

He thought of Peter Hughes-Winterton and wondered how long this combination of heroism and opportunism would bear up under the strain of Anna's condition; at least, he thought, Anna seemed well enough aware of where the strains would be. It might all be more possible than he had immediately thought.

But there was this fact, the pregnancy. The thought of abortion repelled him, and in connection with Anna stirred his body into shuddering too. Morally he had nothing against it, he thought. It might be best. But . . . should he fix it himself, or pay, or leave it to Peter, or . . . ? It was so much what should not have been.

And there was Caroline, who was, he was aware, waiting tactfully in the kitchen until he came to tell her what had been in the letter. What could he tell Caroline? For her own sake? And for Anna's? He stuffed the letter into his pocket, threw back his chair, and went out through the window, into the garden.

Caroline saw him cross the lawn, and thought that Anna had done something really tiresome this time; he was walking violently, straining all his muscles obsessively, in the way he had when he was put out, or under extreme literary pressure. Caroline did not think he was under extreme literary pressure this time. Caroline thought, damn that girl, and, he doesn't know what to say to me, and, he can't keep that up for long, he'll be back. He had been walking a great deal lately, not like this, but slowly, heavily, stopping from time to time and turning, as though he was up against a series of invisible walls. Caroline had assumed that his work was proving intransigent. Now, she watched him into the orchard and began to polish silver, waiting for his return.

Under his feet the leaves were frozen crisply to the ground, in layers, stiff at the edges, soft in the middle, like a galette of potatoes. They creaked and crunched under his shoes like new snow. His breath came in visible puffs and spread on the cold air; the trees were spread with grey, furry frost like fungus. Henry threaded them without much direction, stopping to take his corners like an inefficient horse in a bending race. He had told himself that he was coming out to think, but in fact, he was walking so fast in order to put off thinking.

He came in a zig-zag to the hut and went in. It smelled of damp wood, and there was frost on the outside of the windows. Opening the drawer in what he thought of still as 'Jeremy's work-bench' he found Anna's notebook; a mass of damp empty pages, one page covered entirely with Michael, Michael, Michael, the beginning of the poem, 'Why trees were green once, Was, of course, yourself', and underneath that, in very careful writing, with decorated flourishes, the flat statement, 'We are all very much alone.'

Michael? he asked himself, and had no answer. He had never bothered to learn Michael's name. He turned the limp pages over again, and thought that here, too, Anna had left no clue, nothing which he could take as a sign of a mind burning in her, or a talent to develop; nothing in the light of which he could take the train to York, and say to her, look, you must come home, you must go away by yourself and do this, or this. Nothing, even, bad and gushing and undeveloped, that showed at least the will to work. Only the name, and the final sentence, and the bit of poem. Even her love poetry, at a distance, in the past tense, Henry thought – something which should have been felt urgently, here made remote, in this hesitant language, examined from outside. Had this Michael been past or present when this was written? He thought he knew it would have been the same whatever Michael had been. That was like Anna. She would never go up to things, or grasp them, or let herself in for knowing them.

Oh, Anna, Anna, Anna, he said to himself, I would like to give you something to hold. I would like to start you off again.

'We are all very much alone.'

Ever since he came back from Cambridge, he had been tormented by love; he had thought over and over what he could or should have said to Anna, then, last summer, two summers ago; he would have told her what he knew, he would have taken her to his places and made her see them as he saw them; he would have made her look pleased, and smile, and catch her breath as she had when he first mentioned Mexico. But he could not bring himself to approach her, afraid as he was of Oliver, and unused as he was to action, and he had felt, with this love, he was heavy with a complete helplessness he had not known before. He had not been able to write. At first this had not mattered, had been only a transitory prick of irritation in his trouble. But lately, with a letter from his publisher, and the strain of days spent with nothing done, nothing achieved, no progress, only the same circle of love, and responsibility, and helplessness, and decisions not made, he had begun to worry about the writing too. He felt that he was not a man without it; after he had spent enough time away from pen and paper he lost touch with himself and had no centre to judge from.

He had always known he was spiritually gambling on being able to continue his own cycle of vision and thought and construction and walking into old age without interruption. Then, he assumed tacitly and with no medical evidence, he would pop off with a convenient heart attack. Or at the worst, if something died, and the line of novels petered out, become a meaningless repetition of the same watered down formulas, as he had seen happen with others, he would know, he would give up gracefully and come to grips with his book on romanticism. If he were not capable of reading a little each day, and organizing notes, he reasoned, he would be as good as dead in any case and only obliged to wait with dignity. He was luckier than most; there was no need for his occupation to be gone 'at age sixty-five' as it said in the insurance brochures.

Oh, he had been well prepared for the future, he had taken it into account. He had thought that a man's job now was his religion often enough; the first thing he would bring up in his mind if asked suddenly, 'Why do you think you are alive?' He did not think this generally satisfactory, but in his own case it was a truth; he was a knot of what he saw, and his job, what he made of what he saw, what he wrote – there seemed to be nothing of him except physical functions hanging over to be mistrusted or accused before death. Or so he had thought; a curious over-simplification for anyone pretending to be a novelist, he told himself, looking at Anna's damp little notebook, even a novelist as little concerned with idiosyncratic human relations as himself. Except that it had been a deliberate over-simplification that had worked. A man cannot go down all paths and at the same time travel any distance, he said; a man must choose, and I could not have stayed in my own clearing and explored myself to all ends. I had to close off ways, and to strike out.

It should have been easy enough to act, with Anna's news in his pocket. He touched that, and then pushed the little notebook down to join it, pocketing it a little like a love token, the private possession acquired without the beloved's knowledge, the traditional lost glove, the page of doodled drawings, the magic symbol which gives a secret power over its owner, in other hands.

Anna must be very frightened, he thought suddenly. She's not used to having to act either. And her need to act is more immediate than mine. He could not bear the thought of Anna being frightened, and turned and went in again. Caroline had always told him what to do, and he would have, after all, to turn to her.

When he came in, Caroline looked up, alert for the ordinary tiresomeness she expected from Anna. He said gloomily, 'I must talk to you,' and stood at the window with his back to her, falling into a silence that seemed designed to convey that he had said all that was necessary, all he could. Caroline began to say, 'What has Anna done now?' and changed it, feeling her way more carefully, to, 'When are we to expect Anna home?' 'Not for some time,' Henry said. 'She's staying with some people called Hughes-Winterton. Near York.' He looked surreptitiously at the address engraved on Anna's letter.'Near York.'

'I wish she'd let us know earlier. Will she come home for Christmas? Jeremy will be very upset if the family isn't together for Christmas.'

'I doubt that. No, she won't. She wants to stay there.' Caroline could not think how to get at what he could not say. She asked, rather hopelessly, 'Who are these Hughes-Wintertons?'

'There's a Lady Hughes-Winterton with a husband in the Foreign Office. Sir Walter Hughes-Winterton, I believe it is. And a son, Peter. Up at Cambridge.' He seemed about to plunge into silence again, and then brought out with an effort, 'Anna says she is going to marry him.'

It was Caroline's turn now to be silent. She was willing to rejoice; she wanted Anna married and the Hughes-Wintertons sounded much more possible than she had even dared hope from Anna. Her imagination ran out into *The Times* and the *Telegraph*, her own wise, and friendly, and balanced welcome for Peter on his first visit after Christmas – no rushing at him, but no sense of inspection, immediate acceptance – a summer reception on the lawn? Jeremy in morning dress, how charming, one of her own relatives who was a clergyman, her own hat – something a bit dashing this time, a silk cartwheel on a grand scale – Henry giving his daughter away, looking splendid – and here she came up against Henry's entirely unexplained and disproportionate gloom. She knew that fathers traditionally thought no one good enough for their daughters – even Anna – and would have been indulgently amused by doubt or apprehension. But Henry was plainly miserable. There was something she did not know.

'Do they approve then? His parents?'

'Oh yes. Anna wants it in the papers, she says. They seem only to be arguing over when it shall be. They, Peter and Anna – want it in a few weeks' time. Lady Hughes-Winterton would prefer the summer.'

'I see. We should be rather rushed . . . It takes time to get a dress made . . . People might think . . . Will Anna not finish at Cambridge?'

'No. I don't think that matters. She wasn't doing much good there.' This was obviously what he thought; the trouble was not there. Caroline would have liked to shake words from him.

'Hadn't you better let me read Anna's letter, so that I can make arrangements?'

'No,' said Henry, too quickly. 'I think it was – meant for me.'

'Henry – what is the trouble? Is Anna not happy? Has she . . . is she . . . does she have to get married?'

Henry waited too long to be able to lie convincingly.

'I see. I assume Lady Hughes-Winterton doesn't know.' There was a stridency in her voice, now. 'I should have expected something like this from Anna, I suppose. She can't do anything – she can't keep out of any trouble.' She considered. 'Still, if the wedding is as soon as possible, no one may . . . Henry, I wish you would treat me responsibly. How long has this been going on? This Peter – is he only marrying her because of this? Do they love each other? Because – if he is – he must be told that he need not. Nobody need marry for that. It's a bad beginning. Anna should have looked after herself.'

Caroline believed that trouble of this kind was always the woman's fault. Men were naturally lascivious, even the nicest of them, and out for what they could get. In a curious female way she admired this in them. It was a woman's responsibility to keep out of harm, and her intelligence to know what men were and how to manage them. She must have 'self-control', which she must also know men were incapable of. Caroline finished, 'Anna will not be responsible for herself. She will not think of consequences. I do not want this young man to feel coerced.'

'I don't think he is,' said Henry, not knowing where he was leading himself. 'I think it is Anna who is fundamentally uncertain . . .'

'In that case they had better be married quickly. Anna will never make her mind up. She wasn't uncertain, I suppose, when – '

'You don't understand,' Henry said in spite of himself. 'Peter – Peter isn't responsible.'

Caroline sat down at the kitchen table and looked onto her silver things, spoons and bowls spread neatly in front of her, some shining, some smeared with jeweller's rouge. She looked at them for some time, as though steadying herself. Then she said, almost inaudibly, 'Who is?'

'Oliver Canning.' Henry felt the answer was not unexpected. He also knew suddenly that he had passed a boundary, had made a decision; that the handing over of this piece of information had decided the way things were to be. He felt bad, very bad. And he had never seen Caroline so shaken. She whispered, from a dry throat, 'I knew he was dangerous, that summer. But I thought he went away in time. He was that sort. But I thought he went in time.' She asked, not looking at Henry. 'And Anna – dragged – this boy – into this?'

'He knows – '

'How disgusting,' Caroline cried. 'How disgusting. How horrible.' She put her face down on the table between the coasters and began to shake, and then to weep. Once she cried, 'I don't know how she could, she was taught what was right.' Henry shifted slightly; if you read that line, somewhere, it was almost trite, everyone said it; but here to Caroline it was as though they had all, all the family, lost virtue; a terrible pain.

Henry made no move to help his wife, to pat her on the shoulder, or wipe her tears, or tell her what she wanted to be told, that what fault there was was not hers. Something had happened to him. When he turned round from the window he wore his old look, abstracted, retreating under the camouflage of his generous eyebrows; he watched Caroline's twisting shoulders with a curious compound of sharp interest and some-

248

thing like relief. It was, he remarked with some surprise, as though Caroline's family anguish, Caroline's outrage, Caroline's sense of failure in her part, relieved him of his own burden. As though her misery cancelled his different and more single misery; as though he had handed this too over to her, with the butcher, the baker, the income tax, the journalists, and all the other like responsibilities he didn't even know about. As though to share his knowledge of Anna had changed the face of Anna; to let Caroline see her had moved her into Caroline's world. Caroline's tears moved him in one way more deeply than Margaret's, or even Anna's, whose cause he felt more clearly — Caroline was closer to him, the eruption was within the boundary of his land, and less expected.

But he was not, he thought, a sufferer, any more than he was an actor. He was no Christian, let alone no Christ. He remembered what Oliver had said, in the library — something about 'all of us like dead albatrosses, tumbling out of the sky, to be hung round your neck as evidence of your spiritual progress'. Well, if they were, he didn't feel that he had died with the albatross after all, he did not share its flurry and struggle; if it was round his neck, it impeded his progress a little, and he studied how its feathers lay, white and smooth, and its claws curled, cold and limp.

He remembered now, there was always a point at which misery snapped in him, at which he was impelled to stand aside, and watch, at which he had to say, 'I have had enough of this,' and retreat into solitude. And write? It had been like this after his worst clumsinesses in Cambridge, after his friends had been tortured in Burma — and now, after Anna. He began to recognize himself again, felt down tentatively, and touched a secret excitement over his knowledge of Anna, of Caroline, of Oliver, of Peter, of the way things were working.

Caroline said, 'I'm sorry, Henry, I didn't mean to do that.' She straightened herself and wiped her eyes. 'I can see it's bad enough for you without my getting worked up too.' The thought struck her. 'How long have you known?'

'About Oliver Canning since I went to Cambridge. I saw them both then, but there seemed to be nothing I could do. About the other matter, only since this morning.'

'I see,' said Caroline. She did not ask why he had not told her; that was not the sort of question she asked. 'Why didn't you make Anna come home?'

'I didn't feel I had any right.'

'I would have made her come home.' She was allowing herself to grow angry, and as her anger increased her back stiffened and her hands ceased to tremble. 'What does Oliver Canning think of this latest idea?'

Henry had not thought of Oliver at all, except as a ciphered nastiness who was the cause of the pregnancy; certainly not as anyone who might have any feeling for Anna or personal interest in the possible child. He said, mildly surprised, 'I don't know. I don't know if he even knows. I hadn't thought of him.'

'Well,' said Caroline briskly, 'he's responsible, and he must pay. However much we dislike the idea, we must see him and tell him so. We must move quickly. Anna must come here – we'll see her through, we must do so much – and Oliver Canning must pay. If that poor boy really wants to marry Anna he can do so when the baby's over – and personally I doubt if he will, once he's had time to think. Anna had better go right away. She won't have much future left in this country as things are; she'd better go and teach in the Colonies, and be useful at least.'

'I don't think she wants to have the baby,' Henry suggested, knowing what the answer would be.

'Well, she must. She must take what comes when she behaves wrongly. She can't do anything else – for one thing, it's wicked, and for another, it's dangerous. None of us are going to enjoy the next year, but that can't be helped. You must make her come home.'

'I don't think I can.'

'Someone must. He must – Oliver Canning must, if no one else will. I shall make him.'

'Don't you think we'd do better to leave him out?'

'No,' said Caroline, who was now in a fine rage and was holding herself together with plans and action. 'He must take what he deserves, he must pay, and I shall see that he does. I shall write now.' She looked at Henry with tears still in her eyelashes, quite incapable of admitting that some of her rage was directed at him. She said, 'We must get on with it, quickly,' and then bowed down over the table again, and muttered to herself, 'He was such a nasty little man, I don't know how she could bear to let him touch her. I knew he was like that, he can't leave people alone, he used to look at Anna in a way I didn't like, that summer – and at me, sometimes – he can't bear women who aren't under his power, I know that kind. But I thought Anna was too stupid to notice, that's what I thought, such a lump she was then, not a woman at all, and I didn't think he'd dare, depending on you as he does.'

'That was partly why,' Henry suggested.

'I can see that it might have been. That makes it worse. I blame myself, partly. I instinctively didn't want him in my house, but I was sorry for poor Margaret.'

The thought of Margaret was a small shock to both of them.

'Does Margaret know?' Caroline demanded. 'Was that why she – '

'No. I think she is living in her own quite private tragedy. I don't think she leaves herself time to notice – things like – Anna.'

'It's a pity,' Caroline observed dispassionately, 'that it was only Anna. If it had been someone more – less – more possible, at least Margaret would have been rid of him. She always floundered about him so. Just what he wouldn't like. And she needn't be like that – she'd have made a splendid wife for all sorts of people – almost anyone, except that inconsiderate little horror.'

'Poor Margaret,' said Henry. 'She's going to suffer for all these decisions we've all been making or refusing to make and she's never going to know what went wrong. Like the girl on the roundabout whose skirt got caught up in the machinery, who got rather nastily mangled, quite by mistake. I don't know what we're going to do with her.'

'That's Oliver's business.'

'I'm afraid Margaret won't think so.' Henry's sudden prick of conscience over not having communicated with Margaret gave a further blow to his personal distress for Anna, which had not been grounded on conscience but was now completely shunted into association with it. He was growing together again, alone with himself, only morally associated with all the trouble.

He felt now, guilty in all directions. But lighter, clearer, all the same. Distanced. He stood up, and left Caroline abruptly, and wandered, like a discoverer, back into his study.

FIFTEEN

SO DEALING WITH Anna and Oliver fell into Caroline's hands. She thought of telephoning Anna and ordering her to come home, but she knew that that was not likely to have any effect beyond antagonizing or distressing the Hughes-Wintertons, which, however remote she might judge the real possibility of their becoming Anna's in-laws, she did not want to do. So instead, wanting to find out 'what was really going on', to give herself time to think without having to suffer any period of inaction, and perhaps most of all to take a legitimate revenge on someone for the humiliation, she wrote to Oliver, and summoned him to Darton to explain himself. It was not the way in which Henry would have managed things, perhaps, but Henry, to whom Oliver and Anna and Margaret had all in their different ways delegated the dealing of the affair, seemed to have abdicated completely. He was not writing yet, but was obscurely content with this, certain now that it was temporary. He wandered around the house and garden with an air of confidently waiting for something to happen, and answered all Caroline's questions and suggestions with a vague reassurance that he was certain she knew best. Caroline was not always sure that he even heard her, but that suited her. She needed to deal, at that time, and was really happier if he had no ideas of his own about the dealing.

The letter to Oliver fell into Margaret's hands, who picked it up at lunch-time, when it arrived by the second post. She heard the squeak of the spring and the flutter of paper, and the light flop of the envelope on her doormat, and hurried out of her bedroom in her dressing-gown, thinking it might be the letter of advice – of information – from Henry, for which she seemed to have been waiting so long. Margaret had changed since Henry's visit; she had become passive and resigned, and had not energy or will to try and change anything further, even to the extent of writing letters. She had done all she could in writing to Henry, and had now the sense of having put her life into his hands completely. She sat around in a lethargy which was no longer intolerable because it seemed no longer either final or morally reprehensible. She was waiting for Henry; it was not her weakness that caused the lethargy, but Henry's decree. She was like a woman who has taken religion, abandoned to another putative Will, relieved finally of the need to ask the questions, why am I here, what must I do about it? It would all be revealed in due course. Meanwhile, on the two occasions when Oliver briefly came home, she sat quietly, looking past him, and hardly spoke to him. She felt that she almost needed Henry's permission to do that. What Oliver thought she did not enquire.

She had largely given up the Bloody Marys because one day they had made her sick, which was altogether too violent an activity for her. She had used them as a medicine, and was not really addicted to the alcohol; she was capable of producing her own anaesthetics, which were more agreeable and effective than drink could ever have been. She ate less and less, and had become so thin that the tendons stood out on the back of her hands, and her nose was almost transparent just above the nostrils, bluish and shadowed where it had been live and warm and golden. Her ankles, on the other hand, were puffy from lack of movement, in spite of frequent scrubbings with the loofah in the bath. Her ribs stood out, the skin stretched over them, but the skin over her stomach, where the ribs curved away from each other, hung in a little fold of unrelated fat. In the face, the same pattern repeated itself – the cheeks were pulled taut, the eyes sunk, the jaw like a knife and all of it greyish-blue – but the skin under the throat hung in a little bag, a shadow of the cheerful plumpness of a double chin. She rarely looked at herself now.

She slept a great deal, much more easily than before, sometimes eighteen hours a day, and was learning to sleep longer.

When she was awake, she sat quietly in the living room with the fire on and the curtains drawn, and joined in conversations with Henry and Oliver against a background of soaring melting noise provided by the Light Programme. She felt herself contained helplessly in a great yellow ball, warm as the curtains which bounded it, spotted as they were with large daisies, all bravely turning their stylized pretty heads to the sun within the room. Oliver and Henry spoke with tremendous gentleness to her, they told her that everything was for the best, that in some obscure way she had suffered for them, that she was necessary to them and they loved her.

All this had been more than enough because it was not all, because Henry would write, in the end, and tell her what to do next, when it was time to do it.

She did not at first understand why the letter was addressed to Oliver. It came from Darton, it was postmarked, quite clearly. She was afraid of it when it came to it, afraid in spite of herself that what Henry had to say might make things more difficult for her. But she could not quite believe that this letter was not for her, because she had been waiting for it. Also she did not like the idea of Henry's having anything to say to Oliver that she did not know about. It was really impossible not to open the letter, and it was only when she had the full sheet of paper in front of her that she realized the handwriting was not Henry's but his wife's.

Caroline had hesitated over the beginning of the letter. She had not known whether to put Dear Oliver, or Dear Mr Canning, and had taken some time to decide on Dear Oliver, as a way of showing him that this had always been a mere formality. Since she had also saved most of her anger for where it would be most effective, when she had Oliver in front of her in the house, the letter was not as icy as she had imagined when posting it. It might have seemed obliquely so to Oliver, who would expect it. To Margaret it was numbly bewildering, a series of added complications she was not prepared to understand – what had Caroline, what had Anna, to do with what she and Henry and Oliver were achieving together?

Caroline had mentioned nothing openly, since she did not know whether Oliver knew about Anna's pregnancy, or her move to the Hughes-Wintertons. She assumed that there had been a break between Anna and Oliver, but did not know when; she suspected that Anna's uncharacteristic anxiety to have her engagement posted in *The Times* and the *Telegraph* might be to have Oliver informed, impersonally, of a *fait accompli* – Caroline, unlike Henry and Anna, was not aware of how unlikely it was that Oliver should read either of these papers, still less the Society Column. So her letter had been brief, and vague, and had commanded urgency: the gist was, Oliver must come, and he would know why. Margaret read it and re-read it, gathering only from the urgency and the invitation, and feeling vaguely indignant that Oliver should be asked without herself being informed. And then she thought of Darton, and that Henry would be there, and suddenly everything boiled over, the waiting was at an end, and it was time now, if Henry was at Darton, she must be there too.

She made a muddle of the train journey and was put out to find that there was no taxi and no Henry to meet her at Darton; by the time she reached the house it was evening; too late for a call. When she came round the curve of the drive, she was met by light; light poured steadily through the front windows, light from the lamp over the door in a warm, bright pool on the drive. The place was very still, very substantial, after London almost unbearably silent. She stumbled into a run as she saw the whole house, like a thief coming in for sanctuary. Inside, she would need to do no more, it would be the end, it would be peaceful. She was coming home.

Caroline in a brown dress opened the door for her, with light deep and clear behind her. She had a polite enquiring look, which changed slowly to one of concern.

'Margaret – ' she said. 'I didn't recognize you for a moment. We weren't expecting . . . Come in.'

Margaret began to tremble.

'Are you ill? How did you get here? Give me your umbrella. Let me take your coat.'

'I came in a van with a pig,' Margaret said hopefully. But her teeth were chattering so loudly that Caroline must hear them, and her amused smile would not be formed. She tried to take off her hat, forgetting it was transfixed with hairpins, panicked, pulled at it, and fetched down hat, pins, and all the uncertain structure of her hair. This seemed such a disaster that she turned to Caroline choking with apology, wild and defenceless, with her thin neck lost in the slight decolleté of her black dress, and all her brittle straw-coloured hair crackling on her shoulders. Caroline warded off the apology, addressed her like a child, 'Never mind, let me help with it,' and extracted a comb from the handbag Margaret was still clutching. She tugged patiently at her hair, said, 'Have you ever thought of having it thinned?' and began to coil it neatly in the nape of Margaret's neck. Under her hands Margaret began to relax; she bent her head submissively, and allowed herself to be dealt with. This was something of what she had hoped for, Caroline's cool fingers, touching her, looking after her, taking charge. The result was not very successful. There was not enough pins to secure it very firmly, and no woman can ever treat another woman's hair with the severity necessary to get it under control. There were wisps loose on her neck, and little ends loose all over, lifting with electricity, as though they were in a breeze.

'It's obvious I wasn't trained as a hairdresser,' Caroline said. 'The only hair I've touched beside my own was my daughter's and nobody could say I was successful there.'

This reference to Anna passed unnoticed between them; Caroline remembered it and blushed for it five minutes later. Margaret said, 'You are so kind – ' and began, trembling again, 'Oh, Caroline – '

'No,' said Caroline. 'Don't say anything. You don't have to. I can see you've had a bad day, you must be terribly tired. We'd have met you at the station if you'd let us know. Come into the drawing room. Let me give you a drink and you can relax for a moment. That will be best.'

Caroline talked, and poured sherry, whilst Margaret sat heavily in an armchair and answered questions like – 'Did you have a good journey?' and remarks on the weather, quite automatically in the expected way. She took pleasure in these questions; it was so long since she had been able to answer them, they were guiding lights, as she saw them, to normal human contact. When she said, 'I had a long wait in London,' or 'It has been rather dismal for the last few days,' she felt she was passing an examination, proving herself, establishing herself again as a human being. She began tentatively to elaborate on the London drizzle, took her glass with a bright remark about how rarely one now met with a good manzanilla, began, confusedly, to imagine that this was the end of the struggle, that she was paying a perfectly ordinary call.

Caroline, who in her first revulsion from Margaret's oddness and wild appeal had meant to have precisely this neutralizing effect on her, was now slightly annoyed at the completeness of her success. It was all very well to sit there chattering politely at eight in the evening, but Caroline could not now see any opening for the questions she must ask: where was Oliver, what did Margaret know, why had she come?

She had meant to use Margaret's plight very effectively in the speech she had been preparing for Oliver, but she had not bargained for Margaret's presence, which would make the plain speaking she was looking forward to almost impossible. She did not even know whether Oliver was coming – had Margaret intercepted her letter and come instead, or first, or had she come independently and if so, why, at this time? Caroline could not feel friendly towards Margaret. She asked as lightly as she could, 'Have you had any food?' This question seemed to embarrass Margaret quite disproportionately. She became awkward again, and stammered, 'No, I haven't. I meant to. I really meant to. I haven't for some time, I'm sorry. I came in rather a hurry.' Why apologize, Caroline thought irritably. She said, 'I think there's some cold chicken. I'll fetch it, in a moment. Why did you come?' Margaret did not answer. Caroline repeated patiently, 'Why did you come?' Margaret looked frightened. 'I had to. I had to be here. I thought you understood.'

'Of course I understand,' Caroline soothed her. She said nothing further, only allowed it to be seen that she was waiting for an elaboration. Margaret shifted herself and then added plaintively, 'I got your letter. I didn't quite understand it, but I saw I had to be here.' She managed a little laugh. 'I'm afraid I don't know all that's going on. But that's all right – Henry will. Henry will know what to do.'

'Where is Oliver?' Caroline asked slowly. She wanted to ask,

'Where is the letter I sent Oliver?' She was afraid it was in Margaret's handbag.

'I don't know.' Margaret was more flustered. Her lip shook, she twisted her hands and looked around unhappily. 'I thought he might be here.'

'We have not heard from him.'

'Oh dear,' Margaret cried. 'I'm terribly sorry. Really, terribly sorry. I wish I could help but I don't know where he is.'

'I particularly wanted to speak to him,' Caroline pursued.

'But Henry has spoken to him already. Henry will tell us what to do.'

'Henry hasn't seen him since the latest developments.'

The idea of any development seemed to paralyse Margaret, along with the imputation of even a hint of helplessness to Henry. She murmured, 'Oh dear,' and 'Henry,' and began to twist her head around, first one way and then the other, as if planning a line of retreat. She said vaguely, 'I'm sorry. Such a long journey. Terribly sorry.'

'Margaret,' said Caroline firmly, and was going to ask about the letter point-blank, when Henry came in. He was on tiptoe, a momentary intruder, wearing his secret smile. He said, 'Coffee?'

Caroline said repressively, 'We have a visitor, Henry.' Margaret rose uncertainly to her feet. She could not see very clearly; the sherry on an empty stomach had fuddled her entirely. The room turned slightly, with Caroline like a curl of brown smoke swaying in one corner, and then righted itself for a moment, although still oscillating beneath her feet, so that she could fix the bulk of Henry in the doorway and the soft white light of his hair and beard. She gave a great cry, 'Henry!' and set out across the space of the carpet, holding her hands out to him, and collapsed against him, clinging to his lapels, sagging, so that her head was on his chest, and her knees pressed against his legs. Her hair uncurled and sprang loose again, so that hairpins shot into the carpet and stood there at angles. 'Henry,' she said again, more quietly, and then just clung.

Henry pulled clumsily at the back of her dress, trying to straighten her.

'What is it?' he said. 'What is it, Margaret?' He found it

258

impossible to do anything except clutch her under the arms to support her. 'Why have you come?'

'I had to come. I was waiting for the letter. Then I had to come.'

'I wrote to Oliver, I told you,' Caroline explained in an undertone. Henry looked at her anxiously over Margaret's head; both of them were wondering, where is Oliver?

'I can't go on,' Margaret said, 'any longer, without a meaning. You know, Henry, tell me what to do.' Henry, for want of anything to say or do, held her closer with one arm, and aimlessly stroked her hair with his free hand. It was Caroline who spoke, with an edge to the reasonable kindness of her voice.

'Come now, Margaret, you must sit down. We'll take care of you. Come over here and sit down. Leave Henry alone.'

But Margaret was past Caroline's reason, and only pressed closer against Henry.

'Make her sit down, Henry,' Caroline ordered, faintly flushed. Henry said gently, helplessly, 'Wouldn't you like to sit down?'

'You must tell her,' said Caroline, seeing how Margaret was. Henry said, 'I'd like you to sit down, Margaret,' and she turned her face up to him, with blank eyes swivelling from side to side. Henry hesitated, and then pushed her firmly in the middle, collapsed her, folded her, and carried her effortlessly to the sofa. She allowed herself to be arrange on it, quite passively, but when Henry tried to stand and leave her, she flung her arms around his neck, and pulled him down to her. She said, 'Henry, Henry, no, Henry, don't go,' and then went quite limp, except for her hands, still clasped firmly at the base of his neck.

Henry dropped unhappily beside her, and managed to shift her grip to his own hands. There she clung, and rolled her body over against him, her head on his knee. Once there, she settled herself, and said fearfully, with an undertone of basic cunning, 'You won't send me away, Henry, will you? You'll let me stay?'

'Yes,' said Henry. 'Of course. You mustn't worry.'

'I love you, Henry,' Margaret said. 'You know that?'

'Margaret,' Caroline said, driven by years of protecting Henry, and by her own deepest security, the fact that however little effort Henry put into his marriage, at least he had no relationship outside it; 'Margaret, pull yourself together please.

259

You must pull yourself together and help us. And let go of Henry – it's very inconsiderate to treat him in this way, he has worries enough of his own.'

Even to her own ears this sounded petty. Margaret turned reproachful eyes on her and then burrowed even further into Henry's thigh. She said something indistinguishable, and then, more fearfully, 'Henry?'

'For goodness sake do something,' Caroline told Henry, quivering with anger. 'You've got to put an end to this.'

'What shall I do?' Henry asked neither of them, mildly. He had a look of being at their mercy, Caroline thought, making no difference between them, simply waiting quietly until he could get away. Margaret was now quite still, even more prepared than Henry to wait for the next event. There was only herself who was interested in getting anything done, she thought, standing as still as they were, simply from a lack of something she could do. The door opened, tentatively, then quickly. Oliver stepped into the room and closed it behind him.

'I rang twice,' he said, 'and no one answered. But there were lights, so I came in to look. You are lucky to be able to trust your neighbours enough to leave the house unlocked.'

He wore his gunman's raincoat, and a gunman's soft hat, which he now removed, and held in front of him. He seemed jaunty, even happy, stood with his feet together, as though on parade. His voice dropped into their pool of hysteria like a series of rough, round pebbles, all concrete, all the same, all finite. Caroline said to him, with an edge of relief in her voice which she had not intended, 'I hoped you'd come.'

Henry nodded to him from the sofa, and continued to sit, unmoving. Oliver took things in, his wife, her grip on Henry, Caroline's slight difficulty in breathing and the line of colour on her cheek.

'I see you've been having trouble,' he said. 'I feared you might. I found your letter to me, opened, I was afraid this might have happened. So I came straight here, to see how much I could stop. I'm afraid I didn't think to telephone – it's later than I thought, an unearthly hour to arrive. My apologies. Now I am here, what can I do for you?'

Caroline embarked on her prepared speech.

'I don't suppose you want to be in this house any longer than we want to have you. But there are things I think you ought to know. I can't believe you know them already, but if you do, we have a right to know what you mean to do about it. You know what I'm talking about?'

'I believe so,' Oliver said politely, but with an amused little smile that Caroline did not like. 'I believe so.'

'Good,' said Caroline. 'I want to know when you last saw Anna?'

Oliver's smile drew in, as though he liked answering this kind of question less, when it came to it, than he had imagined. He said, 'I thought you were going to tell me things.'

'I assume you haven't seen her for some time. Do you know where she is?'

'Not here I imagine,' Oliver said. 'She didn't like coming home, overmuch.'

'That's immaterial,' Caroline cried, losing her inquisitorial manner for a moment. Oliver said, quickly and expressionlessly, 'I don't think so,' and drew a breath, sharply.

'Look,' he said, taking charge. 'Let's not hedge, let's not recriminate yet. Let's get it over with. Where is she? Has she done something silly?'

Caroline began to speak, and then could not. Oliver went on, without a trace of a smile, now, 'Or don't you know where she is? Is that what it is?'

'Of course we know.'

'Well then?'

'Do you want to discuss this in front of Margaret? I should have thought you'd have preferred to talk it over with her alone, later. Some of it doesn't concern her.'

Oliver said nothing. Caroline said to Margaret, 'Perhaps you would like to lie down for a short time on the spare bed? I have something private to say to Oliver. It won't take long.'

Margaret sat up, still grasping Henry.

'Oliver,' Caroline commanded.

'Come along, Maggie,' said Oliver, taking a step towards her. Margaret winced, and shrank against Henry. 'Let me take you upstairs,' Oliver went on, neutrally kind.

'No,' said Margaret. She turned to Henry, desperately. 'Don't let them push me out. It's my life they're taking to bits. My life. Make them give it to me back.'

'Lie down now,' said Caroline patiently, 'and then Oliver will drive you home, and you can talk.'

'This doesn't concern you. Honestly,' Oliver said, with a touch of irritation which seemed to drive Margaret to frenzy. She began to cry, with huge tears rolling down her face.

'Henry don't let them take me, let me stay here, let me stay with you. You're all I've got, Henry, don't let them take me.'

'They shan't if you don't want them to,' Henry said, as though it was drawn from him.

'I'm sorry about this, Henry,' said Oliver, who did not sound particularly sorry. Margaret wept at him, 'And you, you must admit now, Henry knows what you are. You – ' She began to elaborate, in the terms of her letter to Henry, telling Oliver graphically and in most vivid language, what he had done to her. Oliver seemed, Henry noticed with a curious relief, genuinely completely taken aback. He said, 'God, I didn't know it had come to this,' and then, directly to her, with that gentleness of his that Henry had never seen before, 'Maggie, don't do that. It isn't as bad as that.'

But Margaret turned to Henry and wept on his neck, crying, 'I can't stand any more. I want my life. That's all. I tried, didn't I, and I can't take any more.'

Caroline said in a small voice, 'Henry, please – ' and Henry stood up and stretched.

'Come along, Margaret,' he said to her with absolute authority, 'you must go to bed now. Caroline will make you a hot-water bottle and you can sleep. No one will make you do anything you don't want to do.'

Margaret stood up suspiciously, and clutched his hand. 'Don't let them come near me.'

'No, I won't.'

'You come.'

'Yes,' said Henry. He took her by the hand like a child, and led her out. Caroline looked at Oliver suspiciously for a moment, as though if she left him he might steal the silver, or at the least abscond. Oliver did not answer her look, but took up a book from the table nearest him, and settled in Henry's chair with it, one leg crossed over the other. Caroline turned against the door, to see whether he had tried to do anything furtive whilst her back was turned, but he was still there, and seemed almost rudely settled and at home. She hurried out to put on the kettle for the hot-water bottle.

Upstairs, Henry turned back the spare bed, found that it was not made up, and hunted in a series of drawers for sheets. Finally he found a pair, sprigged with forget-me-nots, and began to make the bed – something he hadn't done for himself since he left school. He was slow and clumsy, very occupied with the whole business, making unnecessary little journeys round the bed foot, twitching worriedly at the corners of sheets and blankets, pushing pillows into pillow cases and fluffing out the frills. Margaret trotted after him like a dog, making no move to help him, but not letting him out of reach, like the three-year-old that doesn't sink quite as far as clutching his mother's skirts, but will not go from under her feet. The room had not been slept in for some time and was cold. Henry found an electric fire, and plugged it in. Then he turned back a corner of the bed and said, 'There. All ready. All you have to do is get in.'

Margaret sat down on the edge of it. Henry said, 'Shall I draw the curtains?'

'No,' said Margaret. 'They make me feel trapped.'

Henry moved towards the door, and she began to tremble again.

'Henry don't go. Don't leave me. I don't know what's going on, what's happening, but I know it's happening to me. It's terrible.'

Henry came back and said in his voice of authority, 'You must go to bed now.'

'I will if I must,' said Margaret. 'But don't leave me. Don't let them come. There's only you that isn't against me.'

Henry did not answer. He sat down beside her, took her ankles, and lifted off her shoes, one after the other.

'Now, stand up,' he ordered. Margaret stood up. Henry, quite impersonally and quite gently, unzipped her dress and pulled it over her head. Margaret did not resist, and did not help she lifted her arms when Henry moved them. Henry laid the poor black dress across a chair, and looked her over critically.

'You'd be more comfortable without your stockings and that girdle thing, wouldn't you? Won't you take them off?' Margaret nodded affirmatively, but made no move to help herself. Gooseflesh was beginning to form on her thighs and her upper arms. Henry, as though it was his job, undid the suspenders, rolled off the stockings, and unclasped the row of little hooks on her girdle, one by one. It was, he reflected, a parody of a seduction, with himself the victim. He was taking on a great deal that he would have considered himself peculiarly unfit to take on. But it seemed that it did not lie within his choice.

'Now,' he said. 'To bed.' He saw that he would have to lift her in, and was just doing so when Caroline knocked and came in, carrying the promised hot-water bottle, two sleeping pills, and a mug of Ovaltine. She had wondered about the cold chicken and decided against it – the idea of food seemed to upset Margaret so. When she came round the door Margaret's limpness changed to a vice-like grip on Henry's neck.

'Here is your bottle,' Caroline said with forced kindness, 'and a hot drink and something to make you sleep. You'll be all right, won't you?'

'Yes, she will,' said Henry, still making decisions. He slid Margaret's body in between the sheets, pushed the bottle down beside her, switched on the bedside lamp, and tucked her in. She gave a little sigh and settled back into the pillows. Caroline hovered in the doorway; she said, finally unable to endure Henry's patient arranging any more. 'Do you mind coming now, Henry? We really must get this over with.'

'Henry – ' said Margaret in alarm.

'I'll wait outside,' said Caroline. Henry knew as well as she did that she could not bear to go down and sit alone with Oliver.

Alone with Henry again, Margaret became slowly rational. He kept a distant silence, until finally she sat up of her own accord, and drank down the pills and the Ovaltine. She said in an almost normal voice, 'What is all this, Henry? About Anna?'

'That it was Anna Oliver went to see in Cambridge.'

'I see. I hadn't thought of that. I was fond of Anna, I thought she liked me.'

Henry was ashamed that he could not remember enough of

Anna to be able to reassure her about this. He did not want to think about Anna; he came back doggedly to the business in hand.

'Anna hasn't come home, and Caroline thought Oliver might persuade her.'

Margaret did not examine this vague version of the truth, which was as well. She said, 'Everything I've done was a lie. I love him so much, and he wasn't there. What shall I do now?'

'What do you want to do?'

'I don't know. I shall probably just drag about, doing nothing, just keeping alive, eating and sleeping, until I die. It doesn't seem to matter, except when I'm with you. I used to despise people like that, didn't I, Henry?'

'And Oliver?'

'He was all I had. He was all I wanted,' Margaret said in her wild voice.

'I think you should leave him now,' Henry committed himself. Margaret said, 'I know you know better than I do.' She picked up his hand, and held it against her face. 'I'll do anything you tell me, Henry, you know that. You know how to live, you're alive, you're the only person I'm sure is. You'll let me stay here, Henry, won't you?'

'Until you feel better, yes.'

'I'd kill myself if I went away from you now, just for pointlessness. That's terrible. But I love you, Henry. I'd do anything for you.'

'You must do something for yourself.' He saw that this was not something she would want to take in, but was unprepared for her taking it as a compliment, as an expression of his personal sense of a bond between them. She cried triumphantly, 'You do care for me,' and reached for him. He said, 'You must go to sleep now,' and disengaged himself. She settled back onto the pillows, and distaste for himself came over him, as it did every time he exacted this obedience from her. He did not want it, the tie, not the power, not the contact. And now he had apparently brought it on himself indefinitely. He said gently, 'Goodnight,' and let himself out.

Caroline came after him and caught his arm in the hall.

265

'Really, this is intolerable,' she said. 'Quite intolerable. Did you have to undress her?'

'Yes,' said Henry simply. He could hardly bring himself to be considerate in yet another direction; who was he, where was he, where was his occupation, in all this? But he made an effort. 'I don't like it,' he said, 'I don't like having to touch people. But at the moment she can't do anything for herself.'

'You enjoy having power over her.'

'No I don't. You should know it isn't that.'

Caroline did know, and did not want to know that she knew. She would have preferred to be able to think her almost bodily rage reasonable. Henry said, 'Well, Oliver.'

Oliver was still sitting where Caroline had left him. He had smoked one cigarette from Caroline's silver box for visitors, and was beginning on another, his dark face bowed over the flame of Caroline's silver table lighter. Caroline, when she saw him so unconcerned and at home, would have torn at him and shaken him until he was properly distressed, until he bled. Instead, she drove her nails into her own clenched fists, and said, 'Now let us get this over.'

Henry, coming in behind her, moved across the room to the window, lifted a fold of the deep rose velvet curtain, and looked out, distancing himself, detaching a flicker of Oliver's attention from Caroline, making him frown slightly, as though he would rather have had Henry drawn into his circle with his wife. He said to him, 'Did you manage?'

'Yes,' said Henry, his eyes on the dark grass.

'She took two sleeping pills,' said Caroline, 'and is lying down. Although I don't see how it could be much more tiresome for any of us, I'm afraid you won't be able to move her tonight. I don't know how anyone could be so – wantonly destructive. You must have *known* – even you must recognize *some* responsibility.'

'I know what you think about me,' Oliver said. 'I didn't come here to be told that, though I saw I'd have to take some of it if I was to find out anything I wanted to know. Let's take the lecture as read, shall we? And tell me, for God's sake, *where is Anna*?' He turned to Henry. 'Where is she? What do you want me to do?'

Caroline said, 'She is in York. Staying with Peter Hughes-Winterton. She wants to marry him . . . As soon as possible.'

Oliver said, very slowly, his eyes still on Henry, 'That sounds like a happy ending.'

'I want you to tell her to come back.'

'Why? I should have thought you'd have wanted her to stay there. Or don't you think she is fit to associate with the Hughes-Wintertons after sleeping with me? Is that what it is? You want her ashamed? You would, wouldn't you – '

Caroline whitened. 'Henry,' she said, furious with him, 'this is your decision too, you know. You tell Oliver – *Henry* – you tell Oliver, why . . .'

Henry turned his great head from the contemplation of the garden, looked briefly at Oliver, and said, in a colourless voice from a great distance, 'Anna is pregnant.' Then he turned his head back again.

He felt sick for a moment, and for a moment as he said Anna's name his imagination touched at her, and love tore him. But under that, he was still and cold, waiting quiescent. And under that again, the old life stirred, a tiny flame, which warmed him, in spite of himself, which he knew he must protect before anything.

Oliver seemed to shrink for a moment, and caught at one of his hands with the other, as if for support. Then he cried angrily, 'Why the hell didn't you begin with that?'

'I thought you should know,' Caroline said, in charge again. 'Naturally, we feel she must come back here to have the baby, and not put it all on this unfortunate boy. We must look after her, of course, it's our place. But we – don't know if we can make her come. We thought – you might do that – '

'Why me?' Oliver asked, in the same small, outraged voice. Caroline hesitated she was not quite sure why: her greatest need had not been for someone to fetch Anna back, but for someone to punish, someone to hurt. And she did not want to say that she thought Anna might love Oliver enough to listen to him, might trust him enough to see that she must abandon her entrenchment, because she could not say that there was no such love between herself and Anna, and that Henry would not help. She had meant Oliver to betray Anna to them, to her. But it

267

was not, she saw suddenly, moving that way. She said, 'It will be your child. It is your responsibility. You must help to provide.'

'Be quiet,' Oliver said. 'I know, I know it is my child. But I will do this my way. Anna – '

'You must know why she went there. You must tell her to come home.'

'She has no home,' Oliver snapped. 'Let me think.'

'It's clear enough . . .'

'Henry!' Oliver broke across Caroline's talk. 'What does she want, Henry? What does she want?'

'What she wants is immaterial, at the moment,' said Caroline.

'Henry, what does she want?'

'An abortion,' said Henry flatly. His large fingers pleated the curtain, and released it.

'You must see – ' said Caroline.

'All right, I see that. Of course I see that. I'm not having *that*. She's not killing my child for any bloody Hughes-Winterton.'

'He doesn't want her to,' Henry said. 'It's Anna.'

'Oh, but *why?*' Oliver demanded, as though in pain. He said to Henry, 'I love Anna, have you thought of that? More than you – any of you – have guts to begin to imagine. I'd give her anything, anything, something enormous – but I'd have to know what she wants. If I thought she loved me – or could love me – ' He thought fiercely, moving his brows, rapidly. He said, 'Henry, do you think she'd come?'

'I don't know. I don't know if she knows,' Henry said judicially.

'Will you give me the telephone number?' Henry put his hand in his pocket, and hesitated. Oliver said, 'What can you do – what will you do – yourself?'

'I'll give it to you,' Henry said slowly. 'The telephone is in the hall.' He took Anna's letter from his pocket, looked for the number, was about to hand the letter to Oliver, and then instead, carefully wrote out the figures on a piece of card. 'It's late, to telephone now.'

'That doesn't matter,' said Oliver. 'Excuse me.'

He swung out of the room, and a moment later they heard

his voice in the hall, dry and authoritative. 'Operator. Can you get me this number via York. I'm in a hurry. Thank you.'

And then a long silence.

Caroline said, 'I don't understand. What does he mean to do?'

'To take her away. If she'll go. To marry her eventually, I suppose.'

'And you mean to let him?'

'I can't decide for Anna. I think he should see her. I think he has a right.'

'She's too young, and you know it. It's your duty, Henry – you have to stop him, you have to. Can't you see? It's disgusting – '

'You know,' said Henry, slowly, 'there's nothing for her here. Not now. She would be better not to come here.' He thought that was not the whole truth. There was something he himself should have done, and he had not found it. In a short time it would seem as though that had been inevitable, but not now, not quite. He stirred his body, and looked out of the window.

'And Margaret?' Caroline demanded, flinging from one trouble to the next.

'We shall have to look after Margaret for the time being.'

'How could you let him do this to us?' Caroline cried, and was heard by Oliver who had come quietly in again.

'She took some persuading,' said Oliver. 'I told her I had a right to see her. It wasn't nice. She sounds – I don't like how she sounds. She says she will come and meet me in York tomorrow. I think there is only half a chance that she will, but that's a risk I've got to take. So I'll drive up there tomorrow. She didn't want to speak to you. She was very angry with you, incidentally, particularly with you, Henry'.

'Yes,' said Henry. 'She would be.'

There was an embarrassed silence, which prolonged itself. It was broken by Henry, who suddenly, without speaking, almost absentmindedly, dropped the heavy curtain with a swish over the dark glass and the garden, turned from the window, and strode out of the room. He had obviously not felt anything to be intolerable; had not meant to finish anything grandly, or make a gesture. He gave, rather, the impression that he had suddenly realized that he ought not to have been there at all, that his presence was a mistake. Caroline and Oliver, the tidy-minded, the arrangers, swung to each other in momentary sympathy; they felt deeply and indignantly discarded. For a moment Caroline felt that Oliver was nearer to understanding – no, to appreciating – the wrong that had been done to her than Henry would ever be. She clicked her tongue in exasperation, and shrugged her shoulders, as if inviting Oliver to speak. Oliver voiced both their thoughts.

'I don't suppose we had any right to expect him to pay us any more attention. He has better things to do. He always has had better things to do. That's what makes it more difficult for the rest of us.'

'It depends what you mean by better things,' Caroline said sharply, and recollected herself. She lifted her head, and said, more stiffly, 'However awkward it may be, I don't see that you can leave her, tonight, now. I'll make up Jeremy's bed for you.' She had been going to say Anna's bed; she did not like to let anyone else sleep in Jeremy's room, it was his sanctum. But Anna's bed was obviously out of the question, and now she had to resent Oliver on Jeremy's behalf too.

'It may be convenient in a way. We must obviously discuss this matter further. Your – your plans – are obviously impossible, you must try and see what she – Anna – will want in – ten years, say. Henry – believed too much in letting her have her own way, he is over-indulgent, he won't see how immature she is. I should be grateful if you'd wait here whilst I put an electric blanket in the bed. It will need airing.'

Oliver did not answer; he took, and lit, another cigarette, which Caroline took for acquiescence. She went out, head high, and closed him in behind her, like a naughty boy, set to wait in the headmaster's study.

For a moment he stood there, quite still, and smoked, dark and self-contained, leaning against the chimney. Then he turned, wrenching his whole body round violently, and threw the cigarette in amongst the burning logs. He looked around, unsatisfied, carrying his arms tense from the shoulders, bent slightly out and forward, like a prize-fighter moving in for the clinch. His gaze flickered over the silver box and lighter, and came to rest on the tray with the glasses. He took up Margaret's glass, and Caroline's, and all the unused ones, fragile, exquisite, clean-cut and slender, like everything of Caroline's, carried them over and threw them down on the blue and white Dutch tiles in the hearth. After a second's hesitation he pitched the decanter, silver label, contents and all, in amongst them. Then he ground the fragments deliberately with his heel, until they were powdered, and the sherry and glass dust seeped out under the fender onto the hearth rug. Still unsatisfied, he dropped the delicate little brass clock, with its glass dome, in on top of them, where it clucked, and died. He gave it a kick so that it flew against the fireback, and lay on its side. Then, suddenly still again, he wiped his feet carefully on the carpet and mopped his brow. It had only been a moment's work, but he was sweating, and breathing heavily; he straightened slowly, as though a load had eased from him, and went out, closing the door behind him.

SIXTEEN

HENRY HAD COME into his study and taken the unworked manuscript from his desk automatically. The need to touch it, to have to do with it, to revert to that kind of action was absolute on him. He began to read it through from the beginning, and then, slowly, to pencil in comments, corrections, alternative phrases in the blank pages he left opposite his text. Slowly the process became familiar and absorbing, his notes became longer; when he came to the end of what he had written he would be able to continue as though there had never been a break. He was amazedly, triumphantly conscious of the action of his pencil on the paper, and his fingers guiding it, of the action of his mind, now so completely directed onto his own structure of words and knowledge. And his face was stripped of all its vagueness, all its woolly benignity; it set itself keen, purely intelligent; in human terms even cruel.

He took some time to notice that Oliver had come in without knocking and was standing just inside the door, watching him with a complicated expression that might have been amusement, awe, or a kind of sadness. When Henry looked up, Oliver said, 'I see you are working.'

'Yes.'

'I suppose you will work all night?'

'Yes.'

'I want to say goodbye to you. May I sit down?'

'Please,' said Henry, not yet really attending. Oliver pulled up a chair to Henry's fire, and stretched his thin hands blindly to it, warming them, first one side and then the other. The fire glowed red on them, giving the illusions of lighting them through and outlining the bone in deep rose.

'Caroline has gone to make up a bed for me,' he told Henry, examining his hands. 'But I won't stay – it would be in bad taste, wouldn't it? I'll drive north as far as I can; I need to move; and I won't be impossibly late for Anna. Caroline expects me to talk everything over again – but we'd neither of us enjoy it, and we wouldn't do very much good, would we? So I'll slip out now, if I may, and leave you to make my apologies. I suppose I take some pleasure in leaving you with the washing up. Do you think she'll come to me, Henry?'

'I don't know. I honestly don't know.'

'If she does – will you mind?'

'Mind?' said Henry. He considered. 'I shall be less unhappy than I feared, originally. If that's what you want to know. I don't think Caroline will get over it.'

'So you wouldn't "receive us", so to say?'

'I would do what Anna wanted. Whatever Anna wanted. But if – if she comes to you – I imagine it will be precisely because she wants to have no more to do with me. I think that's how she sees it. She may be right.'

Oliver looked up at him, and said, in his old questioning manner, 'What do you think she ought to do? What do *you* think?'

Henry considered. He said, 'I don't think she should stay there. That would be too limiting. Though she may still want that. I don't know if I know her well enough to know what she ought to do. If I were her, I would go away alone now, I would work something out. She has some power, of some kind; she isn't yet, what she will be. I still think that might be best. But she must do what she wants to do.'

'You just don't care enough, do you? I can't understand you. You must know that you're the power of her life – that if you exerted yourself – *really* exerted yourself – and went and fetched her from there, you could stop her marrying him, or me, or anyone, you could make her do anything. For all I know, that's what she's waiting for. But you don't mean to help, do you? You mean to sit here, and work, and wait for the event. Why?'

Henry said, 'I have never been very good at doing things. And I think that – if *I* fetched her – it wouldn't help, it would destroy anything I offered her. I think that's right. I think it is. I don't know.'

'And you don't mean to find out. You mean to let me try, to marry her – in order to take possession of yourself, you said, didn't you?'

Henry looked at him then, directly, resting his grey look for a moment entirely on him.

'I did you an injustice there. I was confused. I can see you love her.'

'You can see that, can you?' Oliver said, less truculently, and sat back in his chair. He said, 'It wasn't entirely an injustice in Cambridge; you know that. I had a tremendous sense of power to have you there, turning on *my* needle, dancing to *my* tune, caring what *I* did. I thought I'd pull you down and show you were human, like the rest of us. But you got away, didn't you? You don't care now, do you? Not really *care*? You must write your quota of pages tonight and the rest of us must shift as we can. Well, we'll shift. I'd respect you more – oh yes, and envy you less – if you did care.'

'I care,' said Henry.

'You don't know what it means,' said Oliver briskly, turning his hands meditatively before the flames. He said, 'People like me have very complicated feelings about people like you. I'm aware that you don't really care whether I tell you about them or not – you'd probably rather I didn't. But I seem to share what's apparently a common urge to explain everything to you

273

– to drop all my little worries and stoppages into the well of your considered silence. Perhaps because one feels that since the worries don't worry you, and the stoppages don't stop you, you've got time to make something of them, whilst one gets on with the struggling. Which I resent; but still, I talk.

'I wanted to be your friend – really your friend – I wanted an intimacy . . . You know what I mean, I believed you could open up the world for me, change things unutterably . . . I've been with you like my wife was with me, waiting to be allowed to share, angry at my own inadequacy, my own lack of touch – oh, and quite sure that if you only knew me as I was, really as I was, myself – whatever that might be – you'd see that I understood, that I was a proper person to be let in, that I deserved your – your trust. But it wasn't so, was it? You'd never trust me?'

'I don't think I have ever been very good at trusting anyone,' said Henry. 'I don't have much I can offer.'

'No,' said Oliver. 'But I hoped – I set about it badly, but maybe it wouldn't have made any difference whatever I did.

'When I was a boy – a little boy, that is – I was clever. I was good at composition, I used to write lyrical descriptions of hedges in flower, animals in the pasture, the sea – you know the kind of stuff – all the clean, bright things we didn't get in the place I lived in. I had a schoolteacher – a sentimental old idiot with a long damp moustache – who used to say beautiful, beautiful, holding the mirror up to Nature, you'll make a writer, my boy, if you persevere. I was going to inhabit the heavenly fields all right, when I'd earned the right to, by describing them so beautifully.

'So I went to grammar school, which wasn't a very good grammar school, but believed in itself – and I learned grammar, and précis, and languages, and a bit of science, and got laughed at, towards the end, by the clever man there, who taught history, and had a Cambridge degree, and was very Left, and he said Think, Canning, think, you've got the future in your hands, you've a duty to society, you're one of the bright boys who'll have to fight. So I went up to University and duly thought – and grew angry, as one must, I think one *must*, at the dirt and the mess, and the asphalt, and the poverty, and the little houses in rows and yellow press – I've told you it all often enough, you must be sick of hearing it, but it's real, and it's evil. And one got to hate the gentlemen – people like you – who can sit here like this, and look at the fields, and write all the time, and think that you've a right to the heavenly fields I used to write about. Partly because I'm no gentleman, and can't, but partly because once one has seen the asphalt and dust and dirt, one wants to take them away and open up the fields to everyone – and whilst one looks at the backyards and plans their removal the fields recede and recede. I speak metaphorically, you understand.'

Henry said, 'I'm no gentleman. I'm no squire. You knew that, really. All this business of – gentleman – non-gentleman – is immaterial here, I think. I live here because I like the land – '

'It isn't immaterial to Caroline.'

'No.'

'And therefore it has not been immaterial to Anna. Remember that. It has harmed Anna. It's been choking her. It's the sort of thing you can say is immaterial if you're on the right side of it. But not from my place. Nor hers.'

'Maybe.'

'You know I'm right. Anna – when I was a boy, girls were things you had to make. You measured yourself against them. You planned – oh, in your head, alone, like a piece of work – a campaign. You got them in a park, and you saw how far you could get. And then boasted appropriately. Margaret was a lady – she laughed, she talked a lot, she had a poise. I was terrified of her, deep in me I was terrified of her. So I planned my campaign, and I tried my technique, and it worked – and I thought ah, I can get *in*, on my brains, I can take possession of all these sure people after all. I know what you and Caroline think about my behaviour there. But I've not been just coldly cruel, you know, I've not just grinned and watched her squirm. I've suffered, if that interests you. I though she'd always be a bit too clean for me, a bit above me – her silliness I put down to her not *having* to think, the way I did. I thought she'd teach me to rest. She had a sort of life. But she wanted a god, and a master – you know what she wanted, it's you she wants now – and I couldn't *be* that man, no one could. And I believe in

275

human relations, I think one must be honest with people, achieve a balance, a trust. This is the first thing. I didn't enjoy my failure, whatever Caroline may think. She'll be better with you, you've no affection to withhold, you don't see her as a parody of anything you believe in, you can be kind, can't you? It doesn't cost you much effort.

'But Anna – Anna is like me. Anna struggles in the same basic gulfs – I loved her that summer, when I saw her struggling against Caroline's care and your lack of it; she was all alive, and no one helped her, or used it – '

He looked up at Henry, and then back at his hands against the fire, and said, as though treading dangerous and familiar ground where he was doomed to lose himself, 'Things are solid for my wife. Here, she says, is a tree, and she walks round and round it, patting its trunk, and sniffing at its leaves, and admiring the pattern of the sun through its branches on her new silk dress, and there *is* a tree – '

Henry sat up, and said, 'Yes.'

'God knows what you see. God only knows. I look, I see there is something, and I see a hole.'

'The tree is there.'

'Oh, I know, you're so certain. A transfigured tree, an ideal and shining tree, a visible witness to the fact that you are there, and you *see* it so, and are alive. Terribly simple, but unfortunately convincing, as you put it. The holes are the same, equally simple, quite damning. I can't get out by saying what do trees matter? They do – I work – Anna works – in the same area. It's not that we've lost faith in Margaret's solid tree, nor that we've not been fortunate or clever enough to see your eternal Tree. It's positively a lack of trees, a space for a tree, *no* tree. *No* tree. But we come back and back to it, it's an issue, all right. We stand in the same field from time to time, and scan the horizon for trees. Why d'you think I spend my time writing about your novels? I suppose you think I don't *know* what you see – '

'Yes,' said Henry.

'Precisely,' said Oliver, with triumph. 'But I occupy myself with it. It's precisely people like myself who do. What good are you doing us?'

'None, very probably.'

'Precisely. But we have to read you, at second-hand we have to see there are fields. But we can't *live* that way – we have to find our own way of living.'

'Anna said something like that.'

'Oh, she is like me, she knows. She knows more than she can bear – '

'We shall see,' said Henry.

There fell a silence; a natural, but uneasy one, between them. Henry looked at Oliver, who kept his head resolutely turned away towards the fire, and then out off the uncurtained window, where the night light lay dark and bright, like another pane of glass against the first. He waited a moment, his mouth tightening, and then, as though obeying an irresistible temptation, he drew his papers towards him and pencilled in a short comment casually, and when Oliver still did not move, several longer ones. When he was entirely absorbed in the paper, Oliver looked up.

'I'll not disturb you any longer,' he said, and stood. 'Or Caroline will catch me. Look after Maggie: she'll find someone to love her, don't you think? I'll let you know what Anna decides.'

'Thank you.'

'I feel as though this is the last time. Not that one can ever tell. But if it is, I'm sorry. As I said, I hoped to make a friend of you.'

'I'm sorry,' said Henry. Oliver said, 'I'll review your next – that one, will it be? Will you mind?'

'No,' said Henry truthfully.

'Will you read my review?'

'Probably not,' said Henry. 'Often I don't. It's one of those things one is better without.'

Oliver hesitated and looked at Henry, and said, 'Goodbye, then.' 'Goodbye,' said Henry. Oliver hesitated for a further moment, as though he was still reluctant to put an end to even so prolonged a parting, as though something would be lost to him for ever when he went out of that room, and its warmth, and its work, and it silence. But Henry only looked at him steadily, and added nothing to encourage him to say, or re-open the conversation, so that in the end he bowed, submissively, and closed himself out.

Henry balanced his pencil, and thought, I should have said something to him, he expected something, it might have changed things for Anna, as well. But Oliver was so far away, so much something he normally did not traffic with, that he could not have said anything, comprehensibly.

He smiled, carefully. Most people, one imagines without thinking deeply about it, are diminished in some way when left alone in a room. One considers them in abeyance, waiting for some human contact, some action, some move in the Aristotelian fable to set them going again and give them substance. This is not true of the object of a hopeless love, who is always so magnified by absence, and it was more importantly in the same and in different ways, and for all of them, not true of Henry, who was now restored to his proper size and weight on their imaginations, and his own.

For a time he sat and watched the fire as Oliver had done, moving from the desk to the chair Oliver had left; he folded his hands in his lap, and watched, and collected his senses. He remembered, and gathered, and stored, and obliterated: the slight grit of Oliver's voice from his hearing, Margaret's tired flesh and Oliver's small, white, pleading face from his sight, Margaret's hair, and Caroline's sherry, and Oliver's trousers, animal and slightly scorched by the sturdy fire, from his smell, the momentary dryness and bitterness from his taste. He reduced everything touched – Margaret's cold thigh, Caroline's troubled woollen shoulder, the rubbed, slightly furry paper of Anna's letter, the light bony dryness of Oliver's handshake – to the feel of the power of his huge hands, clasped loosely one in the other, his firm skin against his firm skin, with nothing between.

He thought, he had tried to tempt Fate, though that was not what it had looked like at the time. He had always been afraid that he was, by virtue of his strength, in for it, in a way those who struggled naturally with greyness, Margaret, Oliver, Anna, were not. He saw his strength, not precisely puritanically, but almost physically, as something he must pay for, for which the bill was always mounting. And his years in the prison camp had not been, as he had half expected, part of the payment; they had been his brightest, most terrible years; his ultimate release from the middle class niceties, the dryads, he had been so hopelessly trying to harness his disproportionate splendour to. His fall, he had always known, was to be smaller, more ordinary, greyer. It was to consist of a real but almost imperceptible loss of solitude, of a growth in him of what Oliver would have praised as humanity. He had had it all planned, he saw now, like a sketch of a novel, the dramatically suitable punishment for hubris, he had quite ludicrously, in some unconscious way, organized – or at the very least, invited it all.

And discovering Anna, and all that he had thought was new about her, that had not been new, but known and ignored, he thought he had uncovered what had been lying in wait for him. And had set out on his 'Fate' with, he now saw, a secret curiosity, a secret excitement over new knowledge, which had after all differed only in degree, not in kind, from his earlier attitudes. He had taken, as Samson must have done, a certain pleasure in offering up his strength to human relations, in lying down and allowing it to be shorn away from him for love.

Well, Henry thought, I tempted it. I exposed myself to it and it wouldn't bite. I tried to dislodge it on my head, and it wouldn't fall. Samson must have known that hair grows again; it's in the nature of things; he had had to gather himself up again after all, balance buildings on his shoulders, and pull down what temples there were to pull down. Mutilated or not. But Samson was a man of action – beside that splendid downfall his own tergiversations seem petty. But he could accuse himself how he would; the flow was one way and would not be turned.

Light welled into the room from somewhere undefined, a new unearthly, wild light, drawing live, singing triangles between the cool sea-green plane of the window, the still white circle of his desk lamp, and the rising flames in the chimney. He finally unclasped his hands, and held them out against the sting of the light, as Oliver had earlier held out his against the warmth.

For a moment, against the shifting backcloth of the fire, he saw Anna and Oliver, two changing grey figures, with bowed heads and tossing arms, dancing a secret and desperate dance, a violent and constricted dance, around a black tunnel of emptiness, stiffly branched, Oliver's tree that was no tree. This, later, was what he would know of them. Then there were only the flames rising, beginning stiffly, erect, cone within cone, and then reaching a point, flickering and wavering wildly, dipping, dissolving, running down, it seems, to rise again. Blue and green and peacock, gold and silver and scarlet and crimson, climbing and striving onto the thick, soft, powdered dark.

Henry stood up, so contained he was hardly breathing, and let the light burn, round him and over him and through him, and watched the accustomed, yet always nearly intolerable, transfiguration of his room. Everything held at first, patterned in an instant brilliant geometrical clarity that was always the first thing. The carpet glittered at him, a forest of shadowed spiked points of coloured light. The furniture glowed gold and living, the papers across his desk shone out like silver stepping stones on a sea of flame. And then as the threads of light tautened, and spun and hummed more and more busily, his surroundings dissolved like the flames. Walls folded and opened like curtains, the light tore at them and probed their flimsiness, the window split and opened finally, an infinite tunnel of bright glass into a live and turning sky.

He was contained now by the light only, he was abandoned to what he knew was not human, to where he was alive. And he stared out now, he was drawn, to whatever it was that was incandescent in the orchard, crackling and powerful in the shrubbery, flames in the bushes, light climbing in nooses over the trees. He flexed himself and opened the window onto the garden, and the clamour of light leaped and increased. The moonlight moved in pale tongues of flame along the grass, and rose in slender twisted towers amongst the trees, and spread, and washed the hill beyond with glory. Henry unknitted his shoulders and went out with it, gathering speed.

SEVENTEEN

ANNA, UNLIKE THE rest of them, was not much concerned with Henry; she was too occupied with her present circumstances. When she had first run to Peter, he had wisely taken her, immediately, to London, where they had spent some days in his parents' empty town flat. Here, Anna lay in the double bed, not moving, and Peter shopped, and cooked, and put on records, and talked and held her hand, and Anna let him slowly construct the story as he saw it; the great emptiness that had been her childhood, Henry's large shadow, Oliver's determined move into the emptiness, how she had managed finally, at what cost to herself, to evade his clutches, and last, almost casually, the pregnancy, as though this solid difficulty was just another strand in the psychological net she was or had been entangled in. Peter took it all, as information he himself with admirable calmness had elicited, because he wanted to understand, and loved her. When they had talked it out, he suggested that they should go home to his mother· it was now understood that they would marry.

Anna had left Cambridge without clothes. Peter insisted on buying her a wardrobe and showed himself surprisingly knowledgeable and concerned about sweater and shoes; he insisted on a camel coat, which was something Anna had always disliked, and a coral felt hat with a deep brim which reminded Anna of Margaret. Coral was Margaret's colour, it should have been Margaret's warm gold face looking out from under that hat, her mouth with a browny coral lipstick she had, just the one for this, Anna remembered clearly, not Anna's own small secretive face, so much too pale, and pinched. But Peter liked that hat, he said it gave her 'poise', and Anna planted it carefully on her head, a badge of good intentions, before they drove north to Lady Hughes-Winterton and a new life.

Peter had warned or informed his mother by telephone of

their arrival, and of the fact that he intended to marry Anna. 'She won't want to have been told by telephone,' he had said, 'but she'd like still less to think she hadn't been told as soon as possible. It's rather difficult, I don't know what's best.' He had spent the journey telling Anna how kind and understanding his mother was, what a refuge she would be to her, how she had always wished for a daughter . . . Anna discounted half of it, but had nevertheless, in some curious way that harked back to Caroline, come to regard Lady Hughes-Winterton's quiet country life as a final means to peace, as something to be settled in, for a lifetime. She had been visited by an uncharacteristic but powerful nostalgia for the things Caroline had known of, had tried for, but with Henry and herself and the war to contend with, had never managed ideally to achieve. It was what she had once been fighting, but that, somehow, no longer seemed to matter. It was silly to prolong old battles.

It was apparent, immediately, that Peter's telephone call had given Lady Hughes-Winterton time to prepare herself for Anna. She came, just quickly enough to suggest eagerness, out into the drive to help them out of the car, embraced Peter, and laid her own solid cheek against Anna's under the coral hat just long enough to make it certain that this was unusual in her, a gracious acknowledgment of Anna's right to special treatment, a signification that she herself intended to make no trouble, to be as helpful as possible. Anna thought, seeing her lucidly during this first meeting only, that she had had all this scene neatly staged before they ever arrived, and wondered how much more of her stay would be simply a matter of finding her own predetermined lines at the right moment, and speaking them. Arriving, with the help of the hat and the camel coat, was easy enough; Anna was soon to find that it was all that was easy.

Lady Hughes-Winterton was not what Anna had expected, which was odd, since she fitted both Peter's description, and Anna's private modifications of it, well enough. She looked as she should have looked, not tall, not dumpy, but giving the impression of a trimness of figure achieved only by ruthless slimming of the hips, and even more ruthless corseting of an abundant bosom: God had designed her to be a cottage loaf, and she had thwarted him. She had the willpower to thwart anyone. She wore tweeds, certainly, oatmeal and a deceptively gentle violet, but the tweeds were not seated, were not worn for comfort, Anna could see how they had been pressed, could observe how Lady Hughes-Winterton smoothed them before she sat down in them although she was nevertheless, paradoxically, one of those women who sit defiantly easily, their knees thrust apart, revealing to those who happen to be facing them from the right angle, a patch of solid thigh, the join of suspender and stocking, the scalloped edge of thick violet silk knickers.

She had the clear soft skin of the woman who is naturally a cottage loaf, and used little make-up beyond an irrelevant splash of bright lipstick. They will *all* wear red, Anna thought, all these women who affect not to care, and it doesn't suit one of them but looks like a uniform; something softer and more subtle would make them, in fact, look slightly overdone, I suppose. The hair was short, thick, and simple, and the colour had been left alone – a tweedy colour, gold and silver, chestnut, chocolate, all mixed, not unattractive, and beautifully set. Caroline's coil would have looked dowdy beside it, just because a coil was an easy way out, which was unfair. She takes trouble where it matters, Anna thought, and watched Lady Hughes-Winterton notice one of her own finger nails, broken and bitten down. She thought she could detect distaste, there, but all Lady Hughes-Winterton said was, 'A *simple* ring would be best, wouldn't it, Peter? Great Aunt Emily's little emerald, maybe?'

Anna came to see that making it up to Peter would involve, largely, a superhuman effort to get on with Peter's mother, and she was angry, because there was no apparent reason why this should not be easy. Lady Hughes-Winterton was so willing. Anna had guessed, from Peter's descriptions, that trying to marry Peter might be like trying to prise Jeremy away from Caroline. But it looked now as though it should have been easier, in a way much easier, because Peter's mother was less distressed and more rational, held and repeated so firmly the view that she had always hoped to see Peter married, she was not like some women, she looked forward, had always looked forward to a daughter-in-law. Anna came to see that she could say this because in fact she believed – even admitted to herself – that unlike most women she was in no danger of losing her son to any daughter-in-law, that she knew too well how not to make demands, or scenes, or side comments, for Peter to need to make any change in their relationship. Anna, or whoever else it might be, would just be added to it. So she accepted Anna easily enough, and made quite a little ceremony over the handing-over of Great Aunt Emily's little emerald, which she fetched from a leather box to give it to Peter to put onto Anna's chewed finger, which it fitted, as Lady Hughes-Winterton had declared it would, perfectly.

Anna liked the ring; it was one she might even have chosen; and she did not care for Peter in a way which made her miss any romantic choosing or handing over of it alone together. But she was now apprehensive. She thought, as the ring-giving developed into a private showing of the Hughes-Winterton jewels — some valuable, one or two very valuable, most purely pretty, with Peter dismissed somewhere to see about something, and Lady Hughes-Winterton handing garnet collars to Anna saying, 'This would suit you; I must see about letting you have this, when you're married' — that what was really meant that Lady Hughes-Winterton should take her, Anna, over, should spend her time with her, whilst Peter went off to do whatever men in the country do do; that she should become, should be, how graciously, how generously, *made* to become, no less, and no more, than part of the household.

Lady Hughes-Winterton had had time between Peter's telephone call and the arrival to buy new copies of all Henry's books, and, more incredibly, to look at them. They stood conspicuously on a bookshelf in the drawing room, with Henry's great face, retiring and challenging, staring sideways from the back of every new cover. Anna did not think Lady Hughes-Winterton could possibly like these books: her own bedroom was furnished with all seventy-two of Angela Thirkell's novels, Trollope's Barsetshire novels in a uniform edition, obviously bought *post* if not *propter* Angela Thirkell, Nancy Mitford, and *Pride and Prejudice*. And a rack of *Harper's* and *Country Life*. But Lady Hughes-Winterton managed to spin an incredible amount of intelligent comment out of her cursory reading of them, comment which might even have interested Henry himself, but by which Anna, whose day was divided between answering it, and answering the more usual motherly catechism about people she ought to have been acquainted with, was irritated to screaming point.

'I think,' Lady Hughes-Winterton would say, 'it's so clever of him to make Teresa's contempt for death so *convincing*, don't you? I mean, it isn't anything we usually feel, is it, and I don't believe people in books when they say they do. I just say, that all sounds very fine, but I'd be more impressed if you said you were terrified. Don't you think? But your father is so overbearing he's quite uncontradictable. His characters make me feel positively *small*. Don't they you? I suppose,' she added, 'that all that can't make him very easy to live with.' This last was Peter's understanding mother, who had been told something, Anna did not know how much, offering a delicate sympathy to Anna. For Peter's sake, Anna must not refuse it, she must offer herself in return, she must allow herself to be understood. But she did not know how to begin. And was made, very gently, to feel that her reticence was a shortcoming, if not a positive failure.

The other line of conversation was as bad. It ran, 'And the Salters perhaps? They must have lived quite near you? Victoria Salter, so nice, was quite an intelligent girl too, went to LMH and married, quite recently, into the Anlotts. You must have been nearly the same age. No? What a pity, I'm sure you'd have liked Vicky, she was so warm and open. Or there were the Wade-Thomases, he was in publishing, your father might have known him that way, he wrote a little book himself, once, *Walks and Anecdotes of Dartmoor*, rather a clever idea, in very good taste for that kind of thing, the son was your age, he was at school with Peter, he hopes to go into the Foreign Office with him. Geoffrey his name is, a nice boy, so clean looking. No? What a pity. If there had been daughters, maybe – they wanted a daughter, but were always unlucky. Like me. I tell Charlotte Wade-Thomas, we must just possess our souls in patience, until the daughters-in-law come along. Not that she's so anxious to see Geoffrey married, they've been very close, and I'm afraid she's a bit *possessive* about him, poor dear. Something one really should have sense to avoid. I say to her, of course you won't like the poor girl if you expect her to be everything you would like someone to be for Geoffrey; it isn't as though she's going to take your place; you must just treat her like every other human being, take the rough with the smooth as we all must, it'd be a pity if being a mother-in-law made *that* impossible. Don't you agree?'

Anna agreed. But she sensed that she herself was not liked; she could not respond openly, that was too demure, too quiet, agreed too much. She could never find an opening in the conversation where it would be possible to disagree, with that rush of frankness, earnestness, even laughter, which she sensed would be acceptable, and could not, to save herself, produce. And she saw that Peter's mother was coming to suspect her of a basic dishonesty – which indeed, with the pregnancy, there was, although luckily she was no longer very sick – and, although this was not what was meant, to suspect her of a scheming, a plot, something to hide, which made the whole thing impossible and fraudulent. Her lack of acquaintance with the people on the list was set down as extra evidence in the count against her, and rather ostentatiously stated not to matter; so far, she was allowed to feel, her being Henry's daughter, which left space for a certain amount of forgiveable eccentricity, just about balanced it out. But she was found wanting; she knew it, and was hurt; she was too tired not to be hurt, and Peter was so much her last refuge that she could not even tell herself it did not matter. And then, she felt that something ought to be done about getting rid of the baby, and, thanks to Lady Hughes-Winterton's arrangements for her own and Peter's time, she saw little enough chance of getting away to manage it quickly enough. She tried, once or twice, to tackle Peter about it late at night when his mother had gone to bed, but discovered that this, too, was nearly impossible – partly because Peter, since coming home, had developed a great guilt about making love to her, and seemed anxious to avoid temptation, partly because he was showing a new reluctance even to talk about the baby, whether because he meant it to survive or wanted to pretend it wasn't there, Anna was not certain; but mostly because he had an old custom of sitting on the end of his mother's bed at that time, and telling her everything, at least when his father was not at home.

Anna could imagine them so well, nested amongst shell-pink satin, Lady Hughes-Winterton in cap and gown of ivory silk and lace, Peter curled up on the eiderdown in stocking feet, and no light but the deep pink silk light on the dressing table – talking 'sensibly', and so earnestly. She had felt, ridiculously, that she must make Peter promise not to tell his mother about the baby, and was shocked to realize, from his slight air of guilt as he promised, how necessary this had been. She wondered what Lady Hughes-Winterton had already been told – Oliver? In what way, in what light? Peter was so sure of his mother's superior understanding, he would never see how her knowing could hurt Anna since she was so certain not to 'mind' This new fear hampered her conversation with Lady Hughes-Winterton even more; she could no longer be sure that anything she said could not be proved to be a lie. And she was aware that this new nervousness was marked, in its turn.

Nevertheless, she took a certain dogged pleasure in dealing with her new circumstances, in surviving at all as Peter's prospective wife, or Lady Hughes-Winterton's prospective daughter-in-law. She hoped for something from Sir Walter – men tended to like her more than women did – and was brought to realize that the present disposition of her time had the advantage of showing her how much she really needed, and liked, Peter. The prospect of living comfortably alone with him became golden, days when the only physical contact between them was a hasty hug in a corridor or a stableyard brought her by degrees to look forward to sleeping warmly with him, all night, every night; she told herself triumphantly that she had known it was something that came gradually, something to be relaxed into. She was ready now. She was positively eager. She could do it.

So that Oliver's telephone call, which she had answered thinking it must be from her mother, made her feel very angry. It was quite outside her calculations that he should make any further move, let alone that he should be angry with her, or have expected to be told about the baby, or feel that he should be consulted about its future. She was angry too that he obviously dismissed her carefully chosen way of life as something quite out of the question, not even worth discussing. What was he to know of the reality of Lady Hughes-Winterton – or was

Peter any less substantial because he was kind, and to be expected? She swore at him down the telephone, cried Don't, don't, don't, and would at first listen to nothing. When he said, finally, that he expected her at least to meet him in the Station Hotel in York to discuss the baby – which was his baby, he reminded her – his small voice was so cold, so tight, that she hesitated a moment, and then said, 'I might well not come. You'll have to risk that.' She had always found making and breaking appointments easier than refusing them outright.

'I'll risk that,' the small voice said, 'because if you don't come that won't be the last of it, and I mean you to know that for certain. When you've thought it over, you'll see it'll be easier to get away tomorrow than to have me badgering Lady Twiddly for access to you. I shall be quite unscrupulous. So I'll expect you. You may have to wait, I don't know how long it takes or when I'll set out. I've not finished with your father yet. Any messages?'

'No. He might have left you out of things. But he'll know that. He'll know I've nothing to say. He'll know why. Let him be.'

'He ought to be shot,' the small voice said cheerfully, 'but never mind. Just hang on, and I'll be with you, and it'll all look quite different. We can deal with this, love.'

He had rung off before Anna could get over her surprise at his incredible assumption that she could be reassured and comforted by his coming. For a moment she was outraged, and then, for a moment, hot with a sudden desire for him, for his sharpness, for his lack of cushioning, for the dry, grey place where they had met and knew each other. She grew hotter and hotter, tears pricked her eyes, she thought, 'He doesn't make me *lie* to him,' and was brought to her senses by a maid, peering round a corner to see what she was doing, so that she went hastily back to Lady Hughes-Winterton's coffee table to assure her that it had been 'only a friend, who might be in York; I told him to ring up if he's free'.

The next day was curiously long and ominous. It began well enough; she had half an hour alone with Peter after breakfast, whilst Lady Hughes-Winterton ordered meals and telephoned tradesmen, and paid bills. They sat together on a long stool (*petit point*, worked by Great Aunt Emily) in front of a newly-lit log fire in the drawing room; outside, frost was on the lawn, and on the gravel in the terrace; inside, the air was clear and thin, and light, and the fire crackled, trying to catch altogether. Peter put his arm round Anna's shoulder, and said, 'Happy?'

'Yes. More than I'd hoped. That was Oliver, last night.'

'I thought it might be.'

'He wants to see me.'

'I supposed he would,' said Peter, who had always been less ready than Anna herself to assume that they had heard the last of Oliver. He could not imagine anyone abandoning Anna with so little struggle.

'No, it's because of the baby. Father must have told him. He thinks he ought to have some say. It's a funny line for him to take – I'd always supposed he was responsible for Margaret not having any – but anyway, he thinks he has a right to – to say what happens. I told you, we ought to have dealt with it by now. I'm sure it'll be dangerous if it goes on much longer.'

'It might anyway,' Peter said. 'I wish you'd have it. They say it – getting rid of them – can mean you can't have any more. I'd rather keep this one, really, and make certain of several more of my own, than risk that. You see, I'm not being heroic, I'm being selfish. But I'm not sure it's right, anyway.'

Anna felt like crying. She said, 'But I don't *want* it, Peter, I don't *want* it, I can't bear the thought of it, I'm not ready.' She did not want any child, she was not fit to have one, she thought, and how would she ever know her place in the world, so hampered; even on the bridge she had not seen, and that may have been to do with it; *femina gravida*, weighed down, weighed down . . . Peter patted her shoulder, and went on, 'Besides, I'm not sure he hasn't a right to – to be consulted, at least. If he really wants to be, I respect him for it, in a way. But you don't have to see him, unless you want to.'

'I don't.'

'Very well then, you don't have to. That's simple.'

'He'll come here, he said as much.'

'If he does, I'll see him. I imagine I can cope with him. He's not a violent man, is he? You needn't have anything to do with it. I don't want you upset – it won't do you any good – and it won't help anything.'

Anna was dubious for a moment about his assertion that he could 'deal with' Oliver, remembering Oliver's contempt for young men like Peter, the grimness with which he went into battle. And then she thought she was guilty of a constant injustice, Peter's honesty was very strong, and it was the kind of strength Oliver would recognize.

He was possessed by a generous indignation, a genuine moral superiority, that would appeal to Oliver's natural puritanism and to a certain extent disarm him. It would appeal more to Oliver, who was more moral than she was, than it did to herself, she thought. But she recognized it, she admired it, she needed it, she thought. People like herself and Oliver found it too easy to dismiss Peter's decency, Peter's simplicity, Peter's real power – except in the last resort. Peter was not precisely what they would have called 'interesting', but ultimately he was necessary, ultimately he was life, to be lived with, to hold her to the earth. She looked up at his golden head and saw it bright and warm in the clear, cold light, and thought that Oliver and Henry did not allow for the kind of reality that Peter was, that she possessed an awareness that they knew nothing about. She said impulsively, 'You won't ever know how grateful I am for you, Peter. You make things seem solid enough to make plans about, and live with. I really think I might manage, married to you. I get to love you more, and more, really.'

'There's a lot to just going on,' Peter said, 'if you're sure things are there to go on with. I love you, so I'm sure.'

'And I am, truly, Peter.'

'I hope so. I mean you to be.'

'And I won't see Oliver.'

'I don't want to make your mind up for you. But candidly, I think better not.'

'Much better not.'

Lady Hughes-Winterton came in and smiled, and said, 'There you are, both of you, how comfortable you look,' and stood in the doorway until Anna felt impelled to move away from Peter, over to the window.

She went on, 'You'll remember about going to see the Porters about those pheasants, won't you darling? And tell them it's quite all right about Daphne borrowing Mayfly for the Meet, she must feel quite free, you'll fix it, won't you? I don't know if you and Anna will be going out that day but there's still Marina, she's quite enough . . .'

'Anna rides very well, mother . . .'

'Yes, I'm sure she does. So will you do that for me, then?'

Peter stood up. 'Would you like to come, Anna?'

Lady Hughes-Winterton said nothing; Anna looked at both of them and neither met her eye; after a moment she looked down and said mildly, 'No – no – I don't think – that is, I think I'll stay in.'

'Take the big car, Peter, in case any of them want a lift later. And do stay to lunch, if they ask you. Anna and I will manage very well together. We've lots to talk about, so don't you hurry back.'

Peter went, striding and upright, kissing Anna on the way and whispering, 'If there's any trouble, hold it, till I get back.' This caused Anna to realize suddenly that the main trouble still had not been met. If she did not go to Oliver, what if he came out here, as was only too likely, when Peter was not there? It was certain that Lady Hughes-Winterton's understanding would not extend to an encounter with Oliver. For a moment she allowed her desolation to show in her face, but Peter went without remarking it, and all she achieved was a quick look of calculation from Lady Hughes-Winterton, who had seen. Another point lost. Damn Oliver, Anna thought savagely. One trails so much mess after one, even into retreat, even back to the land. Not even only the baby, but all this arranging. Like a fly that got away, trailing sticky threads of web, picking up dust, stopping from time to time to try ineffectually to clean itself up a bit. And laying itself open to goodness knows what.

Lady Hughes-Winterton had the day arranged. First they went out, and Anna held the basket whilst Lady Hughes-Winterton collected autumn leaves for the house. Then there were hens and pigs and horses to be inspected, for no real purpose, just because Lady Hughes-Winterton took pleasure in seeing them. Anna would have taken pleasure in them too, she would have liked to stand and talk to the mares in the looseboxes, or hunt eggs; that was the kind of thing she had come to do. But she found her companion's presence irritating. Not because Lady Hughes-Winterton saw the animals as things, which she might have expected. She did not, she obviously cared for them; the horses whickered with pleasure when she came into the yard, and the hand which moved the warm bundle of hen aside in its box and lifted eggs out, so gently, was assured and accepted. It was basically the same feeling that Anna had had over Margaret's admiration of St Anne, or over Cambridge. Some things were solitary things, some things could only be possessed if no one else possessed them or loved them. The hens and horses were Lady Hughes-Winterton's who knew them, and loved them quite adequately. So Anna followed her and carried eggs and admired like a stranger, feeling the sharp autumn air, and the horse smell, and the brittle hedges and the garden paths crackling with frost, beautiful but not hers, like a tourist, or a mere hirer of horses in a stable where someone lives and works constantly.

In the house, they arranged the leaves, and finally confirmed the meals: a simple lunch, since Peter might be out, a large dinner, since he would be in. Then Lady Hughes-Winterton discussed Anna's wedding with her. It occurred to Anna that previous discussions of this had been incredibly tactful. No surprise had been expressed about her own parents' lack of communication with the Hughes-Wintertons, no questions had been asked which would involve a direct statement on Anna's part of their views, their plans, their arrangements. It had all been clothes and timing, nebulous undefined bridesmaids, colours and flowers. Showing an interest, but never forcing Anna's hand. Anna saw that this must be put down to one of Peter's midnight discussions with his mother, and wished he wouldn't. She could not, after all, get married *without* Caroline, even without Henry. It had been only from her first panic that she had wanted to exclude them altogether, but now that she did not know what had been so effectively said to make her family and her own attitude to them unmentionable, she dared not bring up the subject herself. And so she disappointed again.

Lady Hughes-Winterton said, 'And of course, if you do marry as ridiculously early as you want to – don't think I don't under-

292

stand, dear, I ought to, I had enough battles with my parents to get married *at all*, with Walter off on missions all over the place – if you do marry so soon, I shall expect you to live with me here in term time until Peter gets his degree over with. I think that's the best we can do for him, don't you agree? Hardly fair to divide his attention, so close to the time. And then we've to get him through the Civil Service exams, which shouldn't be too bad – and then you really will be able to start house hunting. I do want you to feel that – just like Peter – you always have a home here.'

Anna said that was very kind; she could summon up no more adequate response. Desolation invaded her again. She had had a horrible experience once as a child, going to stay with a family where the children had a nanny and a nursery. They had spent all day living a life shut up, shut away, a half life, a horrible grey unplaced life, visiting the adults for tea, for an hour in the afternoon, to hear a story and return to nursery tea, supper and bed. It had been intolerably less than was possible. And living here with Peter's mother would be like that.

Over lunch, Lady Hughes-Winterton returned to the cat-echism. Anna had been hopeful that it must end, when Lady Hughes-Winterton finally ran out of friends. But although this had happened, almost altogether, by now, it had had no deterrent effect. She assumed an absence of mind which, Anna was certain, was not natural to her, and began again, introducing longer and longer anecdotes about the unknown families, Vicky Salter's strange experience at a Hunt Ball, Geoffrey Wade-Thomas's peculiar skill, no doubt inherited from his father, at finding paths over apparently trackless moors. And then, when they were having tea, after lunch – Lady Hughes-Winterton always took tea after lunch, she was of the opinion that it sat more lightly on the stomach, which was important since she also always took a rest after lunch, owing to a slight cardiac trouble, nothing serious, but it was best to take care – when they were having tea, Lady Hughes-Winterton suddenly turned up what must have been the one name they had in common.

'Or did you,' she asked, clattering her teaspoon, 'by any chance know a young man whose father was a great friend of mine? Michael Farne?'

'Michael?' Anna said stupidly, feeling the colour spreading hot in her face. 'Michael? Of course I know him. I – we used to ride a lot together. He was – we were friends. We spent all one summer riding together . . .'

'Indeed?' said Lady Hughes-Winterton, at a loss now, apparently, over what to do with the information she had elicited. 'I believe he was very good with horses.'

'He was,' Anna said, troubled by this irrelevant calling up of so much she had thought renounced, remembering, far too vividly, far too urgently, the golden figure on the huge horse, trampling off under a burning sun, throwing the dust back at her and Oliver. And everything else that went with it – docks in the stable yard, bridles in the warm dark of the saddle room, the brightness and dustiness of straw stacks, the green and blue and gold perturbation of the orchard at Darton and the burning bracken on the hills over the hedge, Michael in a white shirt like an avenging angel treading the hay and laughing, and herself, imagining something huge, and possible, and bright, and transfiguring, to be met round every corner.

'It was a very hot summer,' she said hopelessly to Lady Hughes-Winterton, almost unable to contain her memory of it enough to speak rationally, 'the hottest for years.'

'Indeed?' said Lady Hughes-Winterton. Anna was still blushing, still so troubled that she did not this time notice Lady Hughes-Winterton looking at her carefully, taking note; she was aware only of a tremendous sense of relief when that lady, a little disturbed, moved off to her rest.

When she had gone, Anna looked round the Hughes-Winterton drawing room with new eyes. It had a birch-grey carpet, and ice-green slipper satin curtains, fluted under a castellated pelmet; it had green and silver damasked walls and would have been airy in the summer, but now in the winter it was chill. In the hearth, the log fire flaked, pink for a moment, into whitish ash. There was a lot of *petit point*, worked on a grey background; a screen, several stools, all in Victorian roses.

She thought, with new clarity, 'I came here because of Michael. I wanted Peter to be Michael. I wanted the country to be bright and the sun shining, and nobody thinking, as they were for Michael, and me to be in it, part of it.'

But Peter was not Michael, and she saw suddenly that however right she may have been about Peter's peculiar strength, or life, her rightness had been purely irrelevant. She had not allowed for herself, or her own modes of knowledge; here she would be half-human; a child in a nursery. Which she might have wanted blindly for a moment, but she could do better than that.

'I was terribly unhappy then but I *knew* something,' she thought, whilst memory selected patches of sun, a heroic gesture from Michael, bright trees from the whole orchard, and significance from a tangle of distress. 'I *did* know,' she insisted to herself, meaning: I have come to know, now. Whatever had been learned, not to be unlearned, on the bridge at night. She would come to remember the flakes of ash in this hearth with the same sense of significance, but that would be years later. Now the past rose bright and decisive; Peter was not Michael; nothing here mattered to her, nothing was live, as Michael had been. She must go away from here, before she could find what was. Not Michael himself, she had never supposed that, but something of the same weight. I thought it was a retreat, a dead end, she told herself, as she searched Peter's jackets in the hall cupboards for the keys to Peter's sports car. But there are no ends and I must do something.

The keys were in Peter's riding-mac finally; Anna had been gambling on his not having taken them; the rich, luckily, have so many pockets to leave things in that the chances are more often that things are not on them or with them. Anna put on the camel coat and the coral hat, because they were to hand, and wrote a note to Peter, which after some deliberation she pushed into his pocket, in place of the keys. It would never do for his mother to find it.

'Dear Peter, I have suddenly come to see that I must do things for myself. Because what one does affects one more than it looks as though it is going to when one does it. Like the baby. So I am going to start by seeing Oliver for myself. I might not come back, it's only fair to say, *but this doesn't mean I won't*. I want to, partly, I mean that. I have taken your car. If I don't come back I'll let you know where I've left it. It's easier to write because I suspect you suspected this might happen. My love, whatever happens, Anna.'

She drove out of the garage as quietly as she could, in order not to wake the sleeper, and out onto the road down through the Yorkshire moors, into York. She felt alive, driving the tiny car over twisting grey roads between dead frost-bitten bracken and grass; she sat up, and felt the wheel live under her hands, and her eyes awake to the road. She had not been alone with herself for some time. She thought of the baby, without bitterness for the first time. Oliver cared what happened to it; let it be born then; it must live its own life, as she must, it was not really a part of her, it was itself. It might be like Henry, or Oliver, or Caroline, or even Jeremy. One might as well let it have its life. Thinking of it as someone who might be like someone held her imagination to it for a moment; it would be difficult, now, to treat it as a thing again.

York came, surprisingly quickly, solid pale gold walls, fine grey Minster, narrow streets, ceremonial gates. Last time she had been there, she had been running away too, she remembered, and had been dreadfully lost. Running away did just as much damage as any other form of activity or refusal to act. After that she had run to school, and from school home, and from home to Oliver, and from Oliver to Peter. And now from Peter, to where? she thought, drawing up Peter's car outside the Station Hotel of which as a schoolgirl she had been so much afraid. This looks very like simple running away, too. But it isn't – it can't be.

Oliver was not inside, that she could see. It was not opening time so she sat down in the main hall, in the well of the great, curving, gilt staircase, in an armchair like a tub, stretched her tidy feet in their countrywoman's shoes, out on a thick carpet, and ate four ruinously expensive ham sandwiches to provide an excuse for being there. She ate them slowly, and when she had finished them Oliver still did not come; this hardly surprised her, though her stomach was tight with expecting him; she did not quite believe in Oliver.

What I always do, she thought, is run not quite far enough. I don't have courage to get right out. To give myself time to take stock and try. The thing to do, when I've dealt with Oliver,

296

would be to go to Mexico or somewhere – London, now, tonight, for a start, and get this baby over, and find someone to want it – the thought crossed her mind of Ernest Pontifex's children, happy in the sands with the waterman – and try to do something. Father will pay. And away from him I might write something, even if I'm not him, and shan't be. After all, I've never tried yet, I've never put pen to paper.

And then she thought, you are doing it again, Anna, thinking you must wait to deal with Oliver, it is just like all the other times, all you are doing is running away from Peter to Oliver. Which is worse, surely. The thing to do is go, now. Alone.

She stood up, in a blaze of decision, her mind humming over the bright summer, and left the hall without looking back. In the Station Hotel's bright, clean pink lavatory, she powdered her nose, and pushed a wisp of hair under the coral hat, seeing her own face, new and shining, and to be cared for, and embellished. She smiled at herself, with love, and went back, out into the entrance hall, towards the main door, and Peter's car. She would leave it in safe hands for him, in London.

In the doorway, Oliver caught her elbow. He said, 'Where are you going, in that inappropriate hat?'

Anna turned slowly to him, waking up out of a dream, seeing that what one did was indeed done, one was what one did, this as well, this above all, watching her last chance, or illusion, which? slip away as Oliver held her from it.

'I was just going,' she said. 'But it doesn't matter. I wouldn't have gone far, I suspect.'

Oliver's grip was like a claw on her elbow; he was holding himself together terribly; he looked at her directly, with a tremendous effort, but his face twitched, and Anna noticed suddenly that his knees were trembling.

'Don't,' she said. 'Don't trouble. Darling. Come and sit down. I couldn't really go far without you, now.'

The relief of her saying this was quite unexpected, to both of them. Oliver smiled slowly, and then more broadly, and said, 'Then we must just get on with things together.' He looked quite incongruous in the furred, palatial hotel. He had not even shaved, and had a raffish air, quite different from his normal constricted neatness. Anna said, 'Yes, it's about time we did.'

Greyness, and remembered brightness, things done and things to do; one had to contain them, and continue somehow. Seeing Oliver, now, Anna saw that it was silly to imagine it could have been done without him. This really was the feared and expected end. At that time, she was surprisingly content.

'Let's have a drink,' Oliver said. 'We've a lot to discuss.'